brutal academy

MAGGIE ALABASTER

Cover design by Atscandare

Edited by Lily Luchesi

Proofread by Nora Hogan

Paperback and hardback interior art by Crooked Sixpence.

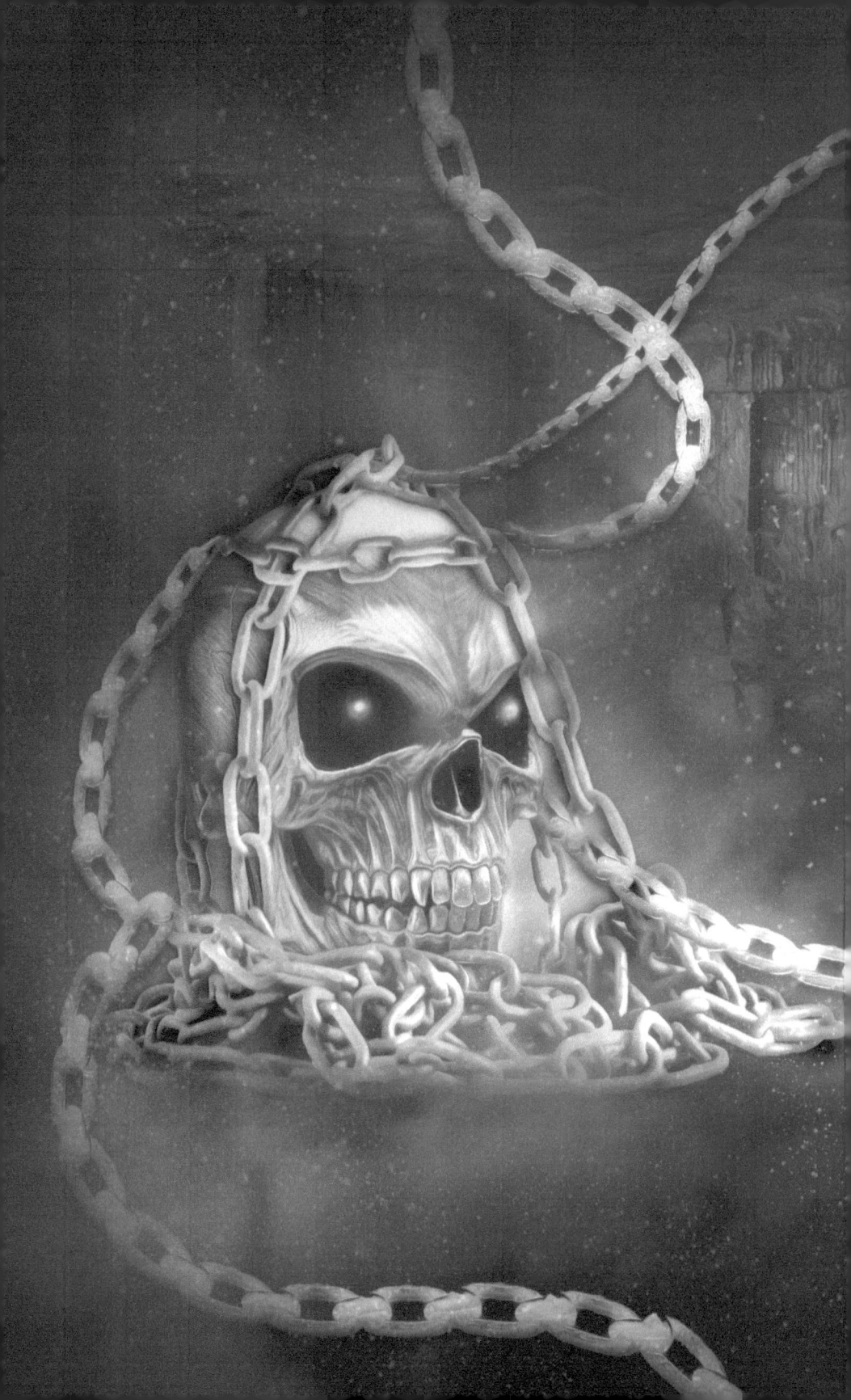

heartless

trigger warnings

Trigger warnings for mentions of sexual assault, attempted sexual assault, past psychological abuse, and human trafficking (not children).

one

HUNTER

I STALKED SLOWLY around the table, hands clasped behind my back.

Every so often, I glanced at our 'guest.' That's a term I use loosely, given he was tied to the chair by his ankles and wrists. His mouth was covered with a ragged slash of duct tape.

He was blindfolded with one of his cheap polyester ties when we brought him here. Parker slipped it off so we could see his fear.

Besides, it was easier to get our point across if he could see our faces and the level of shit he was in right now.

He screamed something into the tape and fought against his bindings. His movement rattled the chair. The feet scraped across the concrete floor, screeching painfully.

Parker shook his head. "Scott, Scott, Scott. There's no need to panic. All Hunter and I wanted to do was have a little chat."

Scott eyed him carefully, pain in his gaze. Maybe even a hint of anticipation.

Considering I already removed three of his toes with pruning shears, panic seemed like a good reaction to me. Presumably he was hopeful of getting out of here alive, before he bled out all over the floor.

I tossed one of his toes down onto the table. It bounced a couple of times before it stopped on the edge, right in front of him.

His eyes widened.

"There's a few more where that came from," I reminded him.

He struggled again. Screamed into the tape.

"He knows what he did wrong, doesn't he, Park?" I asked my identical twin brother. "Did we explain it clearly enough?"

Parker sat back in his chair and placed his hands behind his head. "I don't know if we did, Hunt. I suppose he's wondering why he's here."

Scott gave us both a wary look and pressed himself against the back of the chair. As if somehow he could get away from us like that.

"Would you like to explain, or will I?" I asked.

Parker waved his hand at me. "Be my guest."

I raised the pruning shears and slammed them, blades first, into the table. They embedded a centimetre or two, the handle wobbling from the impact.

Scott flinched and jerked away.

I closed my palms down on the table to either side of the shears and leaned forward.

"You may have been ignorant of the fact that Lila Bell belongs to us." I raised an eyebrow at him.

Scott shook his head.

"You didn't know?" I asked.

He nodded.

My other eyebrow joined the first. "You *did* know?" I knew he knew, but fucking with him was too much fun to resist.

His eyes were wide, unsure what to do now.

I straightened up and sat on the edge of the table. "Let's save us both some time. You did know. You knew when you shoved her out of the way in the corridor. You knew when you almost knocked her off her feet. When you knocked books out of her arms."

I leaned forward until I was almost nose to nose with him. He smelled like terror. I inhaled deeply. Scaring the shit out of people was one of the simple joys of life. Particularly when we had good reason to do it.

Scott shook his head and said something against the tape.

I looked over to Parker and nodded. I sat back as my brother ripped the tape off Scott's mouth.

Scott cried out. "I swear to God, it was an accident. I was on my way to class. I was late. Mr D said if I was late again, he'd make sure they'd kick my ass out of Brutham. I can't afford to—"

I slapped my hand down on the table so hard it made Scott and Parker both jump.

"I don't give a fuck if he threatened to kick you out of a fucking aeroplane," I snarled. "You don't touch our woman, and you sure as fuck don't shove her out of the way."

By the sound of it, we were doing Dane DiMarco a favour by dealing with this asshole.

"Man, I'm sorry. I swear, it will never happen again." He pleaded with us both with his eyes. "I was in a hurry and didn't see her. That's all. I sure as fuck didn't mean to—"

"But you did," I said. "At Brutal Academy, running into another guy's woman can get you dead. Any guy. But Lila isn't any guy's woman. She's *our* woman and will be head of the Bell family someday. That's a dangerous fucking combination to make an enemy of, Scott," I told him.

He looked like he wanted to contradict what I said about Lila leading her family. Chloe, her non-identical twin, was the older sister. If Parker and I had our way, Lila would be the one taking on that role when Samuel Bell stepped down or died. Or, more likely given our lifestyle, was killed.

Life expectancy when you work for criminal organisations, such as our families, was like the shears, short and sharp.

The Bell family and ours were bitter enemies, but Parker, Lila and I would change that. Preferably before her father found out we were fucking her. Our life expectancy would be much shorter than the shears then.

"I swear, I'll look where I am going from now on," Scott whined. "I've learned my lesson. I'll apologise to her again. I'll... I'll do anything, just please..."

His eyes were so wide, I was sure he was about to piss in his jeans. Or shit in them.

Either of those things would make this pleasant chat much less pleasant. I hated when people lost control to that extent. No matter how scared a guy gets, he should be able to control his bodily functions. Unless we're talking about his cock. Some of us just get off on fear, ours or someone else's.

Granted, I preferred other people's fear to my own, but I take no responsibility if my cock gets hard, no matter what the circumstances. He has a mind of his own. In fact, he was quite enjoying this. If it wasn't for the smell of sweat and fear, I might insist Scott blow me off. On the other hand, he touched our woman, so he didn't get to enjoy the feeling of my cock in his mouth. That privilege was reserved for people better than him.

"What do you think, Park?" I asked my twin. I was the older and better looking one of us, and the most ruthless. Parker had a way of making people like him, usually right before they found out it was a bad idea to turn their back on him.

"I don't know, Hunt," Parker said slowly. "He seems genuinely sorry for what he did."

"People usually are when they're tied up and missing a couple of toes," I mused. "It tends to make people say things they don't really mean. If we let him walk out of here, he might just go and knock over someone else's woman."

"I won't, I swear," Scott pleaded. "I'll be more careful."

"What do you think Mr D would do if Scotty here shoved his woman out of the way?" I asked thoughtfully.

That begged the question, how many people knew Brutham Academy's history teacher was fucking Chloe Bell, Lila's older sister?

"He'd be pissed," Parker said. "Without doubt, he'd make sure you'd be kicked out of Brutham. Kicked so far no other university in Australia would touch you. Maybe anywhere in the world."

As a DiMarco, Dane probably didn't have that much influence, but Parker got his point across.

"The question is, what does a pair of Brantley brothers do?" I asked. "Even Zeke would kick Scotty's ass into next month."

One of our older brothers, Zeke, was the lead singer of Wolf Venom, one of the hottest rock bands in the world. He wasn't involved in the family business, but he was as protective of his girlfriend, Abbie, as any of her other six boyfriends were. Including the drummer, Asher DiMarco, Mr D's younger brother.

Yeah, it all seemed a bit incestuous at times.

"Maybe we should give him a second chance," I suggested. "Losing a couple of toes and a lot of dignity, might be enough to teach him a lesson."

Parker peered at Scott's face. "Not to mention the bruising on his pretty boy face."

Scott had a swollen lip and a pair of swollen eyes. His nose was most likely broken.

"I've definitely learned my lesson." Scott looked back and forth between us like he was watching a game of tennis and his life depended on the outcome. This was no centre court at the Australian open. This was far more serious, and a lot more fun.

"Please." Our guest was getting tired. The pleading and the pain was clearly getting to him. His feet must be throbbing like a bitch. The floor underneath was slick with his own blood.

It sucked to be him, as they say. On any given day, I'd much prefer to be me anyway. If I pissed off anyone by touching their woman, and I had many times before meeting Lila, no one would dare to drag Parker or me into one of the sheds beside the Academy building and torture us. Doing that would make them the enemy of our oldest brother, Reuben Brantley. Most people weren't dumb enough to get him offside.

Of course, that meant we got away with pretty much anything we wanted, including fucking other guys' girlfriends.

Of course, after meeting Lila we were one-woman guys, no matter how tempting an offer was.

I glanced at my watch. "We've wasted enough time on this loser. Let's cut him free and get the fuck out of here. I, for one, could use a drink."

I hopped off the table and leaned my hip against it, my arms crossed over my chest.

Parker nodded and gripped the handle of the shears. He yanked them out of the table and stood to snip the zip tie that held Scott's arms behind him. He crouched down and snipped the ones that bound his ankles to the legs of the chair.

"You made a mess down here Scott." Parker clicked his tongue. "You can clean it up."

He grabbed the back of Scott's shirt and yanked him off the chair. He shoved him down onto the concrete floor on his knees and pressed his face down into the puddle of blood.

"Lick it up, asshole," Parker told him.

Scott glanced up at him, but started to lick his own blood off the floor.

For some reason, the sight of the first year student on his hands and knees like a dog, licking at the floor, made me laugh. It was nothing less than he deserved, and it would save washing time later. As a bonus, the floor was rough and not entirely clean. It must be chafing the shit out of his tongue.

That realisation made me laugh harder. It served him right for barrelling around the corridors of Brutham. The moment he laid a hand on Lila, he sealed his own fate. He wouldn't get any sympathy from me or anyone else here at the Academy. We didn't call the place Brutal for nothing.

"This was a good idea of yours, Park," I told my brother.

"I have them once in a while," Parker said. "It's a shame he didn't piss himself though. I'm sure he'd thoroughly enjoy licking that up."

Scott groaned and gagged.

The sound made my cock harder. I reconsidered the idea of making him suck me off, but dismissed it again. I didn't really need his blood on my balls.

Scott stopped licking and sat back on his haunches. He wiped his mouth with the back of his sleeve.

"It's clean. Can I go now? Please?"

I cocked my head at him. "You know what, Parker? I think I changed my mind about letting him leave."

I slipped a gun out from the side of my jeans, and shot Scott once through the forehead.

two

HUNTER

"I GUESS we should call for cleanup." I put my gun away and flicked bits of brain and skull off my shirt.

Parker sighed. Not because he cared whether or not I killed Scott, but because of the hassle that came after. A hassle he put into simple but eloquently resigned words.

"Hunt, we're on cleanup tonight."

"Fuck," I said under my breath. "You could have said something before I shot the prick."

He spread his hands. "I didn't know you were going to kill him. Do I look like a fucking mind reader?"

"You look like me, therefore you should be able to read my mind." I crouched down and grabbed Scott's wrists. "You grab his ankles. Let's get this asshole dealt with."

Parker grimaced. "Why do I have to pick him up by his ankles? You're the one who cut his toes off." In spite of that, he leaned forward and grabbed them before hoisting them into the air.

"You didn't seem to object at the time." We made our way over to the door. I placed the front end of Scott down to unlock and open it.

It was dark out, and quiet. Voices and music came from the Academy building, but down here, near the sheds, there was no one but us.

Unless someone else was down here having fun like we were. That was as likely as not. The sheds were originally built to house animals and gardening stuff, like lawnmowers. When it was turned into Brutham Academy, we appropriated them for different uses. The only animals that came down here now had two legs. However, the lawnmowers were still housed in one of the sheds.

We couldn't have Brutham falling into disarray, could we now?

With Scott swinging between us, we hurried through the darkness and into trees on the edge of the property.

"Hey, *Watch*, turn on the torch," I said roughly in the direction of my wrist.

My watch lit up, illuminating the path through the trees.

"This would be a whole lot easier with a wheelbarrow," Parker remarked.

"Then we'd have to wash out the wheelbarrow," I pointed out. "Besides, this is good exercise. Think how big your biceps would be if we did this every day."

"My biceps are already massive," he bragged.

I snorted a laugh and stopped next to a hole beside some trees. "On three. One. Two."

On three, we swung Scott and hefted him into the hole.

He landed with a thump, half a metre down from the surface of the forest.

"This thing is getting full," Parker remarked.

I shrugged. "When it's full, we'll have another one dug."

"Reuben is going to be pissed off if we keep asking for more money for more holes." Parker walked beside me as we returned to the shed for a pair of shovels.

"Then we'll have to dig them ourselves," I said. "I wish this place would invest in an incinerator. It would be a whole lot fucking easier to drop guys like Scotty inside and not have to worry about him."

"Maybe we can ask Reuben to donate one." Parker grabbed two shovels from beside the door and handed me one.

I accepted it and followed him back out. "And make it easier for us to dispose of the evidence? What would Brutham have to blackmail us with some day?"

They turned a blind eye to anything we did, but there was always something in it for them. Always an angle they could eventually play. If one of us became the head of the Brantley family in the future, we'd owe a very large favour in return for them keeping their mouths shut.

Of course, once we graduated, Reuben would send someone behind us to clean up any evidence. He wouldn't leave that hanging over his head. Ours, yes, not his. If our oldest brother was good at anything, it was covering his ass.

We headed back down into the forest and shovelled dirt from the pile beside the hole, over Scott.

"It would be so much easier to pay someone to do this for us," Parker remarked.

"Easier, but not as satisfying," I replied. "Look at this." I dropped an extra-large shovel full of dirt onto Scott's face, almost completely making him disappear. "Doesn't that feel good after what he did to Lila?"

"Let me try." Parker dropped dirt on the other side of Scott, covering his face completely. "That does feel good. Better than when it's just the kid of one of Reuben's enemies."

Those were all from our first year here at Brutham. Some from before the trials, some from during. Those we dispensed with during the trials, the Academy made us bury ourselves. Something about making us humble, even though we survived the first year here.

"It's true what they say, revenge is sweet." I dumped more dirt on top of Scott and smoothed it down with the back of my shovel.

"It really is," Parker agreed. "It's also making me horny as fuck."

"When are you not horny as fuck?" I leaned the shovel against a tree.

"As often as you," Parker agreed. "Never." He flashed me a grin.

"Exactly," I said. "But there's something about torture and death. It turns me on almost as hard as Lila."

I unzipped my jeans and pushed down the front of my boxers, until my cock sprang free. I wrapped my fingers around my length and stroked my hand up and down until I was hard.

I stood with my feet slightly apart, cock directly over Scott's grave.

In the corner of my eye, I saw Parker pull out his own cock and do the same thing.

I looked away from him and kept on sliding and tugging my hand up and down from my balls to my tip. Pre-cum beaded on my slit and dripped onto the dirt road above Scott's face.

I rolled my hips and pressed my lips together to keep from groaning out loud. The pressure in my balls built to an almost unbearable level. They felt hot, tight and heavy. Begging for release.

Beside me, Parker let out a long, low moan. His movements became faster and faster, before a squirt of cum shot out his tip and over Scott's grave.

Spurred on by my twin, a rush of blood hammered through me and I came, squirting my own cum over the freshly packed dirt. It spread across Parker's, before sinking into the ground.

"That was all kinds of fucked up." Parker tucked his cock away in his pants and did up his zipper.

I laughed softly. "If there's anything we're good at, it's things which are all kinds of fucked up. It comes with being a Brantley."

I shook the last drop off the head of my cock and put mine away too. Coming like this only took the edge off. What I really needed was to sink my cock deep into Lila's pussy and pound her so hard I wrecked her for days. Just the way we liked it.

"It's the best thing about being a Brantley." Parker grabbed up his shovel and lifted it up to his shoulder.

I grabbed my own. "I thought the best thing was being my brother."

"I think they go hand in hand." He shrugged, then broke into a grin. "Or dick in hand."

I laughed louder and offered him a high-five with my spare hand. The best thing about having a twin was getting up to all sorts of shit together. Whatever happened, we always had each other's backs. We never judged each other, not really. We gave each other shit, but when push came to shove, we were a team.

Lila was the last woman we both ever wanted to fuck, but she wasn't the first we both shared. More than one woman had woken up sore from us both.

"As long as you keep your hand off my dick," I told him. We were close, but we weren't *that* close. I was sure women pictured us doing things to each other, but that wasn't our jam.

Besides, we had plenty of women, and men, before Lila; we didn't need to touch each other. With her... She was always willing to go along with whatever we wanted. Neither of us went without.

"Dude." Parker grimaced in the light from a window at the bottom of the Academy building. "I'd have to find yours first."

I snorted loudly before leaning my shovel up against the wall inside the shed. "My cock is so big, you wouldn't get your hand around it."

"I think you're protesting too much." He leaned his shovel up beside mine and cast a look around the room before stepping over to scoop up the zip ties and duct tape.

"Don't make me use this on you." I picked up the shears and waved them at him before hanging them on a hook on the wall.

"You wouldn't do that," he said easily. "You love me too much. Besides, who else would do this shit with you but me?"

"I'm sure I'd find someone." I draped my arm over his shoulder and gave him a bro hug before shoving him out into the night and closing the shed door behind us.

"Who? Zeke?" Parker laughed. He'd staggered a few steps before finding his footing again. Shame, I would have laughed my ass off if he fell on his knees.

I barked a laugh of my own. "Zeke is nothing but a party pooper. Reuben and Caleb wouldn't want to get their suits dirty. Joshua too. Lucas is too busy fucking... What's her name? Amity Fiorelli."

Parker nodded. "I guess that leaves me. Although, there's a few guys outside the family who might be fun to hang around with."

I looked at him sideways. "Yeah? Like who? Mr D?"

"Maybe," Parker shrugged. "I was thinking more of his brother, Asher. Or Asher's cousin Ric. Or better yet, the so-called Devils of Dusk Bay."

He spoke derisively, as if they in no way deserved such a cool, collective nickname. I had a fair idea of the shit they got up to. They deserved it as much as we deserved ours— the evil twins.

That nickname started when Zeke referred to us that way to piss us off, but it stuck. Ever since then, we did what it took to live up to it. If anyone was to blame for the things we got up to, it was him, for encouraging us. That's what big brothers were for anyway, right?

"Ice Miller, Ares Turner and Mannix Cassani?" I stepped around the wide fire pit we sometimes used for toasting marshmallows. "I wouldn't turn my back on any of them."

"Neither would I, but I'd fuck their girlfriend, Kennedy. I'd bet you anything she knows how to use her mouth." He smacked his lips.

"I wouldn't take that bet," I said. "Because you have no way of proving it's true. Not without cheating on Lila."

If not for her, Kennedy would be fair game, boyfriends or no boyfriends. She was cute and I did have a thing for redheads. And blondes. And brunettes.

"You might as well bet on Zeke's girlfriend, Abbie." She was also a singer and someone we'd both had unconscious in our esteemed company. Apart from kidnapping her and putting a tracking device in her earring, we hadn't touched her. She was another woman I would totally would have fucked if not for my commitment to Lila. It would have pissed my brother off, but would have been worth it.

I had to be careful. If I kept going like this, Lila might turn me into something vaguely resembling a good person.

I snorted to myself at the thought. As if I could ever be good. Not when it was this much fun being bad.

three

LILA

I EYED my sister across the table. Since arriving at Brutham, everything had been quiet.

That wouldn't last and we both knew it. Our father made it clear, before we left to come here, what he expected of us.

"One of you will take over as head of the family someday." He'd sat back in his leather chair and regarded us both.

"I expect you to work at proving you deserve it over your sister." He sat forward and rested his arms on his solid mahogany desk. At home, in just our presence, he didn't bother with a suit jacket. The sleeves of his white button down shirt were rolled up to just below his elbows. The face of his chunky Rolex watch caught the light which slanted in behind him from a window overlooking the harbour.

Most people might consider Samuel Bell attractive. Even as his daughter, I saw why.

His dark hair was peppered with grey, but his brown eyes were as shrewd as ever. Power radiated from him. Wherever he went, he attracted attention, especially beautiful women. They flocked to him, enticed by the lure of him and his money.

I'd be naïve if I didn't think he fucked them, but he never kept any of them around for long. Never got attached. After Mum died, he was never with anyone for more than a short while, apart from a brief marriage that ended years ago.

I didn't get the impression he missed any of the women, just no one held his attention. No one was silly enough to think it was because he didn't want anyone getting between him and his daughters. He loved us, but he wasn't sentimental.

"When you say work at proving it?" Chloe asked tentatively.

"Whatever it takes," he said evenly. "This isn't an easy business. If your skin isn't thick enough, you'll be eaten alive. If you let your sister walk all over you, you have no chance out there in the world."

"The trials—" Chloe started.

"You have to make it to the trials first." His eyes took in her, then me. "You know what they say about Brutham Academy."

"It's the only university in Australia with a mortality rate that's higher than the dropout rate," I quoted.

"And do you know why that is?" His expression didn't change.

"To teach us to kill anyone who gets in our way." I was sixteen when I killed my first person, down in the basement of this very house.

I can't claim to have enjoyed it, but I'd do anything for my father's approval and to prove I was a worthy successor to him. If I had to kill again, I would.

But if that person was my sister...

"Yes, but it's more than that," Dad said. He waited for me to elaborate. He was never one for giving us easy answers.

"To stay alive," Chloe said. She gave me the side eye, clearly thinking the same thing I was. She had also killed, but would she kill me if I was in her way? "To make the right connections and allies and use them to further ourselves."

Dad nodded. "Exactly. You're not merely there to learn, although you're there to do that too. You'll both be studying business. Not only will you be in competition for head of the family, you'll be competing academically. Brutham takes your education very, very seriously. This isn't the kind of establishment where you can turn up, not do anything and expect to succeed. Money will not buy a degree from Brutham. Hard work and the right contacts will."

In the corner of my eye, I caught the slight grimace on Chloe's face. She didn't want to study business any more than I did, but we'd both work to excel. We had to. Neither of us was going to hand the position of head of the family over without a fight.

Neither would give the other an advantage of any kind. We were competitive by nature, but the situation Dad put us in made us even more so. We were both equally determined to best the other.

Still, I would have preferred to learn the family business directly from my father. Chloe was the older twin by minutes, but I had what it took to run it. I never hesitated at the things that made her hesitate. Never flinched at things that made her flinch. No one would ever doubt my commitment.

Chloe, on the other hand, would have preferred to take up painting, or playing an instrument, or studying history. Something Dad would definitely not consider to be a worthwhile occupation. A hobby, certainly, but nothing to make a lifelong commitment to.

He'd instilled that in us from a very young age. He wanted us to be well-rounded, but realistic. Useful to the family.

"Something to say?" Dad asked her.

"No," she said quickly. She sat up straighter in her chair. "Nothing."

He cocked his head very slightly. "Good. I don't need to remind you there's a place you can go if you need to think for a while."

She paled. "No, I haven't forgotten," she said quickly.

I had to work to contain a shudder. We both knew what he was referring to.

When he bought this house before we were born, he made rooms underneath it. Several of them. All soundproof, cold and, if he wanted them to be, completely devoid of light.

Built to torture his enemies, both of us spent time in those rooms. So we understood what they were like, he'd explained.

What they were like was a living nightmare. Which was exactly the point. If we put a toenail out of line, the best we could hope for was to only be in there for an hour or two.

Chloe and I did everything we could to avoid going in there at all, but one of his favourite pastimes was sending us down there to give food and water to anyone presently housed there. Thank fuck that didn't happen too often, especially lately. The whole place gave me the creeps.

Dad nodded. "Good. I prefer not to have to put you in those rooms. It gives me no pleasure."

Only the idea of him putting me there made me hold back a snort.

He was a Bell. Putting people down in the basement gave him at least *some* pleasure. Even if it was my sister and me.

He liked to cover it with a pleasant smile, and well-dressed exterior, but he had a sadistic streak at least as big as my own. Why else would he have those rooms in the first place? He could just as easily have his enemies killed. He did that too, but the basement was his special, peculiar pleasure.

I lifted my chin. "We'll make you proud. By the time the trials come at the end of the year, everyone will know who is worthy of becoming head of the family. To take your place. In the distant future, of course."

He was harsh, but he was still my father and I loved him. He and I were a lot alike. Ruthless, sadistic and more than a little bit fucked up.

Chloe was all of those things too, but by the time I was done, she'd be begging me to step into our father's shoes.

Dad smirked. "Of course. What you're competing for, may well be for your children to take over from me. I intend to be around for a long time yet."

I smiled, but at the same time I was thinking, *I hope not.*

I didn't want him to die, but I wasn't going to have this opportunity pass me by and go straight to my future children.

No, by the time I was done, I wanted him to know he could retire and leave everything to me. I'd expand the empire he started. I wanted to take the family business global. I wanted to control governments all over the world.

Chloe, on the other hand, would probably want to legitimise the business. As far as I was concerned, that was bullshit. We'd lose millions by doing that. Billions. Who cared about obeying the fucking law? Living and operating outside the law was much more profitable and a fuck load more fun.

"We will definitely make you proud," Chloe said. "The legacy we'll pass on to our children will last for generations."

She didn't mean her children and mine, she meant hers and whoever she got to fuck her pregnant.

I slipped that thought into the back of my mind for later.

"It will definitely be one hell of a legacy," I agreed. "Nothing will stand in our way."

"What are you staring at?" Chloe's voice snapped me back to the present.

I blinked. "Just thinking about that lecture this morning," I lied.

The one advantage of studying the same degree as my sister was getting to talk about it with her. Often she helped to put things into perspective for me. I did the same for her, but that couldn't be helped.

Chloe groaned. "It was so boring. Is there anything more dry than marketing and economics?"

"Your pussy?" I teased.

She grimaced at me. "I'm not discussing my pussy with you. I don't want to talk about yours either," she added quickly. "I certainly don't want to know if it's full of Brantley cum."

"Jealous?" I raised a perfectly shaped eyebrow at her.

"Why would I be jealous?" she asked. "It means I have a better chance of taking over from Dad. As soon as he finds out you're fucking them, all bets will be off."

That was a possibility I'd considered. The rivalry between the two families was vicious at times. My father wouldn't approve of me speaking to them, much less taking them to my bed.

However, as far as I was concerned, the bad blood was between my father and Reuben Brantley. That shit didn't have to continue with our generation. Hunter and Parker had skills I could make use of, including two skilled tongues and equally skilled cocks. If having a relationship with them put me on the back foot with Dad...I'd just have to work that much harder to get ahead of my sister.

I shrugged one shoulder and pushed my hair back off my face. "Dad will understand. Better than he'll understand you fucking Dane DiMarco. The DiMarco family has no power anymore." Some of them liked to think they did, but in the end they all answered to my father or Reuben Brantley. "How old is he anyway? Forty?"

She glared at me. "He's thirty-four. He's not that much older than me."

I leaned over the table towards her. "Why don't you step aside now? You and Mr D could get married and have a bunch of cute little babies, and leave me to do the real work. Imagine, you could be the wife of a history teacher." If that was all the ambition she had, she had no business competing with me.

"You know as well as I do Dane doesn't want to spend the rest of his life teaching history," she snapped. "He's going to stand by my side when I'm head of the Bell family."

She gave me a venomous smile. "What will you be doing? Spreading your legs for Reuben Brantley's minion brothers? Neither of them will ever have any real power. But you already know that. Honestly, I can't help thinking you're trying to sabotage yourself. Which is fine with me. Maybe *you* should step aside right now."

"I will never step aside willingly," I said coldly. "And I won't let you beat me. It will be Hunter and Parker at my side." I hesitated for a moment. "Or maybe Mr D will change allegiance to me when he realises you're going to lose."

I smiled to myself at the look of doubt in her eyes. I had no interest in Dane DiMarco, but whatever it took to get to her, I'd do it.

four

LILA

THE KNOCK on my bedroom door came early. It always did when it was the twins. All the better for catching people off-guard, according to Hunter.

"Are you decent?" Parker called out through the door.

I struggled to tell them apart at times, but I always knew which twin was which from their voice. Chloe claimed that was bullshit, but I'd never been wrong yet.

"Yeah," I called out. "Come in."

"Shame," Parker said as he stepped into the room, followed by Hunter. "We were hoping to find you naked, lying on your bed waiting for us."

He stepped up behind me and looked at our reflections in the mirror. He cupped my cheeks with his hands before sliding them up my face and tangling his fingers in my hair.

It was almost unfair how good-looking both of them were. One of them that hot would have been unfair, but two? I'd only seen photos of the rest of the family, but all of their brothers were good-looking. Even Reuben, if I was honest with myself.

He and I would make an interesting alliance, if I went there, which I wouldn't. Two Brantley brothers was enough for me.

"What part about that wouldn't be decent?" I teased.

"Good point." Parker gripped my hair and pulled my head back so I was looking up at him. He kissed me with his face upside down from mine. His nose tickled my chin. The stubble from his chin teased the tip of my nose. "Maybe we should stay in tonight instead?"

"I'm not saying that's not a good idea," Hunter drawled. He lay back on my bed and crossed his legs. "But we all know what tonight is. We don't want to miss it, do we?"

He leaned his head against my headboard and looked at us questioningly like he had all the time in the world. If people had past lives, he was definitely a cat. Lazing around in the sun all day, ripping unsuspecting smaller animals apart at night.

"I don't, but..." Parker let go of my hair and slid his hands down the front of my black, V-neck T-shirt. He worked his fingers under my bra and over my nipples.

I shivered. The sensation his touch sent through me was sinfully good. No one would ever accuse me of having a dry pussy, especially around these two. They could make me dripping wet with just a look, never mind their touch.

"We have time for both, don't we?" I asked. "Especially since you're early."

"I'm not saying that's *why* we're early." Hunter grinned. "It might just be a bonus."

"It's totally a bonus." Parker palmed my nipples until I was all but panting. "I bet you're wet as fuck already."

"I bet you're hard as fuck already," I told him.

"Miss Bell, I'm always hard as fuck," he replied. "Especially around you." He drew me up out of the chair and stepped around to press his body against mine. His hard cock poked against my ass. "I will never *not* want to fuck you."

He pulled his hands out of the front of my T-shirt and gripped the hem to pull it over my head.

I raised my arms to help him, but took my T-shirt from his fingers so I could place it carefully over the back of the chair. I intended to wear it later. I didn't need it dumped on the floor and creased.

He unhooked my black lace bra, letting my full breasts fall free. The straps slid down my arms. I caught it before it fell and draped it over my top.

Parker turned me around, admiring my bare breasts while pushing me back towards the bed. He laid me back and let Hunter pull me up until I was lying on top of him.

"You're so beautiful." Hunter lightly gripped my breast in one hand and ran his other through my hair.

"Isn't she?" Parker stood at the end of the bed and looked down at us both. He knelt down beside my ankles and crawled up the bed. He pushed up my skirt, revealing my lacy, black G-string. The front was so sheer he was looking right down at my pussy.

"Gorgeous." He parted my thighs and dove his face straight down between them. He tugged the gusset of my panties aside and went to work on my pussy with his tongue.

"You taste better than honey," he groaned.

"Your tongue feels amazing." I let Hunter manoeuvre me so his upper body was facing me, without dislodging his brother. He kissed my mouth, his tongue sliding over my lips and teeth, before pressing inside.

His tongue was pretty fucking amazing too.

I bent my knees, opening myself wider to Parker before he slipped a finger inside me, then another.

"Definitely wet," he said, his voice muffled by my dripping pussy and clit. "So fucking wet."

I was right on the brink of coming, when he slid his fingers out and lifted his shining face.

"Hey," I protested weakly. I glared down at him, but he only grinned. He knew exactly what he was doing. He could play my body better than anyone else except Hunter. When it came to knowing what I liked, they were equal. Both incredible and addictive.

Parker chuckled and waited until I was almost down from my near-orgasm, before lowering his mouth back to me and slipping his fingers back inside. He worked me inside and out, flicking his tongue against my clit and drawing it between his teeth to bite down gently.

At the same time, Hunter kissed me deeply, thrusting his tongue in and out of my mouth and kneading my breasts with firm fingers.

I loved being with both of them at the same time. Or separately, but there was something about being spoiled like this that I couldn't get enough of.

I closed my eyes and slowly rocked my body in rhythm to Parker's fingers sliding in and out of me, fucking me. Inching me closer and closer to the edge.

Once again, I was almost there and he stopped, pulling out of and away from me. He grinned when I growled, deep in the back of my throat.

"You're such an asshole," I told him.

"Yeah, but you love that about me." He was a cocky prick. But he was right, it was one of the things I loved about him.

I shook my head and glared until he lowered his face back to me. The third time, he only took a matter of moments to get me back to the precipice. If he pulled away this time, I was going to suffocate him with my thighs. Honestly, he might not even mind dying that way. Both guys also had a sadistic streak to match mine. So much so, I knew Hunter would get me off while his twin's body cooled.

Fortunately, Parker didn't pull away this time. He drove me all the way to the edge of the cliff and off the other side, mouth and fingers working me all the way up and not letting up until I came back down.

I sighed against Hunter's mouth and lay against him while I caught my breath.

Parker hooked his fingers into the top of my panties and slid them off. His thumb through one end, fingers gripping the other, he stretched them out and aimed them toward Hunter's face. They hit his twin right in the middle of his forehead. Both of them laughed.

I rolled my eyes at them.

"You two are such little boys," I scolded playfully.

"There's nothing little about me, woman," Parker growled, just as playful. He placed his hands and knees on either side of my ankles and crawled up my body. At the same time, he opened his pants. He nudged my knees apart with his and used his hand to position his cock outside my entrance.

Before I could respond to his claim, he sank inside me until he was seated all the way to his balls.

Hunter worked his way out from under me and undid his own pants. "There's nothing small about me either." He nudged the tip of his cock, which already shone with pre-cum against my lips. "Be a good girl and open up for this big boy."

28

"When have I ever been a good girl?" I asked, but I opened and let him slide his cock into my mouth.

Hunter groaned as he pressed his length almost down to my throat. "Every time my cock is inside you."

"Exactly," Parker groaned. "No one takes my cock as well as you do."

"Or mine," Hunter agreed. "You were definitely made for us." He started to move slowly, sliding in and out between my lips, keeping pace with his twin.

My mouth was too full to respond, so I curled my hand around Hunter's balls and raked over them lightly with my fingernails at the same time as I sucked him hard.

I loved everything about this. The way they both felt inside my body. The way I could control their pleasure with the speed I sucked, licked or rolled my hips. This time, the speed was slow and deliberate. I wanted to drag this out for them the way Parker had with me. I wanted them to suffer the agony of being right on the edge, suspended there until I was ready to let them find bliss.

Nothing in my life made me feel as powerful as this. It was addictive. There would never come a time when I didn't want both of these guys, at the same time or separately.

Parker hooked his hands under my knees and draped my legs over his shoulder so he could pound inside me deeper.

I grabbed a fistful of blanket and dug my nails in. I was on the verge of coming again, but I didn't want to increase the speed, not yet. I focused on breathing and sucking and bucking, until I couldn't take it anymore. I moved faster, pushing all of us nearer.

I was so fucking close. I knew they were too. If I timed this perfectly...

I couldn't stop myself from coming again, but I was only a heartbeat or two ahead of Parker and Hunter. I don't know which of them came first, but it was close enough to almost be in unison. The world disappeared, washed away by panting and groaning, and the rush of blood through my ears.

I arched my back and remembered to breathe while Hunter squirted hot, salty cum down my throat.

"Be a good girl and swallow," Hunter said before easing his cock out from between my lips.

I looked him in the eyes and swallowed every drop.

"So good," Parker groaned. He eased out of me and lowered my legs, but kept my knees apart with his hands. "I'll be right back."

He rolled off the bed and into the small bathroom I had to myself. Fortunately, no one at Brutham had to share unless they wanted to. Otherwise people would get stabbed over things like snoring and leaving clothes on the floor. There was a reason none of the rooms anywhere in the Academy had carpet on the floors. We liked to say it was because cum was hard to get out of the carpet, but so was blood. Not to mention shards of skull and chunks of brain. Hardwood and tiles were much more manageable.

Parker came back a minute or two later with a warm, damp cloth in his hand. He used it to carefully wipe his cum from my pussy.

"Don't want our girl to feel messy, do we?" he asked.

"Not tonight," Hunter agreed. "She'll be messy enough by the end of it."

"Promises promises," I teased.

"We definitely promise." Hunter grinned. "We intend to make you as messy as possible."

five

LILA

"I LOVE THIS PLACE," Hunter said. "I think I might keep studying so I can stay here longer."

Academics wasn't the only thing Brutham took seriously. Under the guise of churning out well-rounded adults, they also took the relaxation side to a whole new level. That, or the school board had a lot of kinks they wanted to explore. Either way, that left us with a space to explore. And drink.

The Academy's bar was located in the basement, in a soundproof space that consisted of several private rooms, and one main area with a long bar down one side.

Music thumped from speakers in the ceiling, playing some song that hadn't been released to the public yet. The bass was as heavy as the tone, while the lyrics said something about fucking someone's mouth.

"That doesn't sound like Wolf Venom," I said teasingly. Hunter and Parker had both threatened people with violence in the past if they played their brother's music down here.

I suspected Mr D would be just as happy to hear it as they would. I didn't mind Wolf Venom's music, but it was weird that Hunter and Parker, and Mr D both had brothers in the same band.

In fact, Zeke and Asher were involved with each other as well as with Abbie. Fuck only knew what would happen if Chloe and I started a war between us. Honestly, if it created trouble between Zeke and Asher, that was not my problem.

My interest was in my own ass, as well as Hunter and Parker's. If collateral damage happened along the way, then too fucking bad.

"It's better than Wolf Venom." Parker grabbed my hand and pulled me over to the lounge area in the corner. "It's Blazing Violet. They were the support act for Zeke's band on the last world tour, but now they're headlining. They fucking rock."

"That is the idea of a rock band, isn't it?" I let Parker pull me down onto the couch and settled in on his lap. Hunter disappeared off in the direction of the bar.

"That depends who you ask," Parker said. "For example, if you ask my brother Caleb, he'll tell you rock bands are a really good way of smuggling contraband. Same with hockey teams."

"Hockey teams?" I said with a laugh. "That's specific."

Parker wrapped his arms around me and slipped his hands under the front of my shirt. He pressed them against my belly, and squeezed the soft flesh there.

"Yeah, he bought one." He shrugged. "The Dusk Bay Demons. As far as I can tell, they suck. That's what you get for signing a bunch of guys who come from our... Lifestyle."

"And then they give them knife shoes and sticks, what could go wrong?" I said dryly.

"A puck ton," he laughed.

I jabbed my elbow into his ribs. "That was terrible."

"Hey," he said in protest. He squeezed me tighter. "That joke was awesome."

"You said *awful* wrong," I told him over my shoulder. "Pucking awful."

He groaned. "Now *that* one was bad."

"What was bad?" Hunter approached with a tray in his hands.

Another man followed behind him, his gaze on me as he drew closer.

He had to at least have been in his late twenties, with dark hair and blue-green eyes which seemed to see everything. When he looked at me, I got the impression he saw into my soul.

"This is Slade Lincoln." Hunter jerked her head in his direction before placing the tray down on the table. "He's the new business law lecturer."

"Someone had to replace Dexter Clifford," Parker said. He leaned past me to offer Slade his hand. "It's good to see you again, dude."

Slade shook his hand, then sat beside him. "You too, bro."

"You don't sound like a business law lecturer," I remarked.

Slade looked at me appraisingly, his eyes dipping to my breasts and back up again. "I don't? I'm sorry to disappoint you."

"You don't disappoint me," I said quickly. "Just, the last one was uptight and old." This one was young and hot. Looking at him made me want to pant.

"Yeah, I try not to be uptight." Slade already had me naked with his eyes. His fingers were mentally circling my clit.

I swallowed. I had my hands full with the twins, but there was something about this guy, something compelling. Something as dangerous as them.

"Slade is an old family friend," Hunter said meaningfully.

I guessed as much. He was no innocent who had the misfortune of landing a job here, only to find out what the university was really like. No, he had the air of someone who knew exactly what he was doing.

"I figured he could join us for the evening's proceedings," Hunter added.

"The more the merrier," I said lightly. I managed to drag my eyes away from Slade as several others, also carrying trays, sat down on the couches with us.

Chloe was among them, with Dane in tow. He and Slade exchanged glances and nods before they sat down on the opposite side of the lounge area.

About twelve of us sat around the table, most appearing eager, some nervous.

Satisfied everyone was here, Hunter rose and gestured for everyone's attention.

"Thank you all for gathering here this evening," he started formally. "It's once again time for our monthly game of—" He paused for effect. "Kink or Drink. For those of you who are new to the game—" He nodded toward Slade.

"Allow me to explain how this works. On the trays in front of you,

you'll see a variety of delicious shots of alcohol. In the middle of the table, is a stack of cards. The rules are simple. Take a card, read it out loud. You have a choice: do whatever the card tells you, or take a drink. There will be no judgement, whatever you decide. There may, however, be some jeering. All acts must take place in this room, in front of all of us. They may incur some wolf whistles, and possibly some advice."

"I must remind you, cameras and phones are not allowed. Anyone breaking that rule will be taken out and shot." He said the words lightly, but could have meant them literally. As far as I knew, no one ever broke that rule. The game was too much fun for anyone to want to ruin it like that, much less die for it.

"One last thing." Hunter held up his finger. "Everything that takes place here must be one hundred percent consensual. If you cannot find a willing partner for the act the card tells you to do, then you must forfeit and take a drink. If you are so drunk you are unable to perform, you may be laughed at. You will also have to either drink or forfeit. Which is another way of saying 'go to bed.'"

He started to sit down, but stood up again. "I should also remind you, anyone who passes out on the couch is fair game for someone to draw a moustache and glasses on their face." He grinned.

"If you do that to me again, I'm going to whip your ass," Parker growled.

Hunter's grin broadened. "Then don't pass out again, bro. Simple."

Parker flipped him off. "Asshole."

"Guilty." Hunter shrugged and pointed over to a woman on the opposite side of the couches. "Posey, it's your turn to go first."

She gave him a nervous look, but leaned forward and picked up a card. Her eyes widened.

"Get spanked."

"My favourite card." Parker rubbed his hands together.

"I'm fond of it myself," Hunter agreed. "The question is, what is Posey going to do? Kink or Drink?" He gestured at her and gave her a questioning look.

She looked around the table. "If someone wants to..."

"I will." Edward Takahashi seemed quiet and shy when you first met him, but he had ties to the Yakuza, and never missed a game of Kink or

Drink. He was always a very active participant. It didn't surprise me he volunteered to spank Posey.

"Ding ding," Hunter said enthusiastically. "Off you go then." He waved them over to the side of the room where a variety of paddles, floggers and various other toys were hung or sat on shelves. "Don't forget the safe word. Banana."

That was the universal safe word for anything that took place here.

Edward waved for Posey to choose her toy of preference. Her gaze skimmed the shelves before she decided on a pink paddle with velvet covering the head and handle. She gave it to Edward before turning around and leaning over the black, vinyl sex couch. That was starting to look well-worn.

She flipped up the back of her short skirt to expose her ass, bare except for a red, lacy G -string.

I glanced over to Slade. He was watching with casual interest, one arm draped over the back of the couch. I couldn't tell what he thought about any of this, but presumed Hunter filled him in before he joined us. This game wasn't for everyone. Better that people knew what they might get into before they took a place on the couch.

Of course, anyone could walk away whenever they wanted to. No one was forced into anything. Pride kept most people from leaving.

I returned my gaze to Posey and Edward as he spanked her ass tentatively with the paddle.

She jumped slightly, but then turned and gave him a smile. In spite of her nerves, Posey wasn't new to the game either. She clearly enjoyed it as much as the rest of us.

"Harder," she said just loud enough to be heard over the music.

He paddled her harder a couple of times on the same ass cheek, before swapping to the other one.

When her cheeks were both red, she turned her face again and said, "Banana."

Collectively we all shouted, "Banana!" We cheered and waited until they sat back down before the next person picked up a card.

That happened to be my sister, Chloe. She leaned forward far enough that her tits looked like they were about to fall out of her dress. She snatched up a card and sat back.

"Fuck the person on your right," she read.

One kink most of us shared in common was that we liked to be watched. That was one of the reasons we were here. Anyone who played this game more than a few times had fucked in front of the group at least once. I had done it several times, as had Chloe.

Unfortunately, Dane was sitting to her left.

She looked at him, then to the guy on her right. He looked keen, but she shook her head.

"Sorry." Dane leaned over to whisper something in her ear, but she shook her head and picked up a shot of tequila. She threw it back and placed the empty glass down on the table.

The guy beside her, Liam, picked up the next card. His face turned pink. "Get blindfolded and fuck whoever volunteers."

"Are you willing?" Hunter asked him, a brow raised.

When Liam nodded his enthusiastic agreement, Hunter gestured at him. "Close your eyes and cover them with your hands. No peeking."

When Liam's hands were safely over his eyes, Hunter waved around the group. "Don't say anything, just raise your hand if you want to play."

Three of the women and two men raised their hands. Posey looked ready to jump out of her seat. Evidently the spanking left her horny as fuck.

"Hands down," Hunter said. "Okay, Liam you're on." He stood and led Liam over to the side of the room. He grabbed a blindfold off the shelf and put it over his eyes. He tied it tightly at the back, then waved at Posey.

Grinning with excitement, she hurried back over to the sex couch and draped herself over it. She flipped her skirt back up again, revealing her bare, still pink ass.

"All right, Liam, over this way." Hunter guided him over until he was standing behind Posey.

Liam lowered his hands as Hunter stepped back, and cupped Posey's ass cheeks. He felt around for a while before he found the top of her G-string. He pulled it down and dropped it onto the floor, then worked two fingers between her legs and over her pussy.

"So wet," he marvelled. He undid the front of his jeans and pushed them down his hips. He positioned his cock carefully before pressing himself into her.

36

There was something incredibly hot about watching someone fuck someone else, especially knowing he didn't have a clue who it was his cock was embedded inside. Seeing him sliding in and out of her pussy turned me on so hard.

I glanced around the couches to see everyone else watching just as avidly. Every guy had a tent in the front of his jeans. A couple had them undone, their hands inside. They wouldn't work themselves too hard, in case they got a similar card, but they would toy with themselves for a while.

Liam wrapped an arm around Posey and drew her back from the sex couch, far enough to slip his hand between her legs and rub her clit. She arched her back against him, tilted her head and moaned. If he was listening carefully, he might know who she was from that sound alone, but he looked beyond lost to me.

She came first, bucking against his hand, but he quickly followed, pounding into her over and over until he came hard, grunting and groaning.

"Fuck yeah," he said breathlessly. "So fucking good." He held her like that for a while before she slipped away, scooped up her G-string and darted back to the couch. By the time he pushed the blindfold of his eyes, she was sitting with her legs crossed, looking innocent.

If he asked, we'd tell him who he fucked, but that was up to him. Some people preferred not to know. It was all part of the game.

Liam shrugged and tossed the blindfold back on the shelf before he sat back down.

Hunter smiled at me. "Your turn, babe."

I leaned forward and picked up a card.

I took a breath before reading it. It was a new card. That wasn't surprising. Hunter liked to change them, so we weren't always doing the same things. Some of them were ridiculous, like run around the Academy building naked.

"Fuck someone you've never fucked before," I said. I thought the twins might get angry and pass me a drink immediately. To my surprise, they both gave me speculative looks instead.

"It's up to you, babe," Hunter said. There was a hint of warning in his eyes. If I was going to do this, I better choose very wisely.

I didn't bother to look in Mr D's direction. No one was going to consent to that, even if I was inclined to try. Especially not in front of Chloe.

Instead, my gaze slid to Slade. I knew beyond a shadow of a doubt, the twins would pass me a drink if I chose anyone else here. But him—

"We don't mind sharing if it's with him," Parker said softly.

I raised my eyebrows at Slade.

"I'm game," he said simply.

The expression on his face made me wetter than hell. Yeah, he wanted me.

He put out his hand. I hesitated for a moment before I took it.

He reached over and pulled me until I was straddling his lap. His erection pressed into the side of my leg. The fabric of his jeans was rough against my ass. I undid his fly and pushed myself up enough so he could work his jeans down his hips. I pulled the top of his boxers down with them, freeing his huge cock.

Oh my God.

I glanced over to Hunter and Parker. They both watched with wide eyes, full of excitement and arousal. Not even a hint of jealousy or annoyance. Of course, they were secure in our relationship. They knew nothing would change things between us. This was all about us adding some excitement to it.

I didn't want to see them with another woman, but they were one hundred percent okay with this. That and white hot heat on their faces turned me on even more than before.

I tugged the gusset of my panties aside and lowered my dripping wet pussy slowly down onto Slade's cock.

Holy fuck, he felt so good. I sank all the way down and stayed still for a while before I started to move, rising and falling up and down his cock.

His eyes half closed. "Holy fuck," he whispered. He pulled down the front of my T-shirt and the cup of my bra and kneaded my breast with his hand.

"They look good together," Parker said to Hunter.

"They do," Hunter mused. "I think we might be sharing more often, Park."

Parker hummed his agreement.

That was a conversation for later, but I wouldn't mind enjoying this cock again another time. Maybe even getting to know the man it was attached to.

Slade squeezed my breast. His other hand slid between us to circle my clit. "Come for me sweetheart," he ordered. "Come for me and then I'm going to come inside your beautiful pussy. I'm going to come inside you while your boyfriends watch us. You want that, don't you?"

"Yes," I said breathlessly.

"I know I do," Parker said. "I want to see you fill her to the brim."

"Me too," Hunter agreed.

And just like that, I was completely undone. I shattered into a thousand pieces, coming hard all over Slade's cock. Blood pounded through me so hard I saw stars in distant galaxies. My whole body sang. I tipped my head back and cried out to the ceiling.

Slade came a few moments later, thrusting hard up into me. "Fuck yes," he panted. "Take every fucking drop. I want you dripping with my cum." He ground up into me, groaning and gripping my breast and my pussy in hard, bruising fingers.

Finally, we both sagged down, slick with sweat and cum.

Between pants, Slade muttered something which sounded like, "I think I'm going to like it here."

six

LILA

I ROUNDED on Hunter the moment we stepped back into my room. I slammed my hands into his chest and shoved him back a step.

"What the fuck was that?"

He looked down at me for a moment with surprise that quickly passed. His expression turned to one of feigned innocence.

"What was what?" He grabbed my wrists and pushed me backwards into my room.

"You know what." I tugged my wrists free and stomped away from him. I whirled back around and glared. "You put that card there. You knew I'd get it. You were the one who chose Posey to go first. You set me up. You wanted me to fuck Slade."

"You didn't seem to mind." Parker closed the door behind us, but stayed at a safe distance from me.

"You were in on it?" I demanded. I wanted to grab the backs of their heads and bang them together, but at the same time I was angry with myself. I got caught up in the moment and now I was worried about the repercussions. Not to mention the reasons why Hunter put me in Slade's path.

"Since when do you share?" I turned my gaze back to Hunter. He was the one who ran the game. If anyone was responsible for this, it started with him, even if it finished with me. Or finished with Slade inside me.

"We've been sharing since we met you." Hunter grinned as though somehow all of this was funny. When I didn't smile, his faded. "Okay, let's all calm down." He gestured downward with his hands.

"I don't want to calm down," I snapped. "I want to know what the fuck happened."

Hunter sighed and flopped down into the end of the bed. "Chloe had an advantage. Dane DiMarco. Not just his contacts, but his influence."

"Because he's a teacher here?" I already knew how much of that he had. Dane could fail students if he wanted to, or potentially influence his peers to do the same. If I failed any of my classes, that was near enough to an automatic loss against my sister. Now I thought about it, I'd be surprised if he hadn't tried to do that already. Any chance I had of becoming head of the family someday... I could more or less kiss it goodbye.

"Exactly." Hunter leaned back on his hands. "I wanted to introduce you to Slade. You need him in your corner. That card was designed to put all of his attention on you. Which it did. Now he's had one taste of you, he's going to want more. You and your pussy are addictive."

"For the record, it was Hunter's idea," Parker said. He leaned against the door, his arms crossed.

"Thanks, Park," Hunter said sarcastically. He rolled his eyes at his brother, then turned back to me. "I didn't necessarily *expect* you to fuck Slade, but I'm glad you did. Watching you with him was hot as hell."

"Did he know about any of this?" I asked. The idea they might have invited Slade along for the sole purpose of fucking me, made me even angrier.

"Absolutely not," Hunter said immediately. "Like I said, it was meant to be an introduction. Whatever came of it, came of it. I thought you might take a drink, but then you were into the idea, and Parker and I didn't mind." He grabbed my hand and pulled me down to the bed beside him.

"Having a guy like Slade around will give you an advantage over Chloe. With two teachers involved, you'd be on equal footing. With Parker and I, you're miles ahead. Between the four of us, we'll make it so your father has no choice but to choose you."

"What happened to taking people out for coffee?" I asked. "Or lunch. Hell, a nice picnic would have worked too."

"We could have done that, but that would have taken time," Hunter said. "This way, you have us all where you need us."

"You mean *you* have us where you need us," I corrected. "You seem to think you're the one calling all the shots."

He grinned. "Babe, the only thing I'm calling is that your father will choose you. Everything else is a small cog in that wheel. You could have taken a shot and then I would have figured out something else to make sure you had Slade's attention."

"She had his attention the moment he laid eyes on her," Parker said. "Did you see the way he had her naked with his eyes? He was all in like a fish taking the bait. All we had to do was reel him in, and Lila did that with her perfect pussy. The guy never stood a chance."

"Do either of us have a choice in this?" I asked dryly.

"You always have a choice," Hunter said coolly. "No matter what that choice is, we support it. All we want is what's best for you. Now you're on Slade's radar, you'll be able to get him to do all sorts of things. I have a few things in mind myself. I'm not saying you have to have a relationship with the guy, but if you want to, that's fine with us. As long as you don't dump us for him."

I shook my head slowly. My thoughts were tumbling around in my brain.

"You don't mind if I have a third boyfriend?" I asked. "It won't bother you if I fuck him when you're not around?"

"As long as you're not sneaking around, we don't mind," Parker said. "If everyone knows what's going on, where's the harm?"

"Right," I said vaguely. I barely knew Slade. The attraction was undeniable, but fucking someone and dating them were two different things. We might have an actual conversation and realise we hated each other. What would happen then? He wouldn't help me the way Hunter suggested he could.

"Do me a favour. If you find some other guy you think I should fuck, warn me in advance. I feel..."

I slipped my hand out of Hunter's and wrapped my arms around myself. "I don't know. Like I cheated."

"You did not cheat," Hunter said firmly. "If you did, Slade would be missing his cock right now." The expression on his face suggested Slade would be missing a lot more than that. "You're right, I should have told you what I planned, but I wanted it to be spontaneous. Natural. And it was. He wanted you and you wanted him as much as Park and I wanted you to want each other."

He frowned, trying to get his head around that sentence. "You know what I mean."

"We've been trying to figure out a way to pry Dane away from Chloe," Parker said thoughtfully. "He seems very attached. Her too. So far, we've been gentle with them. We have some plans we might have to put into action if they keep going the way they are."

"Does it involve killing either of them?" I asked.

How did I feel about that? Chloe was my twin sister, as well as my rival. We hadn't been close for years, but I didn't *necessarily* want her dead.

Dane, I didn't much care about one way or the other. Students got away with a lot here at Brutham, but killing teachers was usually frowned upon. Hunter and Parker got away with it once, but the Academy would probably fail them if they did it twice.

Their oldest brother Reuben, would be pissed if they flunked out. Especially if it was because of me.

"Only as a last resort," Parker said. "We'll play as dirty as we have to, but killing is way too easy. You want to win because you're the best, not by default. Right?"

"Right," I agreed. If I won because I was the only Bell twin left standing, then so be it, but I really wanted to earn this. I wanted to look my father in the eyes and hear him tell me I was the best of his daughters. The most worthy. The most ruthless.

I ran a hand over my hair and gripped the ends. "Do I want to know what you have planned?"

Hunter laughed. "Probably not. Don't worry, it will be epic. In the meantime, you should get to know Slade. Reel him in a little tighter. We're going to need him to pull a few things off. If he falls for you, great. If he doesn't, he's probably out of his mind, but if you two are friends, that will help too."

"I'm starting to feel like a whore." I gave Hunter a dark look.

"You're a *queen*." He slipped his arm around me. "A queen needs a harem to see to all of her needs. To vanquish her enemies and give her lots and lots of orgasms. Slade can help us at least with the vanquishing, if not the orgasms. With the added bonus of helping you pass business law, which I know you despise."

"You think of everything," I said with a slight touch of sarcasm. "Did you interview all the teachers before you chose him?"

He laughed. "Naw, we really have known Slade for years. He went to school with our brother, Zeke. Come to think of it, he went to school with Dane's brother too, Asher DiMarco. They used to be friends. If they still are, that could work in our favour." He looked thoughtful.

I sighed. "I suppose it can't hurt to try to get to know him. He's kinda hot. And he knows what to do with his cock." And he didn't mind doing it in front of other people. This could make the next game of Kink Or Drink very interesting.

Parker groaned. "I can't decide if I'm jealous or horny. Probably both. If he's better at fucking than I am, I don't want to know."

I snorted a laugh.

"You should be used to being told that by now," Hunter said, looking both sly and cocky. "I've been telling you I'm better than you for ages."

Parker flipped him off. "Yes you have, but it's still bullshit. I'm the one who makes Lila make those cute little panting sounds just before she comes."

"Yes you do," Hunter agreed. "I'm the one who makes her make cute *big* panting sounds. I'm clearly better at getting her off then you will ever be."

He gave Parker the side eye, then turned his gaze back to me. "Park has a point though. If Slade is better than us—"

"You only have yourselves to blame," I finished for him. "You introduced me to him. Whatever the consequences of that, you both have to suck it up." Maybe I could have some fun with this. What was the point of dating hot twins if you couldn't dangle them off the end of a string once in a while?

"Only if Slade lets us," Parker said. He grinned, but his expression was dreamy at the same time. Evidently I wasn't the only one who found Slade hot.

Now I was picturing both of the twins on their knees in front of Slade, taking turns to suck his cock.

"On that note, I need to have a shower." I slipped away from Hunter and stood. "I'm still sticky with Slade's cum." I smiled to myself at the glance they exchanged. Yes, this was definitely going to be fun.

"KEEP YOUR EYES AND EARS PEELED." I glanced back to see Parker nod. The best part about having a twin was having someone who always had my back. Some days I felt bad for Lila, because she couldn't say the same about hers.

She didn't have the monopoly on dysfunctional families, but I usually didn't want any of my brothers dead. Not even Zeke that time he held a gun to my head and threatened to kill me. I was almost, mostly, reasonably sure he wouldn't have actually done it, but I was grateful Reuben made him promise not to kill me or Parker at any time in the future. If there was anyone in the world who would keep a promise, it was Zeke. He considered himself above all of the shit our family was into.

Mr Lead Singer of Wolf Venom thought he was pretty fucking perfect and better than the rest of us. Sure, being a rock star was glamorous and all that shit, but this was much more fun.

I slid the key into the lock and turned it slowly. Like the well-maintained contraption it was, the lock clicked easily and the door opened without a sound.

I glanced around at Parker and grinned. "Good work." He was the one who got the key, made a copy and returned it, without anyone being the wiser.

"You doubted me?" The cocky prick cocked his head at me and

grinned. Anyone would think he was the better looking, smarter twin, the way he was acting.

Fortunately, I knew better.

I stepped into the dark room and turned my phone's torch on. We didn't want to be too obvious by turning on the light, or potentially leaving fingerprints. This was by no means our first rodeo.

"If you were a woman, where would you leave your contraceptives?" Parker asked.

My gaze swept the room. It was identical in layout to Lila's, but the bed was covered in blue-grey blankets and pillows instead of the black and red Lila preferred. No clothes lay on the floor here either. No half-damp towels. It was lived in, but not quite as homely.

"If I was a woman, and went to Brutham Academy, I'd probably keep them on me at all times," I said. "In case some nefarious person snuck in and fucked with them."

"Yes, but you're not a trusting person, Hunt," he told me.

"Are you suggesting you are?" I raised my phone and moved it around slowly, taking in everything.

"Not at all," he said with a laugh. "But I know us and what we're capable of. I wouldn't trust us if I was anyone but Lila."

I glanced back at him. "She was pissed about that Slade thing." For a while there I thought we were well and truly in the doghouse with our girl. I never intended to make her feel like a whore. I meant what I said when I told her she was a queen. She was our queen.

Slade could help us secure the crown for her and help her keep it. If he was willing to, of course. Why wouldn't he be? Lila was hot, beautiful and deserving. The whole world should be at her feet, as far as I was concerned. If that meant sharing her with one more guy, then that's what I'll do. Hell, I'd share her with ten more if it got her what she wanted and needed.

I'm not going to lie, I hoped it didn't come down to that. My balls would be so blue they'd probably fall off.

I stepped into Chloe's bathroom. "She might have one of those implant things." I pulled out a handkerchief out of my pocket and wrapped it around my hand before I opened the top drawer.

I smiled. "Bingo." On the top of the draw was half a packet of contraceptive pills. I picked them up and shoved them in my pocket. I pulled out another packet and popped the same amount of sugar pills that she'd already used up, into the toilet.

One by one, they plopped in and sank to the bottom. I flushed the toilet and placed the packet of fake contraceptives in the drawer where the real ones had been.

"Operation fuckery is complete," I declared. I closed the drawer and stepped away from the sink.

"I have to admit, this was a brilliant idea," Parker said.

"Are you admitting that because it was your idea?" I won't lie, I wish I'd thought of it. When I told Lila killing her sister was a last resort, I was sincere. But if Dane *accidentally* got Chloe pregnant, that would throw a spanner in the works.

If nothing else, it might distract her for long enough for her grades to slip. Best case scenario, she dropped out altogether. Samuel Bell wouldn't be happy with her if that happened. Not at all.

Of course, the worst case scenario would be Samuel Bell embracing his grandchild, and basing his decision on their existence. Although, with a DiMarco as the father, the chances on that were reduced somewhat.

Not as low as they would be if Lila had a child fathered by Parker or me. A Brantley father would not be looked down upon well. That was exactly why we made sure Lila was very careful with her contraceptives. And why Parker and I both had vasectomies. They could be reversed later if we wanted to, but the chances of an unwelcome accident were greatly reduced.

I knew Dane hadn't done the same thing, because I hacked into his medical records and checked. All of this would have been pointless otherwise. Although, breaking into Chloe's room and messing with her was fun anyway. After turning off her security camera, obviously. Neither Parker nor I were born yesterday.

"I might be," Parker said. "It was definitely one of my more inspired ideas."

I turned and raised an eyebrow at him. "Inspired by what? You're not starting to think you want children, are you?"

He grimaced. "Fuck no. I just like to come up with creative ways to screw with people that aren't us. Like Penn that time."

I grinned. Messing with the keyboardist of Wolf Venom was one of the most fun afternoons I'd ever had. The guy was so fucking uptight, he needed some loosening up. The fact he could have died was another item in the 'not my problem' basket. He hadn't died, so no harm was done in the end.

"How long are we going to—" He stopped mid-sentence and froze. "Fuck," he whispered.

Shit, I heard them too. Voices in the corridor outside. Chloe and someone else. A male voice. It sounded like Dane, but I didn't give a crap if it wasn't.

I had a vested interest in whoever she was fucking, but I didn't give a hoot if she was cheating on Mr D.

I dropped to the ground and rolled under the bed as Parker did the same thing. I grunted as he rammed into my shoulder, but fell silent. Now wasn't the time to punch or poke him back.

The door clicked and opened a moment later.

"It's so good to finally get some time alone," Chloe said.

"Tell me about it." That was definitely Dane DiMarco. "It seems like the school board keeps finding things to occupy my time. And yours. I haven't had a moment's peace since the other night's Kink or Drink. Between that and keeping an eye on that Slade guy..."

The door shut and locked. "Can you believe that?" Chloe asked. "Lila fucking him in front of everyone, including the evil twins."

I grinned at their favourite nickname for Parker and me. If she thought we were evil, she hadn't seen anything yet. Not that she could talk. Behind their backs, people called her and her sister the wicked sisters. They did their best to live up to it.

"When it comes to those three, I'd believe anything," Dane said. "The last thing you need is a guy like Slade Lincoln getting involved with your sister as well. He would complicate things."

Hell yes he would, I thought. *Ain't that awesome?*

"Can we stop talking?" Chloe asked, her tone low and husky.

I have to confess her voice made my cock hard. I would totally fuck Chloe given the chance, and if it didn't complicate things, which it would.

Parker stifled a groan right next to my ear. "Tell me they're not," he whispered.

The mattress dropped to just above my nose as their weight bore down on it. Judging by the sound of wet kissing and zippers, they absolutely *were* going to. And we were going to have to listen to it until we found a chance to sneak out again.

It felt as though only a couple of minutes passed before Chloe started moaning. "Oh my God, your tongue is amazing."

I stuck out mine and made a face at the slats above my head. I would much rather watch than listen and imagine Dane's tongue on Chloe's clit.

On the other hand, the sounds she was making made me harder than hell. I slipped a hand down silently and undid my jeans. I pushed them and my boxers down and curled my fingers around my cock. The harder Chloe moaned, the more she bounced the bed, the harder my hand slid up and down my hot length.

I bit my lip to keep my body as still as I could, and to stop from making a sound. Nothing would give us away faster than screaming when I came.

From the soft but steady pants beside me, Parker was working his own cock.

"Oh, oh, ohhh. I'm going to come," Chloe groaned. "God, yes, right there. Ohhh." Her body went still, but she cried out, long and loud. She sounded a lot like her twin when she was having an orgasm.

The mattress shifted and Dane let out a moan of his own. I pictured him with his cock deep inside her, pumping and grinding. With any luck, he was getting her pregnant right above our heads.

I could be an uncle of sorts to the kid, since I was so involved in their potential conception. I grinned to myself.

The mattress shifted again. It sounded like they'd rolled over and Chloe was now on top of the history teacher. I bet she got good marks for spreading her pretty little legs for him.

As for him, if I was a teacher here, I'd probably fuck half the students. Was it frowned upon? Sure. Was it illegal? No. Did anyone really give a fuck what went on behind closed doors? Not at all.

Alliances were made and broken against mattresses all over the Academy. It was one of the unwritten rules of Brutham. Don't ask, definitely don't tell. Do whatever you have to do to get through your time here. What doesn't kill you in a place like this will one hundred percent make you stronger. If you don't lose your mind in the process.

"Ride me," he said. "Be a good little slut and make me come."

"Mmm, yes sir," she replied, a smile in her tone.

Fuck, that was hot. Could I get Lila to call me sir? Maybe that was reserved for people like Slade and Dane. That was a conversation that would have to wait until later.

"You're such a good fucking slut." Dane drew out the words as though saying one per thrust up into her pussy. "I'm glad this pussy is mine. You are mine. I... I own you... Ahhh..."

When he came, so did I, hot cum squirting out of my cock and onto my hand and the bottom of the mattress. Oops.

I wiped the rest of it off above my head while Chloe and Dane bounced around for a while longer. By the time they went still, so did I. I closed my eyes and sighed. We'd have to wait until they left or fell asleep before we could sneak back out again.

It might be a long, uncomfortable night under here.

eight

LILA

"WHAT THE HELL DID YOU DO?" Chloe waved something in my face.

Apparently she didn't give a crap that we were in the middle of a busy corridor outside the library. A couple of students stopped to stare. We both glared at them until they hurried away.

I grabbed her wrist to take a better look.

"What the hell?" I squinted. "Why are you waving contraceptive pills in my face?" I shoved her wrist away from me.

"They're not contraceptive pills," she snarled. "Someone changed them out."

I snorted a laugh. "It wasn't me. Don't tell me you're pregnant."

"Thankfully not." She lowered her hand to her side. "I noticed they'd been moved slightly and got suspicious. I had the Academy lab look at them. They're nothing more than sugar." She looked at them in disgust before flinging the packet into a rubbish bin.

"Maybe Dane did it," I suggested. "That sounds like the kind of thing he'd do."

It also sounded like the kind of thing the twins would do. If they had, they hadn't told me. They were going to have some questions to answer when they got back from yet another business trip for their brother, Reuben. He usually sent them during the holidays, but once in a while something 'urgent' came up that only they could handle.

The last time, Parker came back with a broken nose and some story about an unprovoked attack by an asshole he wouldn't name. Apparently it was better if I didn't know. Sooner or later, I'll get him or Hunter to tell me the details. For the time being, I was content to let it lie.

"Dane wouldn't do that," Chloe said, but she looked uncertain. "Are you sure it wasn't you? Some kind of fucked up way to try to get to me? Did you think I'd get pregnant and drop out of Brutham?"

I raised my hands to either side. "I had nothing to do with it. If I did, I would have put something stronger in them than sugar. Nothing would get you kicked out of the Academy faster than taking illegal drugs."

They didn't care if we got drunk off our faces, or stabbed each other, but they drew the line at drugs.

Chloe growled. "Fucking bitch. That is something you'd do, isn't it? Or something you'd have your lap dogs do. No wonder you and they get along so well. You're all degenerates. You'll bring the Bell name down into the gutter."

I rolled my eyes. "You'd know all about the gutter. It's the favourite place of most people with the last name DiMarco. You know the only reason Dane is with you is for his own ambition, right? He'd suck Dad's cock if it got him power. Or Reuben Brantley. Hell, he'd suck them both and call them ice cream if they threw him half a bone."

Her face turned pink. "Dane has more integrity than you ever will. He—"

"What's going on?"

I didn't know Slade was there until he stood beside me.

He looked from me to Chloe and back again. "You two are getting loud."

Chloe regarded him for a moment and forced a smile. "Sorry, sir," she said with saccharine sweetness. "My dear sister and I got a little carried away. We didn't mean to be a bother." Past all the mock sweetness, she was giving him 'bend me over your desk and fuck me' eyes.

Would she really do that? Potentially.

She might have the kind of relationship with Dane that I had with Hunter and Parker. The kind where they didn't mind sharing, and were ambitious for me. Slade taught my weakest subject. It would be an easy matter for him to fail me if Chloe got him on her side.

The prospect should have made me nervous, but it was pushed off my radar by the idea of them together. That gave me an unexpected stab of jealousy right in my heart. My competitive nature flared, along with my anger.

If Slade was going to be with either of us, it would be me. I'd make certain of that.

"Chloe was just wrongfully accusing me of tampering with her birth-control," I said frankly.

He gave her a long look, then turned his gaze to me. "Did you?"

"I can one hundred percent promise I did *not*," I told him. "I don't know who did."

I had a fair idea, but I wasn't exactly lying. I *didn't* know for certain. He understood that as well as I did.

He rubbed a hand over the stubble on his cheek. "I'm sure you appreciate what the penalty would be for doing something like that."

His gaze seemed to bore right into me, stripping off my clothes and a layer or two of skin. He was definitely not talking about expulsion. The punishment he had in mind probably involved a paddle and restraints.

My tongue darted over my lips. I was wet as hell thinking about it. I almost wished I *had* changed Chloe's pills. Let him spank my ass until I screamed for him to stop. And then a few more times after that.

"Yes, sir." I looked at him through my lashes. "The punishment would be very severe. I would feel the repercussions for days." Including a pussy so wrecked I wouldn't be able to walk for a week.

His eyes darkened. Hell yes, he was thinking exactly the same thing I was. With Hunter and Parker away, I was already suffering from a terrible case of blue clit. If he kept looking at me the way he was, I was going to come right here in the middle of the corridor.

Chloe made a sound of disgust. "Just so you know, I've already had the lock on my door changed. And the code to access my security camera. Whatever it takes to keep myself safe." She gave Slade a last smile before she turned and walked away down the corridor, ass wiggling as she went.

"I love her, but she can be so paranoid." I sighed dramatically. "Anyone would think I'm out to get her."

"Aren't you?" Slade asked bluntly. Before I could respond he pressed a finger to his lips to signal silence. "Let's not talk about it here. Come with me to my office."

I didn't miss the double meaning. If he wasn't careful, I was going to start dripping down the insides of my thighs.

"Yes, sir." I walked beside him down the corridor and into another one that led to the back of the Academy building. A lot of the teachers had offices here, with views that overlooked the lake and the forest beyond.

He gestured for me to step inside and closed the door behind us.

"I think you have some explaining to do." He leaned against the edge of his desk and crossed his arms. He made no attempt to hide the tent in his pants.

"What do you want to know?" I crossed my arms too and pushed my breasts up higher. His gaze dropped to them before flicking back up to my face.

"That whole Kink or Drink game. Was it set up?"

"Yes it was, but I wasn't in on it," I replied. "Were you?"

His expression faltered for a moment. He clearly hadn't expected me to throw the question back at him like that.

"No. I've known Hunter and Parker for years. Hunter invited me along for some fun. What happened between us... It was unexpected."

"Yes it was," I agreed. "It was a spur of the moment thing. Do you regret it?"

"No," he said immediately. "The opposite. The moment I saw you, I was drawn to you. Like a moth to a dangerously hot flame." The side of his mouth twitched. "All I could think about was touching you, fucking you. When I realised you were the twins' girlfriend—"

"You figured that was that?" I asked.

He worked his mouth into a slow smile. "No. I figured I'd have to find a way to steal you away from them." He lowered his arms and stepped towards me. "The minute I saw you, I decided you were mine. Whatever I had to do, I would have found a way to make that happen."

His smile became boyishly lopsided. "Students go missing all the time around here. If it came to that..."

I should have been as disturbed as hell to hear him say he would have killed Hunter and Parker to win me, but it was hotter than fuck.

What girl doesn't want a guy who's prepared to go to great lengths for her?

"And now?" I asked.

He cupped my face with his hands. "They seem all right with sharing."

"They are." I locked my eyes on his. If I wasn't dripping before, I was now.

I took a steadying breath before things got out of control. "Hunter and Parker had an ulterior motive for introducing us to each other." I quickly explained the rivalry between Chloe and me and the reason for it. And why the twins thought Slade could help.

"If you want to walk away right now, I understand," I told him. The electricity crackling between us was undeniable, but the reality was we were playing a dangerous game. A game that wasn't for everyone.

"You don't understand." His voice was barely above a whisper. "The moment I saw you, I couldn't walk away. Whatever this is between us, I want that and everything that goes with it. If that means doing some dubious things..." He shrugged. "It wouldn't be the first time. I teach law, but I've broken plenty of them. But that's a story for another time. I need you."

He dropped his hands to my hips, turned me around and pushed me until I was bent forward over the top of his desk.

He flipped up my skirt, pulled my G string aside and slid two fingers straight into my soaking pussy.

"You are so fucking wet," he marvelled. "How badly do you want me?" He slid his fingers in and out, stroking my flesh and threatening to drive me wild.

"Badly," I panted. "So badly, sir."

"I like the sound of that." He grabbed a fistful of hair and pulled my head back while he continued to fuck me with his fingers. "Do you want my cock?"

"Yes. Yes I do. Please, sir." The blood was racing so fast inside me I could barely think or breathe. I needed to have his cock inside me so, so much.

"If you want my cock, you have to earn it," he said. "You have to come for me." He slipped his fingers out and turned his hand so he was rubbing the heel over my clit. He slid his fingers back inside and worked me harder than ever.

I placed my palms down to the desktop to either side of me, my chest pressed against the cool wood. I spread my legs as far as they'd go, opening me out to him further.

"I'm going to come, sir," I said between breaths.

"Good, come... Right now."

His demand pushed me over the edge immediately, as though my body had no choice but to obey his order. I groaned into the desktop as he worked me all the way through my orgasm and back down the other side.

I lay puffing lightly and trying to get my breath as he slipped off my G string and replaced his fingers with his massive cock. He eased into me slowly, giving my body time to get used to him.

"All my cock has wanted to do since the other night was get back inside your body." His voice was low and husky with desire. "I'm going to fuck you everywhere. All of your holes are going to be mine. But for now, I'm going to claim your pussy. I may have to share her with two other cocks, but right now, she belongs to me." He pushed himself all the way inside me until he was seated to his balls. He placed his hands on the top of the desk beside me and started to thrust slowly.

He took his time, fucking me with slow, even strokes, savouring the sweet friction between our bodies. Fucking me into the oblivion of a second orgasm before he joined me, tipping over the edge and filling me with his cum.

He slipped his arms around me and pulled me up while his cock was still deep inside me. He buried his face in my hair and inhaled deeply.

"This is just the start," he promised.

nine

LILA

PARKER HANDED me a drink and flopped down beside me. How he managed not to slosh beer over the side of his glass, I have no idea. He had an interesting skill set.

"So Chloe figured it out, hmmm?" Hunter reclined in a chair opposite us. A private room in the Academy bar was a favourite place for us to drink and plan world domination.

"So it would seem," I said. They told me how they snuck into her room, changed her contraceptives and spend half the night under her bed waiting for her and Dane to stop fucking and fall asleep. They'd managed to sneak out again a couple of hours before dawn.

Both of them thought it was hilarious. So did I, but at the same time, it served them right, getting stuck under there. Without doubt, they'd do it again. They were slightly out of their trees, but that was part of their charm. There was nothing they wouldn't do for shits and giggles.

"She was definitely not happy about it." Slade sat in a chair beside Hunter. He looked at us over the rim of his glass. He'd grinned when the guys told their story. If he was bothered by it in any way, he showed no sign. If anything, he seemed to admire the twins' audacity.

"The question is, what do we do next?" Parker asked.

"I recommend practising for the trials," Slade said. "We can deal with whatever Chloe throws at Lila, but during the trials, there's only so much we can do. The more prepared you are, the better. You'll be able to focus on going after her, or protecting yourself, rather than on the trials themselves."

A flutter of fear passed through me. The trials were Brutham's way of separating the stronger students from the weaker. The ones with strong connections from the ones without.

During the trials, we'd be taken to a particular location. From there, we had to make our way to another location. That was it. In terms of rules, there were none.

If anyone got in our way, we could remove them. By any means. The trials were often used as a way for students to resolve past grudges. Few students who survived the trials came out of it unscathed.

"I should know what to expect, I suppose," I said slowly. I could ask them for help, but if Chloe came after me somewhere remote, they may not get to me in time. And vice versa. Slade was right. The better prepared I was, the more chance I had of getting through the trials in one piece.

"We'll make it fun for you." Parker grinned. "By the time the trials come around, you'll be looking forward to it."

"That sounds like a big ask to me," I told him. Excuse me for being sceptical. Cynicism went hand in hand with being a Bell.

"Do you trust us?" Hunter gave me a searching look, although his tone was light.

"Yes," I said without hesitation. "Of course I do." They hadn't blinked an eye when I told them I fucked Slade in his office. Or when I included him in this meeting. It felt natural to have all three of them here. Like Slade was the final piece of our puzzle.

"Then trust us when we say we can make this good for you," Hunter said. "We've all been through the trials, we know what to expect."

"You two had each other's backs," Slade pointed out. Not accusing, just stating a fact.

"That's true," Hunter conceded. "But Reuben has a lot of enemies who would have paid to have us eliminated."

"It just so happens, we're smarter, faster and more resourceful than they were." Parker looked smug. "They were never going to catch us."

"So I may have more than Chloe to contend with." I grimaced. "My father has some powerful enemies too, including Reuben."

"Any chance Reuben would pay you to eliminate Lila and Chloe?" Slade asked bluntly.

"There's every chance he'd try," Hunter agreed. "There's no chance we'd take it."

"Does he know that?" Slade cocked his head at the twins.

They exchanged glances.

"He does," Parker said carefully. "Zeke was nice enough to fill him in on that. He's not happy, but we're still alive, so I guess he still needs us for...things."

"He wouldn't have made Zeke promise not to kill us if he didn't need us for, like Parker said, 'things,'" Hunter agreed.

"Like potentially killing Lila and Chloe?" Slade pressed a little harder.

"Chloe maybe." Parker shrugged. "But only if we have to, not because our brother paid us to do it. If we have to choose between Lila and him, we'll choose her every time. If she needs Chloe dead, then she'll be dead." He nodded as though that was the end of the conversation.

Hunter sat forward, forearm across his thighs supporting his weight. "I know what you're trying to do. You want to know exactly where our loyalties lie. They're with Lila. Where are yours?"

"You're the one who brought me in here," Slade pointed out.

"Answer the question," Parker said. His eyes narrowed dangerously. He smiled a lot, but sometimes it was good to remind people he was as dangerous as fuck as well.

Slade matched Hunter's pose. "In the same place. My loyalty is with her. I'd like to think the four of us are a team. With one ultimate goal. Lila's happiness."

"And giving her lots of orgasms," Parker added.

Slade sat back and smiled. "Definitely lots of those."

"Are you all done?" I asked. "Would you like a moment to pull out your cocks and compare them for size?" This conversation was gratifying and in some ways necessary, but it wasn't getting us any closer to making any plans. Not that I didn't appreciate every single one of those orgasms.

"No need, we all know Slade's is the biggest," Parker said. He didn't seem too concerned about the fact. "Mine isn't as big, but I know how to use it." He glanced over at me and grinned.

"Yes, you do," I told him. All three of them did. Better than any other guy I ever fucked.

With the possible exception of my stepbrother Zachary. The only guy, as far as I knew who both Chloe and I screwed. Thinking of him reminded me of my stepmother. She and my father weren't together for very long, but we got along well enough. When she left my father's life, she left mine as well. Only Zachary stayed in contact these days.

"Apart from the trials, what else can we be focusing on?" Hunter asked.

"I've offered to tutor Lila," Slade said, looking smug. "And by that I mean actual study as well as orgasms. I'll make sure no one has any excuse to fail her."

Hunter nodded. "That's a good idea. I'd suggest you try to make friends with Dane, but I doubt he'd take the bait. If he doesn't know you're also involved with Lila, he soon will. Shame, we could have used someone keeping an eye on him. He's a slippery fucker."

"I'm sure he could say the same about you," Parker said.

"That's because I am a slippery fucker," Hunter agreed. He grinned. "I know the kinds of things we get up to, which makes me nervous. After what we did to Chloe's birth control, we can expect them to do something. They're not going to take that lying down."

"Any idea what they might try?" Slade asked. He sipped his beer, with his brow creased in a slight frown. He was sexy as fuck when he was that intense.

"Chloe likes to sell herself as the nicer twin," Parker said. "If she does something, it's going to be something subtle. Preferably something she can pin on someone else."

"That's exactly what she'd do." I sighed softly.

I hated having to be wary of my sister. I would have loved a relationship with my twin like Hunter and Parker had.

Although, if they were pitted against each other, it would get even uglier than this. They had no filter, or much in the way of a moral compass. What was the expression? Morally grey. My guys were closer to morally charcoal; so dark they were almost unforgivably bad.

To people who weren't me and now Slade anyway. I loved them all the more for it.

I'd hate to have them off side. Chloe must lie awake at night wondering what they'd do next. Honestly, I doubted there was anything *close* to a limit to what they might pull.

Parker wrapped his fingers around mine. "Whatever happens, we'll deal with it. She's not getting past us to get to you. And if she does, we'll deal with that too. The four of us are an unstoppable force. Sometimes for good, sometimes for evil." He grinned.

Hunter frowned at him. "When are we a force for good?"

"Whenever we have our tongues on Lila's clit," Parker retorted. "Or our hands. Or our cocks. Or a vibrator, for that matter. Any time we're giving our queen orgasms."

Hunter pointed a finger gun at him. "You have a point, bro. That's definitely good."

"Of course I have a point," Parker said. "I am the smarter twin." He pretended to fluff the back of his hair.

"In your dreams," Hunter said with a laugh.

I turned to Slade. "Do you have any siblings?" He'd been watching the conversation with a combination of curiosity and amusement. Like a guy would watch his younger siblings banter and squabble. I realised I knew almost nothing about him.

"I have two sisters," he replied. "One older and one younger. Kirsten and Darcie. They don't get along very well either."

"You went here, to Brutham?" I sat against the back of the couch and crossed my knees.

"I did, yes," he agreed. "We all did. I... I had an older brother who didn't survive the trials. He got too cocky and made too many enemies. That put a lot of pressure on us to succeed. Everyone assumed we'd be like him. But we all got through and we're stronger for it."

"What do your sisters do?" Parker asked. He pulled my feet onto his lap and took off my shoes. With his drink in one hand, he started to massage my toes with the other.

"Kirsten works with Mack D'Antonio, the businessman," Slade said slowly. "Darcie works for the twins' brother, Caleb. They're both ambitious and career driven."

I nodded. I'd never met either man, but I knew *of* them. If Slade's sisters worked with or for them, then they were as up to their eyeballs in this lifestyle as I was. None of which I could or would judge them for.

Although, neither were fans of my father, so we may end up rivals someday. Or, if I had my way, we'd merge everything Bell with everything Brantley. If we could achieve that, we'd be virtually unstoppable. Above every law and government. Rich beyond most people's wildest dreams.

"How receptive are they going to be when they learn about your current situation?" Hunter turned his pointer finger around in the air in a circle, to gesture to all of us.

Slade shrugged indifferently. "They'll deal with it or they won't. That's a bridge I'll worry about when we get to it. But on a woman to woman level, they'll adore Lila. They love women who are as tough, independent and smart as they are. If nothing else, they will respect you." He nodded to me.

"They better," Parker growled. "Lila deserves all the respect she can get."

"And then some," Hunter agreed.

I sipped my drink and smiled at them. They were right. Whatever Chloe threw at me, we'd be ready for it. How could I not be with three incredible, hot guys on my side.

ten

LILA

"WHERE THE HELL ARE WE?"

We were at least an hour from Brutham Academy, deep in the bush. We could bring people out here, bury them and they'd never be found. On the other hand, neither would we if we got stuck out here.

"This is where the trials are held," Slade said. "Technically only people who have been through them before, or who work at the Academy should know the whereabouts of this place. Of course, some rules are meant to be broken more than others."

"And frequently are," Parker said. "We're not the first to bring people out here for this."

"We won't be the last," Hunter agreed. "But we are going to have the most fun."

"Getting me lost in the forest?" I eyed the trees doubtfully. The Academy was situated in a nice setting, with countryside all around it, but I was a city girl at heart. This kind of bushland was not the kind of place I frequented. I preferred my wildlife in the form of the three guys who stood around Slade's SUV, each looking hot and cocky.

"We are not getting you lost," Slade assured me. "You have a compass on your watch. All you need to do is head east. The location you need to reach is only five kilometres that way." He jerked his head.

"Only," I echoed. It would be slow going with heavy scrub, rocks and fuck knows what else. "It's all fun and games until I run into a yowie."

"If they exist, you won't find them here," Hunter said. "Past trials would have scared them off. You might see a fox or two, but they'll run from you." He folded his arms around me and pulled me to him. "The only predators around here are us."

"That's where the fun part comes into it," Parker said. He rubbed his hands together. "We'll give you a head start before we give chase."

A flutter of excitement passed through me. I should have known they planned something.

"What happens if you catch me before I get to the finish line?" I asked.

Parker grinned. "Whoever catches you first gets to fuck you."

"And if two of you catch me at the same time?" I asked.

"Then we both get to fuck you," Hunter said. "And the unfortunate guy that gets left behind has to watch." He sounded very certain that wouldn't be him.

Were they giving me incentive to run, or stick around and have a good time? My competitive instincts quickly kicked in, overriding any doubt or hesitation. That rush of adrenaline that lit me on fire. I wanted to beat them all. I wanted to stand at the finish and laugh at their expressions as they saw they were beaten by a woman.

"And what if I get to the finish line before any of you catch me?" I raised my chin in challenge.

"Then you win our undying admiration and we all get to fuck you," Hunter said. "It's a win-win situation for everyone."

"You're not going to be competing with each other, are you?" I asked. The last thing I needed was for them to injure or maim each other so they could keep up with me.

"If you're asking if we have dirty tricks to pull on each other, the answer is no," Hunter said. "At least, nothing specific. If I happen to trip either of them over, then so be it."

"The point of this is so you have a feel for the landscape," Slade said. "The rest is a bonus, to take the pressure off you. If we do this enough times, you'll reach the finish line within an hour or so, hopefully bypassing any trouble. The rest of the students will be busy getting lost and causing problems for each other. By the time they realise you're not, you'll be long gone."

"Not just that, but you may see places you can use to your advantage," Hunter said. "Places where you can deal with Chloe if she tries anything."

"Dane is going to bring her out here for the same reason, isn't he?" I asked.

"Highly likely," Slade agreed. "All the more reason to know where she may set traps for you."

I made a face. "Other universities just have exams." Which were their own special kind of hell. Brutham had them too, but this on top of those? It was next level torturous pressure.

"Other universities don't turn out students who are ready to deal with everything life throws at them," Hunter said. "Brutham is brutal, but those who survive are tougher and smarter than anyone else. It's easy enough to pass an exam. It's a lot harder to survive each other. Do that, and you'll be unstoppable."

"I know." I sighed. "It's just... Extreme. Who came up with this anyway? Whoever they are, they're a sadistic fuck."

All three of the guys grinned.

"They really were," Slade agreed. "But there's no feeling like crossing that finishing line and knowing you survived your first year. You feel invincible."

"Slade is right," Hunter said. "It feels amazing. But today will feel even more amazing. And don't worry about getting lost. We put a tracking device in your watch and a backup one in your earring, just in case."

He frowned briefly. "It might be worth putting one in a clit piercing as well. In case someone tries to pull them out during the trial itself. A few people last year had piercings torn straight out. Most won't think to look at your clit."

"They better not," Parker growled. "I'll push them off a fucking cliff if they go anywhere near her clit."

"Get in line, bro," Hunter told him.

"We can push them together," Slade said placatingly. "Hunter is right though, a clit piercing would be a good idea. Not *just* to have somewhere to put a tracker though." He grinned.

"Only if you get a cock piercing," I said to all three in general. I'd get a clit piercing if it meant not getting lost out here, but I'd never thought about getting one for any other reason.

"I will," Parker said immediately. Of course he did, he was the more adventurous of the twins. It must be a younger twin thing. I was the same way, where Chloe was the predictable, reliable twin. At least, that was the picture she painted of herself to the world. I'd seen her do some pretty wild shit in the past. Nothing I wouldn't do though. I preferred to take life by the balls and live it.

"In the meantime, let's get this hunt started before the sun goes down." Hunter jogged on the spot to warm up. He gave me a predatory look that set my blood on fire.

I forgot I was going to be running through trees and bushes and started to see it for what it was. Something primal. Three gorgeous guys chasing me, hoping to catch me and pin me down under their bodies. I was the rabbit and they were the hungry wolves, desperate to sink their teeth into my flesh. To tear me to pieces. To wreck me completely.

I nodded. "How much of a head start do I get?"

"Five minutes." Slade glanced down at his watch. "Your time has started, little bunny. If I was you, I'd run."

If he thought he was going to give me the nickname 'little bunny,' we'd be having words later. In the meantime, I pressed on the compass on my watch, turned until I was facing east and started to run.

I didn't look back until I reached the line of trees. All three of the guys stood side by side, backs to the SUV, arms crossed. Each was trying to give the impression he was relaxed, but the tension in their bodies said otherwise. They were ready for this, as though they chased women through forests on a regular basis. As though they were just doing this for fun, but for the continuation of the species. Only the strongest, fastest, smartest got to fuck.

I smiled. Only if they could catch me.

I turned away and ducked down into the trees.

It was a good thing I was dressed for this, in solid boots, jeans and a sturdy long sleeved shirt. Anything else would have been ripped to shreds on the branches as I ran past. I would have tripped in the kind of shoes I usually preferred. If they really wanted to torture us, they'd make us do the trials in heels. That sounded like the perfectly sadistic thing whoever came up with this would do. Assholes.

I held my hands up in front of me, protecting my face and sweeping branches away in front of me. Every so often, I glanced down at my watch to make sure I was still heading in the right direction. I had to turn to the south to run around a particularly thick section of bush.

The moment I could, I headed back east, I turned but slowed to a quick walk. Running through the trees sounding like a herd of elephants would be the quickest way for the guys to find me.

I glanced back a few times, but saw no sign of any of them. Once in a while, I heard a shout that suggested they were following quite a way back.

Good, I thought. *Stay back there*. I was not going to let them catch me. I had to be fast like that little bunny, but I also had to be smart. Outrunning them wouldn't be enough. I had to think like them. What would they do?

Parker would barrel on through the trees, shoving anything and everything out of his path. He'd want to head in a straight line and hope to catch me in the middle of it.

Hunter would live up to his name. He'd be looking for signs of the direction I went, tracking my every move and trying to anticipate where I'd end up next. He knew the terrain. If he saw me skirt around the thick bushes, he'd know where the next one was and figure out the best way around them.

I might outrun Parker, but I'd have to out think Hunter.

Slade— He was the most difficult one to figure out. He zeroed in on me the moment we met. He knew what he wanted and set his sights on getting me. He'd also done the trials before, and knew the terrain.

I mulled it over for a minute or two before I realised. I knew where he'd be. I'd have to be very careful to avoid him.

I reached a place where several large boulders stood in my way. On the other side was a drop down into the valley below. It was exactly the sort of place I wouldn't want to be pinned down during the trials. A couple of people wanting to dispose of me and I'd be pushed down off that drop. If the fall down the sheer rock didn't kill me, the landing would.

The question was, how did I get past?

Almost as soon as I had that thought, I had another realisation. It wasn't just how I got past, it was about how the guys *expected* me to get past. They'd be waiting for me to reach places like this. They'd be expecting me to behave in a certain way. I had to do something unexpected. For the first time, I understood the point of the trials. It wasn't just a test of loyalties and who wanted who dead, although it was also that, it was about using critical thinking skills.

I stepped back and crouched down in some bushes.

Directly east was straight over the edge of the cliff. In order to get by, I had to work my way around the ridges on either side. One looked easier to navigate than the other. The easier way would be the logical choice.

I turned towards the more difficult ridge.

eleven

HUNTER

I TOOK my time following Lila through the thick forest of gum trees. I loved the smell of them, and the way the scent clung to clothing and hair. We'd all smelled like dirt and sweat and gum trees after this. Earthy and real.

Don't get me wrong, I liked civilisation and city living as much as the next guy, but there was something compelling about being here in nature. Hunting down our mate like a pack of wild animals.

Parker was moving through the trees a few metres to my south, sounding just like that. A pack determined to trample everything in his path. I adored my twin, but he was about as subtle as a hippopotamus on steroids.

Slade was somewhere to the north. At least, I presumed he was. He drew the short straw and had to leave last. He'd looked so smug, I was sure he had a plan to get around us somehow. Or maybe that was what he wanted us to think. That was all part of the game. It wasn't just a chase, it was also a mind fuck. My second favourite kind of fuck. Unless it was my mind getting fucked with.

Either way, I wasn't going to let him psych me out.

I reached a thick section of bushes and tracked Lila's movement around them. Here and there were snapped twigs and sections of disturbed ground coverage. At this time of year, the leaves were thick on the ground and dry. The signs they left behind were almost as good as a neon arrow pointing the way.

I smiled to myself. Lila couldn't be too much further ahead. When I caught up to her, I was going to pin her cute little ass to the trunk of a tree and fuck her silly. I was going to fuck her so hard, the other guys would hear her scream from kilometres away.

They could listen all they wanted. She was going to be my prize. The hunter would catch and claim his prey out here in nature.

This whole thing was so primal, it set my blood on fire. I was so hot it didn't bother me that until now I hadn't thought to insist Lila wear a remote control vibrator as she ran. I made a mental note to include that next time.

If she had one inside her now, I'd turn it on and grin at the sound of her squealing. That would slow her down like nothing else.

I pushed on through the trees until I reached the boulders. I stopped for a moment to reminisce about the trials. Parker and I had cornered Brinson Smith here. The smug prick was on our radar for quite some time. He seemed to have a thing for every woman we set our sights on. Back then, it was nothing serious, just a fuck here and there, but he was always hanging around.

Not after the trials he wasn't. I gather it was a difficult process to recover his body from the bottom of the cliff.

"Sorry not sorry," I said to myself. Seeing the expression on his face as he scrambled to grab on to something, anything, only to be shoved backwards by Parker, was one of my most satisfying memories. If we hadn't done it then, we would have had to do it later. He would definitely have been sniffing around Lila. No one did that and got away with it, unless we'd agreed upon it. Which, apart from Slade, we never would. One of our many mottos was 'touch her and die.'

Fortunately, Slade agreed with that sentiment. Lucky for all of us, we didn't view each other as rivals, or shit would get really ugly really quickly.

"Now, which way would you go?" I asked Lila under my breath. One of the ridges was easier to navigate than the other. I would bet anything she realised the same thing. And that I would expect her to take the easier way, rather than risking stepping so close to the edge of the cliff.

That being the case, she must have taken the more difficult ridge.

She wouldn't have minded the challenge. She had more balls than most guys I knew. Or a cast iron pussy.

I turned towards the easier ridge and started to make my way carefully around the edge. Both ridges led to the same place, but this one would get me there more quickly. Taking the difficult route was unexpected, but it would, potentially, slow her down.

I kept my eyes and ears open. If this was the actual trials, it was exactly the kind of place I'd expect an ambush. That wasn't going to happen here, but it was treacherous nonetheless. The last thing I wanted was for me to end up at the bottom of a cliff. That would not help Lila to claim her throne. And it wouldn't end with me fucking her against a tree, or on the bare ground. Or...

I pushed the thought out of my mind for now. If I kept thinking like that, my heavy balls would drag me down. I needed my blood in the head on my shoulders, not the one in my pants.

"Focus, Hunt," I told myself. I pressed my lips together and kept moving.

The sound of snapping branches and grunting from behind me told me my brother was on the same ridge, making his way as loudly as he could. It wasn't laziness or carelessness on his part. No, there was strategy in everything we both did, including this. The amount of noise he was making was his way of trying to psych me out. If I knew where he was, I'd know he was close. He'd expect me to freak out and make mistakes.

Fuck that. I had no intention of doing either of those things. I moved carefully and kept my head as clear as possible, ignoring the sounds from behind me. And trying to ignore the frustration at not knowing where Slade was.

Was he so far behind us I wouldn't hear him anyway? That was possible, but for some reason I knew that wasn't the case. From past experience, I knew to rely on my instincts. They'd never let me down yet. Doing otherwise would get me killed. Or worse, I'd lose.

That wasn't going to happen.

"Ouch!" Parker cried out behind me. "Fucking tree." A branch cracked off and flew through the air. It sailed over the side of the cliff and disappeared. A thud followed a moment later.

I grinned. Only Parker would stop to take vengeance on a branch at a time like this. He wasn't acting out of anger though, not really. He knew better than to get pissed off with inanimate objects. This was just another trick to remind me he was right on my heels. To make me stop and look back.

Keeping as silent as I could, I swept my gaze back and forth, looking for signs of Lila or Slade. She couldn't be that far ahead now. I stepped off the ridge and headed back east. I knew I closed the distance between us, but by how far? Was it enough to catch her before Slade did? Where was the slippery motherfucker anyway?

And where was Lila?

I caught a glimpse of movement up ahead. Just a flash. I stopped mid-step and watched, but I didn't see anything more.

I held my breath. Wait, there it was again. Something dark moving slowly through the trees. I couldn't tell if it was Lila or Slade. It wasn't both of them, because there were no groans of pleasure yet. Good, he hadn't caught up to her.

I stepped carefully in the direction of the movement, keeping eyes and ears open. If that was Lila, Slade might not be far behind. If it was Slade, I didn't want to catch up to him, in case he decided to pull something. Even though we weren't officially competing, that didn't mean he wouldn't try to psych me out, or slow me down the way Parker was.

I was so busy looking ahead of me, I almost missed the trap in the ground in front of me. A hole carved out by nature, but covered by a person. Presumably left here from the last trial. Maybe to catch Parker and I out. Judging by the dry branches scattered haphazardly across the top of the hole, they were here for a while. Definitely not placed there by someone in advance of this year's trial.

I stepped around the hole, but stopped to crouch down beside it. I peeled off a couple of branches and peered inside.

It was empty. I half expected it to be full of bones from missing students. Every few years or so, one or two would go missing during the trials. The Academy would send out search parties and sniffer dogs, but once in a while they never turned up. I wouldn't like to be on the school board and have to explain that to their parents. Some may insist on the Academy being shut down. Having their children die was one thing, going missing was another.

Whatever, either way the Academy remained open and the trials continued.

I placed the branches back over the hole and stood. If Parker was dumb enough to fall in, he could stay there until I was finished with Lila. Or until he got himself out. The hole was deep enough to break a bone on landing, and the sides were difficult to climb, but a few hours in there wouldn't kill him.

I stepped away carefully, trying to leave no sign I was right there. Parker might be trying to pretend to be the proverbial bull in a china shop, but he wasn't stupid. He knew as well as I did how to look for signs of people passing this way.

We practised before the trials in a bunch of different places. We followed people and had people follow us. We worked through a bunch of different scenarios, some of which were useful on the day. Others not, but they'd come in useful since. It never hurt to add to my skill set.

"Fuck," Parker growled. That was followed by a soft thud and a groan that sounded like he pulled himself back to his feet. I guessed he tripped, but didn't fall through the trap. Not yet anyway.

I smiled to myself as he let out a string of curses before staggering on.

In the corner of my eye, I saw another flash of movement. Closer now. I was almost certain it was Lila. She was so close I could almost taste her. Could almost hear her heart beating as she pushed her way through the trees, trying to keep ahead of us. The sweat would be slick on her body like it was on mine. When I caught her, our skin would slide against each other, slapping wet when I thrust.

I slipped through the trees like a fox, weaving my way through and trying not to make a sound.

There it was again, movement. A flash of long dark hair, tied back in a ponytail.

The finishing line wasn't far ahead either. We made it sound vague, but she'd know when she reached it. That was the point. Everyone who undertook the trials would start to wonder how they were supposed to know when they ended. That little bit of fear, the paranoia, was yet another layer to the challenge.

She slowed to walk around some wattle bushes that grew up in her path.

I smiled to myself and went the other way. I slipped in between two trees and waited.

She cursed under her breath as she reached the boulders I knew she'd find. When she turned around and headed back to go the other way around the wattles, I was waiting for her.

"Caught you."

I spoke at the same time as Slade.

twelve

HUNTER

I STARED AT HIM.

"What the fuck, dude? Where did you come from?" I caught up to Lila and grabbed her arm. She and Slade looked at me like I should know the answer.

"Oh, hey... What?" Parker caught up to us. "Howinhell? Slade started after us."

"Yeah, he was just about to explain." I didn't take my eyes off Slade.

The asshole grinned and jerked his head back behind him. "I drove. The rules were to catch Lila before she got to the road. No one ever said how." He looked even more smug than Parker after we disposed of Scott. Or anyone else we ever killed, for that matter. Rolled into one.

My gaze went from Slade to Lila. "You're not surprised."

I half expected her to encourage us to find a nice shallow grave for him. For her, I'd be happy to oblige.

"I figured he'd do something to get ahead of you two," she said with a smile. "How better than to jump back into the SUV?" She actually seemed impressed by his cheating ass.

I shoved down my annoyance to a place I could get at it later. No doubt it would come in useful. It always did.

I shrugged as though I didn't give a shit. "I still won. I caught Lila." I pulled her over to me. I was hard as hell. Even when I was annoyed, my cock didn't let me down. Right now, all he wanted was to be buried deep inside her.

"Actually, it was a tie," Slade said. "But I don't mind sharing." He stepped over to her and slid his hands up the back of her shirt.

"Crap," Parker grumbled.

"You're welcome to watch," I said over my shoulder.

"I was planning on it." Parker flopped down under a tree and pulled a packet of salted nuts out of his pocket. "I should have brought some beers too."

I laughed and gripped the front of Lila's shirt. I ripped the front of it apart, sending buttons flying. It wouldn't be primal if I didn't literally tear the clothes off her body. I shoved what was left down her arms.

Slade grabbed it before it could fall to the ground.

He unhooked Lila's bra and pushed it off. The black lace slid to the ground and lay splayed apart. Slade grabbed her wrists and pulled them behind her. He wound her shirt around her wrists and tied it firmly. "Wouldn't want you running away again."

She gave us both a look, then twisted away from us and started to run through the trees.

I glanced at Slade and grinned. If that was how she wanted to play it, I was here for it.

He grinned back and we gave chase.

Running as awkwardly as she was, it didn't take us long to catch up to her again.

Slade grabbed her arm and yanked her back so hard he almost pulled her off her feet.

She fell back against him, giving me time to undo the top of her jeans and drag them down her legs. She kicked out at me, but I grabbed her ankle and pulled off one of her boots.

"Hold her." I dropped her foot and grabbed the other.

Slade wrapped his arms around her upper body and gripped her while she squirmed and fought.

I pulled off the other boot and tossed it aside before tugging her jeans the rest of the way off.

I smiled at her briefly before tearing her panties off.

"Open up." I pressed her panties against her lips.

She shook her head until I gripped her chin and forced her mouth open. I shoved her panties inside and slipped my hand between her legs.

"As I suspected, she's drenched." I shoved her legs apart and slipped a couple of fingers inside her. She wriggled and growled, but I knew she was enjoying every minute.

I slipped my fingers out long enough to undo my jeans, my grateful erection rock hard in my hand. I gripped the back of one one of Lila's thighs and Slade gripped the other. Between us we lifted her high enough to slide her onto my cock.

She wriggled and writhed, but the moment I was seated deep inside her, her eyes shone with excitement and pleasure.

"That's my girl. Always ready to take me." She felt so fucking good.

I gripped her hips so tight I knew I would leave bruises, and slid out of her. I slammed back in so hard she let out a cry of pain. That sound made my balls heavier than ever. I slammed into her again, harder than before. Again and again until tears poured from her eyes.

She rolled her hips to meet me. Her head tipped back, eyes closed before she came around my cock, clenching me so tight she forced an orgasm out of me. My balls contracted, exploding my cum inside her. I pumped and went on pumping until every drop was milked dry.

I sagged forward and stood for a few minutes before sliding out of her and lowering her legs to the ground.

Slade pulled the panties out of her mouth and pushed her down to her knees. He already had his cock out, but now he pressed it between her lips.

I grabbed a fistful of her hair and tugged her back, before guiding her forward until she was gagging on him. Over and over I shoved her on to him while he bucked, fucking her mouth hard.

"Fucking hell, her mouth," Slade said with a grunt.

"It's something else isn't it?" I agreed. Every time she gagged, Slade drew closer to the edge. "That's it, babe. Take him all the way down your pretty little throat. He's going to come in your mouth and you're going to swallow down every bit of it. Every drop."

In the corner of my eye, I caught Parker, cock in his hand. His eyes were half closed, blissed out but watching. He looked close to coming too.

Slade went still, hands in fists at his sides. He pressed himself in deeper still before groaning long and low as he came.

Lila gagged again and swallowed hard a couple of times. By the time Slade slid out of her mouth, she was gasping for breath.

I kept my fingers tangled in her hair and let her recover before helping her to her feet.

"I'm guessing if I get caught during the trials it won't be that much fun." She stood still while Slade untied her shirt from her wrists.

"If it goes anything like that, I will be killing people," I said. If anyone touched a hair on her head against her will I'd strangle them with my bare hands. After slicing them to bits.

"We'll make sure they won't," Slade said. He slipped what was left of her shirt around her shoulders.

I tucked my cock back into my jeans and did them up.

"You did so well," I told her. "The road is only a few metres away." I nodded in that direction.

She turned to see the SUV parked under some trees beside the road.

"That didn't seem so difficult." She pulled the sides of her shirt tighter around herself.

"With only us chasing you it won't be," I agreed. "The actual trials will be different." I rubbed my chin and draped an arm around her shoulders. "I'm sure everyone would agree this was much more fun."

"Speak for yourself." Parker was tucking his cock back into his pants. "It could have been a bit more fun for me."

I grinned. "I guess you'll have to try harder next time, bro. But next time, no one drives." My annoyance came back to the surface and I gave Slade a dark look. So it wasn't an official rule, but it was an unspoken one. Up until now. If he did it again, I'd come right down on his cheating ass. Teacher or no teacher.

"No flying or anything else like that either," I added. I wouldn't put it past Parker to organise a helicopter if I didn't make the rules clear.

Although, now I thought about it, maybe I should have kept my mouth shut and done just that. I could have had Lila all to myself. On the other hand, having someone else hold her down added another layer of excitement to the chase. Just thinking about the way she struggled made my cock harden again.

I'd always had a thing for being dominant, but if she'd consent to a little role-play, I'd be a hundred percent there for it. The other guys too, by the look of them.

Without giving her any warning I was about to do it, I scooped Lila up and started towards the road. "One of you grab her jeans and boots," I called out over my shoulder.

She squealed in surprise, but then nestled into me, her arms around my neck.

"You enjoyed that?" I asked.

"More than I thought I would," she admitted. "Is that...weird? The way both of you were holding me and making me do what you wanted? It was... It was hot. I liked relinquishing control, but at the same time..." She thought as I stepped carefully over a fallen tree.

"At the same time, I was in control. I knew you would have understood if I said banana, even with my mouth full. You would have known if I really wanted you to stop. And you would have stopped. Both of you."

"Yes we would," I agreed. Stopping would have been difficult, and my balls would have hurt, but I would have backed right off. There was nothing in this world I wanted less than to hurt her. That would be like hurting the best piece of myself.

"I felt powerful, because I could let go and enjoy what you were doing. I didn't feel like the victim. Is that wrong? I mean... You were forceful." She looked up at me tentatively. Lila Bell was such a tough badass on the outside, but on the inside she had places that weren't broken. Places that were still soft, still sweet. Most people never saw that side of her. That I did right now was a testament to her feelings for me. We never spoke about it, but we both knew it for what it was. The woman held my heart in a vice, and I couldn't be happier.

"Nothing you could ever do would be wrong," I assured her. "There's no shame in wanting to be dominated once in a while. Or all the time. As long as you know you're the one calling the shots, there's no harm in it. If anything, it says how much you trust me and Slade. How many people do we know that we can really let go around and know they won't screw us over?"

"I know three," she said. "And all of them are right here."

"Is it Slade, me and yourself?" Parker asked jokingly.

"Fuck off," I told him. "If she's including herself, and she should, that makes four. If she's not, then clearly she meant herself, Slade and me."

"I meant you, Parker and Slade, dickhead," Lila told me. "But you're right, I should include myself. If I can't trust myself, then who will?"

"I will." I trusted this woman more than I trusted myself. If she told me the sky was pink, then it probably was. If she said I needed to kill someone for her, then I did. There was nothing I wouldn't do or say for her.

I turned sideways to the SUV and opened the door before placing her on the back seat. Before I could blink, Parker was around the other side and all but throwing himself in beside her.

He draped her jeans over her lap. "I couldn't find your panties. You won't need them for the ride home anyway." He grabbed her legs and turned her to face him, before opening her thighs and pressing his face between them.

I closed the door behind them and slipped into the front passenger seat. Just because he hadn't won didn't mean she shouldn't miss out on an orgasm or two on the drive back to the Academy.

I watched out the window as Slade drove and Lila groaned in the back seat. We didn't say a word most of the way, but that gave me time to think.

thirteen

LILA

I SLIPPED my headphones off my ears and frowned.

When the knock came at the door again, I knew I wasn't hearing things. I also knew it wasn't Hunter or Parker, because they'd made their own keys and let themselves in when they felt like it. I should be annoyed at them, but I couldn't bring myself to be. Not even when I woke in the middle of the night with one of their cocks inside me.

I set the headphones aside and closed my laptop.

I rolled off the bed and unlocked the door. I opened it a crack and peered out.

I blinked in surprise.

"Zachary? What are you doing here?" I opened the door wider to let my former stepbrother in. He was tall and dark, with blue eyes that reminded me I definitely had a type. The attraction didn't go beyond the physical though.

I liked him, but there was no chance of us hooking up again. Certainly no chance of a relationship. That didn't mean I wasn't happy to see him. I was, it was just strange for him to drop in unannounced. Honestly, it was strange for anyone to drop in to Brutham unannounced. The Academy was tucked away from any major city and we weren't even close to the beach.

"Can I not pay my favourite stepsister a visit?" He kissed my cheek and stepped into the room. "Nice place."

I closed the door behind him. "It's no harbourside mansion, but it's all right," I said. "It's only for another couple of years." The rooms here were comfortable, but half the size of my room at home.

"Yeah, I guess so. I brought you something." He drew his hand out from behind his back and handed me a gift wrapped package. The paper was black, red and gold. My favourite combination. It was sweet of him to remember.

He sat in a chair while I flopped down on my bed and placed the package in my lap.

"You didn't have to get me anything." I pressed my hands into the sides of the parcel, like it was Christmas Day. My fingers sank into something soft.

"Of course I didn't, but I felt like it." He shrugged.

"This is the only reason you are here?" Call me cynical, but it was difficult not to find an ulterior motive wherever I looked. The whole competition between Chloe and I, and the trials at the end of the year, had me jumping at shadows. I knew well enough to know shadows were often more than shadows.

Without answering the question, he nodded towards the package. "Open it."

He crossed his legs, propping his ankle on his opposite thigh. He had the pose of a future master of the universe down pat. Then again, he'd been practising all his life the same way I had. My father was still one of his role models, although they weren't legally family anymore.

I looked down at the parcel. "It doesn't seem to be ticking."

Zachary chuckled.

Chloe would have peeled back the tape carefully, trying not to damage the paper.

Personally, I could never understand the point of having that kind of patience. I grabbed the slides and yanked them apart, tearing the paper down the middle.

Inside was a teddy bear the size of my arm, from my elbow to the tips of my fingers. He wore black trousers, red shirt, gold suspenders and a black, red and gold bowtie. His smiling face looked up at me, begging to be cuddled.

"He's so cute." I drew out the last word. I picked up the plush toy and wrapped my arms around him.

Zachary grinned. "The moment I saw him, I thought of you. I know you like those colours and you're probably homesick. Teddy bears make everything better, especially homesickness. I'm assuming here, because I've never had a teddy bear in my life." He wiggled his brows slightly.

"That is such a lie," I said with a laugh. "I remember Mr Snuggles. And that huge purple elephant you used to have. And the plush cocka-too. And—"

He raised his hands in surrender. "Okay, okay. You caught me. I'm a sucker for soft, squishy animals. Especially brightly coloured ones. Happy now?"

"I'll be happy when you admit to sleeping next to one of them," I said slyly.

He dropped his hands, letting them slap on his thighs. "I will never admit something like that. Anyway, I prefer my soft, squishy bed mates to be alive. And human," he added quickly when he saw me about to suggest he fucked animals.

I wrinkled my nose. "I don't think I want to hear about your bed mates. There are things a girl doesn't want to know about her brother." I would always see him that way, regardless of what happened between my father and his mother. That was their business. My relationship with Zachary was mine.

"Shame, because the details are juicy." He grinned.

I pulled a face. "I'll take your word for it." I doubt he wanted to hear about my sex life any more than I wanted to hear about his.

"Does he have a name?" I nodded down at the teddy bear to change the subject.

"You'd trust someone who calls his bear Mr Snuggles to name yours?" Zachary gave me a lopsided smile.

"Good point," I said. "If it was up to me, I'd name him Ted E Bear."

"In that case, let me think of something. How about Reginald?"

I snorted a laugh. "I'm not calling a teddy bear Reginald."

"Fine," Zachary drawled. "How about Francisco? Laurence? I know, Terence. You could call him Terry Bear."

I aimed a kick at the front of his leg, even though I was too far away to reach. "I swear, these suggestions are getting worse."

"You try then." He lifted his chin in challenge. "What would you call him, Brantley?" Something flickered in his eyes, but it was gone before I could pin down what it was.

"It's a better name than Terry Bear." I could just picture the expression on my father's face if I named the plush that.

He'd be only slightly less horrified than he would knowing I was still with Hunter and Parker. Some day that penny would drop and I was dreading it. That revelation had to wait until after my father chose me to head the family. Otherwise, he may choose Chloe instead.

I was almost certain the only reason she hadn't told him was because she was screwing a DiMarco. In the eyes of my father, that would be just as bad. He probably had some ally of his lined up to marry me, but that wasn't going to happen. Not if I could help it.

"I think I'll name him Herman," I said finally. That was cute and wouldn't raise any eyebrows or cause any trouble.

"Herman it is then," Zachary said. He glanced down and I knew he was finally ready to talk about what he'd really come here for.

I waited.

He looked back up. "I heard about your father pitting you and Chloe against each other. Herman is kind of a peace offering. Before you say anything, I got one for Chloe too. I have no intention of coming between you two, or taking sides one way or another."

"Do you wish he chose you?" I asked gently.

Zachary was older than Chloe and me, and male. If he was dad's biological son, he would have been the logical choice. Chloe and I would have been put to good use on behalf of the family, in some capacity or other. Whether that meant being married off or trained to work in some particular arm of the business, I didn't know. Maybe both.

There was a time when I thought Dad might insist Chloe or I marry Zachary. Then he could legitimately hand the business over to him and whichever one of us he married. But as time went by, the possibility became less and less likely. Just as well, I didn't want to hurt Zachary by refusing. There was no way Hunter, Parker and Slade would share me with him as well. Even if I was inclined to ask them to, which I wasn't.

"Sam would never have chosen me," Zachary said. "Even if he and Mum were still together, I'm only the step kid."

"Dad loves you," I argued. "So do I. You're not *only* anything. You're Zachary Sinclair. You're a card-carrying badass, motherfucker."

85

His smile was brief. "Literally. But I'm not a Bell. That makes all the difference."

I sat Herman aside and moved over to sit in the seat beside Zachary. I took his hand.

"I'm sorry if anyone made you feel like you're not enough. Who do I need to kill? Don't say my father, that would make all sorts of things more complicated."

His smile was more genuine now, the bitter edge dulled. "If anyone else asked that, I'd think they were joking. Not you though. You'd totally go out there and stab someone for your family." He made a repeated stabbing motion with his other hand.

"Yes, I would." I gave him a short nod. "Or better yet, I'd send someone to do it. Blood is a bitch to get out of clothes. Actually, when it comes down to it, poison is a lot less messy."

It was slower and more satisfying to watch the victim's eyes bug out and their face swell. They knew what was going to happen and were powerless to stop it. If they did something so terrible to warrant the poison, they deserved every moment of what they got.

"Will you give me a job when you're head of the family?" Zacahry asked, tugging my thoughts back to the present. "I know I won't be a Brutham graduate, but I have some useful skills. You know I'm good with my tongue." He grinned.

"Yes you are, and yes you do," I agreed. It would be better if I didn't think too much about his tongue. That was the past and we wouldn't revisit it again.

"I'd be more than happy to give you a job. Hell, I'd give Chloe a job if she stepped aside now and agreed never to undermine me." Which I knew full well she would never agree to. That was probably just as well too, because I didn't think I'd ever be able to trust her again.

"Is that why you came here, to ask for a job?" I teased. "I'm sure you have prospective bosses lining up at your door to hire you." Why wouldn't they? He was intelligent, resourceful and charming. He'd be an asset to any business, including mine.

"You'd think so, wouldn't you? Maybe there are, but I know who I want to work for. Besides, the Bell's have better perks than anywhere else."

"We're slightly less inclined to get angry if you kill a coworker?" I only half joked.

While that did occasionally happen, they had to have a very good reason for doing it, like the person they killed was stealing from the company, or betrayed us somehow. If you killed someone who looked at you the wrong way, you'd end up in a shallow grave beside them. Neither my father nor I had time for any of that bullshit.

"Exactly," Zachary agreed. "Anyway, I've kept you long enough. I should be getting back to Sydney. I have an exam in the morning." He grimaced.

I matched his expression. "Me too." The only reason the guys weren't here was because we were all studying for exams, and they distracted me too much. If they had their way, they'd be chasing me through the forest in the dark, rather than letting me study. While I preferred their idea, I couldn't afford not to do well. Chasing would have to wait.

When he stood, I stood with him and gave him a hug.

"Thank you for coming. And for Herman. It's been good to see you." I kissed his cheek.

"You too." He kissed mine back. "Herman will help you to sleep well tonight. Have sweet dreams. Goodbye."

His words lingered in my mind long after he slipped out the door, but I put them out of my mind and got ready for bed.

fourteen

HUNTER

"ARE YOU SURE ABOUT THIS?" Parker asked. "She has an exam in a few hours. You know how she gets when she's woken up before an exam."

His face was still sleepy from falling asleep on my bed while we studied for our exam. I tried to sneak out without waking him, but of course he heard me. Nothing I could say would persuade him to stay and go back to sleep. I considered handcuffing him to my bed, but it was too much of a hassle, and my cock needed to see Lila.

I flashed him a grin. "That's half the fun. She gets pissed off with us and we get to make it up to her." I pulled the key out of my pocket.

"Wait." He caught my wrist before I could put the key in the lock. "What is that?"

I was halfway to assuming it was some kind of joke. An attempt to shove me out of the way and get in first.

A moment later, I caught his tone and froze. My gaze dropped to the base of the door.

Wisps of something white drifted out from the gap at the bottom.

"Fuck." I shoved the key into the lock frantically and pushed the door open. We both almost tumbled inside. I staggered a step or two and caught a whiff.

The smell wafted through the corridor. How had I not noticed it until now? It was sickly sweet and slightly nauseating. My eyes watered and my nose started to run.

"That's not smoke." I grabbed the bottom of my shirt with one hand and pulled it off over my head. I pressed it against my mouth and hurried into Lila's room.

The fumes were thicker here. Not as thick as smoke, but thick enough to be visible. And to sting my skin and eyes. I wiped away tears and blinked several times to clear them.

"Shit."

Lila lay on her bed like she was asleep, hair fanned out across her pillow. Her long lashes lay against her cheeks. Her lips were parted slightly. Her skin was pale as death.

Something lay on the bed beside her, fumes winding their way toward the ceiling. It looked like a teddy bear.

What the fuck?

"Don't breathe it in," I told my twin. I coughed a couple of times into the cotton of my shirt. The fumes coated my lungs, making it harder to breathe.

"We need to get her out of here." I tied the arms of my shirt around the back of my head to keep it in place and scooped her up. I'd be no use to her if I inhaled too much of the stuff and passed out. If that happened, we'd all be screwed.

"What the fuck?" Parker stood staring at the teddy bear. "Wild guess, we need to get this out of here too." He threw the bed covers over the teddy bear to cut off the gas, gathered it up tight and carried it out of the room behind us.

"Be careful of that thing. I'm guessing it's some kind of nerve agent. We need to get her to the Academy hospital."

She was limp in my arms, barely breathing. If she died, whoever left that fucking teddy bear would regret the day they were born. Fuck it, when she made a complete recovery I'd still make sure they regretted the day they were born. No one messes with my queen and gets away with it.

"What do we do with this thing?" Parker was holding the covers firm around the teddy bear, his own shirt pressed against his face. He looked as angry as I was. Between us, we'd rip whoever did this to Lila, to shreds.

"We need to bring it with us," I said. "The sooner they know what it is, the sooner they can treat her." For the first time, I regretted studying cyber security. If I'd studied medicine or chemistry, I may have some idea of how to fix this. If she wasn't all right...

I pushed the thought away and trotted through the corridor. I couldn't let myself think that way. She'd be fine. She had to be. My heart would shatter irreparably if she wasn't. The pieces left would be smaller than grains of sand. A Brantley with a broken heart was the definition of dangerous. I'd end worlds if she didn't recover.

I turned around and pushed the hospital door open with my back.

"I need help!" I shouted. I didn't care who else was in here and what injuries they might have. Lila was my priority. The only priority. Everyone else could fucking wait.

A nurse immediately sprang to her feet and hurried out from behind the long wooden desk. "Bring her through." She waved towards a door to the side of the room and pressed a button on the wall. "The doctor won't be long."

"By *not long* you better mean no more than a minute," I snarled. I'd grab a scalpel and make the doctor treat her right now if I had to. I didn't give a fuck if someone else was dying in another part of the hospital.

I carried Lila through into the examining room and gently laid her down on the narrow bed in the centre. She looked so small and vulnerable lying there. Like a doll at the mercy of a child with a pair of scissors, or one who liked to remove the heads from their toys to swap them around.

She would have hated seeing herself like this. If there was something she couldn't stand, it was being vulnerable. I hated it too, because it reminded me she was only human. Fragile.

I forced breaths in and out. I had to be calm. She didn't need me losing my shit now. If anyone could fix her, it was the medical staff here.

Like everything else here at Brutham, the hospital was the best money could buy. Better than the average infirmary. Better, if I was honest, than any other hospitals. It was rarely very busy and, lucky for them, was well staffed.

I tore the shirt off my face and tossed it aside.

"What's happened?" The doctor on duty's name was Racquel. In her mid-thirties, I knew her from previous injuries and several fucks before I met Lila. When she hurried into the room, she was all business.

"Someone tried to poison her with some kind of gas from this." Parker held out the pile of covers.

Racquel nodded and stuck her face out the door. "Henry, come and take this. Figure out what was in it."

I didn't look up to see who Henry was. I didn't give a shit. All of my attention was on Lila and how shallow her breathing was. I leaned down and pressed my cheek to hers.

"You're going to be okay, babe. You're in the best hands here. They'll take care of you."

If I thought there was any better, I'd send a helicopter for them right now. But Brutham had the best doctors, all of them highly skilled and paid well to turn a blind eye to everything they saw here. If they ever wrote a book about their experiences, no one would believe it anyway. Not that they'd get to write it, because the Academy would never allow that.

Racquel started on all her doctor things, checking Lila's pulse and pupils. "Any idea how long she was like this?"

"We found her five minutes ago," Parker said. He moved to the other side of the bed. His arms were empty, his shirt gone from over his face. "No idea before that. Although, she usually goes to sleep around midnight."

Racquel glanced at the clock on the wall. "It's almost 3 AM. Potentially three hours. Probably less. If it was that long, it's unlikely she'd still be alive."

Fury burned a path through my body. If we hadn't snuck in, she'd be dead. Murdered by whoever left that fucking teddy bear.

When I found who did this, they'd regret the day their parents were born, nevermind themselves. Their death was going to be slow and very, very painful. I might play with them for a couple of weeks first. Make them beg to die.

"You both need to step back and give us room," Racquel barked. She ordered the nurse to bring over an oxygen mask and tank. In moments, the mask was over Lila's face, pumping the precious substance into her.

I stood back beside Parker. If they thought that would make us leave, they'd need to think again. We weren't leaving her side.

Parker pulled out his phone and sent off a text. "Slade," was all he said.

I nodded vaguely. All I cared about right now was Lila.

A man slipped into the room and said something to Racquel before slipping back out. Something about chlorine and level two nerve agent.

Racquel grabbed a needle of something and tapped at it to get out the bubbles. She inserted it into a vein in Lila's arm and pressed the plunger.

"The next hour or two will be critical," she said, addressing everyone present. "Much longer and it would have been too late, but I'm confident she should make a full recovery."

"She better," Parker growled.

Racquel looked at him, unflinchingly. "It depends on her and how strong she is. She's young and fit, she should be fine. I can't guarantee there won't be long term side effects. The best you can do right now is focus on her recovery." She turned back to Lila, quickly assessing her progress.

I put my arm around Parker. "Lila is a badass bitch. She's too stubborn to be taken out by a fucking teddy bear."

"This was Chloe, wasn't it?" Parker gritted his teeth together, barely containing his anger. "We knew she'd do something, and she has. I'm going to rip her fucking face off. And that prick, Dane, while I'm at it. This was probably his idea. Motherfucking son of a whore's bitch."

Slade came barrelling into the room. He skidded to a stop right before he ran into us. He took one look at Lila and his face turned red. We didn't need to exchange words. We were all thinking the same thing. By the time we were done, there was going to be nothing left of any of Lila's enemies.

"This is fucked up." Parker didn't take his eyes off our queen. "If she dies—"

"She's not going to die," Slade said. "She has too much unfinished business to take care of. Too much life left to live."

But Lila looked so pale and helpless laying there, mask over her mouth and nose. Her eyelids twitched once in a while, and her chest rose and fell. If it wasn't for those and the machine monitoring her vitals, I would have thought she was dead.

Chloe won.

If she did, the bitch wouldn't win for long. Samuel Bell would lose both of his daughters. I didn't care that it would start a war between him and my family. Fuck the consequences. Chloe was going to pay for this.

"Has anyone informed her sister?" Racquel asked. "Or the rest of her family?"

"We are her family," Parker snapped. "We're the only family she needs."

"That may be so," Racquel said slowly, "but I'm obligated to inform her biological family."

"We'll tell them," I said. "They should know. Leave it to us."

Racquel nodded and ducked out of the room.

Parker glanced at me. "What the hell? Chloe doesn't deserve—"

I interrupted him. "Look at Lila. She's alive. Don't you want to see the expression on Chloe's face when she finds out she failed? When she realises we know she's behind this and that we're going to come after her for it?"

His mouth turned up in a slow, humourless smile. "Yeah, I do want to see that. Slade?"

"I'll stay here with Lila." He pulled a chair over to the bed and sat before taking Lila's hand in his.

"We won't be long." I gave her a long look. For the first time, I seriously considered suggesting Lila concede the role of head of the family. Let Chloe have it. Then, when the time was right, we'd destroy everything Samuel Bell built and bring Chloe to her knees. Was it worth putting Lila at risk anymore? If Chloe did this, then hell only knows what else she might pull.

Fucking with her birth control was one thing, but this was war. One I was determined to win, no matter how dirty we had to play to win it. If she really thought screwing with us was a good idea, she was wrong.

So, so fucking wrong.

fifteen

LILA

I WOKE to the sound of whooshing and soft beeping. Something was on my face. I moved my head from side to side slowly, but couldn't dislodge it. Panic started to rise. The beeping increased in speed.

What the absolute fuck?

"Hey, Lila. It's okay. Calm down. It's just an oxygen mask."

Who was that? My sleepy mind took a while to register who it was. Slade.

Oxygen mask? What the hell?

I opened my eyes a crack, closed them again immediately. The glare was too much.

"Lila, I need you to open your eyes," a female voice said. "I need to look at your pupils."

"Do what the doctor says," Slade ordered. "Open your eyes."

I tried to tell him to fuck off, but the mask and my sluggish brain wouldn't let the words come.

I opened my eyes again and winced at the glare of a torch shining into them.

I wanted to tell the doctor to fuck off too.

"Good. You're doing well. Let the oxygen breathe for you for a while longer. We should be able to take the mask off soon." She turned the torch off and the room went darker.

"Is she going to be okay?" That was Parker's voice. He sounded worried, tense. People should get out of his and Hunter's way when they were like that. Someone was likely to die if they looked at them wrong. Why was he worried though? What happened?

"It's too early to tell, but the signs are positive," the doctor said.

"She'll be all right," Hunter snapped. His face appeared above me. He looked tired. His eyes were red. "Right, babe?"

All I could do was look back at him and make a sound in the back of my throat. I regretted that immediately. My throat was dry, like someone had run sandpaper up and down the inside of it.

"Let her get some rest," the doctor said. "I'll be back in an hour. Hopefully she won't need the oxygen then and we can see if she's up to eating. The rest of you should get some breakfast."

Breakfast? How long was I asleep? Fuck, I had an exam this morning. What time was it anyway?

The beeping increased speed again.

"It's okay, babe." Hunter took my hand. "Don't worry about anything except getting better. Relax. We've got you, I promise."

I forced myself to relax, if only because the doctor might sedate me if I didn't. I hated the idea of being given drugs because I couldn't control myself properly. That wasn't me. I was Lila Bell. I was the one in full control.

Me.

The beeping slowed.

"Funny story," Hunter said. "I went and told Chloe you were still alive. She tried to pretend she had no idea what was going on, but I knew she was full of shit. She definitely knew who put that teddy bear in your room."

I blinked hard. Teddy bear?

Herman.

Zachary.

Zachary did this to me? My head spun with the implications of that. I thought he cared about me. He came to me to say he wasn't getting involved...

He fucking lied. Everything he said was bullshit. That whole time, he was there on Chloe's behalf. He was working with her or for her. The only thing he said that was honest was that the teddy bear would help me sleep. He meant it when he said goodbye.

He knew when he left that the bear contained a booby-trap meant to kill me.

No wonder Hunter thought the conversation with Chloe was funny. She must have been pissed when she learned she failed. She'd tried to kill me, but I survived. I was stronger than that. I'd make a full recovery and then I'd go after her.

"You know too, don't you?" Slade asked. "Someone was in your room?"

He looked ready to rip their arms off and strangle them with them. Teddy bear or no teddy bear, he was furious at the idea of someone being in my room and him not knowing about it.

Hunter looked equally unimpressed. He and Parker knew about Zachary, but neither of them were fans of my former stepbrother. When they found out what he did...

I managed to nod in spite of the mask.

"You can tell us as soon as the doctor lets you take that off," Parker said.

Hunter looked to the side.

"What? I can be the voice of reason once in a while," Parker protested. "The most important thing here is that Lila gets better. We can worry about revenge later."

"Right." Hunter looked back at me. "It will be sweeter after they've stewed for a while anyway. Let them think we aren't coming after them. When they least expect it." He grinned. "We'll fuck them so hard they'll wish they hadn't touched you."

He sounded like he was very much looking forward to doing just that. Hell had no fury like me and one of my guys when someone fucked with us.

"Didn't you two say something about having exams?" Slade asked. "Go and get something to eat and get them done. You're not going to help Lila if you fail."

He stepped over to the other side of me and brushed hair back off my forehead. "Don't worry about yours, you can take it when you're better."

"Don't you have a class to teach?" Hunter asked.

"Not until after lunch," Slade replied. "I'll stay with Lila until then."

Both twins hesitated before Hunter nodded. "We'll be back as soon as the exam is over." He leaned over and kissed my cheek.

Parker shoved him out of the way and did the same.

I turned my head to watch them step out of the room.

"You're safe with me," Slade said softly.

I held his gaze. I wanted to believe him. I *did* believe him, but I believed the same of Zachary. Now, I realised how naïve that was. It never crossed my mind he might do anything like this to me.

I trusted him.

I trusted him and he tried to kill me. All this time he was on Chloe's side and I didn't have a clue. Did Dane know? How could he not?

"We got lucky," Slade said. His expression was closed except for a hint of suppressed emotion in his eyes. He was also used to being in control of himself and those around him, to keeping himself guarded against the world. I suspected if he was with anyone else he wouldn't let it even slip this far.

I frowned at him.

"If the twins hadn't found you in time, we would have lost you. Yeah, we haven't known each other for long, but losing you would..." He cleared his throat.

"I suck at all this expressing emotion shit. I just wanted to say I'm fucking glad we didn't lose you. Not only because if we did, the twins would probably burn Brutham to the ground." A faint hint of a smile brushed his lips.

That was exactly what they'd do. With Chloe and Dane inside. They'd sit outside on the front lawn with beer and pizza, and watch. And laugh while my sister and her lover screamed.

No one would ever accuse them of being too sweet.

I gave Slade a questioning look.

"You're wondering what I would do?" He mused on that for a while. "I'd probably drive the getaway car, and be their alibi. I'd like to think I have enough credibility that if I say they were with me, I'd be believed. I might even help them spread accelerant all around the building before they lit a match."

He mimed striking a match against a matchbox and throwing it. Followed by his hands rising in the to signify fire, or an explosion.

His boyish smile made him look younger. Evidently, he had the same violent streak as the twins. I wondered if they were related some-how. Or maybe I just attracted sadistic men.

That suited me just fine.

Imagining the guys destroying the place shouldn't have been hot, but it was. All three of the guys would do more than burn the Academy down. They'd burn the whole world down for me. And then dance in the ashes. They'd get off on doing it.

"It won't come to that," Slade added. "We'll deal with this. We'll teach them they fucked with the wrong people. By the time we're done, they'll wish Chloe hadn't relinquished everything to you. They'll wish she ran, dropped off the face of the earth while she could. But she didn't and that was her mistake. Like Hunter said, when we fuck back, we're going to fuck back hard."

He emphasised the last word with a nod, his nose slightly scrunched, teeth bared.

I closed my eyes and exhaled softly. I was tired, but more than that I was angry. At myself for letting Zachary in and accepting that present. For listening to his lies and not seeing them for what they were. For knowing there was meaning in what he said but not taking the time to think it through and realise something was up. For not realising he brought a Trojan horse to my door and welcoming it with open arms and even cuddles.

I even named the fucking thing. I was naïve and stupid and I could have died because of it.

I was angry at Chloe for being a spineless bitch. She couldn't even come at me herself, she had to send Zachary on her behalf. Even if he swore up and down this was her idea, she'd deny it. She'd go to the grave denying it.

Somewhere in the back of my mind, I was angry at my father too. Sure, Chloe did this, but this whole competition bullshit was his idea. He could have chosen one of us and been done with it.

Even as I was thinking that, I realised it wouldn't have been that simple. If he chose Chloe, I would have insisted he change his mind. If he chose me, she would have done the same. We would have resented each other and him until one of us was dead.

Maybe that was the idea. He wanted one of us to kill the other, because he was too gutless to do it. Too much of a coward to cut one of our throats. Instead, he pitted us against each other, forcing us to do his dirty work for him. Making us hate each other more and more, until our relationship was shredded into nothing.

I hoped he was satisfied, because that was exactly what was happening. If Chloe was in front of me right now, I'd wrap my hands around her throat and squeeze until her body went limp, her lips blue, her eyes lifeless.

I'd stare at the dead body that looked a lot like me and know I'd won.

The only thing I knew for certain right now was that I *would* win. This attack made me more determined than ever.

Creeping around in the shadows, sending Zachary with a teddy bear, that was unbecoming of the Bell family. Both of them should be ashamed of themselves.

Zachary was right, he wasn't a Bell; he never would be. He didn't have what it took. Neither of them did.

I would head the family with Hunter, Parker and Slade by my side. And the whole fucking world would tremble.

I DROPPED my books onto the top of the table with a thud that made Chloe jump. Smiling in satisfaction at her response, I flopped down in the chair opposite her. Arms on the table in front of me, I sat looking at her.

"You're up out of bed, I see," she said sweetly. It would be obvious to anyone listening that she wasn't only referring to the hospital.

I ignored her attempt to slut shame me —as if she could talk anyway—and smiled.

"Yes, I've made a full recovery. The doctor says I won't have any lingering side-effects." That was almost the truth. The doctor said she *thought* I wouldn't, but I may suffer problems in the future. In the short term, I tired more quickly, but that would pass.

"That's wonderful," Chloe said, as if she wasn't seething on the inside. "I'm so relieved. I was worried about you. I popped in to visit, but you'd already been discharged. I figured you'd be resting."

You're full of shit, I thought.

"Always so thoughtful," I said sarcastically. "Where did you get the teddy bear from?" I was done tiptoeing around the truth. We both knew I knew exactly what happened. The only reason I didn't jump over the table right now and strangle her was because there were witnesses. That and I wanted her to suffer.

"Zachary gave it to me," she said with mock innocence. "She's so cute, with her little blue tutu." She cocked her head. "What's wrong? He didn't give you one too?" She clicked her tongue in mock sympathy.

"You know he did," I snapped. "Inside it was a capsule of toxic gas and a timer to release it. Which you know all about, because it was your idea. Yours or his. How long have you been working together?" I hadn't meant to ask that. I didn't want to talk about Zachary, but the words were out and I wanted the answer anyway. Not that I was naïve enough to think she'd give me one.

"I have no idea what you're going on about. Why would Zachary work with me?" She laughed, but the sound was higher than usual, as it was when she was nervous.

I rested my elbows on the table and clasped my hands in front of me. The black gloss polish on my nails caught the light.

"I've been asking myself the same question. The only answer I can come up with is a momentary lapse of judgement on his part. Or maybe he *wanted* to be on the losing side. Why—I assume it involves you sucking his cock."

Chloe leaned forward, resting her own elbows on the table. Her own nails were baby pink.

"Has it crossed your mind I had nothing to do with what happened? Have you, even for a second, considered he was working alone? You should be flattered. Out of both of us, he went after you. He could just as easily have tried to kill me too. Then what would have happened? Dad would have had no choice but to make Zachary his heir."

"Dad would choose Kennedy before he chose Zachary," I said. Our older half sister had already renounced any claim on any part of the family inheritance, but if we were gone, Dad would find a way to convince her to change her mind. He could be persuasive when he needed to be.

"Then perhaps you should warn Kennedy that Zachary might come after her." Chloe shrugged.

"He won't go after her if he didn't go after you," I said. "And the only reason he didn't go after you was because you and he are working together. By your own reasoning, he has no reason to leave you alive."

"Unless he thinks he can use me for something. Hell, for all I know my teddy bear has a capsule inside it that hasn't gone off yet." She sat back.

"Prove it," I said. "Show me this bear."

"Don't you have a make-up exam to study for?" she asked.

"After I see the bear." I couldn't entirely discount the possibility Zachary did this all by himself. Getting rid of us and Kennedy would force Dad's hand. Dad would be pissed if he killed us, but he'd appreciate Zachary's ambition.

Chloe sighed loudly. "Fine. Let's get this over with then. Some of us have work to do." She snatched up her books and laptop and stomped away.

I scooped up my own books and strode after her.

* * *

I hadn't been in her room since we first arrived at Brutham. I'd helped carry a couple of boxes from the car, but hadn't had a reason to be here after that.

Like our rooms at home, mine looked like a bomb went off inside a wardrobe. Clothes were always scattered all over the floor and on the top of the desk and chair. A bra often dangled over the edge of my bed.

Like always, Chloe's room was spotless. If I didn't know better, I'd think she didn't live here. The space was too tidy for a normal person.

"Here it is." She snatched up the teddy bear and all but threw it at me.

I grabbed it and squeezed its torso. "I need a knife."

"What makes you think I keep a knife here?" she asked, like cum wouldn't melt in her mouth.

I gave her a sidelong glance and held out my hand.

She rolled her eyes but stepped over to the table beside the bed and opened the drawer. She pulled out a knife and handed it to me, blade first.

I eyed her carefully, before taking the blade between my thumb and forefinger and slipping it out of her hand. I wouldn't put it past her to take this opportunity to stab me. I would have seriously considered it myself, but she didn't.

I moved a neat pile of books stacked on her desk, to the side and placed the teddy on the scratched, mahogany surface. I slashed the knife across the plush torso, exposing the stuffing. Placing the knife out of reach of my dear sister, I started to pull the stuffing out of the teddy bear.

I got halfway when something caught the overhead light. A glint of something shiny. Something familiar.

I glanced up at Chloe before digging my fingers in and pulling out a metal tube with a rounded end, like an elongated capsule. It was connected to a small, plastic device.

Her mouth dropped open. For the first time in I couldn't remember how long, she seemed genuinely surprised.

I won't lie, so was I.

"That fucking asshole," she growled. "He dared to come after me?"

"You didn't seem too worried when you thought it was just me he tried to kill," I said dryly.

She took the capsule for a closer look. "It's more personal when someone tries to kill you. Especially when you didn't realise *that* someone hates your guts."

For some reason, her words actually stung.

"I don't—" I started to say.

She glanced up at me. "You can't finish that sentence, can you?"

I pressed my lips together. "Chloe, I don't hate your guts. I hate this situation. I hate that in order to get the one thing I want in this world, I have to step over you."

She opened and closed her mouth a couple of times. "And now Zachary is trying to step over both of us."

"Yes, he is." We could agree on that at least.

"Are we going to let him do that?" She placed the capsule back inside the teddy bear and covered it with stuffing. "We should get rid of this before that goes off. I don't want to assume it failed. It might be on a different timer to yours."

I glanced around the room.

"Open the window."

She frowned at me. "I don't —"

"Open the window!" I didn't wait for her to move. I picked up a chair and slammed it straight into the glass. It cracked, but didn't break. Of course it didn't, the windows here were a couple of layers thick. Not quite bullet-proof, but close to it. Thank fuck they weren't bullet-proof, I'd never get through that. Not with a chair.

I pulled it back and slammed it into the window again. And again until finally a small section broke. It wasn't much, but it would have to do.

I grabbed up the whole teddy bear and shoved it through the hole. It dropped out and onto the ground below. Grabbing Chloe by the wrist, I pulled her down low to the floor. I threw myself down beside her, landing hard on my shoulder. I winced with pain but manage to throw my arms over my head.

"What the fuck—"

Her words were cut off by a bang loud enough to rattle the glass in the windows on the floor below this one. That was followed by a cloud of dust and smoke.

I lay with my face pressed to the hardwood. My heart pounded. My body was damp with sweat. I struggled to get my mind around what just happened.

When I was finally able to speak, I said, "Are you flattered now? He came after us both." I coughed lightly as smoke drifted in through the hole in the window.

Chloe choked on a laugh and managed to sit up. Her usually neat hair was in disarray, strands stuck out all over. She swept it back off her face. "How did you know?"

"I guessed," I admitted. "If there were cameras in your room, when would it be better to let off a bomb? He might have intended it just for you, but when the gas didn't kill me, he had to improvise. He could have taken us both out at the same time."

She looked disgusted. "This just got very, very fucking personal." She leaned her back against the side of her bed. I know we're supposed to be competing with each other, but he's pissed me off." She sucked in an angry breath.

"Why don't we call a truce until we deal with him? Otherwise, he's going to go on using our animosity towards each other, against us. I don't know about you, but I don't want to fight a war on two fronts. If we keep doing that, we both lose."

She offered me her hand.

I looked at it for a good minute before I finally accepted it and shook. "We can't let him take what's ours." Relinquishing control of the family to her would be difficult enough. Seeing Zachary running it wasn't something I could allow. Even if he was a Bell by blood, he'd done something I couldn't forgive. He'd tried to kill me, twice. That really, really pissed me off.

"No we can't." I scooted over and leaned against the bed beside her. "He's going to regret fucking with the wrong sisters."

I didn't know how long this tentative truce would last, but between us we'd fuck back against Zachary harder than we ever would have against each other. It might even feel good to be on the same side as her for a while.

"Yes he is. And you owe me an apology." She gave me a sly smile. "You thought I sent that bear."

I flipped her off. "For one thing, I had good reason to think that. If the tables were turned, you would have thought I attacked you. Also, I just saved your ass. I could have walked out the door, closed it behind me and let that bomb go off with you in the room."

"You wouldn't do that," she said. "Deep down, you love me. Besides, you couldn't know how powerful that bomb was. It could have taken out the corridor with you in it."

"You're right in the second count." I wasn't going to say anything about the first point. Maybe she was right. That wasn't something I needed to dwell on right now.

When Zachary was dealt with, we'd go back to being bitter enemies. I had no reason to assume otherwise. At this point, we'd been at each other's throats for so long, I didn't know if we could do any different.

She snorted softly. "There's something you should know."

"You're sleeping with Dane DiMarco, everyone knows that," I said lightly.

She rolled her eyes to the ceiling. "I don't care who knows that. Dane is—" She shook her head. "That doesn't matter at the moment. When Zachary was here, he told me he was transferring to Brutham. They're going to make sure he does the trials along with us."

We exchanged knowing looks.

"That is interesting," I said slowly. "He may regret that choice."

"If he lives long enough to regret it," she said. "Personally, I'd be okay with him being long gone before that."

"So would I," I agreed. "Although...after what he did to us, I'd be just as happy to make him suffer for a while."

seventeen

HUNTER

"OR WE COULD JUST RIP his balls off and shove them down his throat." I bit into my apple like I might tear a piece off Zachary and spit it out.

Parker and I were in class when we heard the explosion outside the window. Although it was several metres from where we sat, the whole building shook. The windows rattled. The bomb left a crater the size of my outstretched arms in the manicured lawn. Small in the scheme of things, but big enough to kill Lila and her sister if it went off in the same room as them.

Needless to say, I was pissed off. Coming after Lila once was bad enough. Twice was a one way trip to the perpetrator's worst nightmare. That was a ticket I was happy to spring for.

Sitting opposite Chloe and Dane, on the same side for once, was as surreal as it was temporary. I trusted them as much as I trusted Zachary, but if Lila said they were working together, then I'd play nice.

For now.

"I'm not ruling that out," Lila said. "I don't want to kill him outright just yet."

"Why?" Parker asked. "You'd be surprised how many problems can be solved by killing someone outright."

"I hate to say it, but Parker is right," Dane said. He sat beside Chloe, his arm draped across the back of the couch behind her. He was tense. Ready to defend her if any of us made a move.

Parker grinned. "Thanks, dude. I keep telling Hunter that but he thinks I'm biased."

"I didn't say you were biased," I argued. "I said you were full of shit. There's a significant difference."

He flipped me off. "I love you too, bro."

"Anyway," Dane drawled. "This asshole tried to kill both of you and you don't want him dead?"

"Oh, we want him dead all right," Lila said. "But we want to toy with him first. Make an example of him. Killing him would be too easy. We want this to be memorable."

"Exactly," Chloe agreed. "We want people to know what happens when they fuck with the Bell family. We want what we do to him to serve as a deterrent to anyone else who thinks we're pushovers because we're women."

"The only people who think that are people who haven't met you," Slade said. He sat quietly in the corner until now. Watching and listening, his eyes following the conversation back and forth across the room.

"See, Slade is all for killing Zachary and getting it over with," Parker said.

Slade raised his eyebrows. "On the contrary, if this helps to deter other people from causing problems later, then I'm all for playing cat and mouse with Zachary. Although six of us against one of him... I almost feel sorry for the asshole."

"Don't," Lila told him. "There's nothing to feel sorry for him for. He made his bed and now he has to lie in it."

She lifted her chin, her dark eyes darker than ever. She was absolutely fucking gorgeous and glorious. She was the flame and I was one of the moths drawn to her heat and light, not caring if I got burnt to a crisp. I couldn't think of a better way to go.

"Why would he come here?" I asked. "He failed to kill you. He must know he's not gonna get away with that."

If I was him, I'd be shaking in my shoes, not packing up to come to Brutham. Although, I wouldn't be him, because when I tried to kill people, I succeeded. That was one of the reasons I preferred the direct approach. Bombs and gases, they're too hit and miss. A good gunshot to the brain, or sliced throat, were much simpler and more effective. Not to mention much more personal.

Waiting to hear through the grapevine whether or not your victim died, would be very unsatisfying. That was a level of patience I didn't have.

"If he wants to be considered for the head of the family, he has no choice but to come here," Lila said. "It might be that he didn't necessarily intend to kill us. That was his way of throwing his hat into the ring, of letting us know he's in contention too."

"Nothing says 'I'm not necessarily trying to kill you' like a bomb," Chloe said dryly.

"It wasn't a very powerful bomb," Lila pointed out. Her brow was furrowed, contradicting her own words with an expression that clearly said she was remembering the explosion. She tried to let on that she wasn't bothered by it, but I knew her better than that.

I sat forward. "Enough to kill you if you were too close to it." For a while there, I thought we'd lost her. For the second time in only a handful of days, I was worried. Seeing her alive and whole...

Words couldn't express my relief. And my anger.

"But I wasn't." She gave me a soft look. One that melted me in places I hadn't known existed before I met her. I would have said I was made of stone and cum. I refused to be soft, but for her I'd be slightly less rigid.

"So we're supposed to let him transfer here and welcome him with open arms?" I asked, borderline disbelieving.

"Exactly," Lila said. "You've made no secret you want to build a bridge between the Bell and Brantley families. Let Zachary think you were using me to achieve that, but now he's put his hand up, you'd rather work with him. Tell him you think men deserve to be in charge. Whatever you have to do. When you've won him over, then we can strike."

"We're going to have to be very convincing for him to believe we're on his side." Parker looked doubtful.

"If anyone can bullshit, it's you two," Dane said. "You've had lots of experience. I, for one, would totally buy the suggestion you're only using Lila to get what you want." He gave Parker a scathing look.

Chloe put a hand on his knee.

"You can be next in line to have your balls ripped off and shoved down your throat, if you like," I said darkly. "In fact, I don't mind if you're first in line."

Dane rolled his eyes. "Typical Brantley. You throw out the threats, but we all know you're not going to follow through. Your brains are as big as your dicks."

"Thank you," I replied. "Both are very big. It's nice of you to acknowledge that." I gave him a nod, coupled with a sarcastic smile.

Dane barked a laugh. He opened his mouth to say something else, no doubt something derogatory.

"That's enough," Lila snapped. "I know we've been at each other's throats all year, but we need to put that aside. This may come as a shock to some of you, but we're all adults here. It's time we started acting like it. If we don't, we'll be dead at the end of this. If you want to keep carrying on like this, you can fuck off right now, because I'm not going to let childish behaviour get me killed." Her gaze swept across all of us.

I turned to Parker. "That was hot."

"It really was." He nodded. He raised his hands to either side. "I can be a mature adult. If the rest of them can."

"I can," I said. "Lila is right. Fighting amongst ourselves is going to work in Zachary's favour. Him and anyone here who is working for or with him. That's another thing. We can't assume he's going to act alone. It would be naive to presume it's six against one. He's not stupid enough to come here with odds like that. Especially not while Lila and Chloe are alive."

"Good point," Slade said. "There were a couple of new transfers in the last month or so, but no one that stood out. No one else with the last name Sinclair, or anything that ties them to his mother or Samuel Bell."

"It's more likely whoever they are, they already attend Brutham," Dane reasoned.

"Or work here." Parker raised an eyebrow in Dane's direction.

"Or work here," Dane agreed. "But I'm not one of them. My loyalty is with Chloe. To the point where I've put myself off side with the rest of my family." He didn't look too worried about that. Of course not. He was more ambitious than he was sentimental.

"Asher wouldn't care," I said. "No one has seen Mina for years." That was the official story anyway. I'd find myself smothered by a pillow in the middle of the night, courtesy of Reuben, if I deviated from that.

"That leaves Rose. I can see why you'd be worried." Rose DiMarco was intelligent, tough and connected. If anyone wanted to cover their tracks, they went to her. If she couldn't deal with it, no one could. If she was pissed off enough at Dane, she could make him disappear without a trace, and never break a sweat.

Dane shrugged. "I can handle Rose. The point is, I'm not working with Zachary Sinclair." He turned his head to look at Slade.

"Don't look at me," Slade said. "I've never met the guy. He's lucky he's not studying business law, because I won't be teaching him. From what I've seen, he's studying chemistry."

"With a little bit of bomb making on the side," I added. "Useful skills to have, unless he's the enemy. In which case, not so much."

"Lucky for us, we have three computer nerds in our corner," Parker said. "Me, Hunter and Kennedy. Between us, there's nothing we can't hack."

"There's nothing *Kennedy* can't hack," Chloe said. "Maybe she can make a virus like she did with Dad's computer."

"Can't hurt to ask." I shrugged.

"Unless her boyfriends get pissed off at us for asking," Parker remarked. "Then we can look forward to a couple of weeks chained to the ceiling and tortured by Ice Miller. Actually, from what I've heard of him, we wouldn't need to piss them off. He'd just do it for fun."

"He probably has a grudge against you two for turning Kennedy and him in to Dad," Lila said.

Parker grinned. "Nothing we can't handle. All of that turned out fine in the end."

"I doubt Ice sees it that way." She rubbed her eyes. She looked tired. Almost dying would do that to a person. So would almost dying twice. "I suspect he'd happily chain me up beside you two."

"If he tries, his life expectancy will be very short," Slade growled.

"Fuck yeah it will," I agreed. "Better if Lila stays away from Dusk Bay altogether. At least from Ice, Mannix and Ares. All three of them seem like the type to hold a grudge."

Me, I didn't bother, unless it was someone like Zachary. Even Chloe was all right when she wasn't trying to make life difficult for Lila. Dane wasn't so bad either, more or less. And it was easy to get a rise out of him. That was a bonus.

Of course, the minute Lila called an end to their ceasefire, all bets would be off again. We'd be right back to finding ways to make their lives hell, or shortening them.

"Let's see what this Zachary asshole has to say for himself when he gets here," I concluded. "Parker and I will do whatever we have to do, then we'll hit him hard. The prick won't see us coming."

"Dane and I will keep an eye out for any students we suspect might be acting with Zachary," Slade said. "In the meantime, it's probably a good idea for Lila and Chloe to pretend they're still at war with each other. If he sees they've joined forces, is much more likely to suspect they will come after him."

"Right," Dane agreed. "From what I know about this guy he's not stupid. He's probably desperate. We can use that against him."

I rubbed my hands together. I wasn't sure if killing Zachary immediately wasn't the right way to go, but if this was how Lila wanted to play it, then I might as well have some fun.

When we were done with him, Zachary would be lucky to recognise himself in the mirror. If he looked in it. Even his reflection was going to hate him when we were done with him.

eighteen

HUNTER

"HEY." I flopped down on the grass beside Zachary. Parker on the other side of him. "Welcome to Brutal Academy."

Zachary didn't turn his eyes away from the rugby match until the big forward smashed the hooker into the ground in a bruising tackle. Only when they were staggering to their feet did he turn to look at me.

"Brantley," he said by way of greeting.

I held out my hand. "Hunter. That's Parker." My hand still out, I gestured to my twin.

Zachary looked at my hand for a while before shaking it. "Zachary Sinclair. But you knew that already."

"Yeah, I did." I crossed my legs at my ankles and leaned back on one hand. I turned my gaze to the rugby as the referee called a knock-on and stopped the play for a few moments.

"You like a bit of football? The Brutham Bears aren't bad."

"I like anything where blood is spilled," Zachary said. "As long as it's not mine." He glanced over at me again.

I chuckled. "Man after my own heart. I much prefer other people's blood be spilled than mine."

"Me too," Parker remarked. His eyes were on the game, but he was listening to us.

"So... You grew up with Chloe and Lila Bell." I might as well cut to the chase. We all knew this wasn't a social call.

"Yeah, and you're dating Lila. Both of you." Zachary smiled as the big forward tackled another player. When the man rose, he had blood pouring out of his nose and down his face.

Zachary looked as though the sight made him want to pull out his cock and get himself off.

I couldn't judge. I was turned on by worse things.

"I wouldn't say we're dating her," I said lightly. "We're both fucking her. So have you."

The thought of it made me want to tackle him to the ground and punch the crap out of him. Even though that happened before we met Lila, the idea of him touching her...

Parker snorted. "Who hasn't? She's not exactly a blushing virgin."

Zachary relaxed slightly. He was a long way from trusting us, but he was almost sure we hadn't come to kill him. Not today.

"She was before I got to her," he said with a shrug. "After I fucked Chloe, Lila practically begged me to fuck her. She couldn't stand her sister having something she didn't. Of course, I was happy to oblige. If there's something she's good at, it's spreading her legs."

I laughed as naturally as I could. For talking about her like that, I wanted to slowly slice his dick off.

Instead, I said, "She really is. Her and Chloe must have fucked half the school by now. On the other hand, so have Parker and I. Out here in the sticks, there's nothing much else to do when we're not studying. We might as well stick our cocks into anything that stays still long enough. Right, Park?"

"Yep." Parker grinned.

"So, I was thinking," I said after we watched a couple more minutes of the game. No more blood was spilled, but one of the guys left the field with a head injury that would probably result in a nasty concussion. No one ever said rugby was a pleasant game. It was a brutal blood sport that spoke to the primal part of me. One I preferred to watch than play.

Cricket and tennis were more my speed. Less chance of getting myself badly injured.

"Don't hurt yourself," Zachary teased lightly.

Parker and I both laughed, him a little louder than me.

I clapped Zachary on the back. I would have preferred to knife him there. For Lila's sake, I'd keep playing this stupid game. It would be Zachary who won the stupid prizes.

"Seriously though. Park and I both appreciate the way you went after Chloe and Lila. Teddy bears?" I mimed a chef's kiss. "Genius. I'm definitely stealing that idea and putting it in my playbook. But I want to know why."

Zachary stiffened. "Why what?" He was very much on alert now.

"Why go after them in a way that they didn't end up dead? Was it your intention to kill them or are you sending a message?" I looked hopeful.

He chose his words carefully. "If I wanted to kill them, they'd be dead."

I doubted that, but I played along. "So, you were trying to tell them something? Or were you trying to...encourage them to step aside? I mean, you're older than them and you're a guy. It seems to me you're the easy pick to take Samuel Bell's place some day. They needed a reminder of that. Right?"

I could see the wheels of thought turning in his brain. He wanted to agree with everything I said, but could he trust me? If I was him, I'd tell me to fuck off. But then again, I knew me better than he did.

Finally, he let out a frustrated sigh. "He should have chosen me instead of pitting the girls against each other. Neither of them have the balls to take Sam's place."

"Exactly," I agreed. Lila had bigger proverbial balls than he would ever have. Although, he was smart enough and ruthless enough to have been an asset if he hadn't gone after them. Whatever, that was his funeral.

"They don't have balls at all, which is half the problem." I uncrossed my legs and crossed them the other way. "Sooner or later, they'll get pregnant and get all weak and weepy. You know what women are like. That's why men rule the world."

I caught a glimpse of Parker's smirk at my words. He didn't buy them any more than I did, but only Zachary had to.

"They should both step aside before they break a nail," Parker said. "It's bad enough when that happens."

"What are you saying?" Zachary asked. "I was under the impression you supported Lila."

I gestured vaguely. "Like I said, we're fucking her. For a while we thought maybe she'd be the one to back. Over Chloe anyway. That was before there was a viable alternative." I clapped him on the back again.

"What's in it for you?" He narrowed his eyes at me.

"Power," Parker said.

I nodded my agreement. "The possibility of joining the Bell and Brantley families together. Reuben will never agree to work with a woman. But someone like you— You could change all of that. Imagine how powerful the three of us could be."

"Do you mean how powerful Reuben and I would be?" Zachary asked. "He is the head of your family."

"That's what we want him to think," Parker said. "But Hunt and I have been building contacts over the years. At some point we may move to take Reuben down and replace him. For now, he's useful to us."

If Reuben heard any of that, he'd have someone slice the skin of our bodies as slowly as possible. He was already suspicious that we might not toe the line forever. Anything that sounded like an active plan to overthrow him would get us dead quickly.

The truth was, we had no such plan. Parker and I took every day as it came. Besides, we had several other brothers we'd have to step over first and taking all of them on would take time and resources.

Resources we'd have when Lila was head of her family.

"You'd support me against Chloe and Lila?" Zachary asked carefully.

"Absolutely we would," I agreed. "In fact, I'd like to nominate you to join the Brotherhood."

"The Brotherhood?" Zachary echoed.

"It's a very exclusive club of the most powerful men in the world," I said. "There's a chapter here at Brutham. Most of us join here, but only when invited and nominated by a current member. Once you join, you're in for life. The Brotherhood of Kings has connections you could only dream of."

"I've never heard of it." Zachary shook his head.

Parker laughed. "It wouldn't be a very good secret organisation if you had. Trust me, you know the names of a lot of the members. They're basically the who's who of the most rich and powerful, and the up-and-comers in the world. But don't ask us to tell you who, because you don't get to know unless you join."

"Both of you are members?" He still looked doubtful.

"We are," I said. "We were nominated by our brother Joshua. Most of our brothers are members." The only one who wasn't was Zeke. He had no interest in any of that. Sometimes I wondered if he was adopted. He was certainly not as much fun as the rest of us.

"What do I have to do to join?" Zachary asked.

"There's a meeting two nights from now," I said. "If you want to go, the committee will interview you and if you pass that, you'll go through initiation. Don't worry, it's nothing you can't handle."

Zachary nodded. "I'm there."

Of course he was. No one could resist the lure of a secret, powerful organisation. I certainly couldn't. Like him, I'd had no idea it existed before I started at Brutham. If every member was in the same place and we were attacked and killed, the world would fall into chaos. We were exactly that influential. Nothing happened in the world that didn't involve one of us in some way.

"Excellent." I grinned. "I don't know about you two, but I'm thirsty. Let's go to the bar and celebrate our new arrangement." I could use a beer or three to wash the taste of bullshit out of my mouth.

I climbed to my feet. Before I could take more than a step or two, Zachary put a hand on my bicep.

"There are no women in this... Brotherhood are there?"

I laughed. "Of course not. Unless you count the Fillies. Women who connect themselves to members of the Brotherhood. Some work at the Brotherhood's clubs in the hope of catching the eye of one. We usually pass them around until either someone marries them or we get tired of them."

They were usually gorgeous and ambitious. If the Brotherhood allowed women, they'd be the first to join. Instead, they stayed on the fringes, pouring drinks and spreading their legs. Most of them benefited by receiving gifts, or marrying a rich husband.

Lila would throw herself off the roof of the Academy before she became a Filly. If they ever changed their policy, I'd nominate her in a heartbeat, but the Brotherhood had operated the same way for at least two hundred years. It wasn't going to change now. Not unless Parker and I could work our way into the ruling committee. Then we may have a chance. That would take decades. No one was going to listen to a pair of twenty-year old university students.

Zachary smiled. I could almost see him hungering for women willing to fuck him for his power. If he wasn't careful, that shit would go to his head.

"So, about that drink," I said.

"Let's go," Zachary said. "You two aren't what I expected, but we definitely have something to celebrate here. The beginning of something immense."

"It couldn't get bigger than you heading the Bell family," Parker agreed. He rubbed his hands together. "This is going to be so much fun. And hey, we can talk about helping you through the trials. We know all the good spots to dispose of your enemies. If they're still standing by then."

"By the time the trials come, Chloe and Lila will both be on their knees," Zachary said. "Where they belong."

"Choking on our cocks." I grinned.

nineteen

HUNTER

I GROANED. My head pounded. My whole body felt heavy, like it was weighted down. I must have lain in the same position for too long.

I tried to roll over, but I couldn't move. Had I really drunk that much? I couldn't remember beyond my second beer.

Zachary had peppered Parker and I with questions about the Brotherhood, and ways we could help him with the trials. I'd been as evasive as I could without looking like I was avoiding the questions, and stuck to small talk, like what courses he was taking and whether he had any ambitions outside heading the Bell family.

Everything after that was blank.

I groaned and tried again to roll over. At first, I thought my body felt like lead. In the back of my aching mind I realised something else was going on. It wasn't that my body didn't want to move, but that I *couldn't*.

I opened my crusty eyes a crack and blinked to clear them. The room was dim, but this was not my bedroom at the Academy. Not Lila's either, nor Parker's. It didn't look like anywhere inside the Academy building.

The floor underneath was cold and hard. Concrete. Judging by the faint smell of decay and dirt, I wasn't in Brutham anymore. Unless this was one of the outlying sheds. If it was, it wasn't the one Parker and I usually used.

"Hunt?" Parker's voice sounded dry and raw.

I swallowed and found my throat to be the same. It tasted of something nasty. Not beer or even vomit, but something sickly sweet and medicinal.

"I'm right here, Park," I whispered. God, I could use a drink of water around about now. If my headache didn't kill me, my thirst would.

I tried to raise my arms, but they were heavy as fuck. Chained, with metal bound firmly around my wrists.

I was into being tied up as much as the next guy, but not like this. My strong preference was for consent.

"Where is here?" Parker asked. "What the fuck happened? My head is killing me."

"Mine too and I don't know," I said. "Shhh."

"What—"

I hissed at him to be quiet. Footsteps approached, accompanied by voices.

"I'm sorry I doubted you." That was Zachary. "I didn't think they'd fall for any of that, but they all did exactly what you said they'd do."

"Of course they did."

My whole body stiffened more than it already was. That was Chloe. She sounded as smug as hell.

"Everything went almost exactly as we planned," she continued. "It might have been easier if Lila died from the shit in that teddy bear you gave her, but this worked out better, don't you think?"

"Yeah, it did; Lila still thinks you're working with her." Zachary sounded amused. "And we got these two assholes out of the way."

Who was this prick calling an asshole? As soon as I got out of here, he was going to hell, because I was going to send him there. After torturing him for a while.

"Which one can I kill first?" Zachary sounded excited for the possibility.

"Neither one for now," Chloe said. "While they're alive, we can use them as leverage. Once they've outdone their usefulness, I'll decide. Or better yet, we could get them to kill each other."

Zachary laughed. "That would be good for shits and giggles."

I was going to send both of them to hell. As slowly and painfully as possible. I'd start by cutting off their toes, and gradually work my way up, avoiding vital organs and too much bleeding as I went. Just for fun, I might even carve my initials into their foreheads. And then, into their bones. If Parker was lucky, I'd let him join in too.

Parker grunted softly in annoyance. Only loud enough for me to hear. He obviously realised it was better they didn't know we were awake and listening.

"And Lila?" Zachary asked. "Are you going to kill her too?"

He was obviously very much her minion, just like Lila suspected he was. They must have planted that second teddy bear and timed it to look like Zachary went after Chloe.

That was fucked up bullshit. Chloe wanted Lila to trust her and she had; enough to let her guard down. Enough to send us to make friends with Zachary. If the taste in my mouth was any indication, he'd spiked our drinks with something nasty but nonlethal.

No, I'd watched him carefully, keeping my drink to myself. Parker had bought the first round and I'd bought the second. Zachary hadn't gone near my drink. It was the asshole behind the bar, working with Zachary and Chloe.

He was going to hell with them.

"I don't see any reason we can't continue with our original plan," Chloe said. "Things will be so much easier with Dad if she tells him she's dropping out of the running. He'll accept her quitting better than he'll accept me killing her. He always had a soft spot for her." She sounded bitter.

"He thinks she's as ruthless as he is, and you're not," Zachary said. "But she doesn't know you as well as I do." A slight slap of skin hitting the wall was followed by the wet sound of them kissing.

Did Dane know Chloe and Zachary were involved? More than involved, if their already rapid breathing was an indication.

A zipper slid undone, fabric rustled. She sighed low, from the back of her throat.

"Fuck, you always feel so good," Zachary moaned. "So. Fucking. Good." He was obviously thrusting with each word.

How long had they been fucking each other? I guessed it was a while.

"I'm so glad you transferred here." Chloe's voice was breathless. "I missed you."

"You missed my cock," he growled. "You missed being my whore. Didn't you? *Didn't you?*"

"Yes," she moaned. "Yes, I missed being your whore. Mmmm, I'm going to... To come."

"Good, come for me, bitch," Zachary told her.

Evidently she liked dirty talk from him as just much as she liked it from Dane. She cried out Zachary's name, moaning loudly as she came.

If my head didn't hurt enough before, it was worse now, listening to them fucking. For once, I wasn't even slightly turned on. If anything, my cock was softer than it had ever been in my life. No doubt that was the side effect of whatever drug was still in my system. It better wear off, or they'd be lucky to go to hell.

The sound of skin hitting the wall came faster, over and over, accompanied by Zachary's grunts and groans and growls.

"I'm going to come inside you, you dirty slut." He growled one more time before he came.

Was ear bleach a thing? Because I was going to need a butt ton of it after this.

I thought listening to Chloe and Dane was traumatising, but it was nothing to this. Neither of them had tried to kill Lila at the time. Now, I was tied here, listening to my enemies make each other feel good.

Ugh, kill me now.

What did Parker and I do to deserve this? Okay, we did a lot of shitty things and killed people, but this was a cruel and unusual torture. Mercifully it was over quickly. Apparently Zachary didn't have much staying power. Certainly not as much as Dane.

They were silent for a while, catching their breath.

"Are we leaving them here?" Zachary asked finally. "We're too close to the Academy for my liking."

"For now," Chloe said easily. "No one will find them here. No one will think to look." She sounded certain of that.

Did she really think we could just disappear off the face of the planet and no one would notice? If she did, she was delusional.

"Dane said no one ever comes here," she added.

"He better be right," Zachary growled. "What about his involvement in all of this anyway? He's a DiMarco."

It sounded like there was trouble in paradise. Maybe Zachary-boy didn't like to share his stepsister with a teacher.

"He's useful," Chloe said. "Just like you are. He's in this with us until the end."

"I have to keep sharing?" Zachary sounded pissed off.

"You knew going into this there would be other men," she scolded. "I'm with you and I'm with Dane. And I'm with anyone else who is useful to me. I will fuck whomever I have to fuck, whenever I have to fuck them. And if I tell you to fuck someone—"

"I won't cheat on you," he argued.

"It's not cheating if I tell you to do it," she said. "You know what's at stake here. More power than you and I could ever dream of. We need to do whatever it takes." Her tone turned sultry. "Would you do that for me?"

"I'll do anything for you." He sounded sulky. It seemed he had the impression she'd drop everyone for him. "You're not going to ask me to screw Lila, are you?"

I curled my hands into fists. If that prick touched a hair on her head I would personally place his feet into acid, then pour some of that onto his cock and balls. Better yet, I'd cover them with honey and tie him on top of an ant's nest. The ways I'd make him suffer would be worse than anything his worst nightmares could conjure.

"I doubt she'd trust you, but it wouldn't hurt to try." Chloe said. "With the twins away, she may need consoling."

"But Slade—"

"We need to deal with him," she said with a sigh. "Dane is keeping an eye on him for now, but we definitely shouldn't underestimate Mr Lincoln. I wish I'd got his attention before she did. I might work on him, he might come over to our side yet."

"If you fuck him..."

"It will be because it's necessary," she said firmly. "Besides, he's kinda hot. I can understand what Lila sees in him."

Zachary made a rude noise. That was followed by the sound of skin hitting skin like she was patting his cheek.

"You'll forget your jealousy when you have more pussy than you know what to do with."

"I only want yours." He sounded frustrated.

"You say that now, but that will change. You'll have them lining up to wrap their lips around your cock."

"Speaking of that," he said slowly. "They wanted to nominate me for something called the Brotherhood."

His words were followed by her sharp intake of breath.

"So it's a real thing?" he asked.

"It is. I didn't expect them to suggest that to you," she replied. "It's not something that's offered around to someone you barely know. Did they seem sincere?"

"I guess so," he said uncertainly. "Probably not now. Should I have abandoned the plan to bring them here?"

Silence was followed by, "I don't think so. You can always ask Dad to nominate you. Unless he's used all his nominations. Each member is allowed six in their lifetime."

"They really don't allow women?" he asked carefully. He sounded like he didn't want to admit he liked the idea of women being passed around the organisation. He wasn't sure what she'd think if she knew.

"They really don't, but beyond that I don't know much about it," she admitted. "If anyone offers to nominate you again, say yes. Getting you in there could really help us."

"Yeah, if they do. Anyway, we should get to class."

"Yes we should, I'll be back later to check on our guests." She laughed softly.

I can't fucking wait, I thought.

Their voices and footsteps faded before a door opened and closed somewhere a few metres away.

"Well this is fucked up," Parker said.

"That's one way to put it," I agreed. I swallowed and winced at my dry throat. "We need to find a way to get the hell out of here. Whatever that bitch has planned, I don't think either of us are going to like it."

twenty

LILA

"IS EVERYTHING ALL RIGHT?" Chloe flopped down beside me as I clicked out of my messages and threw my phone down on the table.

"Yeah." I pretended to be interested in my laptop screen, but I hadn't read a word of anything on it for the last hour.

"Just a message from Parker to let me know Reuben needed him and Hunter to do some urgent business." It wasn't unusual, but the timing sucked. Although, the timing always sucked. Reuben seemed to have a knack for knowing when the worst times were, and sending the guys off somewhere.

"It must get really tiring," Chloe said.

When she didn't elaborate, I decided to take the bait anyway.

"What must get tiring?"

"The guys always prioritising their brothers over you." She pulled her phone out of her pocket and toyed with it for a while. "Any time Reuben tells them to jump, they jump without thinking. Have they ever told him no? After what happened to us, there's no way Dane would leave me here alone."

Her words hit too close to home. As far as I know, they never told Reuben they wouldn't do whatever he asked them to. They enjoyed working for him. But to leave now, when so much was at stake?

When I was head of my family, I'd have to consider my options where Reuben was concerned. There may be a time when assassinating him was my only option. He may prove impossible to work with, especially if he was going to keep pulling the strings with the twins. I didn't care for it in the short term, but in the long-term it was definitely not going to work.

"Slade is still here," I reminded her. "And you."

She flashed a brief smile. "Of course I am."

There was definitely something off about her expression. I put it down to this uneasy alliance. *Temporary* alliance. As soon as we dealt with Zachary, we'd be back at war. For all I knew, she was planning her next move.

"Have you spoken to Zachary?" I asked.

She looked even cagier, but shrugged. "I have. He claimed to know nothing about any explosive devices in either of the teddy bears. He actually suggested he was set up by Reuben Brantley. What better way to get rid of us, while pinning it on someone else?"

I mulled that over for a minute. "Is there any chance that's what happened? Maybe Zachary is innocent in all of this."

I *wanted* to believe he wouldn't do anything to hurt me. He'd seemed so sincere when we last spoke. Setting up others wasn't necessarily Reuben's style though. He usually didn't care who knew he was behind attacks like this. Perhaps he saw an opportunity and took it.

"At this point, anything is possible," Chloe agreed. "Maybe we should cut Zachary some slack. Have you talked to him?"

I shook my head. "Not since that night. I saw him arrive, but that was all."

"Maybe you should talk to him," Chloe suggested. She glanced around. "In the meantime, we're still supposed to be on opposite sides. We wouldn't want anyone to see us talking and think we're friendly toward each other."

"Definitely wouldn't want that," I said with an edge of sarcasm. "I guess I could speak to him. I just wish the guys told me what he said to them before they left. I tried calling them, but it went straight to voicemail. I'm sure they'll call me back as soon as they're able to."

They fucking better. Taking off without a word was bad enough, but leaving me in the dark where Zachary was concerned, was worse.

"I'm sure they will." Chloe stood and shoved her phone into the pocket of her skirt. "No doubt, wherever they are, they're pining for you." The smile she gave me before she walked away gave me chills for some reason.

"They better be," I said under my breath. I closed my laptop with a sigh and gathered it up. If I couldn't concentrate in the quiet of the library, then I had no chance. I slipped it under my arm and headed out the oak trimmed doors and up the stairs at the end of the corridor.

Brutham had elevators, but I preferred the stairs. They were good exercise and not an enclosed space like an elevator car. I couldn't step foot in one without being terrified they'd break down and I'd get stuck in there. In my nightmares, the lights would go out and I would hear no sound except my thoughts.

I'd probably never know if my fear of enclosed spaces was due to being locked in the sensory deprivation room in my father's basement as a child, or if it was a phobia I was born with. Either way, I avoided them as much as possible.

I trotted up the steps and around the corner to Slade's office. The door was ajar. I tapped on it before pushing it open.

He glanced up from his computer and gave me a smile that made my heart flip. He was so fucking gorgeous I could hardly believe he looked twice at me, much less tangled his life with mine so quickly.

"I was just thinking about you," he said.

I grimaced playfully and set my things down on a table to the side of the room. "Don't tell me, you're marking my essay?" I closed the door and twisted the lock until it clicked.

"If I said I was, what would you do for a higher grade?" He leaned back in his chair and laced his fingers behind his head.

I stepped over toward him, moving slowly and deliberately. I walked around his desk and knelt down beside him. I ran my hand from his knee, up his thigh and over his cock.

I glanced up at him before working the button of his pants loose and sliding down the zip. He lifted his hips to allow me to ease his pants down to expose his already half hard cock.

I gripped his length in one hand and stroked my fingers down to his tip and back up to his balls until he was rock hard.

I looked back up at him and watched his expression as I licked his tip like it was a tasty lollipop. I slid my tongue over the bead of pre-cum that formed on the head. He was deliciously salty.

My eyes still on his face, I wrapped my mouth around his cock and took him in as deep as I could. Deep enough for him to tap the back of my throat.

I watched him watching me suck him, getting more and more aroused by his clear enjoyment. I loved nothing more than giving pleasure to the guys I cared about. Controlling their pleasure turned me on harder than anything.

His hips rose and fell off the seat of the chair, as he fucked my mouth in rhythm with my sucks.

"Fuck, that's good," he groaned. "I'm going to come in your mouth."

I smiled around my mouthful and sucked harder, his cock hitting the back of my throat with every thrust. Forget lollipops, cock was better than any of them. So thick, warm and hard.

He grunted in bliss and ground against me as he came, squirting warm, salty cum into my throat so hard I gagged.

I went on sucking until he sagged. Slowly, I slid my mouth off him and smiled as I swallowed down every drop like it was melted chocolate.

"Does that give me an A?" I asked teasingly.

"I think I can give you a B+. If you want an A, you're going to have to sit on my desk."

Whether or not I wanted an A, I definitely wanted an O. I scrambled to my feet and onto the top of the desk in front of him.

He gripped my knees and drew them apart, making my skirt ride up my thighs.

He held my thighs open, leaned in and exhaled deeply. "Your pussy always smells like perfection."

He pulled the gusset of my G-string aside and ran the pads of two fingers around my pussy and over my clit. He looked like he was admiring one of the wonders of the world.

He slid his fingers down to my entrance and worked his fingertips inside. "So wet for me too." He pressed his fingers in deeper.

He'd slid them all the way to his knuckles when his phone rang. Rather than ignoring it, he picked it up and pressed it to his ear. At the same time, he slid his fingers in and out of me. The heel of his hand brushed my clit.

"Hello?" he said into the phone. He listened while he worked me with his skilled fingers. His brow crinkled in a frown and his nose scrunched slightly, adorably.

He glanced at me and mouthed, "Shhh."

I bit my lip to keep from moaning when he hooked his fingers around, massaging me inside and out while whoever was on the other end of the phone spoke.

"I see," he was saying. "That could be a problem."

I leaned back on my hands, hooked my fingers around the edge of the desk while my back arched. I bucked my hips and bit my lip harder to stop myself from screaming at the ceiling. Fuck, his touch was so good.

"Yes. No, I agree. It's nothing we can't deal with." He glanced up at me, a wicked glint in his eyes. He knew I was close and fully intended to stay on the line while I came.

I ground against his hand as he pushed me closer and closer to the edge.

A groan slipped from between my lips.

He glanced at me sharply. "No, don't worry about it. Trust me, I have the situation well in hand." He grinned.

I made a face at him, but went on rocking until I tipped over the edge of the abyss and into a rolling tide of pleasure. I came so hard around his hand I left his fingers drenched. I dug my nails into the wood to hold back my cry.

My heart raced as I drifted back down to earth.

"All right, I'll talk to you later," he told whoever was on the other end of the phone. "Okay, bye." He ended the call and placed his phone down on the desk.

"Well, that was fun." He slid his fingers out of my pussy and pressed them between my lips. "Suck."

I sucked, tasting myself on his skin.

"You're fascinating," he told me. "You like to be in control, but you know how to relinquish it and do what you're told. You could have screamed the building down while I was on that important call. But you didn't. You were nice and quiet, just like I told you. Except that one groan." He looked stern.

"Sorry, sir," I said sweetly. "I couldn't contain myself with you touching me like that. Does that mean I don't get an A?" I pouted playfully.

I knew for a fact I wouldn't earn my marks on my back. If my work sucked, no amount of blowjobs would convince him to give me a higher grade. I would have hated that anyway. I worked hard to do well with my brain, not my mouth. Not my pussy either. Not to mention the fact Brutham wouldn't turn a blind eye to our relationship if he did that.

"You already got an A," he growled. "Your essay was beautifully done, but for that groan, you've earned yourself punishment."

I smiled. "Are you going to give me detention?"

"Detention is for high school," he replied. "What I have in mind will be a lot more fun."

He took my hands and pulled me forward until I hopped off his desk. "Come with me."

"Yes, sir." I followed him out of his office.

twenty-one

LILA

ZACHARY LOOKED up in alarm as I stopped in front of him. His beer was halfway to his mouth. He hesitated, then lowered it.

"Hey," he said warily. "May I remind you there's a lot of people in the bar right now. Lots of witnesses if you try to kill me."

"Funny," I slid onto the couch beside him. I tried to suppress a wince at the lingering pain in my ass cheeks. Slade wasn't kidding when he said he was going to punish me. I loved every moment of it. I even loved the bruises he left on my thighs and wrists and the bite marks on my breasts and throat. The man was feral, in the best way possible.

"I was going to say the same to you." I crossed my legs, not missing the way his gaze slid up my jeans-covered legs and over my chest. He always looked at me like I was a tasty snack.

"Why would I want to kill you?" he asked. "You're my sister." He shrugged but he hadn't lost the wary expression.

"You tell me," I said smoothly. "Where did you get that teddy bear?"

He sighed. "Is that what this is about? I swear, I had no idea there was anything dangerous inside... What was his name? Herman."

He looked desperate for me to believe him. "I bought both bears online from what looked like a reputable website. Not one on the dark web that sells booby-trapped plush toys. If they even exist. I had no way of knowing someone set the website up for me to find it, or changed the bears out, or whatever. All I wanted was to do something nice for my sisters."

He raised a hand as though he might put it on my knee, but then lowered it back to his own leg.

Wise move, given Slade was only a few metres away, watching surreptitiously. I couldn't guarantee what he might do if Zachary touched me. I doubted it would end well for my former stepbrother.

"Do you want to take over the family from Dad?" I asked bluntly.

He licked his lips. Picked up his beer and took a gulp.

"Honestly... If he offered it to me, I'd accept. But he's not going to offer it to me. The best I can hope for is that you don't blame me for what happened with the bear, and keep an open mind about letting me work for you. I can prove my loyalty. I can prove that my tongue is still as skilled as ever."

He forced a smile. For the first time in years, he gave me the impression fucking me was something he was reluctant to do.

I put it down to his not wanting to share me with the twins, and Slade. Maybe he met someone here at Brutham already. That wouldn't surprise me. No one here wasted time snapping anyone who would be an asset to them, now or in the future.

Either way, it didn't matter. I wasn't going to go there with him.

"You can keep your tongue to yourself," I told him. "I have enough of those to keep me busy." I took the beer from his hand, gave him a cheeky smile and sipped.

"You really had no idea Herman was full of deadly fumes? What about the bear you gave to Chloe? The one that exploded after I threw it out the window. I had a feeling someone was watching, waiting for the right time."

He shrugged and crossed his arms, relinquishing ownership of his drink. "Would you be so surprised if Reuben Brantley had a camera in your sister's bedroom?" He scoffed. "Hell, I wouldn't be surprised if Hunter and Parker put it there. Maybe you should be having this conversation with them."

"I will when they get back from their business trip." I hated to admit that he might be right, but if there was a camera in Chloe's room, chances were the twins put it there. Not so they could blow me up. They

131

might have done it at Reuben's request, or so they could keep an eye on Chloe.

Zachary was watching me closely. "Are you sure you can trust them? They seem ambitious and very, very... Brantley. Betrayal is in their blood. I wouldn't put it past either of them to get a kick out of using you until they're done with you."

Before I could respond to that he added, "Or you might be using them to get some dick while you keep an eye on them. You know what they say about keeping your enemies close."

"Of course I can trust them," I argued.

I didn't want to admit he planted the seeds of doubt in the back of my mind. I'd always known I needed to be careful of Hunter and Parker. They weren't referred to as the evil twins for nothing. Their whole family was known for stepping on other people to get what they wanted. I wasn't naïve enough to think they might do the same to me.

I didn't want to believe that though. My feelings for both of them ran deep. The idea they might be planning to betray me, made my heart twist. If they did, it would be the last thing they ever did.

"I know you better than that," Zachary said softly. "The Lila Bell I know doesn't go around trusting people easily. You're always on alert for anyone putting a toe out of line. Nothing gets past you, because you don't take things at face value. You're always thinking, evaluating and planning. Just like your father."

It wasn't an accusation, just an observation. An accurate one, most of the time.

"You're right, I don't trust people easily. Including you," I told him.

I wasn't sure I believed a word of what he said about the teddy bears. The best lies always have enough truth in them to make them plausible. Would I have been like this if I grew up with my mother?

I felt as though I spent my life surrounded by men and shadows, and a sister who always seemed to be looking for ways to take advantage.

"Including me," he agreed. "And Chloe. You need to consider the possibility she did this. She might have been planning something with the other teddy bear, that you ruined by turning up when you did. She said something about you cutting it open and finding the bomb inside. Maybe doing that set it off? Explosives are fragile. If you do the wrong thing at the wrong time, they can blow up in your face. Literally."

"Maybe you and Chloe are working together," I said lightly.

He stiffened slightly, then snorted. "Maybe. Did hell freeze over?" He leaned over towards me.

"I meant what I said, I want to work with you. In whatever capacity that may be. I'm not asking you to marry me or have my children, just let me be a part of this." He spread his hands and gestured towards me. "I don't think that's too much to ask."

He seemed sincere, but there was something about his tone that set off warning bells in the back of my mind. Nothing I could put my finger on. Just a sense that something was... Off.

"If I do have you work for me," I said slowly, "it won't be in teddy bear acquisitions." Even if there was such a thing, which there probably wasn't. Although, those teddy bears had to come from somewhere.

He laughed. "I promise not to buy any more teddy bears. Or plush elephants. Or plush pigs. Or plush anything."

"Good, because I don't think I could trust a plush anything ever again." I finished the last of his drink and placed the empty glass on the table in front of us.

"That's the Lila Bell I know," he said. "Mistrustful of everything, including plush toys."

"It might not be my preferred lifestyle choice, but it is what it is." I shrugged.

A frown brushed his forehead. "What would be your preferred life-style choice? If you could be anything you want. Anything at all, what would you choose? Would you choose the same lifestyle as Sam and the rest of the Bell family? Or would you walk away and do something completely different?"

"I don't get to choose—"

He cut me off. "If you *did* get to choose. If you could walk out the door right now and go and live your best, ideal life, what would you do?"

"I don't know," I said slowly. "Maybe I'd just get a regular job, get married and live in the suburbs." That sounded harmless, but as boring as hell.

He raised his eyebrows at me. "Doubtful. Try again."

I rolled my eyes at him. "Fine. I think I'd start a company and build it from scratch to something huge. Maybe an airline, or a line of boutique clothing stores."

"CEO of an airline," he mused. "Lila Air, to rival Devlin Air."

"Something like that." Devlin Air started as a small company, but under the leadership of Anderson Devlin, the oldest of the six Devlin Brothers, was now a billion-dollar company, with offices all over the world. Apparently Anderson Devlin was a massive asshole, but he was a wealthy one.

"If anyone could do that, it would be you," Zachary said. "Have you ever thought about walking away? You have enough money to start whatever company you want. A legitimate one."

I snorted. "You sound like Chloe. Maybe you should have this conversation with her. That would solve all of our problems." Some of them anyway.

"You could both walk away," he suggested.

"And leave you to take over from Dad?" Was that what he was getting at here?

"Would that be so bad?" he asked. "Look, I'm not saying you should walk away for my benefit, but think about doing it for yours. How long do you think the family can go on defying the law? What if it catches up and you're at the helm? You would be locked away for the rest of your life. Is that what you want?"

I smirked. "Have you forgotten how easy it is to pay to have any number of things disappear? Even if the law caught up, there's nothing they can do. No one I can't pay off. Honestly, any investigator would know that and not bother to come sniffing around anyway. They could spend years trying to pin things on us and we'd just walk away from it. Their time would be better spent investigating matters that can be prosecuted. Or crimes that aren't victimless, like husbands hitting their wives."

There was nothing I hated more than a bully. If anyone in my organisation was violent towards their partner without their consent, they could look forward to being buried alive. I didn't tolerate it.

"I guess so." He didn't look convinced. "I want what's best for you, okay? I'd hate it if you looked back someday and regretted not walking away when you had the chance. Once you're head of the family, it's going to be a lot more difficult to untangle yourself from that web."

"This is what I want," I said firmly. "If Chloe wants to turn her back on the family, she's welcome to do that, but I won't. Hell, if you want to walk away with her, I'll support that. But I've never backed down from a fight and I'm not going to start now."

"Neither am I," he said quickly. "Whatever happens, I'm not backing down either. I'm in this thing until the bitter end." He nodded to punctuate that declaration. "So, you believe me about the teddy bears? That it wasn't me?"

I sighed. "I don't know what to believe. But I will say this. If I find out it was you, or if you do anything to betray me, I will kill you. With my bare hands if I have to."

He sat back, a guarded expression on his face. "Noted." He looked like he had more to say, but he fell silent after that.

twenty-two

LILA

"THE TWINS?"

I looked up from frowning at my screen to see Slade watching me with concern.

He nodded towards my phone. "You were looking at that like you weren't impressed. Is it the twins? Have they finally checked in?"

It was five days since they went off for whatever Reuben needed them for. Apart from a couple of text messages, I hadn't heard a thing. They'd probably turn up in a couple of days with tans, and act like nothing happened.

"No, it's not them." I put my phone aside and finished my coffee. Like everything else here, the food was amazing. The best coffee money could buy. Of course it was, we did better with a good breakfast every day. Whatever Brutham Academy had to do to maintain a high academic standard, they'd do. The school board ruthlessly hunted down the best chefs and the best ingredients and paid well for them.

Slade raised an eyebrow at me expectantly.

I sighed. "My father is coming. He'll be here in about twenty minutes."

"Let me guess, he likes to spring visits on you at the last minute?" Slade bit down into his toast and washed it down with tea. I'd never seen him drink coffee. As far as I know, he didn't.

"Exactly," I said. "If I knew he was coming, I'd have time to run."

Slade grinned at the expression on my face. "You wouldn't really run."

"No, but some days it's tempting." I looked at him over the rim of my cup and wondered if I dared to ask.

"I'm coming with you," he said before I could ask. "I'm not leaving you to go into the hornet's nest alone. He's your father but I trust him as much as I trust anyone else in your family."

"Only an idiot would turn their back on my father," I said. "I sure as fuck wouldn't. On some level, he loves me, but he's not above using me to get what he wants. You know what they say about blood being thicker than water? The only thing thicker than that is ambition, and my father has plenty of that to spare. If it was in his best interest to burn Chloe and me, he'd do it. He wouldn't even think twice."

"He sounds like my father," Slade said sympathetically. "Mine was always looking for an excuse to use the belt on me. My sisters felt it occasionally too, but mostly it was me."

"He sounds like an asshole," I said. My father punished me, but he never hit me. Although, that might have been better than being locked away in the basement.

"He *was* an asshole." Slade shrugged. "One day I had enough and I wrapped that belt around his neck and pulled until he stopped struggling. None of us shed a tear at his death."

My lips dropped apart. I won't say I haven't been tempted, but I've never seriously considered killing my father. To be that desperate must be horrible.

"How old were you?" I asked softly.

"Twelve." He downed the last of his tea. "I left him lying there on the floor and went off to my first day of high school. The police ruled it a suicide and that was it. They knew what a prick he was, they just couldn't pin anything on him that would stick. I think they were glad to be rid of him too. And I learnt a valuable lesson. That I was capable of standing up for myself and that killing people who deserve it is enjoyable."

"I feel like I shouldn't find that a massive turn on, but I do," I said.

He grinned. "It's part of my charm. So you know, I still have that belt and I'll use it on your father if he gives me a reason."

"I have a feeling that belt has a long history of being around people's necks." I glanced into my coffee cup to find it already empty. I set it aside and rested my elbows on the table.

Slade leaned forward until we were almost nose to nose. "Yes, it does, and you know what? I'd like to put it around your neck while I fuck that pretty little pussy of yours."

That made me all sorts of hot. "How many people have you killed with that belt?"

He looked thoughtful. "Fourteen. It would have been fifteen, but I was only trying to scare the last guy. I almost got carried away."

"Will you get carried away with me?" His breath brushed my cheek, making my heart race.

"Definitely," he agreed. "But not to the point where I squeeze the last breath out of your body. I know exactly how far to go for us both to enjoy it."

"I would much rather do that right now than speak to my father." As it was, I was wet and probably flushed. If that bothered Dad in any way, that was too fucking bad. He could have given me a few hours, or even a few days, warning of his intention to visit. Since he didn't, he got what he got.

"I guess he wouldn't be pleased if we kept him waiting while I fucked your brains out," Slade said with a sigh.

"No one keeps Samuel Bell waiting." I matched his sigh. "He's going to be pissed off enough knowing I'm... Consorting with someone else with Brantley connections."

Which was hypocritical, given Kennedy's boyfriends all worked for the Brantleys.

"Is that what we're doing?" Humour shone in Slade's eyes. "Consorting?"

I snorted softly. "Yeah, that's the fanciest word I can think of for fucking. I was going to go with boinking, but I figured it sounded better."

He laughed. "You might be right. Although, bonking is a very good word. Very descriptive of the way a bed sounds when we're using it right."

I shook my head at him and laughed. "I guess it does. Why do I get the feeling you've given this a lot more thought than I ever have?"

"I'm a guy." He shrugged. "It's my job to make sure your pussy is getting wrecked just right. If I don't, that would be neglectful."

"Would it, now?" I picked up my phone and tucked it into the back pocket of my jeans. "And what happens if you neglect me?"

"I don't know, because I have no intention of doing it," he said. He stacked my plate and cup on his and carried them over to the trolley the staff used to wheel them into the kitchen for washing.

Once we were clear of the dining room, we were free to talk more easily.

"Will your father be seeing Chloe and Zachary too?"

"His message didn't say, but I presume so," I said. "Is not going to come all this way and not at least see Chloe."

"That would be a punch in the guts to Zachary." Slade didn't look particularly sympathetic. He didn't seem to buy what Zachary said about the teddy bears, or much of anything Chloe said.

If I thought I didn't trust easily, I was nothing compared to him. That wasn't too surprising given his childhood. Who would you trust if you were forced to kill your own father at the age of twelve? He was the kind of guy who formed his loyalties and didn't budge.

"My father isn't particularly sentimental." I eyed a couple of students who hurried to get out of my way as I walked down the corridor. They did that everywhere I went. If I didn't put fear into them, my last name would.

"He won't care if he hurts any of our feelings."

"I'm starting to think I should get my belt before we go and meet him," Slade said.

"If we had time, I'd say you should," I said. "He'll be here in two minutes. My father is many things, including punctual." If anything, he was more likely to be early than late.

Slade grabbed my wrist and pulled me to a stop.

"I'm sure my father won't do anything to warrant you getting your belt—" I started to say.

"This isn't about the belt," he said. "This is about you running the family someday. At some point, you need to teach everyone who is in charge. That includes your father."

I frowned. "What are you saying?"

"I'm saying, what's the hurry?" he said lightly. "It won't kill your father to wait for you. What's he going to do about it? Have you killed?"

"No, but he might have you killed if he realises this is your idea." I stepped closer to him and looked up into his eyes. I could happily drown in them. If I wasn't careful, I was going to fall for him and I was going to fall hard. That terrified me almost as much as any dark, silent room. Love made people vulnerable and I couldn't afford to be vulnerable.

On the other hand, sometimes love made people stronger. It was a fine fucking line I didn't dare to cross. Not yet anyway.

"I'd prefer not to give him an excuse," I added. If my father killed Slade, I wouldn't forgive him. What would I do?

How would it feel to wrap Slade's belt around my father's neck and pull it tight? He'd fix his gaze on mine and watch with widening eyes as the air was cut off from his lungs. His body would slump—

I shook my head slightly. He better not give me a reason to act on those thoughts. They were far too compelling.

"I'm not that easy to kill," Slade said easily. "But you know I'm right. If you come running every time he crooks a finger, then he's going to keep doing it. He's going to know he's the boss. Without doubt, he's waiting for you to take the initiative. To stand up to him and show him you're ready to be the boss." He tilted his head slightly, his gaze on my face as his words sank in.

I swallowed hard. The only thing in this world I was afraid of was my father. Specifically what he might do to me if I didn't live up to his high expectations. He wouldn't kill me, but he could do a whole lot worse than that. Worse than choosing Chloe over me. Worse than choosing Zachary over either of us.

If I failed him, he could lock me in the basement and leave me to rot. Or he could... A whirlpool of other horrible things tumbled around in my brain.

Along with that came the realisation Slade was right. If I didn't stand up to my father, he would never respect me enough to choose me to take his place. That was absolutely something he would be waiting for me to do.

"It wouldn't hurt to keep him waiting for a couple of minutes," I said slowly.

"Or longer." Slade looked at me meaningfully.

I licked my lips. "Fine. A few minutes, but he's going to be pissed off."

Slade smiled. "Good. No one ever made their dreams come true without stirring the pot and pissing a few people off. That's what makes people memorable. Not that anyone would dare to suggest you're forgettable."

"They better fucking not," I growled. I had no intention of being forgotten by anyone. That would be worse than being underestimated.

"Come on. Let's walk slowly to the front of the Academy." He let my wrist go and stepped back.

Having an intense conversation in the corridor was one thing, flaunting the fact we were involved with each other, was another. The fact we were fucking was not a secret, but Brutham preferred we exercise some measure of discretion.

twenty-three

LILA

MY FATHER WAS STANDING, leaning against his car when we stepped down the front steps of Brutham Academy. His arms were crossed over his broad chest, gaze watching us through half-lidded eyes. His expression was guarded. So much so I couldn't tell if he was pissed off or not.

He wasn't alone. I expected to see Chloe and maybe Zachary here. I didn't expect to see my half-sister, Kennedy Knight, or her three boyfriends.

I introduced them to Slade one by one. "Mannix Cassani, Ares Turner and Ice Miller. My sister Kennedy and my father, Samuel Bell. This is—" I raised my hand to gesture at Slade.

"Slade Lincoln," Dad finished for me. His eyes lingered on Slade. "You didn't think I'd do a thorough background check on everyone that works at Brutham Academy?"

"I wouldn't expect anything less." Slade shook hands with Dad, then offered his hand to Kennedy.

All three of her boyfriends stiffened.

"I wouldn't do that if I was you," Ice said with menacing pleasantness.

Mannix actually took a step forward.

Slade lowered his hand. "My apologies. I didn't mean to offend any of you." He was clearly not intimidated by their 'touch her and die' vibes.

"What are you doing here?" I directed the question at Kennedy. She was a couple of years older than me, with flaming red hair and freckles.

Beyond those, there was some family resemblance. Not as obvious as Chloe and I, but it was there. I'd noticed it the first time I met her, but I knew to look for it. At the time, she had no idea she was related to us. I felt a stab of remorse for taking her down to the basement, but at the time I was just glad it wasn't me going in there.

"I'm here to see how you are," Dad said. "Kennedy wanted to see Brutham. She happened to be visiting along with her boys."

Ares glared at him, apparently annoyed at being referred to as a boy.

Mannix didn't look too pleased either.

Ice went on smiling, like he always did. He looked sweet, but that was all a façade. He'd happily slice the skin off my body to see what I looked like underneath. I got the impression he'd love to get his hands on Chloe and me to compare the insides of a set of twins. To say he was slightly unhinged was an understatement.

Anyone with a drop of sense watched their backs when he was around.

"We came because Ric DiMarco is concerned he hasn't heard from Hunter or Parker," Mannix said coolly. He gave off an aura of not giving a shit about the twins. "Where are they?"

I frowned. "They went away on business for Reuben." Ric DiMarco answered to Caleb Brantley, who in turn answered to his brother, Reuben. Why come here instead of asking one of them?

Mannix scowled. He grabbed out his phone and stomped a few metres away before calling someone. I couldn't hear what he said, but his tone was respectful. Much more so than I ever got from him.

While Mannix spoke, Dad gripped my chin with his thumb and forefinger.

"How are you? I was worried when Chloe called me and told me what happened to you. It's out of character for you to get out of your sister's way. Especially as comprehensively as you would if you'd died."

"I wouldn't exactly have had a choice," I pointed out. "I didn't expect anyone to put toxic shit in a teddy bear."

His grip tightened to the point of pain. "You *should* have expected it.

You should have anticipated that someone would try something. You let down your guard and you almost died because of it."

I stood still. Tears of pain gathered in the corners of my eyes.

"Chloe let Zachary give her a bear too," I whispered.

"This isn't about Chloe," he said firmly. "This is about you and what you did. You have to be more careful. Next time, you might not be so lucky." He loosened his grip and drew me in for a hug.

After a moment, I hugged him back. He wasn't wrong about anything, but the look of disappointment on his face was a stab straight into my heart.

"I'm sorry," I said softly. "I'll be more careful next time."

"Of course you will. You're a smart, resourceful young woman. You won't make any more mistakes."

"Yeah." No fucking pressure.

He stepped back as Mannix returned.

"I just spoke to Daisy Lasalle, she's unaware of any assignment Reuben might have sent Hunter and Parker on. She's going to contact him and get back to me." He shoved his phone back into his pocket.

"Did you have them killed, Sam?" Ice asked cheerfully. "I'd be disappointed if you did and didn't let me take part." He glanced at me and his mask slipped slightly. He absolutely held a grudge against me and the twins for turning him and Kennedy in to Dad. If he had his way, I'd be hanging from chains in his workroom right now.

Slade caught his look and stiffened, moving over closer to me.

"Not yet," Dad said. "I did tell them to stay away from Lila."

"Maybe they finally took your advice and fucked off," Ares said with a grunt.

"Doubtful. They seemed to have attached themselves to my daughter." Dad gave me a dark look. I shouldn't be surprised he knew that. The walls had ears, particularly here at Brutham.

Only Kennedy seemed sympathetic. Of course she would, he didn't approve of her choice of boyfriends either. It seemed all of his daughters were destined to disappoint him when it came to our relationships.

"They've been very good to me," I said flatly. "All they want is to make me happy. If it wasn't for them, I'd be dead. If they hadn't found me when they did—"

"If you hadn't accepted that teddy bear, none of that would have mattered," Dad said, straight to the point.

"Maybe you should take that up with your stepson." Slade clearly had enough with my father and his tone. "I haven't ruled out the possibility Chloe was involved in that too. Where are they anyway?" He gave me a look to remind me he'd suggested I not hurry out to see Dad. Evidently, neither had they.

"She's coming down the steps now." Ice nodded behind me. He gave her a smile that was more genuine than the one he gave me.

It seemed he'd taken sides. That was something I'd have to work on, or have him killed. I'd rather not do that. I might need Kennedy at some point in the future. Nothing would alienate her more quickly than killing one of her boyfriends. In the end, that was up to him.

"Dad." Chloe hugged him. Then she hugged Kennedy.

Our sister seemed as pleased to see her as Ice was. If Kennedy took sides against me too, then we may have a problem. If I had to deal with her, then I'd have to deal with all three of her boyfriends as well.

When had that headache started? My forehead throbbed.

Mannix's phone rang. He pulled it back out, glanced at the screen and took a few steps away again. He frowned as he listened and spoke to whoever was on the other end of the phone. The conversation lasted less than a minute. He stalked back over to us.

"Daisy Lasalle said Reuben knows nothing about where Hunter and Parker are. He didn't send them anywhere."

"What the fuck?" I stared at him. "Is she sure?"

He glared at me. "That's what she said Reuben told her. Either they don't know, or they don't see any reason for us to know. For what it's worth, she said Reuben sounded pissed off."

"Reuben always sounds pissed off," Dad said. "It's part of his asshole persona."

"Reuben would have good reason to sound pissed off if the twins went missing," Slade said.

"Oh, I don't know," Chloe said slowly. "It seems like that pair has caused him a lot of trouble recently. It wouldn't surprise me if he decided to deal with them." She looked all too fucking smug.

I wanted to scratch the expression off her face.

"They've never given him a reason to dispose of them," I said firmly.

"Are you sure about that?" Ice asked. "They've given a lot of people a lot of reasons to dispose of them. The list is long. Reuben, me, Mannix, Ares, Sam, his brother Zeke, that dude who plays keyboard for Wolf Venom."

"Penn," Kennedy said with a sigh.

Mannix actually growled. "Don't give me an excuse to have him killed."

She smiled adoringly and kissed his mouth. "You'd never kill the members of my favourite band. I'd never forgive you if you did."

He hooked an arm around her waist and pulled her hard against him. "You would forgive me if I had to paddle your ass until you do."

Dad cleared his throat. He turned cold, brown eyes to me.

"First you accept a present that almost kills you, then two of your... boyfriends go missing. I'm starting to think maybe Chloe—"

"I'm sure there's a reasonable explanation for whatever Hunter and Parker are doing," I said quickly. Surely he wasn't going to hold me responsible for events I had no control over?

Of course he would. Because I should have control over everything.

"They'll turn up in a couple of days with an explanation even you'll be impressed with," I added.

Dad snorted softly, clearly disbelieving.

In the corner of my eye, I saw Chloe looking even more smug. Would anyone mind if I strangled her with my bare hands right here?

Dad's gaze turned to Slade. "When I spoke to you a couple of days ago, you said the situation was under control."

I gaped. They knew each other?

Wait, when Slade was finger fucking me on his desk, was it was my *father* on the other end of the phone? He heard me groan. Fucking hell.

"It was," Slade said. "I didn't anticipate that Hunter and Parker weren't off doing a job for Reuben."

"What the fuck is going on?" I demanded.

"When I heard you were involved with Slade Lincoln, I contacted him," Dad said unapologetically. "I've used his services in the past."

I gave him a blank look.

"He's an assassin," Ice said louder than could possibly have been necessary.

I turned to Slade. He shrugged and nodded.

"It's true. I was trying to explain that, but it's not the kind of thing that comes up in regular conversation."

"The belt," I said slowly.

"Just the beginning of it, and one of many methods. This shouldn't change anything." He was telling me, not asking. Nothing in his expression suggested he thought I'd turn away from him because he was a hitman.

"It does, though," Ice said. "It makes you cooler than I thought you were."

"You're out of your fucking mind," Ares told him.

"Yeah, but not about this," Ice said. "If I didn't do forensic medicine, I would have become an assassin. I would have been good at it too."

"Yes, you would." Mannix patted him on the shoulder.

I rubbed my temples. This was all a lot to process.

Slade slipped an arm around me. "For what it's worth, I think your father approves of me."

Dad granted. "That might be a stretch, but I approve of you more than I approve of Hunter and Parker. If they don't turn up again—"

I was done with his bullshit. "If they don't turn up again, I'm going to be devastated. I know they can be trouble sometimes, but I care about them."

If I thought my words would sway him even slightly, I was wrong.

He waved dismissively. "I expect better from both of you. I don't know who got the better of who here, but I'm seriously considering the value of Zachary taking over some day. Perhaps there are more important things than blood."

His words made me want to spill some.

Instead I lifted my chin. "You won't when I'm finished. I'll show you who deserves to be head of the Bell family."

I wished I felt as confident. Everything Dad said had me doubting myself and wondering who the hell I could trust. Including myself.

One more slip up and I could be totally fucked.

twenty-four

HUNTER

"ANY GUESSES on how many days have passed?" Parker asked.

"Same as the last time you asked me," I snapped. "I have no fucking idea. At least a couple."

Apart from Zachary and Chloe dropping in once in a while to throw us some food, literally, the hours blended into each other. Parker found a bucket in the corner, but that was starting to get full.

The smell was no fucking joke either.

I took a long, slow breath. "Sorry, bro. When I said we needed a vacation, this wasn't what I meant. It's getting to me a bit."

"Yeah, me too," Parker said softly. "I'd rather be paddleboarding on some island somewhere. Or jumping out of a plane."

"We can do those things when we get out of here," I promised. "You, me, Lila and Slade can run off somewhere. Stay away from all the bullshit for a while."

"You'd be bored in the first two hours," he pointed out.

"I'd last at least three," I protested. "All of them with my cock buried in Lila."

We'd tried to break the chains that kept us bound, but they were firmly attached to the wall. They wouldn't slide or break off our wrists, no matter how hard we tried. I'd even placed one against the wall and had Parker slam his foot against it over and over.

Unable to see well enough in the dark, he kicked me more than he kicked the fucking restraints. He tried, but in the end I had to tell him to stop. Keeping going was more dangerous than quitting.

I fucking hated quitting.

Once we realised all we could do was bide our time, I sat leaning against the wall, or trying to sleep. I couldn't think of anything but Lila and what was happening to her.

Did she know we were missing or had Chloe and Zachary spun some bullshit story to explain our absence? If they were doing anything to her... Touching her...

"You're grinding your teeth again," Parker said. "I'm just as pissed off about this as you are."

I unclenched my teeth. "I know you are. I just—"

Footsteps approached. The door creaked open. A light flashed directly in my eyes. The chain gave me just enough slack to raise my hand and shield them.

If one of the assholes got close enough, I could wrap it around their neck, but neither of them did. Maybe they were hoping we'd do that to each other. No such fucking luck assholes.

"Good news," Zachary said cheerfully. "You're getting out of here."

"It's about fucking time," I growled. "Undo these things and we'll be on our way."

I shook my wrist to rattle the chain. The first thing I was going to do was kill this asshole. I didn't even care if it was quick and painless, as long as it happened.

Zachary chuckled. "You misunderstand. You're leaving here, but we're taking you somewhere else. They finally figured out you're missing. If it took them this long to notice, I guess they didn't give a shit. We still don't want anyone nosing around looking for you."

"Funny, because that's exactly what I want," I said. "How about you fuck off and we'll sit here patiently and wait for them?" I lowered my hand and crossed my arms as best I could over my chest.

"We could leave you here." Chloe's voice came out of the dark. "But the only thing they'd find is a matched set of dead bodies. Fortunately for you, you're still useful to us."

"If you think we're going to come quietly, you're wrong," Parker said.

"Parker is right," I said. "When we come, we do it loud enough that everyone knows."

"No one wants to think about you coming," Zachary said.

"I do," Parker said. "I'd much rather think about that than being stuck here."

"I'm starting to think we should have taken out their tongues the last time they were knocked out," Chloe said.

"We're glad you didn't; Lila likes our tongues," Parker said.

"Then shut the fuck and you might get to keep them," she snarled.

Parker glanced sidelong at me. "She's not very nice, is she? She pretends she is, but then when you get to know her, she's really not."

"I've noticed that," I said.

"Enough," she snapped. "Zachary, Dane."

I didn't realise Mr D was here too. I squinted at a dark shape in the shadows. He'd stayed back until now.

"Now we have a party," Parker said. He reeled back as Zachary slammed his fist into his face. Parker's head bounced off the wall behind him. He let out a short cry of pain.

Dane grabbed his arm and held it while Zachary jabbed a syringe. He slid the needle into Parker's vein and depressed the plunger.

Parker tried to jerk away, but they held him down hard until his body sagged. They lowered him onto the floor where he lay still, his breathing shallow.

They rose and stepped over to me. Zachary pulled out another syringe.

"We can do this the hard way or the easy way," Dane said. His expression was ice cold, with a faint aura of triumph. He always was a motherfucker.

"I choose C, neither of the above," I replied lightly. "Also, I'm reporting you to the Board of Education, because I'm pretty sure there's laws against drugging your students."

He laughed. "There are also laws against killing teachers. Who do you think will get in more trouble?"

"The one doesn't have a rich family to bail him out." I gave him a smug smile.

He might have forgotten the DiMarco family was sorely lacking in power and influence these days. Exactly why he hooked up with Chloe in the first place. He was desperate to get back on top, literally and figuratively.

There was nothing worse than someone who was desperate as well as ambitious. If I was him, I would have gone crawling to Ric DiMarco. His cousin was having more success than he was. Whatever, I didn't really give a shit.

I didn't see Dane move until his fist landed on the side of my face. He connected so hard he drove me back with a grunt of pain. Only dropping my head at the last second stopped me from slamming it into the wall.

He drove his booted foot into my ribs a couple of times for good measure before grabbing my wrist and holding my arm out for Zachary.

Yeah, Dane was going to die after that. A bit of witty banter was one thing, punching and kicking a guy when he was chained up was another.

Zachary drove the needle into my vein. Before he pushed down the plunger he crouched with his mouth next to my ear.

"I just want you to know I'm having a lot of fun with Lila. She totally believes that I'm on her side now. She couldn't spread her legs fast enough for me. No wonder she didn't notice you were missing, she was too busy coming around my cock."

"You're a delusional prick," I spat. There was no way Lila would fuck that asshole. Would she? I didn't want to believe it, but if he somehow managed to convince her he was innocent, maybe charmed his way into her pussy as well.

"Maybe, but we have something in mind for her. She's going to love every minute of it." He chuckled.

"If you touch a hair on her head..." I slurred.

Several creative ways to kill him flashed through my mind before everything went dark.

* * *

Lila

. . .

I woke slowly. My thought were groggy, strained. My head ached like my brain was thumping against my skull. The headache that started when Dad was here, was worse now.

He, Kennedy and her boyfriends hadn't stayed much past that conversation. Slade had to go to some meeting.

What happened after that? I must have lain down for a nap. I didn't remember doing that. I also didn't remember my bed being so hard.

Beside me, someone groaned. A female groan.

What the fuck?

They protested, but I forced my eyes open. The light was dim. Barely enough to illuminate beyond a half a metre or so. Enough that I made out a small space, warmth pressed against me on three sides.

Not warmth, I realised. Bodies.

Breathing, whimpering, groaning, female bodies.

Panic started to rise. Where the hell was I?

On the fourth side of me was a wall. I managed to claw my way up until I was sitting.

The smell hit me. Sweat, urine and terror. How many of us were pressed into this small box?

The box was moving. The light in the gaps showed the world flashing by. We must be in the back of a truck.

"Where are they taking us?" I asked, hoping to get some kind of answer. Even as I said it, I knew.

One of the many pies my family had their finger in was human trafficking. It wasn't something I gave much thought to, until now.

Until I realised my sister found a way to sell me.

cruel

one

LILA

(10 YEARS ago)

Every part of me trembled. My hands, my feet. My lips. Those most of all

    "Please, Daddy..." I looked up at him. His face was like stone, cold and hard. Unyielding.

    "I'll be good," I pleaded. "I promise."

    He put a hand on my head. "This isn't about being good or bad, Lila. This is about you understanding what we do and why we do it. You're old enough to grasp the impact of the decisions we make. The more you understand, the better you'll be at making the right ones."

    I lowered my gaze and eyed the thick, solid door. Made of some kind of metal, it didn't reflect a drop of light. If anything, it seemed to suck it in and keep it. I was careful not to touch it, in case I was sucked in too.

    "I don't want to go in there, Daddy. It's dark in there."

    In spite of his reassurance this wasn't about me being bad, I was absolutely sure I'd done something to deserve being put into a pitch black room by myself. Why else would he do it? What had I done? Specifically, what had he caught me doing?

    My twin, Chloe, and I got up to all sorts of things, but Dad, he always told us to be careful getting caught. He made out that was the biggest crime of all. That and betraying him. Which I would never, ever do.

He laughed, but it was a bitter, humourless sound. "Of course it's dark in there, sweetie. That's the point. You'll go in there for a little while and understand the reason for these rooms down in the basement."

He ruffled my hair. "Nothing can hurt you in there." As if that somehow made everything all right.

Tears welled in the corners of my eyes. I blinked them away. Crying was a sign of weakness. If there was anything my father hated, it was weakness. Especially from one of his daughters. Even at the age of nine, I was well aware of the need to control myself.

Was that what this was about? Had I, at some point, done something that wasn't controlled enough? Had I cried? Laughed too loud? If it wasn't one of those, then what was it? I worked hard at school. Chloe and I competed to be top of the class. We competed at everything. With each other and with other people. I beat her at most things, except making friends. She had loads of them wherever she went. I had a couple who stuck with me through everything. Everyone else thought I was stuck up bitch. I didn't care.

Most of the time.

Not even when Chloe was invited to all the birthday parties and I wasn't. Or I was invited because people thought it was rude to invite her and not her twin. No one wanted me there, including me. I'd be the one hiding in the corner, waiting for the earliest opportunity to leave.

"In you go." Dad waved me inside.

I swallowed and looked down at the floor as I stepped inside.

It wasn't until the door clanged shut behind me that I let the tears slide down my cheeks.

The room was completely black. The only sound, the pounding of my pulse in my ears. I wanted to turn around and hammer my fists against the door, but no one would be able to hear me. That was the point. I was completely and utterly alone.

Instead, I sank down onto the floor and sat with my legs crossed.

"I'm sorry, Daddy," I whispered. Somehow, I'd figure out what I did wrong and I would never, ever do it again.

* * *

Lila

. . .

(Present day)

The truck ground to a stop, pressing all of us tight against each other. The woman beside me groaned. That was the only sound she'd made in the last few hours. That and dry retching. Her stomach must have been empty by now.

The smell of vomit was strong, sickening. It clung to the insides of my nostrils.

Thank fuck I didn't get motion sick. I was going to need all my strength to get the fuck out of here.

When I did, I was going to get my revenge on Chloe and whoever was working with her. Dane for sure. Zachary, probably. Someone else... I didn't know.

I'd spent hours thinking over the hours before I woke up here. I still couldn't remember the details. I had a cup of coffee in the Academy dining room. Everything after that... My mind was blank.

Muffled voices shouted from outside the truck. A gate clanged. The truck moved again, driving slowly over what sounded like gravel or dirt. The gate clanged closed.

The truck rumbled on for a minute or two, daylight flashing under the edges.

We passed over a bump. Several of the women groaned. More than one started to cry. I couldn't see any of them beyond vague shapes in the dim light. None sounded older than me. Of course not. Anyone that bought trafficked women wanted them young, pretty and undamaged.

I once overheard my father impress that on one of his employees.

"Customers don't want apples with bruises on them. Even one bruise reduces their value. If anyone leaves visible bruises, they can at best look forward to joining the girls on the auction block. At worst, a nice, slow death will serve as a sufficient deterrent to anyone else who thinks to touch my wares."

"Yes, sir." The man sounded both respectful and amused. "No... *Visible* bruises." He chuckled as though he said something hilarious.

The truck drew to a stop again. The front doors opened and closed, sounding like the driver and a passenger or two climbed out.

Their footsteps crunched around to the back. Metal ground against metal as the bolt holding the door locked was drawn aside.

I scrambled up to a sitting position and drew my legs in as tight as I could. I covered my bare breasts with my arms. As far as I could tell, no one touched me when I was unconscious, apart from removing my clothes. Nothing was painful or sticky. That wasn't a shitload of consolation. I was still naked in the back of a truck.

One, then the other door swung open on protesting hinges.

I raised my hand, blinked against the sudden glare of the late afternoon sun.

The light was a relief after the relentless darkness. A relief that lasted about five seconds before I glanced around.

I was packed in with about twenty other women. Most were around the same age as me. A couple were slightly younger and a couple slightly older. Three were blonde, one or two red. The rest had dark hair like me.

How long had my sister been planning this? Long enough, apparently.

A couple of men appeared in the doorway. One placed his fists on his hips.

"Good afternoon, ladies. You can call me Hades. Firstly, that's my name, and secondly, some of you will come to think of me as the worst kind of hell." His grin was a vicious slash across his face.

The man with him laughed. "He ain't wrong. Asshole is the worst motherfucker I know." He clapped Hades on the shoulder.

Hades laughed. "Listen to Brutus here. That's not his actual name. It's more of a description. Behave yourselves and you don't have to find out why."

Several of the women whimpered.

I bit my lip to keep myself from doing the same. More than anything else, I hated feeling vulnerable. I couldn't remember a time when I ever felt more so. Not even when I lay in the Academy hospital, with an oxygen mask over my face. Not even when my father put me in the basement room.

All of that was that was nothing to being naked in the back of a truck in front of people who intended to sell you to someone who wanted to use you as a fuck toy.

I had to get out of here before that happened. I couldn't assume Hunter and Parker would come for me. If they were, they would have stopped the truck hours ago. Or they'd be here right now, shooting Hades and Brutus, and making jokes.

And Slade— Where was he? Had he noticed I was missing yet?

No, right now I was on my own.

"If you treasure your pretty little skin, you will hop out of the truck and walk inside like we tell you to." Hades spoke as if the request was perfectly reasonable. As if somehow there was nothing wrong with what they were doing.

As if my father or someone like Reuben Brantley weren't paying them to do it. Did my father know where I was? Part of me would like to think he'd stop all of this if he did.

The realistic, cynical part of me remembered the last time I spoke to him. The way he blamed me for letting my guard down.

Maybe he thought I deserved this.

Maybe I did.

I wiped a tear from the corner of my eye before it could trickle down my cheek. Clearly I let my guard down again, somehow. I let my sister and her allies do this to me. If my father knew and approved, there was a chance no one was coming to stop any of this. That if I got away, I'd get no support from anyone.

I was completely, utterly alone.

The other women exchanged teary-eyed glances, but none moved. They were too terrified. Frozen to the pungent spot with fear.

I curled up in a smaller ball of misery. Even the dark, enclosed space that stank of sweat, urine and hours of fear, felt safer than stepping off the back of the truck. Here, it was harder for anyone to see me. To potentially recognise me. In the shadows, I was anonymous. I was no one. Just another piece of meat for the auction block.

If I wanted to move, my body wouldn't comply. I was paralysed in what little of the golden sunlight penetrated the back of the truck. Twilight was settling in. Soon night would fall. With night came more darkness. More terror, or perhaps a chance to escape this place.

As I finished that thought, one of the women jumped up. She leapt out of the truck, past Hades, and started to run.

Either he nor Brutus gave chase. Brutus looked dumbstruck, but Hades crossed his arms and looked amused.

"Looks like we get to have some fun after all," Hades remarked.

The woman reached the gate. She gripped the bottom of it and started to climb.

A moment later, she screamed and was thrown backwards. She landed on the gravel with a thud and a cry of pain.

"That's going to leave marks," Brutus remarked. "Stupid bitch."

"Mm-hmmm," Hades agreed. Over his shoulder, he addressed the rest of us. "You will have noticed the fence is electrified. It's currently on a lower setting. At night, it will be in a higher setting. We'd prefer you didn't damage your skin."

He turned around to face us. "There's worse if you don't cooperate."

Several of the women sobbed harder.

One by one, they started to climb out of the back of the truck, keeping close together. Several put their arms around each other, as though somehow that would keep them safe.

I was one of the last to slip down, trying to keep the trembling in my hands at bay. I didn't want to show fear, but suppressing it was difficult.

Brutus looked me up and down, but Hades only gave me a disinterested glance. He strode over to the woman who tried to escape, as she struggled to her feet. He stepped around her, appraising the grazes on her back.

He clicked his tongue. "They'll heal. You better hope they don't leave scars. You don't want to be bought by the kind of client who likes scars on his women."

He grabbed her hair and pulled over to a dam a few metres from the truck. She struggled against him, sobbing. His expression unchanged, he forced her to her knees and shoved her face into the water.

"In case anyone was wondering what happens if you disobey." He held her down for about ten seconds before yanking her back up again. She gasped for breath. Water poured down her face and dripped off her chin. She tried to jerk away from him again, but he shoved her head back under the water.

Her arms flailed, legs kicked out behind her. He held her down for another ten to fifteen seconds, before pulling her back out.

Once again, she gasped and sobbed, but she didn't fight him. She sat back on her knees and cried while the water trickled down her bare body.

"Are you going to fight me anymore, sweetheart?" Hades asked. When she didn't respond, he lowered her face back towards the pond.

"I'll behave," she squealed. "Please—" Her eyes were huge with absolute terror, and the certainty that, if her face went under again, he'd hold her there until she was dead.

He'd be in trouble with his employer if one of us died, but if we all obeyed after this, he'd probably think it was worth the risk.

If anything, Hades looked slightly disappointed she wasn't giving him the chance to kill her. He wouldn't be the first person to get plea-sure out of killing people. Hunter, Parker and Slade all seemed to get enjoyment from it. Right now, I'd take some enjoyment from killing Hades and Brutus.

This woman, she was innocent as far as I knew. Her only crime might be the same as mine—letting her guard down. Trusting the wrong person.

Hades shoved her away from him. "See you keep behaving. That goes for the rest of you too. You'll only be here for a few days before you're moved on to the auction house. From there—that's up to your buyer to decide." He grinned as if that wasn't completely fucked up.

"Brutus, get them inside. They all need a wash and something to eat. Our gentlemen clients don't want them to be skin and bones, do they?"

Brutus chuckled. "No, they don't. And neither do I." He turned his face and his gaze settled on me.

two

LILA

THE INSIDE of the building was nothing more than a large shed. Foldout beds sat in lines along one side. Along the other were open-fronted shower cubicles. We could get clean, but our captors would see everything.

Clean shift dresses sat folded on the end of each bed. A welcome relief from the assumption they'd keep us naked the entire time.

With the promise of being able to cover myself, I hurried to one of the showers and turned on the water. I thought it would be ice cold, but it was actually warm. A few degrees cooler than I'd prefer, but better than freezing.

A spout sticking out of the shower wall delivered liquid soap to my hand. Another was for shampoo. I lathered myself and rinsed in about a minute and a half flat, all with Brutus watching me, his hand beside the telling bulge in his jeans.

I shuddered at the thought of him touching me, and turned the water off with a snap. I plucked a towel from a nearby shelf and dried myself faster than I ever had in my life.

His gaze still on me, I hurried over to one of the cots and scooped up the dress. I was shaking it out when I became aware of his presence behind me.

"What's the hurry?" he asked. He placed a finger in my shoulder blade before running it down my back and over my ass. "You look good like this. I bet you're a lot of fun."

I slipped the dress over my head and tugged it down into place. At the same time, I tried not to be too obvious about jerking away from him. Electrified fences and dams might be the least of the punishments they'd use on us if we pissed them off.

And nothing pissed off some men more than rejection.

I turned around to face him. "I don't know about that." According to my guys, I was a ton of fun, but he didn't need to know that. He was only a handful of years older than me, but if this was what he did for a living, he could fuck off.

He chuckled. He raised his hand and pressed two fingers slightly to my cheek. He trailed them down my face and over my lips.

"There's one like you in every batch. Smart. Sassy. Clever enough to know what it takes to stay under the radar, but with enough spirit to be interesting. You try to act cool and calm, but when push comes to shove, you'll fight back." He leaned in to whisper in my ear. "I bet you squeal really pretty."

I swallowed. "I don't—"

He pressed his fingers to my lips. "Shhh. No need to say anything. We both know. You and I, we're alike. We're survivors. We don't let people push us around and tell us what to do, what to be and what to think. We grab life by the balls and live it."

He dropped his other hand to mine and pressed it against his semi-hard cock.

"If you look after my balls, I'll look after you."

I forced myself not to flinch. I wanted to jam my knee into his groin.

He rubbed himself against my hand, making himself harder.

"See, you're already a lot of fun. How about you get down on your knees—"

"Brutus," Hades snapped. "Stop toying with the merchandise and put the truck away." He gave me a look like it was all my fault.

Asshole.

Brutus grunted softly but let my hand go and stepped away. "Later, baby," he said. He gave me a wink before he sauntered away, back out of the barn. A couple of minutes later, the truck engine kicked over and rumbled away from the building, the engine so loud the walls shook.

Hades and a couple of other men watched over the women while they washed. Hades himself leaned against a wall, legs crossed at his ankles, eyes half closed, taking in everything.

One of the women, a petite blonde with a silver septum piercing, grabbed up a dress and started to pull it over her sweat-streaked body.

"No you don't," Hades snapped. He straightened up and stalked toward her.

"Get clean first. No point dirtying a perfectly clean dress." He grabbed the fabric and pulled it out of her hand.

She lunged for it, but he slapped his hand against her chest, holding her back.

"You can stay naked if you prefer," he said easily. "I don't give a shit. The dresses are only a courtesy, not a necessity." He shoved her back.

She bared her teeth.

"Want to play, do you?" Like he had with the first woman, he grabbed her hair. He pulled her over to a shower and turned the water on.

No steam rose from it. He'd shoved the woman under the flow that must have been frigid. She squealed and tried to jump out. He held her under.

"Wash," he barked. "The quicker you do it, the faster you can get out from under this fucking cold water." His sleeve was already drenched to his elbow. He disregarded it and held her still.

She hissed, either at him or with the cold. Maybe both. She soaped and washed faster than I had.

He let her go long enough to wash her hair before stepping away and drying his sleeve with a towel. He tossed it at her to dry herself after she turned the water off. It must have been freezing, because his skin was slightly blue. And the towel was more than slightly wet.

She eyed the shelf of dry towels but must have realised he wouldn't let her use one. Instead, she rubbed the damp towel over herself and scurried away to grab her dress and pull it on.

Seeming satisfied the rest of us were going to behave, Hades strode around the room like he owned the place. More than one set of eyes followed him, full of fear, hate and anger.

When he got to me, he stopped.

"Well, what do we have here?" His blonde hair was slicked back off his head. His blue eyes were as piercing as the twins'. As ruthless and determined. Familiar somehow. If he worked for my father, I might have seen him before. Maybe I should tell him who I was. This could be nothing more than a case of mistaken identity. Even as I had that thought, I dismissed it. This was all deliberately planned. Right down to securing so many women who looked enough like me that if anyone was searching for a brown eyed brunette, they'd find over a dozen. That would make it harder for anyone to track me down.

I dipped my gaze to the tops of his cheeks, rather than looking him in the eye.

"I'm no one," I said.

He tipped back his head and laughed. "If you were anyone else here, I'd commend you for learning so quickly. All the other women in this room are no one. Bodies, mouths, pussies. There for the taking by whoever buys them. They'll go wherever they're taken and disappear. But you..."

He stepped around me, his eyes on me. "You're here because someone wants you to disappear."

"I don't know what you're talking about," I lied. How could he tell me from anyone else here? Unless he and Brutus picked me up from Brutham Academy. If that was the case, he might have an inkling of who I was. I didn't recognise any of the other women around me, but I didn't know everyone from the Academy. For all I knew, I wasn't the only one. If that was the case, why had he zeroed in on me?

"Don't you?" He flicked half dry hair off my shoulder. "I think you know exactly what I'm talking about. Let me tell you a story. I knew someone once who had some trouble with his family. They pissed off the wrong people. It happens, am I right?"

He moved around in front of me. "Sometimes families prefer to dispense family members who don't toe the line." He drew his finger across his throat.

I hadn't noticed a scar across his neck until then. It looked as though someone tried to cut his throat, but failed.

Shame.

"But sometimes, families prefer to make their family members disappear in a different way. They like the idea of thinking their dear sibling is suffering. They get off thinking they'll be used until they're broken. The particularly sadistic ones like to see their family members later. To see how they have changed. How they've fallen apart. Because some families are—" He considered for a moment. "Fucked up."

"I guess so." I shrugged. That sounded like something Chloe would do. Hell, it sounded like something *I'd* do. When I got back to the Academy, it was exactly what I would do to her. If she thought this was the end, she was wrong.

"I see you know what I'm talking about," Hades concluded. "Why else would Lila Bell be in a place like this?" He smiled at my expression, clearly amused he'd caught me by surprise.

"I don't know who that is," I lied badly. My pulse was racing so fast I thought my heart might leap clear out of my chest. I half wished it would. At this rate, I'd need another shower to wash away a new layer of sweat.

His smile widened. "Yes you do. For the record, I don't work for your father. But a couple of people send you their best wishes." He looked thoughtful. "Or the opposite of best wishes. Worst curses?" He shrugged indifferently. "Close enough. Whatever they are, they come from Chloe, Dane, Zachary and... Slade Lincoln."

three

PARKER

"OW, FUCK." I tried to roll over, but the chains gave me nowhere to go.

I forced my eyes open. The relative glare made me blink a couple of times.

The room was dimly lit, but bright compared to the darkness the assholes had kept us in for the last few days. Was it three days or four? Hell, it might be five or six for all I knew. Too fucking long.

"You here, Hunt?" My mouth was so dry my voice was little more than a croak. The last time my throat felt like this was after screaming my lungs out at one of Wolf Venom's concerts.

Hunter wasn't a fan of their music, but I secretly liked it. Or not so secretly, but I didn't flaunt it. I loved my twin, but he was always jealous of Zeke and his musical ability. Me, I long ago accepted the fact I had none, and happily left it to those who did. I had talent in other areas. My cock was probably bigger than Zeke's anyway.

"No, I'm lying on a beach in the Bahamas," Hunter said sarcastically. "That pounding in your head is because you drank too many cocktails by the pool last night."

"I wish. We should do that when we get out of here. I hear there's a nice little resort in—" I stopped as the sound of an approaching truck rattled the walls around us.

"I don't suppose someone is coming to..."

The truck rattled closer before roaring past, tyres crunching on gravel. It sent up a spray against the metal side of the building.

The sound of the big engine gradually faded away and disappeared.

"I'm guessing that would be no." I scrunched up my face and shook my head, trying to clear the last of the fog from my brain. I was getting really tired of being drugged. Everything hurt, but at least we were alive. More or less.

The chain left enough slack for me to sit up, albeit awkwardly, since my ankles were duct taped together.

"I can probably pull off your tape." Hunter's feet were right in front of my face.

Normally I'd complain about the smell, but there was a slight chance I didn't smell much better. Besides which, I was grateful they hadn't killed either of us yet. Nothing would suck more than lying here next to my twin's body. Except lying beside Lila's. Honestly, I wouldn't be too happy if it was Slade either. A guy couldn't help admiring his dedication to our girlfriend. That was something all three of us shared.

I started to tease the corner of the tape away and tugged it bit by bit, unwinding it until Hunter's ankles were free.

He groaned and shook them out.

"They were dedicated." I tossed the tape aside. "That was around four times. I personally only wind it three."

"Looks like you need to up your duct tape game," Hunter remarked.

I snorted a laugh. If nothing else would get us through, humour would. "I'd hate to have a duct tape game inferior to these assholes. I can't decide if I'm offended or not."

"Save your energy," Hunter suggested. "Move your ankles over here."

I shifted over and lay still while he worked the duct tape off from around my ankles.

"You know, you're right. This is some next level tape work. It's almost like they knew what they were doing."

"You don't need to sound like you admire them quite so much." I pretended to pout. "They aren't *that* good."

He chuckled. "No, they're motherfuckers. Soon to be dead mother-fuckers."

Blood rushed into my feet, both painful and a relief at the same time. Who knew how long they'd been like that? Too long. I rolled my ankles and waved them around in the air for a while, reducing the stiffness.

"Thanks, bro."

"Any time, bro." He threw the tape aside and sat up. "Given these guys are assholes, they don't seem to be idiots; they're going to have some idea when the drugs wear off."

"Are you suggesting we need to get the fuck out of here?" I asked, fully knowing the answer.

"Yes, Parker, I am," he replied.

"Hunter, I think that's an excellent idea." I glanced down at my wrists. The handcuffs were the same ones that were on there the last time I was awake. We already knew they weren't coming off, not without a fight. Or a key.

That left the other end. The chains were attached to the wall by a bolt, but the wall looked less than sturdy.

Perfect.

I placed my feet against the base of the wall, raised my hands in front of me and pulled.

The wall groaned and buckled slightly.

I leaned forward and threw myself back with everything I had.

The bolt loosened.

I threw myself back again once, twice. The third time the bolt flew out of the wall, throwing me back onto my ass. I landed with a thud on the dirt floor. Thank fuck it wasn't concrete or I could have broken my tailbone.

I caught my breath for a minute or two then staggered to my feet. My wrists were still handcuffed tightly and I was trailing about a metre of chain, but this was a significant improvement in my circumstances.

"Good job, Park," Hunter waited for me to step aside and copied my amazing—if I may say so myself—example. He grunted hard with the exertion, but managed to pull his bolt out of the wall.

I didn't even mind that it took him one try fewer than it took me to get free. There was a time for envy and trying to one up each other, and then there was a time to be fucking glad to be standing.

"Excellent work, Hunt." I helped him to his feet. "I'm guessing the door is locked."

"I won't take that bet, because if I was an asshole, I'd lock us in," Hunter said. He stepped over to the door and tried the handle. An awkward manoeuvre at best with his wrists also handcuffed.

The door swung open.

"Fuck," Hunter grumbled. "I could have won if I'd taken that."

"You win by getting out of this shithole," I pointed out.

"That is very true." He nodded and carefully stepped out through the door.

I followed close behind after gathering up as much chain as I could and holding on to the bolt. It would suck to make it this far only to trip over. Especially if I needed my feet for running away.

"Does this place look familiar to you?" Hunter asked.

I squinted. "Vaguely. It looks a bit like one of the properties owned by..." I stopped and squinted around.

"Caleb," Hunter finished for me. "If he's in on this, he's dead meat."

"You won't hear any argument from me." I loved our second oldest brother as much as Hunter, but chaining us up was not all right. "Although, if I had to guess, I'd say this place isn't used very often. He might not even know anyone is here."

The grass was almost up to my waist. The trees and bushes were overgrown. So much so, the shed behind us was almost entirely obscured on three sides by bush. On the fourth side was a gravel road in a state of disrepair.

"It's no Toorak mansion, that's for sure," Hunter agreed. "Caleb wouldn't be seen dead in a place like this."

"Or alive." I stepped over to the track and peered one way, then the other. "I'm guessing that's the way out." I nodded the direction the truck went. Assuming it wasn't heading to some location deeper in the bush. Either way, we had to pick a direction and try.

"You were wrong about the door being locked," Hunter said thoughtfully.

"So were you," I pointed out.

He ignored me. "Let's go this way." He started walking in the direction I'd already suggested.

I rolled my eyes at his back, but followed regardless.

"Keep your eyes and ears open. If they—"

We both heard the rumble of an engine at the same time. We dove off the track and into the thick of the grass.

It wasn't until I was crouched down as low as I could get, that I remembered the existence of snakes. Right now, I couldn't bring myself to give too much of a shit. If a snake wanted to kill me, the fucker could get in line. The same went for any spiders of whatever else might be lurking around. Enough people wanted us dead, we didn't need animals as our enemies too.

An old SUV drove past slowly. They didn't even slow down when they reached the shed. They went on rolling down the track and disappeared behind the grass and gum trees.

"Let's keep going." Hunter rose, but made his way slowly through the bush, stepping carefully, moving slowly.

We walked parallel to the road. I kept half an eye out for cars and trucks, and the other half for snakes. Apart from the occasional rustle of sound, and cry from a magpie or some other bird, the place was silent.

"This gives me the creeps," Hunter said over his shoulder. "Give me a dirty, smelly city any day."

"You need to think bigger," I told him. "I'd rather be between Lila's legs than here or a city." For one thing, she smelled better and was better looking.

"If you're not careful, people are going to start to think you're the sensible twin," he teased.

"Fuck that," I shot back. "That's your domain. I'm the goofy, better looking, but surprisingly smart one. With the bigger cock." With all of that, who needed to be sensible? Not me. I was more than happy to leave that to him.

"I'll give you goofy." He looked back and grinned. "The rest... I think all the drugs they've given you have messed with your brain."

He'd turned back the way we were headed so I said, "Consider yourself flipped off." I didn't want him to miss out on that.

He chuckled in response. "Love you too, bro."

We walked in silence for a while, some unspoken sense that we must be close to the road. Or close to— Something. What the hell we'd do when we got there, I didn't know. We were us, we'd figure something out. We were nothing if not resourceful.

"What do you think she's doing right now?" Hunter asked after a few minutes.

"Judging by the position of the sun, she's in class," I replied. "Unless it's later than I think it is. In which case, she's probably naked and wet in the shower."

We both groaned at the mental image of our queen naked, water dripping down her glorious body. I almost felt her mouth around my cock. I heard sucking and moaning sounds from between her lips. Thinking about her made me hard, my balls tight and heavy. The things that woman could do with her mouth. There was no one in the world like her.

"I don't know what I want more right now, to eat her or to eat a hamburger," Hunter said wistfully. "I think it's a tie."

Yeah, I would have liked something to eat right about now too. I might even go as far as to prioritise food over Lila's pussy. I was that hungry.

Hunter held up a hand. "There's a bigger shed in front of us. And a dam if you're feeling thirsty enough."

I was that thirsty, to be honest. I stepped up behind him and peered over his shoulder.

"And a gate beyond that shed." I nodded forward. "Here's where you tell me we're going to have to wait until dark, aren't you?"

He glanced up towards the sky. "It should only be a couple of hours."

I sighed with annoyance, but sat back down amongst the bushes to wait.

"IT'S EMPTY." I peered in through the grimy window. The windows had no curtains, enabling me to see all the way across to the window on the opposite side. The moon was high enough to illuminate the inside of the large shed.

"It looks like someone was here recently, but they're gone now." Foldout beds were stacked in a corner, alongside a pile of what looked like thin blankets and towels.

"Ah," Hunter replied. "No prizes for guessing what Caleb uses this for."

Our brother's favourite pastimes included smuggling. Whether it was people, drugs or guns, he had his hands in it. Heading up that side of the family operation let Reuben keep his hands clean. Clean of that, anyway. Reuben preferred to dirty his hands in other ways.

"What are the chances they keep a spare key in there?" I mused. "Or a sandwich?"

"Judging by the apparent lack of anyone around, it wouldn't hurt to try to find out," Hunter said. "Maybe we can find a chainsaw, or something to get these fucking cuffs off."

He stepped around to the door and turned the knob. The door swung open silently.

"They don't believe in locking things around here, do they?"

"I suspect they're more interested in keeping people in here, not out," I suggested. I followed him inside, stepping carefully over the concrete floor.

It only took us a minute or two to come to the same conclusion. The place was empty of tools, or food. I managed to take a drink from a tap that hung over an old sink, but I almost got as much on myself as I did in my mouth. It was worth it.

"That was a bust." Hunter scratched at his thigh as best he could with cuffed wrists. "We—"

A flash of headlights shone through one of the windows.

I immediately dropped into a crouch. Hunter was only a fraction of a second behind me.

"Fuck," he swore. "I don't think they saw us."

"I fucking hope not." I stayed down as the gates clanged open. "Do you think whoever was here has come back?"

"No idea."

We got that answer a moment later when a car rolled past. It continued down the track towards the shed we'd woken in.

Before I could even suggest we make a run for the gate, it clanged shut.

"They're going to come looking for us pretty fucking quickly." Hunter rose and hurried towards the door. "It's not going to take them long to realise we're missing."

I followed him out and we hurried towards the gate.

"If I know Caleb at all..." Hunter bent down to scoop up a handful of gravel and throw it towards the fence. The moment it touched, the fence seemed to sizzle. The rocks rained back on us.

I threw up my wrists to protect my face. "Fucking hell," I growled. "Caleb is very quickly becoming my least favourite brother."

"I'm sure if he knew we were here, he wouldn't have the fence turned on." Hunter didn't sound so convinced.

"We need to figure out how to turn it off," I said. "How the fuck did they turn it off when they came in just now?" I jerked my thumb in the direction the car went.

"Remote-control." Hunter shrugged.

"Then there needs to be somewhere for the signal to go," I reasoned. "Look for a box on the side of the gate."

"You look for a box," he said. "I'm going to keep an eye out for the car, or someone coming after us."

I nodded and knelt down to scoop up a decent sized rock. You never know when a rock might come in handy for smashing boxes or heads.

I stepped out onto the track and approached the gate carefully. I was out in the open here, vulnerable. I wasn't used to the sensation and I didn't like it. People were going to die for what they did to me and my brother. People who weren't us.

It didn't take long to find a small metal box beside the gate. A red light flashed in the centre every few seconds.

Gotcha.

That was the easy part. The hard part was trying to position the rock in my hands so I could smash it against the box without touching the fence or smashing the crap out of my fingers. On a scale of one to a hundred, all of that would suck.

"You've got this, Park," I told myself.

"Get it quickly," Hunter snapped. "It sounds like they've found out we're not there anymore."

"They shouldn't be surprised, their hospitality sucks." I drew my hands back and smashed the rock into the flashing light. I pulled them back quickly, before any electrical charges could surge through me and fry the fuck out of my pubic hairs. That part of my body was on fire a lot of the time, but I didn't want it to burn like that.

The light winked at me like a teasing son of a bitch, then went on blinking.

I growled under my breath and smashed the rock into it again and again.

Finally, the sound of electricity shutting off buzzed through the air.

I lowered the rock and stood panting for a moment.

"You know what would have been even better?" Hunter asked. "If the fucking gate opened."

I twisted my upper body around to glare at him. "Excuse me for not being a fucking miracle worker. We can climb the fence now. You're fucking welcome."

I flung the rock down onto the ground and stomped away off the road.

Hunter swore under his breath. "Hey, Park, look I—"

The rumble of a car engine in the deepening dark sounded impossibly loud.

"Get the hell back into the bushes," Hunter barked.

"What do you think I'm doing, dickhead?" I knew he was sorry for implying that I should be doing better somehow, but I wasn't ready to forgive him yet. He knew I would soon enough. We always bit at each other, but at the end of the day we were virtually inseparable. The Brantley twins against the world. Us, Lila and Slade.

"Whatever you're doing, do it quicker," Hunter snapped.

We dove back into the bushes as headlights swept towards us.

The car skidded to a stop in front of the gate. The doors swung open. A couple of figures stepped out, the lights on their watches turned on.

"They can't have gotten far," one of them said. Male, but with an unfamiliar voice.

"With any luck, a brown snake got them." Also male. Also unfamiliar. Neither was Dane or Zachary. Not surprisingly, neither were Caleb.

"Two against two," Hunter whispered in my ear. "I like those odds."

I rose just high enough to peer over the top of the bush. If there was anyone else in the car, they were hiding, ducked down like us. I decided that was highly unlikely and my brother was right. The odds were even, even with handcuffs on. Even with heavy chains dangling from our wrists. With empty stomachs.

We were still Hunter and Parker Brantley. No one fucked with us.

Hunter whispered the plan quickly. I nodded before ducking down low while he snuck away.

I watched the lights flash as they searched for us, and counted in the back of my mind. We were going to have to time this perfectly. If we didn't, we were highly likely to be screwed. There was at least a one hundred percent chance these guys had guns.

I counted to about two hundred before I slowly crept forward toward the car.

I got into position and crouched still, watching and waiting.

Somewhere in the darkness, a tawny frogmouth called out. Once, twice, three times.

On the third, I rose and rushed forward, keeping low. I sprinted towards the closest guy and looped the chain around his neck. This would be much easier if my wrists weren't bound, but I managed to get it around and yank it tight.

At the same time, Hunter came running out of the bush on the other side and looped his chain around the other guy's neck.

They both struggled, but we had size, surprise and desperation on our side. Not to mention no hesitation when it came to killing. Especially if it meant getting the fuck away from here.

I pulled the chain harder and harder, savouring the grunting and gurgling as my victim struggled to breathe. He let out a choked cough, before he finally sagged. When he fell to the ground, he took me with him, tangled in the chain and, tired from lack of food and being drugged, I lay there for a while until I was sure the stubborn prick had stopped breathing, stopped twitching.

Only then did I dare to breathe and lift the chain off over his head.

Hunter was on his knees behind the other guy, shaking him back and forth as though he could take his anger out on the man's corpse.

"I think he's dead, bro," I drawled.

"Just being sure." He lifted the chain and shoved the guy onto the ground. He fell into the dust with a thud. "Any guesses on the chance these assholes have keys?"

"If they don't, I'm going to resuscitate one of them so I can kill them again," I growled. I rolled my victim over, pulled a gun out of the front of his pants before rifling through his pockets.

They were empty.

"Nothing," I spat. Not even something useful like a packet of nuts. Yeah, it was getting more and more difficult to stop thinking about food.

"I may have something," Hunter said.

I pulled the watch off my guy's wrist and used the light to illuminate the ring full of keys in Hunter's hand.

"I have to admit, that looks promising." I crawled over on my knees and held out my wrists while he teased one key out from the others. After three or four different keys, one finally clicked and the handcuffs fell away from my wrists.

"I've never been so happy to get handcuffs off in my life." I shook out my wrists for a minute before taking the key and unlocking his.

"Yeah, that *does* feel better." He shook out his own wrists. "I think I might be cured of ever wanting handcuffs on me again. Unless they're covered in pink velvet or feathers."

I laughed softly. "Everything is better with velvet or feathers." Almost everything anyway.

"Let's go. Nice of them to leave us a ride." I nodded towards the car.

"We need to take care of them first," Hunter said. Always the voice of fucking reason. He was right though. Two dead bodies within view of the gate wouldn't go unnoticed if anyone came looking for them. They would, there was no doubt of that. Whatever was going on here was bigger than Hunter or me. That was saying something, because we're pretty big.

I brushed dust off my jeans and grabbed the legs of the closest asshole. He was heavy, but I managed to pull him into the bush and dump him there.

I lifted the watch to look at the faces of both assholes. "Anyone we know?"

"Nope," Hunter replied lightly. "I've never seen either of them before. Which is ironic, because no one is ever going to see them again." He grinned, but the expression was strained, tired.

"Let's see if these pricks have food in the car. Or money to buy some."

We started back towards the car, but froze as another set of headlights stopped on the other side of the gate.

"Fuck," I muttered. "What now?"

The doors opened and a couple of silhouettes stepped out and moved around into the glare of the headlights.

"Fancy meeting you two here."

five
PARKER

I GROANED.

"Asher fucking DiMarco," Hunter drawled. "What a surprise."

"Hey, Zeke." I waved at our brother through the fence. "What are you two doing here?"

It seemed like a strange place for a couple of members of the biggest rock band in the world to turn up. On the other hand, Zeke and Asher both grew up in the same world we did. Hell, Hunter and I have disposed of bodies for them and their bandmates. What else are little brothers for?

"We could ask you the same question." Zeke cocked his head at me. "Slade Lincoln got in touch with us."

"He noticed we were missing?" I pressed a hand to my chest. "I'm touched."

"He did, but he wasn't as worried about you as he is about Lila," Asher said. He rubbed a hand over the back of his neck. "If I had to guess, I'd say he doesn't give a shit about you. Would you agree with that, Zeke?"

Before Zeke could answer, Hunter interrupted.

"What do you mean he's worried about Lila? She should be at Brutham, with him."

"That's what he said." Zeke leaned his hip against the side of the car. "She went missing a couple of days ago. Slade had Kennedy Knight hack into the tracker on Lila's earring. Her last location was here before the tracker stopped transmitting. Asher and I happened to be closer than Slade, so he asked us to come here."

"But there's no one else—" The blood drained out of my face. "There were people here."

"That truck," Hunter growled. "It went straight past us. If she was on it..."

Asher stepped forward and pressed his head against the wires of the fence. Any other time, I would have found it hilarious if the fence was still electrified. Seeing the smart ass drummer flying back through the air would be funny as fuck.

Right now though, thinking about what might be happening to Lila, nothing was funny.

"Wild guess here, but people that come here don't usually do it with their consent," Asher said.

"We think Caleb uses this place to run his human trafficking operation," Hunter said, with barely contained rage.

"That tracks," Asher said. "That sounds like exactly the kind of shit Caleb would be involved in." He had no more reason to like our brother than I did right now. "Can you call him and ask him where the truck is headed?"

"I don't exactly have a phone on me." Hunter patted the sides of his jeans.

"I'll lend you mine," Zeke said. "I'd do it myself, but Caleb would want a favour in return for information like that."

"Caleb really is a special kind of asshole, isn't he?" Asher observed.

Zeke shrugged and pulled a phone out of his back pocket. "No more than any of my other brothers." He gave us both a dark look.

"Burned by a guy who makes a living singing," I said sarcastically.

"I could always not lend you my phone." Zeke started to put it back.

"No, we need it," I said quickly. "Also, Hunter and I are both armed so you can hand it over or we'll shoot you and take it."

"Whatever happened to asking nicely?" Asher asked. He glanced at the gate, his gaze up and down. "You might have to climb out and get it."

I gave an experimental tug on the gate, but it didn't budge. There was probably a remote-control in the car, but after smashing the box to turn off the electricity, I doubted it would work. Finding out would only waste valuable time. If Lila was on a truck, on her way to fuck knows where, we needed to hurry to catch up.

I grabbed hold of the fence and scrambled up and over the top, narrowly avoiding snagging my jeans on the barbed wire.

Hunter was right behind me. He all but snatched the phone out of Zeke's hand and stomped a few steps away. He smashed his finger down on the screen a few times before putting the phone to his ear.

While he waited for an answer, I peered into the back of the car.

"You didn't bring Abbie with you," I said, disappointed. "I would have loved the chance to say hello. That woman has some of the best tits—"

"I wouldn't finish that sentence if I were you." Asher's tone was pleasant, but menacing at the same time. He'd probably love an excuse to put a bullet in our brains. Honestly, the feeling was more or less mutual. He was a DiMarco and they were on my shit list right now. With Dane right at the very top.

"You guys promised Reuben you wouldn't kill us," I pointed out.

Asher smiled. "We don't need to kill you to make your life hell."

"What are you going to do, sing?" I grinned. "I've heard you sing. Hell is reasonably accurate." Like usual, I was using humour to cover my anxiety. Although, Asher's singing was pretty bad. There was a reason he was the drummer.

Asher flipped me off. "I'm starting to think Lila came here voluntarily after all. To get away from you."

Zeke grabbed the back of my shirt when I lunged at Asher.

"Don't fucking touch him," he growled. He shoved me hard against the side of the car and held me there. He leaned forward until his cheek was almost pressed against mine.

"In case you hadn't noticed, dickhead, we're on the same side here. I don't give a fuck about Lila Bell, but I care about women being trafficked and abused. And Slade is a friend of mine. If you keep being a fuckwit, we'll leave you here." He shoved me a little harder before he stepped away.

I straightened up and moved away from the car, like I wasn't bothered at all.

"So violent." I brushed dirt off the front of my clothes. "I don't suppose you have a sandwich with you." I shot a glance at Hunter. He looked frustrated, angry.

"What do you mean you don't know? It's your fucking job to know shit like this. You're in charge of these operations. Reuben would be pissed if he—" He shook his head. "Our girlfriend is on that truck. If anything happens to her..."

I heard— *heard* Caleb's laughter through the phone. If he was right in front of me, he'd be missing his balls in three, two, one... I'd hand them to him before I dragged him over to the dam and held him and his Armani suit under until he stopped struggling.

The fact Zeke and Asher looked equally pissed was no consolation.

"Listen here, you motherfucker," Hunter growled. "I want the destination of the truck and I know you can get it for me. I'll wait." He listened with a scowl on his face. His expression hardened. He glanced over at me.

"Whatever he wants us to do in return for that information is going to suck," I observed.

"You won't get any sympathy from me," Zeke said.

"Me either," Asher said. He opened the front passenger door of the car, reached in and pulled out a sandwich. He bit into it and smiled at me.

"Did I mention I have a gun?" I asked.

The asshole smiled broader and went on eating. I should have killed him back in Perth. Or Melbourne. Or Sydney. Hell, there were a bunch of places I could have done it and didn't. That was what I got for being too nice.

"Yeah, yeah," Hunter was saying. "Whatever we have to do. Just get us that information." He was silent for a moment. "Fine, call me back on this number."

He pressed the screen and glared at the phone as if somehow it was in on some conspiracy against us.

"He said he doesn't know the specifics, because he leaves that to the asshole who works for him. There are several different places they could take Lila to be auctioned. They keep it random so the police can't figure it out and they don't tell Caleb until they get there. They know what will happen to them if they try to screw him over, but this way if the police go after Caleb, he can't give them a thing and they can't pin anything on him. The dickhead in charge will take the fall."

"That sounds like Caleb," Zeke said. "Did he say who the dickhead in question was?"

"Hades fucking Turner," Hunter growled. "His brother, Ares, is dating Lila's sister, Kennedy. He's an asshole, but Hades is a thousand times worse. If he touches Lila, I'll rip his bloody arms off."

"Get in line," I snarled. "Hades is a massive prick. I'm not at all surprised he runs this part of Caleb's operation. It's exactly the thing he'd get off on. Having power over other people, especially helpless women." Lila was far from helpless, but when it came to Hades, I hated to think of them in the same room, much less him holding her in the back of a disgusting truck with other women.

Hunter paced back and forward in front of the headlights. With the fence behind him, he looked like an angry, caged tiger. One with claws ready to tear people apart.

"Any idea which direction the truck went?" Zeke asked. He looked up and down the otherwise empty road. We were in the middle of nowhere. Kilometres away from anything. Of course we were. Caleb wouldn't run an operation like this in the middle of the suburbs. That was more Samuel Bell's style.

"None," I replied. "Hunter and I were chained up back from the road."

"Chained up?" Asher huffed a laugh.

"Yeah, in case anyone gives a shit, we were drugged and kidnapped." I glared at the drummer.

That made Asher laugh even more. "Wait until I tell Abbie that. She's going to find it hilarious." He pointed a finger at me. "Don't say you didn't deserve it. How many times have you kidnapped her? Twice?"

I shrugged. "Something like that, but no harm came to her."

"It doesn't seem like much harm came to you either," Zeke observed. "Excuse me if I don't give you any sympathy either. I'll save that for Lila and the other women in her company."

"Who kidnapped you anyway?" Asher asked. "Not that I care or anything."

"Funny you should ask, one of them was your brother, Dane. Helped by Zachary Sinclair and Chloe Bell." Otherwise known as a pack of assholes.

"How about that, Dane getting his hands dirty." Asher spoke lightly, but he looked disgusted. For once, we agreed on something. Had hell frozen over?

Zeke's phone rang. Not with a Wolf Venom tune as I would have suspected, but one from Blazing Violet. There was hope for Zeke after all.

Hunter answered before the first bar was done. "What?" He frowned as he listened. "Yep. Yeah. Okay. We know the place. Yeah, we know we owe you one for this. You know where to find us after we find Lila." He sounded like he wanted to tell Caleb to fuck off to hell, but for now we needed him. As long as we did, we'd play more or less nice.

He mashed his thumb down on the screen and handed the phone back to Zeke. "Let's get the fuck out of here. We need to get to her before —" He shook his head and didn't finish his sentence.

He didn't need to. We all knew what might happen if we didn't get there in time.

"I'll text the location to Slade," Zeke said. "He can meet us there."

I slipped into the back seat of the car and tried not to look like I was freaking out on the inside.

We're coming. Hang on a little while longer.

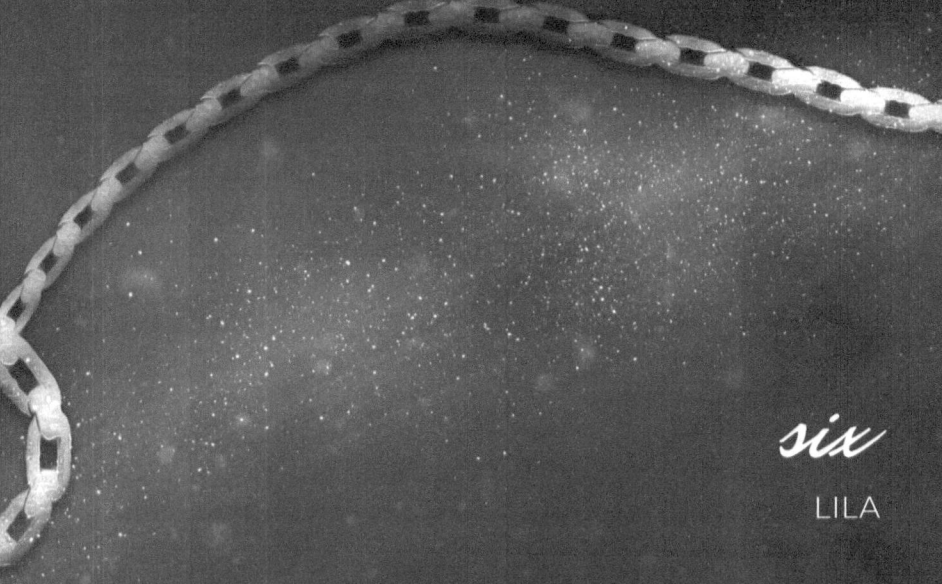

six

LILA

THE ROCKING of the truck made my stomach turn and twist. What made me even more nauseous was Hades' words tumbling around and around in my mind. I was naïve to consider trusting Chloe or Zachary, but Slade... Was he really working with my sister? Was I that bad at judging who I let into my heart? Into my bed?

The twins trusted him, and I trusted them more than I trusted myself. Had they misjudged that badly?

I didn't want to believe any of it. Once the seeds were sown, I couldn't get the thoughts out of my mind. To make it worse, I finally realised why Hades looked familiar. He worked for the Brantley family. I wasn't surprised to learn they were behind this. What I couldn't figure out was how my sister was involved. I didn't doubt she was, but the fact she might be working with another Brantley against me and the twins, was new. Unless...

Unless Slade organised this on her behalf.

The thought he was in it that deep made my heart hurt. And made me want to stab him in his.

I shifted my position to try to get comfortable and lifted a hand to my ear. Hades had made us take all our jewellery off shortly after we arrived at the big shed. He and Brutus had thrown every piece into a machine that ground them all down to nothing. Tracking chip and all.

The girl with the septum piercing, Danica, had refused to remove

189

hers. Hades had held her arms while Brutus laughed and tore it out so hard it bled. While Hades ground down the ring, Brutus grabbed her hair, forced her to her knees and undid the front of his jeans.

I stood and opened my mouth to protest, but Hades cut me a look.

"Unless you want to take her place? Maybe you'd prefer to suck my cock?" He grabbed his groin and grinned.

I backed down and turned away, but couldn't shut out the sound of her sobs. Those hadn't stopped for hours. She was only silent now because she was asleep.

I suspected she would have preferred if she was dead.

"How long?" the woman beside me whispered. What was her name? Mary. Her skin and hair were a shade or two darker than mine, but she was about the same age as me.

"How long what?" I whispered back, my tone more curt than I intended.

She licked her lips. "How long do you think it will be until we get... wherever they're taking us? It feels like we've been in here for hours."

"Yeah, it does." It was hot, dark and uncomfortable, but the hours in here would be better than what was coming after. What Brutus did to Danica was going to happen to all of us. We didn't talk about it. We didn't talk about much of anything, but we all knew.

I had no intention of letting anyone do anything to me without one hell of a fight, but I planned to get the fuck away before it came to that.

Whoever did this to me, I was done being a victim. I would escape, and when I did, I would find out exactly who was behind this and they'd pay dearly for it. Breaking them wouldn't be enough.

"Why does Hades treat you differently?" Mary surprised me by asking. "Are you someone famous?"

I choked back a laugh. "Infamous, more like it. But no, I'm no one special. He just... Singled me out." Better to pretend he planned to toy with me when he got the chance, than admit who I really was. If she'd heard of the Bells, she'd know my father had a hand in doing this to other women. In her mind, that may make me as bad as Hades and Brutus. As bad as Caleb Brantley.

She should think that, because I was thinking it myself. What had I done to stop this from happening to other women? Nothing, because I never gave it any thought. Not for a moment. My father did what he did to make us rich and powerful. I was so far removed from the consequences, I didn't consider there were any. Especially consequences that involved innocent women. These weren't hardened criminals or corrupt politicians who deserved to be fucked with. They were women going about their daily lives when they ended up here.

It went without saying that when I became the head of the Bell family, I would shut down any operations like this. I'd insist the twins make their family do the same. I wouldn't stand for it a moment longer. There were dozens of other ways to make money.

"Why did he single you out?" Mary pressed. "He seemed to know you somehow."

"He's probably seen lots of women like me over however the fuck long he's been involved in this," I said. "No doubt he chooses one in every batch. Brutus too."

The other asshole had his eyes on Danica every time I saw him. He'd do a lot worse to her if it wouldn't leave her more damaged than she already was. Honestly, it was Hades' presence that stopped him. Men like him only gave a shit to a certain extent.

Mary shuddered. "Brutus is horrible."

As if saying his name woke her up, Danica resumed sobbing softly in the corner.

"Do you think they'll find us in time?" Mary asked.

"Who?" I frowned at her.

"Our families. They must be looking for us. The police must be looking for us. This many of us going missing, they'll be looking everywhere." She looked heartbreakingly hopeful.

"Of course they will," I said with as much certainty as I could muster, considering I felt none at all. The twins were missing. Slade might be behind this. My sister certainly didn't give a shit. My father wouldn't be looking for me if he blamed me for letting my guard down. The rest of the Brantley family would be happy to be rid of me, especially if they made a lot of money from selling me. The only consolation there was that maybe they'd be inspired to do the same to Chloe. If she did this to me, then she deserved nothing less.

"They might be waiting for us at... Wherever they're taking us," I said with a shrug. "A whole bunch of cops, ready to arrest their asses. They can lock them away to rot."

"I hear the guys in prison don't take kindly to fellow inmates who do horrible things to women." Mary looked surprisingly pleased at the thought.

I have to admit, I didn't mind it myself. "I hope some big, ugly asshole makes Brutus his bitch."

Mary laughed softly. "That would serve him right. I bet she's not the first one he's done something like that to. But she might be the last."

"She's definitely not the first," I agreed. I didn't want to think too much about how many went before her. Mary was right, Danica should be the last.

"Any idea when they're taking us?" Mary asked. "Are there just... Places men go to... To buy women?"

"I don't know," I admitted. "I suppose there must be." My father never told me and I never asked. Part of me wished I had, but the knowledge wouldn't help me now anyway. Not unless I knew a way out.

"I've never—" Mary whispered. "You know, been with anyone."

I didn't know why she was telling me that until she added, "I was waiting for my first time to be special. Not... Forced." Her voice was choked with emotion.

"I don't think being raped gets any better even if you've fucked a bunch of times," I said, more coldly than I meant to sound.

"I didn't mean to suggest it was," she said quickly. "I just... I want to go home." She sniffed.

"We all do," I said gently. As gently as I was capable of anyway. "We will get out of this. Didn't we already agree the police would be waiting for us at the other end of this? Or our families."

Was there any chance the twins were looking for me? Was there even a chance Hades lied and Slade was looking for me too? Hell, I'd even cling to a kernel of hope that my father was looking for me. If I didn't hold on to that, I might consider giving up and that was something I wasn't going to do. I couldn't let despair get to me. If I did, it would cloud my judgement and force me to make mistakes.

I needed a clear head and rock solid determination. If I was going to fall apart, it would have to wait until later.

"Yes, we did agree on that," Mary said. "Do you think it's possible?"

She was clearly looking to me to keep her spirits up. If she only knew who I really was, she'd be looking in every direction but mine.

"Not only is it possible, it's probable," I lied. "Brutus and Hades and the other assholes should be pissing themselves right about now. And whoever they're working for. I hope they're enjoying their last moments of freedom. They're about to lose that."

Mary's teeth flashed white in the dim light. "I can't wait," she said breathlessly. "I hope we get to see the looks on their faces. That moment they realise how screwed they are."

"Yeah that would be... Good." It would be better than good if it ever actually happened, but what were the chances? Not as good as I would have liked them to be.

"What did you mean when you said you were infamous?" She brushed tangled hair off her forehead.

I suppressed a wince. I'd hoped she hadn't picked up on that and wouldn't ask.

"I just meant I'm good at getting into trouble," I said evasively. "I mean, I ended up here, didn't I? What happened to you? How did you get taken?" Anything to change the subject.

She sighed. "I went on a date with a guy I thought was nice and decent. I thought we had a nice time. He took me to dinner. It was nothing fancy. We talked about all sorts of things, you know? Work, family, shit like that. I guess he slipped something into my drink, because I woke up on the back of this truck."

"What a prick," I said. She struck me as the innocent, naïve type. Someone all too easy to take advantage of. The opposite of me, most of the time.

"He really was." She nodded. "What happened to you? How did you get here?"

"I think it was about the same thing." My brow furrowed in thought. "The last thing I remember was getting a coffee in the... My university coffee shop." If she didn't know about Brutham Academy, then I wasn't going to enlighten her. The rest of the world wasn't ready to know about the existence of such a fucked up place.

"The next thing I knew, I woke up here too. I guess the barista put something in my drink too."

"Shit," Mary said softly. "I'm so sorry. I'm guessing they did that to most of us, if not all of us. Why do men suck so much?"

"I've often wondered the same thing," I said. I couldn't even say 'not all men,' because fuck knows the twins did plenty of similar things. I knew for a fact they'd drugged Abbie at least once. Not for the same reason, but they did it.

"That's why women go to the toilet in pairs. Because too many men can't be trusted. When I get out of this, I'm never going on another date ever again."

"I'm sure you'll find someone nice," I assured her.

We had to get out of this shit first.

seven

LILA

THE TRUCK SLOWED TO A STOP. The rumble of a garage door echoed, the gears grinding it closed behind us. Steel hit concrete with a harsh, resounding clunk.

The truck rolled forward for another minute or two before coming to a full stop. The engine turned off, plunging us into silence.

Mary gripped my arm, trembling fingers pressing into my flesh. We sat like that, huddled together until the back of the truck swung open.

"This is it, ladies," Brutus said cheerfully. "Holiday is over. Time to get out and earn your keep."

Danica sobbed and shuffled away from him, but she had nowhere to go.

None of us did.

Brutus pulled out a gun and waved over several men. They gathered around the back of the truck, each looking more shady as fuck than the last.

"Let's not have any trouble, ladies. Out you get." Brutus waved the gun at us before he stepped back to give us room.

Mary's grip tightened, her nails digging harder into my skin.

"Those aren't police," she whispered.

Brutus aimed the gun at her. "Anything you want to share with the class?"

She shook her head hastily, hair flying this way and that. "No." Her voice trembled as hard as she did.

"Good, then get the fuck out of the truck," he said with a vicious smile. He kept the gun on her until she let go of my arm and scurried out.

I sighed and followed. Instinctively, I kept my eyes down, looking for ways out, while giving the appearance of not making any trouble.

"Do I have to drag you out by your hair?" Brutus snarled as I stepped over near him.

I contained a flinch, but froze until I realised he wasn't addressing me.

A red-eyed Danica was staring back at him. Her cheeks were wet with tears. She didn't bother to wipe them away. She skirted over to the end of the truck, as far from Brutus as she could get, and climbed out.

"Shame, I would have enjoyed that." Brutus laughed. After a moment, the other men joined in.

I forced my eyes back down before I shot daggers at them. Now would not be a good time to provoke Brutus.

"This way ladies." He gestured with his gun.

A wave of panic threatened to wash over me. It lasted until I realised he wasn't referring to the elevator, but the concrete steps beside them. They led up, out of the parking garage.

Cold and dank, they were better than the confined space of an elevator car. Being stuck in one of those with Brutus was 'worst nightmare' material.

The men formed a loose semicircle around us, presumably in case we decided to run. Where they thought we'd go, I had no idea. As far as I could see, the only ways in and out were from the garage door, the elevator or the steps.

The concrete felt like ice under my bare feet, but I trudged up along with the other women. Mary stuck close by my side all the way.

"What is this place?" she whispered. "I was expecting an abandoned warehouse, but this feels..."

"Not abandoned?" I suggested. We were clearly in a city, but I could only guess at which one. If I had to, I'd bet on Melbourne. At this time of year, Brisbane would have been hotter. The two journeys in the truck were too long, too far for to only be in Sydney. Unless we were driving around in heavy city traffic. That didn't seem likely. The outer fringes of Melbourne were a much safer bet.

"Maybe they use this place a lot for... Things like this," she said. "We're not the first."

We were definitely *not* the first, but she was so sweet and naïve, it clearly hadn't occurred to her until now this operation was something ongoing. Something much bigger than any of us.

All I could say in response to that was, "No. We aren't." I glanced at her to suggest we should stop talking. I didn't want to draw the attention of Brutus or any of the others. If I was going to get out of this, I needed to stay under the radar.

Luckily, she got the message and fell silent.

We passed two landings before the stairs stopped at a third. The door was open. Hades stood in the doorway.

"It's good to see you again, girls," he said with a smile that was more menacing than warm. Especially when his gaze lingered on me. "Come with me."

I missed neither the innuendo nor the wink he directed at me. At any other time, and any other place and context, I would have responded with, "in your dreams." Here and now, I kept my mouth shut and followed as he moved out of the doorway and across a carpeted room.

Along one end of the room was a stage, approximately up to my waist. The rest of the room was filled with chairs, all of them currently empty. It didn't take a genius to figure out what this room was intended for. We'd be paraded on the stage for the viewing and bidding pleasure of those who would be seated comfortably.

Assholes.

"Step up to the stage and through the backstage," Hades directed. "There you'll find showers and a change of...clothes." He chuckled.

I started up the steps, hoping to find a door that led out. Or a window with a fire escape. Or...something.

The backstage area consisted of a long table which spanned the wall. Across the wall, several mirrors hung. Chairs sat in front of each, so people could sit and apply make-up. At the end of the room was another door that led into a bathroom. I made out several showers and a couple of toilets.

The top of the table was covered with piles of bras and panties, each lacy and sheer.

Change of clothes my ass. I should have guessed that was what he meant. Of course buyers would want to see what they were getting before they placed any bids.

I spied one heavy door that led out of the dressing room, but it appeared locked. I was going to have to wait and try to figure out a way to get the fuck out. I was patient. I could bide my time a little longer.

Wrinkling my nose, I chose a black bra and panty set that should fit and hurried into the relative safety of the shower. There were no doors, but none of the men followed us in. They must have felt secure that we had nowhere to go.

Like I had in the big shed, I showered in about a minute flat and dried myself on one of the towels that hung off hooks on the wall. I wriggled into the bra and G string and glanced at my reflection in a mirror that was quickly becoming steamed up.

Hunter and Parker would have loved what I was wearing. The lace was so sheer it was practically transparent. My pussy and nipples were clearly visible through the silk.

"That looks good on you." Hades looked me up and down and grinned. "There's hairdryers, hairbrushes and make-up over there." He waved in the direction of the long table. "Go and make yourself extra hot. And before you—" he directed the statement toward all of the women "—think that making yourselves look messy will mean that you avoid being sold, think again. Firstly, we'll make you wash it off. Secondly, the better you look, the better quality buyer you'll attract. Trust me, you don't want to attract the cheapskates. Unless you want to end up with someone like Brutus over there." He nodded towards the other guy.

Brutus flipped him off, but grinned. "I don't mind taking the leftovers. If they've got a pussy and like to cry, they're exactly my type." He leered at Danica.

She looked back at him with a devastated expression on her face. She was clearly terrified exactly that might happen.

I didn't blame her for being scared. Life with Brutus would be short and brutal.

"You're such a ladies man," Hades teased. He gave Brutus a nod before heading towards the doorway and back down the stairs.

"I really am, aren't I?" Brutus eyed Danica again. He laughed when she shrank away from him. "Where do you think you're going?" He stepped over towards her slowly, like a lion stalking his prey. "I might as well make you dirty before you get clean."

She whimpered. And again, when he grabbed her hair and pushed her down to her knees.

"Don't," Mary said, surprising me and herself. "Leave her alone." She lunged towards him, hands in fists in front of her.

"Mouthy bitch." Brutus raised his gun and fired a single shot into Mary's stomach.

She staggered forward a few steps, her eyes wide with shock. Her hands clutched her middle, blood quickly coating her fingers. She dropped to her knees before collapsing to the floor with a soft thud.

The whole room froze.

Brutus laughed. He shoved Danica away so hard she fell on her shoulder with a cry of pain. She rolled over and scurried away to curl up beside the wall.

"You fucked that up, didn't you?" Brutus stood over Mary, gun held loosely in his hands. "You're ruined goods now, stupid bitch." He scowled like it was her fault, then shrugged.

His expression changed to a vicious smile that chilled my blood.

Would he really...

He knelt beside her. "Might as well have some fun."

He shoved her legs apart with his knees and shuffled forward between them. Grinning with anticipation, he pushed her dress up to her waist and undid his fly with one hand.

I didn't wait to see him pull out his cock. Without thinking, I grabbed one of the chairs and slammed it into his back as hard as I could. The impact jarred my hands.

He grunted with pain and slumped forward.

The moment he dropped it, I dove for his gun. My fingers closed over steel still warm from his hand. Acting on pure instinct, I found the trigger and fired off a shot into his head.

Then one each for the other two men who pulled out their weapons.

The women jumped to grab their guns and aim them on the other three men.

"You're not—" one of them started to say when Danica unloaded straight into his chest.

The other two raised their hands and dropped their guns to the floor.

What would Hunter and Parker do if they were faced with an unarmed enemy who surrendered?

I answered that question with a bullet in each of their brains. That was what they got for being involved in an operation like this.

I lowered the gun and dropped to my knees beside Mary.

"Holy shit," I whispered. This was beyond fucked up. My stomach rebelled, but I swallowed my last meal back down. I grabbed a fistful of fabric and tugged her dress back in place to give her some modesty.

"Mary?" She was so still, covered with so much blood. It soaked into the fabric of her dress and spread like a stain.

I'd never seen so much blood in my life. So much innocent fucking blood.

"We need to get her to hospital," one of the women spoke frantically.

I choked back my emotions and took a long moment.

"It's too late."

Brutus must have hit a vital organ for her to have died so quickly, but she was definitely gone. He would have raped a corpse.

I closed her eyes and wiped back tears. She deserved better than this. She should have gotten out of here with the rest of us. She would have met someone who treated her like a queen and had a long, happy life.

Now, none of that would happen. Not for her. It was so fucking unfair.

As for the rest of us... We needed to get out of here before anyone else came.

"Try the door." I nodded towards it.

Danica stepped over and rattled the knob. "It's locked." She aimed the gun at it, but quickly realised it was empty. She looked back at the man she killed with dawning horror on her face.

She'd killed him.

"Panic later," I snapped. I aimed at the lock and fired. The bullet tore through that and decimated a chunk of door.

"I don't know about you, but I'm ready to get the fuck out of here." I pushed the door open with my bare foot.

I froze.

"Slade."

"IT'S GOT to be around here somewhere." I glanced at the screen of Zeke's phone, then out at the street signs as we slowly drove past them. "Unless Caleb gave us the wrong address."

"If he did, it's the last thing he'll do," Hunter growled. "Zeke, pull over here. Let's take a look around."

"Whatever you say, bro," Zeke said with a hint of sarcasm. He pulled the car over to the side of the road and killed the engine.

Hunter was the first one out, but I was close behind. I half expected Zeke and Asher to drive away, but they got out too. I didn't kid myself that it had anything to do with Lila. It was the other women they cared about. Whatever. As long as our girl got out safe, sound and untouched.

They both slipped on caps and sunglasses, because nothing says 'famous person trying to go incognito' like an obvious disguise. Most people wouldn't give them a second glance if they just walked around like normal human beings.

I mean, being members of the biggest rock band in the world wasn't that big a deal, right?

I glanced back at the screen. "According to this, it's back there about fifty metres."

"Wait," Asher said suddenly.

"What the fuck for?" Hunter snarled.

The drummer nodded forward. "That. If we rush up there, we'll draw everyone's attention."

I squinted in the direction he indicated. Several men in Armani and Zegna suits were making their way toward a particular building, all walking like they owned the place.

Of course it wouldn't be everyday riffraff who wanted to buy women like Lila. Men like this wanted the best of the best. They'd pay well for it.

Assholes.

"Parker and I will go," Hunter said. "You two stand out like dog's balls." He glared at them as though daring them to disagree.

"You think no one will notice two dirty guys turning up at an event like this?" Zeke raised an eyebrow at Hunter. "If anyone stands out like dog's balls, it's you."

"Fuck," I said under my breath. "The last thing in the world I want to say is that Zeke is right, but..."

"Zeke is almost always right," Asher said. He gave my brother a fond look. They were so adorably cute together it was sickening.

"Thank you," Zeke told him. "I think. We'll talk about the 'almost always' later. In the meantime, let's find another way into the building. There has to be a back door."

I rubbed my forehead. It was starting to ache.

"It sucks when your big brother is right twice in as many minutes," Zeke said lightly.

"It's a new world record," I said sarcastically. I looked down at the map. "According to this, if we go down to the end of the street, around and back up again, we'll be at the back of that building."

I glanced back up and watched the businessman pass through the glass front doors. The place looked like some sort of underground gentlemen's club. That was likely exactly what it was. A place so exclusive it didn't need a sign. Potentially an establishment owned by the Brotherhood of Kings.

Even though Hunter and I were members, that wouldn't assure us that we'd be allowed to enter.

Sneaking around and breaking in it was then.

I handed the phone to Zeke and hurried up the street after him and Asher. A couple of people gave them funny looks, but most didn't look twice. None of them stopped to ask for autographs or selfies, which was just as well because we didn't have time for that shit and killing them in broad daylight wouldn't go unnoticed.

I resisted the urge to run, instead walking as quickly as I could while looking like I wasn't hurrying. Sneaking wouldn't work very well if we drew attention to ourselves.

"This is it," Hunter said as we reached the back of the building.

A driveway ended in a garage door, which was covered in an interesting variety of graffiti. From the look of it, it was painted recently, presumably to cover other graffiti. There was nothing more welcoming to a graffiti artist than a blank canvas. No doubt whoever owned the building painted it frequently.

Beside the driveway, a door led into the building. A surveillance camera kept watch on anyone who might approach.

At least, it did until I pulled out my gun and shot it.

The sound was loud enough to make me wince.

"Let's get inside before someone comes to investigate that." Hunter cut me a look that suggested he wished I hadn't done that.

I shrugged and tucked the gun away.

The door was locked, but when Hunter grabbed hold of the bottom of the garage door, it rolled up easily. He pushed it high enough for us to duck underneath and slip into the building.

We stood in a parking garage big enough for at least a hundred cars. Parked in the middle was a massive truck. The rear doors sat open.

I trotted over and peered inside. "It's empty, but it smells like... People."

Had Lila been in the back of that recently? She didn't like to let on, but I knew she hated enclosed spaces. They always made her shiver and her pupils dilate. From what I gathered, Samuel Bell didn't mind putting people in dark, enclosed spaces as some form of punishment. It wouldn't surprise me at all if he did that to her and Chloe. Shame he hadn't left Chloe and Zachary inside. Together or apart, it wouldn't matter. Dead was dead.

"She has to be around here somewhere," Hunter said.

I jumped as shots rang out from somewhere else in the building.

"That wasn't me," I said quickly, in case there was any doubt.

"No shit," Hunter said. His face was paler than usual, worry etched on his features. I didn't need any twin to twin telepathy to tell me what he was thinking.

Those gunshots might have meant we were too late. Worse than that, they might have seen us coming and decided to dispose of Lila before we got to her. If that happened, my heart was going to splinter into approximately seventeen billion pieces, each smaller than the last.

"There are—" Asher started to speak, but was interrupted by the garage door opening behind us.

Fuck. We all ran to hide behind the truck.

"The shots came from upstairs. If this has gone all pear-shaped, Caleb is going to be pissed."

I knew that voice. *Hades fucking Turner.* How many people did he have with him?

I chanced a glance around the side of the truck. Hades and four other men. No, three other men and a woman. So much for the sisterhood.

I stepped back and held up five fingers to the other guys. They all nodded and pulled out guns. Figured Zeke and Asher would be carrying too. You can take the boy out of our lifestyle, but you can't take our lifestyle out of the boy. They weren't in it as deep as us, but they couldn't escape it entirely.

Footsteps disappeared up the stairs, suggesting Hades and his people went that way. If they went that way, so would we.

Typically, it was Zeke who took charge. He gestured for us to fall in behind him after taking off his hat and sunglasses and stashing them behind the truck's tyres.

Asher did the same before following close behind Zeke.

Hunter and I exchanged glances and nods, then we too were stepping towards the stairs and up as silently as we could go.

Shouting came from somewhere above us. A woman screamed.

We trotted up the stairs faster, keeping to the side to stay out of sight of anyone who might look back down. Every so often, I glanced up, gun ready to blow out brains.

"They went that way," someone shouted.

"Get after them," that was Hades.

At a signal from Zeke, we started to run. It was clear by now, no one was looking back. Their attention was all focussed ahead.

We bolted past a couple of landings, all the way to the third floor. A room full of chairs and a stage was empty.

"Backstage," Zeke said. He wasn't even puffing.

We slowed down and headed up the stairs onto the stage.

"This is more familiar," Asher remarked.

I rolled my eyes and resisted the temptation to shoot him in the back of the head just to shut him up. Only because I didn't want to waste a bullet.

We stepped into a dressing room. A woman's body lay on the floor. For a heart stopping moment, I thought she was Lila. Her hair was the same colour, the same length. There was so much fucking blood.

My brain finally registered that it wasn't Lila. I released a ragged breath.

Several men lay dead around the room. One had so many holes in his chest he looked like Swiss cheese.

"Anyone want to bet our girl was here?" I asked.

"Without doubt," Hunter said proudly.

"I'm guessing they went that way." I jerked my head toward an open door that also looked shot up.

"Let's go carefully," Zeke said. "If those women did this, the assholes might get desperate. We don't want them to shoot first and ask questions later."

"No, we fucking don't," Hunter agreed.

Guns raised in front of us, we stepped carefully through the doorway. It led to a long corridor lined with doors. At first glance, there was no sign of Hades and his people.

We walked silently across the worn linoleum floor. This section of the building wasn't meant to be seen by men in Armani suits. This was for staff. The doors must be offices or storage.

"Put your guns down," a male voice said from around the corner, just beyond the end of the corridor.

"You first."

I grinned. I knew that voice. Lila. Thank fuck she was alive. No doubt she was the one leading this escape. We were just here to help if necessary. The woman was a motherfucking badass.

"We have you pinned down in there." He sounded very confident.

"We can wait here for reinforcements to arrive. You have nowhere to go. Put your guns down and no one will get hurt."

"We already have been hurt." That was a female voice I didn't recognise. She sounded distraught. Honestly, who could blame her? This whole situation was sixty-nine different kinds of fucked up.

"You can be hurt worse if you want," the man growled.

"Or you can fuck off," Lila replied. She sounded like she was past done with their bullshit. Honestly, she had a low tolerance level for bullshit in the first place. The last couple of days would have stretched her to the limit and beyond. She was going to need lots of chocolate, bubble bath, cuddles and orgasms after this. I knew just the three guys to give them to her. Especially me.

"I suggest you do what the woman says."

I frowned. That sounded like Slade. He must have gotten here right before we did. Evidently he hadn't bothered to wait for us.

Rude.

"Fuck this." Hades' minion sounded pissed off. "Let's just—"

Whatever he was going to suggest, he didn't get to finish.

Zeke flew around the corner. His movement was immediately followed by a shot, then another.

The three of us didn't hesitate to follow.

One minion lay dead outside a doorway. The other three turned their attention to us. There was no sign of Hades.

I got off a shot before one of the minions could shoot my older brother. Zeke, that was. Hunter was busy taking care of the other man.

Asher aimed at the woman but hesitated.

She didn't. She aimed at him and fired.

"FUCK!"

The bullet missed Asher by a hair.

I don't know who killed the woman in the end. Hunter, Zeke and I all fired on her at the same time. The impact of the bullets threw her back against the wall. She slid down slowly, leaving a trail of blood behind her.

I stepped forward carefully and peered into a room full of women. And Slade.

"Anyone else?" I asked with a grin.

"It's okay, he's with me," Lila said quickly to a blonde who aimed at me.

The other woman looked uncertain but lowered her gun.

"Don't worry, I only bite Lila." I put down my own gun and stepped over to embrace her. "You look hot."

Her bra and panties were virtually transparent. If I wasn't hard from all the excitement, I was hard from looking at her.

She snorted at me and accepted Slade's T-shirt when he slipped it off and handed it to her. It fell to mid-thigh. Somehow it was even more adorable than transparent underwear.

Hunter shoved me aside so he could put his arms around Lila and give her a squeeze.

"It's good to see you. You too, Slade."

"Looks like we got here just in time." I scanned the room, smiling at the scared, anxious faces around me.

"We had things under control," Slade said evenly. As if he wasn't as happy to see us as Lila was. He could thank us later.

Lila glanced at him sideways. "You still haven't explained how you got here. How did you know where to find me?"

I knew that expression. That was the same one she had when she looked at her sister. Wary, mistrustful.

"The twins told me." Slade frowned. "What the fuck is going on?" He put out a hand to her, but she jerked away.

"The asshole running this operation, Hades, said you were working with my sister." Her voice was tight with stress and emotion.

He stared at her, open shock on his face. "Why the hell would I do that?" He lowered his hand and balled it into a fist. "Wait, did you say Hades? That explains it."

I slid the back of my knuckles down Lila's cheek. "I wouldn't believe a word that comes out of Hades' mouth."

"Absolutely not," Hunter agreed.

"My guess is Chloe told him to say that to fuck with your head," Slade said slowly. "I'll swear on anything you want me to swear on, I am *not* working with your sister. Or with Zachary. Or Dane for that matter."

"Wise man," Asher remarked. "I wouldn't work with him either." Neither he nor Zeke did more than glance at the half-naked women in the room. They also seemed to be oblivious to how many were staring at them in clear recognition.

Slade looked intently at Lila. "You believe me, right? I was trying to help you get out of here."

"They found us in this room pretty quickly," she said, still wary.

"They followed the sound of gunshots," Hunter said. "We were right behind them." He looked around the room, then back out in the corridor. "Where the hell is Hades?"

"Knowing him, he ran at the first sign of trouble," Slade said. "If there's anything he's good at, it's saving his own ass."

"To be fair, most of us are good at doing that," I said. "In the meantime, I don't know about you all, but I think we should get out of here. They did mention reinforcements."

"Yeah." Hunter nodded. "We need the quickest way out of this building."

"That's probably the way I came," Slade said. "I found a side door and ducked in while they were delivering crates of champagne. That led into the kitchen."

His words reminded my stomach I was starving. It grumbled but I ignored it. Food would have to wait until we were clear of this place.

"Lead the way." Zeke nodded to Slade. "You and Hunter at the head. Parker, Asher and I will go last. Women in the middle."

As usual, everyone jumped to do what Zeke said. Not literally, because that would be feeding his ego.

"You should have joined the army," I told him.

"You too," he replied. "They might have taught you and Hunter some discipline."

I flipped him off.

Asher grinned but didn't say anything, instead gesturing for the women to move ahead of us. He took off his shirt and offered it to the petite blonde who almost shot me. She took it gratefully and slipped it on.

Of course then the rest of us were obligated to do the same. A few of the girls wore white shift dresses, but the ones in underwear, with damp hair, were soon wearing oversized T-shirts.

Who said chivalry was dead?

Not that long ago, I would have been disappointed at all of those women covering up.

Today, I didn't care. If they needed modesty, then fine. I hadn't known where to look anyway. I couldn't really stare anyway. Not without Lila potentially shooting me in the balls. That wouldn't work well for me or her.

We hurried down the corridor and descended another set of stairs, this one as cold and dank as the one on the other side of the building. The smell of food reached my nostrils long before we passed the kitchen. I was sorely tempted to bolt in, grab some food and bolt back out again.

The word 'reinforcements' kept me in line.

Caleb was going to be pissed off enough that we'd killed his people without us having to kill more of them.

Not to mention I was *almost* certain he didn't want three of his brothers dead today.

Don't quote me on that though. Fuck only knows what goes through Caleb's mind. He liked to think he was suave and sophisticated, but without doubt, his thoughts were as firmly in the gutter as the rest of us. After all, he was trying to sell women here. Hunter and I have done some dubious things, but never anything *that* dubious.

"Here's the door," Slade was saying. He glanced back at Zeke.

Zeke nodded. "Everybody down. Open the door carefully. Parker, Asher, keep an eye out behind us."

"So bossy," I mumbled. In spite of that, I turned around and readied my gun, just in case.

Daylight and air rushed in as Slade opened the door.

I glanced over my shoulder.

He and Hunter weren't killed with a barrage of bullets. Lila stood right behind my twin, gun in her hand too. She was so fucking hot. Of course she'd made it through and brought all those women with her. If anyone could do it, it was her. She was beyond incredible.

I turned back in time to see an asshole in a suit walk around the corner behind us. I knew he was an asshole, because he was my brother Caleb. I won't lie, the temptation to shoot him then and there was strong.

He was surrounded by a couple of ridiculously burly bodyguards, who would definitely kill me if I killed him. Fuck that, I wasn't in the mood to die today.

"I see you found your girlfriend," he said smoothly. His eyes grazed all the women before settling on Lila.

"Your powers of observation are on point as always," Zeke remarked. "Observe this. We're leaving and we're taking these women with us." He was never impressed with Caleb's arrogance and posturing.

"I don't see any women," Caleb replied mildly. "None I know anything about. I'm merely here on business. What a surprise to run into all of you."

"See no evil, speak no evil." Zeke looked unimpressed. "Typical Caleb. You never were good at taking responsibility for anything you did."

Caleb raised an eyebrow. "You have no proof I have anything to do with this. If you walk out the door, I won't stop you."

"What, not going to offer us a share of the profits?" Asher said dryly.

Caleb raised his other eyebrow. "Would you take it?"

Asher barked a laugh. "Fuck no."

"Asher is trying to think up a reason not to put a bullet in your head," Zeke said.

"He's right," Asher agreed. "But we've wasted enough time here. These women have been through hell already."

I glanced back at Lila. She held her gun like she had the same internal conflict as Asher.

On one hand, Caleb had a part in what happened to her. On the other, killing Caleb might put the rest of the Brantley family offside and she may need them if we were ever going to form an alliance.

"If I was you, I'd look for things to smuggle that aren't people," I remarked. "I have a feeling it won't end well for you next time."

"Don't threaten me," Caleb said coldly. "I have connections you could only imagine. Several who would be more than happy to slice your throat while you sleep."

"Back at you," I told him. I wasn't going to be intimidated by him. "Can we go now?" I asked Zeke. "I've had enough of this family reunion for one day."

Zeke nodded. "Let's go." He gestured for Hunter and Slade to lead the way out the door, but kept his eye on Caleb the entire time. So did I.

I didn't trust that he'd let us walk away with hundreds and thousands of dollars worth of what he considered merchandise. The only reason for him to do it was because if he tried to stop us, that would be his admission of his involvement with the operation. He'd rather lose money than get his hands visibly dirty.

I had no doubt in my mind at some point he'd make us pay for this. When he did, I'd be ready. If Hunter didn't decide to strike out at him first. With any luck, he'd piss someone else off first. I more or less loved Caleb, kind of. I didn't really want to be the one who killed him. I doubted he shared the same sentiment about me.

I walked backwards, following the others while keeping an eye on Caleb's bodyguards. I couldn't tell what they thought of all of this. They were like a pair of stone walls, dressed in expensive black suits. No one would ever mistake them for what they were. Trained hitmen who worked as my brother's protectors. They wouldn't hesitate to kill if he told them to.

Lucky for everyone involved, especially me, he didn't. I stepped over the threshold and outside into the shade between buildings.

No one stopped us, but people passing paused to stare before hurrying on. It probably wasn't the first time they saw strange happenings here. It probably wouldn't be the last.

"My only regret is not being able to watch Caleb explain to all those buyers that they're here for nothing," Asher remarked.

"You can go and watch if you like," Zeke said.

Asher grinned. "No thanks. My imagination is pretty good. Now, how are we going to get all of these women out of here?"

"If anyone suggests we go into the back of the truck, I will shoot their balls off," Lila growled.

"No one was going to suggest that," Slade assured her.

No one suggested calling the police either. Everyone was well aware Caleb was already telling all the men in suits to vacate the building. Or making up some excuse for being there. By the time the police arrived, the place would be cleaned up, dead bodies removed. Same with the sheds where we'd all been held. Even if the police believed what the women told them, they'd have no proof. Nothing they could pin on anyone. Apart from Hades, everyone involved in the operation was either dead or distancing themselves.

"I have an idea." Asher pulled out his phone, pressed the screen, and put it up to his ear. "Jackson—"

ten

LILA

"NOTHING SAYS subtle like a massive bus with Wolf Venom written down the side." I leaned back against Hunter and let him wrap his arms around me.

Hunter chuckled and nuzzled his face in my hair. "Sometimes being subtle is underrated."

"What would you know about being subtle?" Penn asked. The band's keyboardist glared at us. At the twins in particular. "You two are as subtle as a pimple on the end of a cock. Two pimples."

Parker laughed. "I see you still have your sense of humour intact."

Penn flipped him the bird.

The rest of the band was gathered near their manager, Jackson. Older than the rest of them by about a decade, I gathered he was also involved with Abbie. Three guys was plenty for me. I didn't know how she coped with seven. Unless they were all trained to put down the toilet seat.

"We also have another several of the tour cars coming," Jackson was saying to Slade. "We would have brought a rig truck, but Asher said no trucks." His denim blue eyes regarded the women before sliding over to me and the twins. The sides of his mouth pulled back slightly before he looked away from Hunter and Parker.

"Anyone would think they don't like us," Parker remarked.

"We don't," Penn told him. "You're a pair of assholes."

"What Penn said," Channing remarked. The band's saxophone player gave us a dark look, which was ironic given the things he got up to. Things, according to the twins, they'd helped him with.

"They're not worth it." Landon grabbed Channing's hand and pulled him over to where Abbie stood beside Zeke.

She was pretty, in spite of giving the twins the same look as all her guys did. Okay, in her case it was slightly understandable. They *had* kidnapped her. Twice. Up until now, I wasn't particularly sympathetic.

Now, I had some idea how it felt. Still, the twins were never going to do anything to her.

"Yes we are," Hunter said. "We're totally worth it."

Parker laughed and they exchanged high-fives.

"I see you two haven't grown up," Abbie told them.

"Nope," Parker agreed. "Still singing with these assholes?" He gestured around at the band and Jackson. "I bet you 'sing' really pretty."

The grin evaporated from his face when Penn lunged at him, and gripped him around the throat.

"You fucking little—"

Without thinking, I pulled away from Hunter, raised my gun and pressed it to the side of Penn's head.

"Get. Your. Hands. Off. Him," I growled.

In the corner of my eye, I saw Abbie pull out the gun Asher had at his hip. She aimed it at me, her blue eyes steel.

"Back the fuck off," she said coldly.

"You're not going to use that," Hunter told her.

"Don't count on it," Tully Cole, the band's lead guitarist, told him. His tone was cool and calm, almost amused. A trained assassin, not much ruffled his feathers.

"Zeke, don't make me threaten your girlfriend," Slade warned.

"Don't make me threaten *you*," Zeke replied.

"For love of..." Jackson sighed. "Everyone put your guns down. Have your pissing matches later. Right now, we need to focus on getting these women on the bus, in the cars and away from here."

Penn grunted something under his breath. "One more smart ass remark about Abbie and I'll break your nose again." He shoved Parker away and stalked off without even glancing back at me.

I looked at Abbie for a few long moments before we both lowered our guns. She handed hers back to Asher, but I kept hold of mine. The situation might have been deescalated for now, but the tension remained.

Parker rubbed at his throat. "You really would have killed Penn for me?"

I shrugged and stepped back into the circle of Hunter's arms. "No one gets to touch one of my guys like that."

If it was me, they wouldn't have hesitated to act either. Part of me was relieved I didn't need to kill anyone else. Yet.

Although—

"It was Penn who broke your nose?" For that, maybe I should put a bullet in his brain.

"Yeah, but it was no big deal," Parker said lightly. "Just a little misunderstanding."

"Nothing you didn't deserve," Penn said over his shoulder. He opened the door of one of the tour vans as it pulled up behind the bus, and started to wave several of the women over to climb in. A couple of them didn't seem to have a clue who he was, but most of them stared. If he noticed, he gave no sign. It was just another day in the life of a guy like him. People looked at all of them wherever they went.

The women would have a story to tell when they got home. It wasn't every day they got rescued by rock stars.

"He's such a prick," Hunter said softly, unexpected emotion in his tone.

I turned around to look at him. He wasn't quite as outspoken as Parker, but he wasn't usually gentle either.

He gave me a faint smile. "I let you down. What happened to you never should have happened."

I shook my head. "I don't even know what happened to you and Parker."

"Chloe, Zachary and Dane happened," he replied. "Your dear stepbrother had someone at the Academy slip something into our drinks. The assholes had us chained up until we managed to escape. We stumbled upon Zeke and managed to find you here."

There was clearly more to the story than that, but that was all the explanation I was getting for now. Or maybe ever. I didn't suppose the details mattered all that much.

"That same someone drugged my coffee," I said darkly. "I woke up in the back of the truck."

He locked his eyes on mine. "Did any of them touch you?"

I shook my head slowly. "Someone stripped me, but that was as far as it went."

I couldn't know what they did to me while I was out, but I preferred to assume nothing happened. If it did, I might be better off not knowing. Seeing what Brutus did to Danica was bad enough.

Hunter growled in the back of his throat. "That was more than too far. When I find out who did that, I will fucking kill them."

"I believe you." I stood on my toes and kissed his mouth. "But you may need to get in line. The next person whose head I hold a gun to may not be as lucky as Penn."

Hunter grinned. "I love it when you threaten violence. It's so fucking hot." He kissed the tip of my nose.

"All right, that's everyone but you four," Jackson was saying. "I can have the driver take you back to the Academy on the tour bus, if that's where you want to go."

"We were hoping you'd drive us," Parker told him.

"As tempting as that is," Jackson said sarcastically, "I have a tour to manage. As it is, you're lucky the guys and Abbie have a concert tomorrow night. Otherwise we wouldn't have been anywhere near here."

"I have my SUV," Slade said.

Parker grimaced. "Fuck. I was looking forward to travelling on that." He nodded towards the tour bus.

"You still can." Slade grinned.

"No deal," Jackson said firmly. "If you have alternative transport, you can take it. I'd prefer not to have the tour bus gallivanting all over the countryside."

"Has anyone ever told you you're a spoilsport?" Parker asked him.

"Of course not," Jackson said at the same time as Asher said, "Frequently."

Jackson turned around to raise an eyebrow at Asher.

Asher stuck his hands up to either side. "I know, I know. Drum machine."

Apparently that was some kind of private joke, because the rest of the band, and Abbie, laughed.

"Can we go?" I asked. A crowd was starting to gather around and stare at us. Of all the trafficked women, I was the last one. I didn't need people to gawk at me and wonder what I was doing standing on the street with a rock band. Especially since a couple of them, and Slade, were still shirtless.

"Of course we can, sweetheart," Hunter said. He slipped the gun out of my hand and put it away in the waistband of his jeans. "For safe-keeping."

I nodded. "As long as you give it back if we see Hades." I wouldn't hesitate to use it on him if he showed up. I had a feeling he was long gone by now. If I was him, I'd be in another state already. I'd keep a very, very low-profile for a while.

"Definitely," Hunter agreed. "If I don't kill him before I have a chance to give it back. I can't guarantee what my instincts will do in that situation. I also can't guarantee I won't kill Caleb the next time I see him."

"If he and Reuben agreed to stop trafficking women, he can live," I said. "He might come in useful someday." Fuck knew what for, but I couldn't afford to alienate too many people, even if their last name was Brantley and they weren't the twins.

"Agreed," Zeke said. "I knew he got up to some shady shit, but this is not okay. If he did this to Abbie, I'd rip his head off with my bare hands." He exchanged looks with the twins and something passed between them. Like, suddenly they had something in common. A shared goal.

"If anyone is interested, I'm not too happy with my brother right now either," Asher said. "I knew he'd do a lot to get power, but I didn't think he'd stoop this low." He actually gave me an apologetic look. As if he had any more control over Dane than I did.

"That makes several of us," Hunter said. "He wanted power, but what he's got was some powerful enemies."

"Including Caleb," Zeke said. "There's no way he would have asked anyone to take Lila. He would have known it would end badly. There's a reasonable chance he had no idea until we told him. One of his subordinates was acting outside his orders. Working with Dane, Chloe and

Zachary. I'll let you guess what that subordinate's chances are of living until the end of the year. Or week."

I exhaled softly. "It won't matter. Hades will pin everything on Brutus and he's dead. Anyone who could contradict Hades is probably dead too. Or they soon will be."

"Either way, Caleb prefers to use people than be used *by* people," Zeke said. "He may not shut this operation down forever, but he'll probably do it until he knows who was behind this. He'll want to avoid shit getting messy like this again."

"If there's anything Caleb hates, it's a mess," Hunter agreed. "But we will work on him to shut this down forever. There's plenty more shit he can get involved in."

He rubbed a weary hand over the back of his neck, reminding me he and Parker went through hell too.

"Maybe if we sit back for a little while, Caleb, Dane, Chloe and Zachary will take each other out," Parker said. He rubbed his hands together in gleeful anticipation of that possibility. If that was what happened, he'd be the first to suggest we bring popcorn and watch. Maybe a few beers and pizza.

"As awesome as that would be, that's too messy for Caleb," Hunter said. "He'll sit back and bide his time. Give them enough rope to hang themselves."

"Or he'll let Lila deal with them for him," Zeke said. He cocked his head at me. "Are you going back to Brutham?"

"Of course I am." I lifted my chin. "I'm not letting a little kidnapping and some human trafficking get in the way of my education." I didn't need to address the rest of what he said. We all knew I had every intention of dealing with them. I wasn't even close to broken, but by the time I was finished with them, they would be. Broken and begging for mercy.

eleven

"HOLY FUCKING HELL," Parker groaned. "This is so good." He closed his eyes and bit into his fifth slice of pizza. "Pizza is always good, but when you haven't eaten in weeks, it's even better."

"It wasn't weeks," Hunter told him. He looked no less blissed out.

"Id elt ike id," Parker said, his mouth full. He chewed and swallowed before saying, "I said, it felt like it."

"That was what we thought you said," Slade said over his shoulder. "Are you making a mess back there?"

"Not yet." Hunter grinned. "So far, we're only eating food." He grinned at me before biting into his slice.

I smiled back and ate with only slightly less enthusiasm than the twins. It wasn't very good pizza, but it was nicer than anything Hades and Brutus fed us.

Honestly, I only ate because I had to. All that killing and misery robbed me of my appetite. Remembering Mary and the way she died made my eyes sting. She was so sweet, so innocent. And me, who was far from being either of those things, survived. Some would say that was unfair. Others would say that was life.

I didn't know which was right. Maybe both, maybe neither.

"Are you all right?" Parker asked me.

"Yeah," I lied. "Just a little tired." I bit and chewed to avoid any more questions. For the moment anyway. I knew them better than to think they'd stop asking.

"You've all been through a lot," Slade said. "I feel as though..."

"None of this is your fault," I told him. "None of us knew Chloe had someone working for her, ready to drug drinks."

He said what I was thinking. "We should have anticipated it. Or better yet, beaten her to it."

"We didn't," I said. "But we're still standing. Imagine the look on her face when we step back into the halls of Brutham Academy. She's going to be livid her plan didn't work. Assuming she was working with Zachary and Dane."

"She definitely was," Hunter said. He glanced past me to Parker. Parker nodded.

"You should know, Chloe and Zachary are fucking. Dane was in on what happened to us, but fuck knows if he knows what their relationship is."

I wrinkled my nose. The last thing I wanted to imagine was my sister and my former stepbrother screwing each other's brains out.

"If Dane doesn't know, he should be told," I said.

"That's what we think," Hunter agreed. "We don't mind being the ones to tell him."

"I hope he doesn't know." Parker grinned. "Filling him in will be fucking awesome."

"With any luck, they'll tear each other apart." Hunter finished his slice of pizza and reached for another one.

"With even more luck, they'll take Chloe with them." I finished my own slice and licked my fingers.

"That would simplify matters," Slade said. He pulled the SUV to a stop at a red light. "It confirms what we all suspected though. Chloe was in on that teddy bear stunt."

"Chloe was in it balls deep," Parker said. "The bomb was some sort of decoy. Or a backup plan if the first one didn't get Lila. Or it might have been meant for Hunter and me. Either way, it wasn't meant to kill her. Zachary seemed smitten, from what we saw. But very much eating out of her hand. If she told him to curl up and suck his own cock, he'd do it."

I snorted a laugh and narrowly avoided choking on water when I opened the bottle to take a sip.

"Did you really ask Zachary to screw you?" Hunter asked. "That was the claim he made. Which we didn't believe, of course."

I grimaced and lowered the water bottle. "I might have been slightly... Pissed off when Chloe told me she fucked him. I mean, why her and not me?"

"That doesn't say much about his taste," Parker said. "I would have chosen you and only you."

"Of course you would," I told him. I wasn't naïve enough to think they wouldn't fuck my sister if I wasn't around. Before we were together, they'd fuck anyone who let them.

"Chloe led me to believe it was something magical and romantic between them. After Zachary and I screwed, she told me they were drinking and it just happened. I wondered if Zachary told her to make it out to be something special so I'd spread my legs for him."

Which was exactly what I did. I was young and dumb back then. I wouldn't fall for shit like that now. No, now it took a fake bomb to trick me.

Never again. There were only four people in this world I trusted and we were all in this car together, right now. Everyone else, I'd treat with suspicion. No one else would get close to me. Ever.

"I'm starting to dislike this Zachary asshole more and more." The light turned green and Slade moved the car away from the traffic light and toward the highway.

"Funny, I was just about to say the same thing," Parker remarked. "I've known some snakes in my time, but this dickhead is starting to piss me off."

"Bro, you're a long way behind if he's only *starting* to piss you off," Hunter told him. "He's been doing that to me for a while now. *Touch her and die* works in retrospect, right? Because the thought of him doing anything with you, makes me... I don't know, turn into a raging beast or something."

I patted his thigh. "The time will come that you can kill him if Dane doesn't do it first. I like the idea of you being a rage beast though. That's kinda hot."

"I'm a rage beast too," Parker said quickly. "I'm just the goofy rage beast."

"Yes you are," I told him. "You're *my* goofy rage beast."

"And you're my hero, because you would have shot Penn for me." Parker shoved the last of his pizza in his mouth and grinned.

"Do you think Abbie would have shot me if I shot him?" I didn't know her well, but she had a similar vibe to me. The kind that takes no shit from anyone. That explained how she dealt with seven boyfriends. Plus she had killed before to protect her guys. Only once, that I knew of, but that was all it took sometimes. Once you take that step, there's no going back.

"It would have been the last thing she did," Hunter growled. "And then killing her would be the last thing *I* did."

"And killing whoever killed you would be the last thing *I* did," Parker said. "And I wouldn't care because I don't want to live without either of you."

Slade cleared his throat.

"Or you," Parker said. "I think we can all agree we've grown attached to Slade too."

Slade looked up at the rear view mirror and grinned. "I've grown attached to you three too. When I realised all of you were missing..." His smile faded. "I don't think you've seen a raging beast until you saw what I would have done if anything bad happened to all of you."

"A few students would have failed?" Parker guessed.

Slade choked back a laugh. "That for starters. Things would get uglier and uglier from there."

"Has anyone offered you a drink?" I asked. The twins both turned to look at me. "They went after the three of us. They weren't going to leave without going after Slade too."

"That's true," Hunter said slowly. "Unless..."

"I'm not involved in anything that happened to any of you," Slade said quickly. "I've already told Lila I—"

"I believe you," I said. "Either they swung and missed, or they were hoping we wouldn't trust you because they didn't do anything to you. In which case, they swung and missed there too."

"Interesting." Hunter nodded.

"It really is," Parker said.

I frowned. "What is?"

"The fact they apparently think we don't trust each other," Hunter explained. "That might be because they don't trust each other. They might assume we're like them."

"Oh." He was right. "If that's the case, we can use that to our advantage."

Hunter smiled slowly.

I knew that look. That meant he was up to something. Something I may or may not want to know the details of. Sometimes, I was better off not knowing, if only for plausible deniability. If I didn't know what they were doing, I couldn't stop them.

"Should I ask?" I cocked my head at him.

"Definitely not." He looked like the proverbial cat that got the cream. He usually did, but he was particularly smug right now. "There's only one thing you should do right now."

He shoved the pizza box onto the floor in front of us, grabbed my legs and swung me around until my back was pressed against Parker.

"You should enjoy yourself." He pushed up my oversized T-shirt and smiled at my sheer panties. "I'd prefer none, but I like these."

He parted my knees with his hands and leaned over to the full extent of the seatbelt to bury his face between my legs.

He pulled my panties aside and licked my pussy from bottom to top, then back down again. "You taste better than any pizza ever could." He kissed all around my pussy while tracing circles on my inner thigh with the pad of his thumb. He had me trembling in moments.

"I don't think I've been compared to pizza before," I said breathlessly.

"Favourably compared," he said. "Always favourably."

"Definitely." Parker gripped my chin and turned my face around just far enough to kiss me.

"You both realise how unfair this is," Slade grumbled. "I'm going to have to drive with a painful boner."

"Keep your eyes on the road," Parker told him. "I'm sure you had plenty of time with our girl while everyone thought we were off working for Reuben."

I remembered how he got me off on his desk while speaking to my father on the phone. My face and neck heated.

Hunter lifted his mouth from me and smiled. "Lila's blush says it all. I'm glad you were having fun while we were chained up."

He wasn't even being sarcastic. He was genuinely happy we were enjoying ourselves in spite of their absence and the reason for it. Of course, he wouldn't want me to go without orgasms. The twins were sweet that way.

"We have some time to make up for," Parker said. He pulled the T-shirt up further and slipped his hands into my sheer bra. He palmed and pinched my nipples while Hunter worked my clit into a shallow, quick orgasm followed by a deeper, longer one.

I felt as though I was floating above the earth, above the atmosphere. Somewhere out in space surrounded by stars. Weightless and tangled in bliss. A moment of precise perfection and pleasure. A place I would have liked to stay forever. Carefree and happy.

By the time I came back down from the second one, his face was shining, wet with my juices.

He sat up a little and licked his lips. "Best meal of the day. Of the year."

Parker slipped his hands out of my bra and pushed the T-shirt back down. "We have a long drive back to the Academy. Get some sleep. We'll keep an eye out for trouble."

"You should rest too." I tried to stifle a yawn but failed.

"We'll rest when we get back," Hunter said. "Right now, you need it more than we do. Don't stress, we'll be right here." He smiled and added, "I love you."

"I love you too." I nestled back against Parker and closed my eyes. I probably shouldn't sleep, but I was exhausted. That was the last thought I had before sleep claimed me.

twelve

PARKER

"HOME SWEET HOME," I said as Slade pulled his SUV into a parking space and cut the engine. "Are you sure you want to do this?" I wound a thick strand of Lila's hair around my finger. I let it bounce free before winding another strand. Her hair was so soft, I could play with it all day. Currently it smelled like roses mixed with some kind of spice. Not her usual scents but compelling nonetheless.

"No, I'd rather spend the rest of my life in the back seat of this car," she said sarcastically.

Hunter grinned. "Funny, I was thinking the exact same thing." He twisted his upper body and pretended to crawl over to her.

She batted him away. "Save it until we're inside. I probably look like shit anyway." She sat up and looked at her reflection in the rearview mirror.

I clasped her shoulders and drew her back down. "You could never look like shit. Even if you looked like a potato, you'd still be gorgeous."

"Because the main ingredient of most of your favourite foods is the potato," she said. "If they added potato to pizza, you'd be in heaven."

"I'm not saying you're wrong about that," I said slowly, "But I am saying you're my favourite food, not the humble potato. Although, heaven would involve somehow adding beer to potato pizza."

When it came to actual food, I had relatively simple tastes. Especially compared to Reuben and Caleb. Joshua too. They were all born

226

with a silver spoon up their asses and a taste for the finer things. Zeke, Lucas, Hunter and me, we preferred burgers to caviar. And beer to Bollinger. Although, I wouldn't say no to a glass of champagne most of the time.

Caleb, Reuben and Joshua would probably say it was because our mother didn't have the class as theirs. Since our father probably murdered their mother to marry ours, I'd never know.

Our family was nothing if not complicated. The only thing we knew for certain was that Zeke was conceived before our father's first wife died. If my father wanted someone out of the way, they were removed.

Until Dane and Asher's father removed him and my mother. That was the main reason for the DiMarco family's downfall. They made a bid for power. They failed. Sucked to be them.

"That's disgusting." Lila wrinkled her nose.

"You say that now, but if someone invented it, you'd try it. You might even like it." I opened the door and stepped out before turning back and taking Lila's hand. I didn't want to let her out of my sight, much less let go of her physically. We were all going to have to be a lot more careful from now on. I thought we were before, but Chloe and her merry assholes proved us wrong.

For now.

"I'd settle for a long hot soak in the bath, a glass of wine and a platter of cheese, crackers and grapes." She sighed.

"We can organise two of those." Slade locked the car after us. "The only thing this place is missing are bathtubs in all the bathrooms. Or any of them."

"That was remiss of them." Hunter looked around slowly before leading us across the car park toward the Academy building.

"Remiss? That was downright neglectful," I said. "The school board should be ashamed of themselves. A person can get spanked, but can't have a long soak afterwards. What the absolute fuck?" I was only half joking.

"At least a person can get spanked." Slade's gaze slid over to Lila and he smiled.

"I knew you two were having fun without us." I sniffed. "I can't believe I missed a perfectly good spanking. It was good, right?"

Lila snorted the softest laugh. "It was definitely good. Don't worry, we can recreate it. Later. I'm sure Slade wouldn't mind spanking you."

Slade regarded us both, his eyebrows slightly elevated. "Is that what you want to see?" he asked her.

Her smile widened. "It might be." She clearly wasn't sure what, if anything, there might be between Slade and me or Hunter.

Honestly, I didn't know either. Right now, I felt like we were busy staying alive. That might have to be our priority at the moment. We had plenty of time to explore possibilities when we weren't dodging spiked drinks, assholes with guns and dickheads like Hades Turner.

"Let's get inside and worry about that later," Hunter said. "I don't like being out in the open like this. We don't know what might be waiting for us. Everyone be on alert."

He didn't need to tell us that, we all were anyway. So far, everything seemed normal. Music pumped out from the vicinity of the Academy bar. Voices shouted and laughed. They probably moaned as well, but I couldn't hear any of them.

Dozens of the windows, and the side of the building were lit. Windows sat open to let in the breeze, leaving the spaces inside protected by the not-quite-bullet-proof screens outside the not-quite-bullet-proof glass.

Apparently actual bullet-proof glass was both expensive and a safety hazard for people needing to get out of the building. Personally, I thought it was a corner the school board shouldn't have cut, like having baths, but I doubted they gave a fuck what I thought. Even Reuben and Samuel Bell, who both sat on the school board.

Hunter trotted up the steps in front of us and pushed the doors open.

Nothing exploded, imploded or collapsed. No one shot at us. The building didn't catch on fire. There wasn't even a stampede of man eating chickens, or fuck knows whatever else Chloe might think up.

"Okay." Hunter gestured for us to follow him before he stepped inside and hurried over to the staircase.

A few students gave us funny looks as they passed by, but no one seemed surprised to see us. They didn't even seem surprised us three guys weren't wearing shirts. Then again, we were us. Strange behaviour was kinda our thing. Hunter liked to refer to it as keeping them guessing, but whatever.

Either way, no one took any notice of us.

We walked up the stairs like we owned the place. Nothing to see here. No one was chained up. No one was trafficked. We just went out to do some stuff and now we were back. That was the impression we tried to convey. Whether or not we pulled it off was another matter.

I mean, of course we did. Totally.

We stopped outside Lila's door.

"Fuck," Hunter said softly. When we all turned to him in alarm, he added. "I don't have a key."

Slade grinned. "Thank fuck I do then." He separated one from the others on his keyring and slipped it into the lock.

"Do I want to know how you got that?" Lila asked.

He flashed her a grin. "Probably not. The fact is, I have one and this lock is being changed in the morning. Along with some other security measures."

She raised a hand to her ear. "Including a new earring with a tracker in it."

"And a clit ring?" I asked hopefully. "And cock piercings for Hunter and me. And Slade."

"I thought you loved me." Lila stepped into her room once Slade gave her the all clear.

"I do." I frowned at her.

"Then why would you want all three of your cocks out of commission at the same time?" She sniffed.

"We still have tongues," I pointed out. "And fingers."

"Personally, I'd prefer a nipple piercing," Hunter said. He closed and locked the door behind us. "Then Lila can have my cock all she wants while yours heal." He grinned.

"I've always wanted to get my ears pierced," I said. As curious as I was to know how a cock piercing felt, I didn't want to disappoint Lila. I especially didn't want to watch Hunter fuck her while I couldn't. That would suck in sixty-nine different ways.

"Let's worry about who is getting what pierced later." Slade inspected the window frames before pulling the curtains closed over them. "Everything seems safe here."

"Good." Hunter slipped into the bathroom and started the shower. "Queens first." He gave Lila a low bow and a cheeky grin. He pointed a finger at me as I was about to open my mouth. "You're not a queen."

"That depends on who you ask," I retorted. Still, I was happy to help Lila out of her oversized T-shirt and into the steaming shower. I tugged off my jeans and followed her in. While she grabbed the body wash and started on the front of herself, I pumped shampoo onto my hand and washed her hair.

"Take a step back." I rinsed her hair, then applied conditioner and rubbed it in. I washed my hair and body quickly, then stepped out to let Hunter step in and rinse the conditioner out of Lila's hair.

Slade climbed in with them and ran his hands over her wet, shining breasts.

Both guys washed her legs, occasionally bumping hands until she was clean. While she languished under the water, they washed themselves. Shame, I was kinda hoping they'd wash each other.

By the time Hunter turned off the water, I was dry and holding out a towel to each of them.

"Thanks, bro." Instead of drying himself, Hunter turned to dry Lila. She raised her arms to let him rub the towel all over her, then handed him the dry one to use on himself.

While Slade and Hunter dried, I took Lila's hand and led her over to her bed. I lay her down, then lay over her, my weight on my knees and elbows.

"I missed you." I kissed her mouth slowly, careful not to push her too hard. After what she'd been through, I wasn't going to assume how ready she was for anything more than my tongue on her clit. If that was all she wanted, I was only too happy to oblige.

She surprised me by wrapping her legs around my waist. "I missed you too."

"I love your voice," I told her. It was so husky and hot. It never failed to make me hard, no matter what she was saying. She could read out a shopping list and my cock would pay attention.

"I love yours." She kissed me, her tongue sliding across my lips and pressing inside my mouth.

I wanted to devour her, starting with her tongue and working my way down from here. I wanted to touch every centimetre of her. I wanted to bury myself deep inside her.

"Leave some for us." The bed dipped as Hunter lay down on one side of us.

A moment later, Slade joined us on the other side. "Do you three mind if I..."

"You're one of us now," Hunter told him. "As long as it's all right with Lila."

Lila broke off our kiss. "It's more than all right with me. I want to be with all of you." She kissed me again.

Hunter slipped his hand between us and down to the top of her thighs.

She lowered her feet to the bed. I rolled to the side just enough to give him access to her clit.

"You're so wet for us," Hunter marvelled. He drew his hand back to let Slade feel how wet her pussy was.

"Very wet," Slade agreed. He rubbed his fingers over her clit in tiny circles. "So warm, wet and gorgeous."

Hunter slid his hand under Slade's and pressed a couple of fingers inside her.

"Mmm, that feels so..." Her words were lost in a moan and the rolling of her hips against both of their hands.

"Come for us," Hunter said softly. "Let us give you this."

"I... Mmm..."

She came, panting and moaning, the most beautiful singing I ever heard. Her back arched, breath fast. Just watching and listening almost made me lose my load then and there. She was a fucking goddess. One I fully intended to worship forever.

Finally, she flopped down against the mattress and lay still for a while, catching her breath until both guys pulled their hands from her delicious pussy.

I waited until she was ready and rolled us over until she was straddling me. She looked down at me and smiled before she lowered herself onto my cock.

"Holy fuck." She always felt like the best kind of heaven.

Hunter opened the drawer beside the bed and pulled out a bottle of lube. He handed it to Slade.

"Only if you're sure?" Slade said to Lila, his head cocked to the side.

Her eyes were round. "God, yes please," she panted.

Under Hunter's gentle guidance, she leaned forward.

Slade slathered lube over her rear hole. He tossed the lube aside and stretched her slowly and carefully with a finger, then another.

"Please," she breathed.

He positioned himself behind her and slid inside her gradually, stopping every few moments to stretch her before he slid in all the way. The tip of his cock bumped into mine, separated only by a wall of muscle. An eloquent grunt slid from between the teacher's lips.

"So fucking good."

"Fuck yeah," I breathed. Sheathed in her warmth, while feeling Slade filling her ass was beyond bliss. I don't know what it was. There's no word for anything this incredible. It doesn't need one. This moment was just for us.

Hunter knelt beside her and slid his cock into her mouth.

I glanced over to see the same more-than-bliss expression I probably wore. We went through hell and we fucking survived. We deserved this moment for ourselves. This and more.

I looked back at Lila, her mouth full of cock.

"I love you," I told her.

Her smile around Hunter's dick was all the answer I needed. She loved me too.

Slade set the rhythm, thrusting into her and pushing her onto us. Over and over, slow as honey at midnight in the middle of winter, but warmer. Definitely that sweet though. Sweeter.

No one hurried. None of us wanted to. This could be our last night together. We needed to make it last as long as we could. To cherish every sensation.

Finally, Slade increased the rhythm. He drove us all harder and harder until one by one, we all came. Shattered apart into a million fragments before we came back together, sweating, but oh-so fucking satisfied.

thirteen

PARKER

"HEY, ASSHOLE," I said cheerfully. That wasn't the customary way to greet a teacher, even at Brutham, but in Dane DiMarco's case, it was appropriate.

He glanced up from his computer screen. A flicker of surprise crossed his face. He composed himself quickly. Not quickly enough, but he tried.

"Well, if it isn't the Brantley brats." He leaned back in his chair and laced his fingers behind his head. His resemblance to Asher was subtle. Where Asher was blonde, Dane had dark hair to match his soul. Asher got the smiles and personality, while Dane got the suspicious nature and asshole vibe.

"Not expecting to see us?" Hunter sat on the corner of Dane's desk. "I bet you weren't. Not until Chloe told you the time was right anyway."

I sat on the other corner. "Dude, you are the very definition of pussy whipped."

Dane laughed. "Pot, meet kettle. What are you doing here?"

"You were expecting us to be dead?" Hunter's tone was ice cold, dangerous. Even I was freaked out when he spoke like that. Crossing me was a bad idea. Crossing my brother was the closest thing to a death sentence a person could get without an actual bullet through their brain.

"Or chained up for a while longer?" I glanced over at my twin. "Maybe the plan was to auction us off too."

"Now there's an idea," Dane said slowly. "I'm sure we could find someone who needs a couple of boys who know how to dig."

It was my turn to laugh. "I didn't realise you were a comedian."

"I would have thought a pair of clowns would recognise one," Dane said dryly. "What do you want?"

If he thought he'd insult us by calling us clowns, he'd have to think again. We'd been called a lot worse by better people than him.

"Did you know Chloe and Zachary were fucking each other?" Hunter asked bluntly. "Park and I had the...pleasure of hearing them while we were chained up."

"We'll be sending them the bill for our therapy," I said. "It's going to take a long time to get past hearing that." Spending the night lying under Chloe's bed while she and Dane fucked was bad enough.

"If anyone needs therapy it's—" Dane started.

"Most people," Hunter snapped. "There's nothing wrong with admitting you have issues. You didn't answer the question. Did you know about Chloe and Zachary?"

One side of Dane's mouth drew back. "Yes, I know. If you thought you could come here and stir up trouble by telling me that, you were wrong."

Hunter glanced at me. "Sounds like trouble in paradise to me." He looked back at Dane. "So you knew, but you're clearly not happy about it. Don't like sharing?"

"I'm not going to discuss this with you." Dane closed the lid of his laptop. "I'm sure you have enough problems of your own without coming here to bother me about mine."

"Not at all," Hunter said lightly. "We don't mind. Consider it a complimentary therapy session from us. Go ahead and vent." He gave Dane a 'give it to me' gesture with his fingers.

When Dane didn't speak, Hunter continued.

"Zachary is a prick and you don't want to share Chloe with him. Maybe you don't want to share with anyone else. But you want her and if that's the only way you'll have her..." He cocked his head at Dane. "Am I getting warmer?"

"Is there a point to this conversation?" Dane snapped. "Because, if

---

there isn't, you can both fuck off. We'll be sure to do a more thorough job next time."

"Ouch," I said with a laugh. "I think he's threatening us, Hunt."

"Yeah, I got that vibe too, Park," Hunter agreed. He fixed his gaze on Dane. "Here's the thing. We don't like Zachary. We're pretty sure you don't like him either. I'm not entirely convinced his agenda is—how do I put it—Chloe-friendly. It's certainly not Lila-friendly. Do you think you can trust him or do you think he would shove both of them out of the way to take Samuel Bell's place if he got half a chance? Be honest with yourself if not with us, because we think we have a common enemy."

"If you think I'm working with you..." Dane scoffed.

"Fuck no," Hunter replied. "You're missing the point."

Dane looked at him coldly. "What is the point then?"

"The point is, neither of us wants Zachary to push Lila and Chloe out of the way. Parker, Slade and I are going to keep a close eye on Mr Zachary Sinclair. I suggest you do the same."

Hunter leaned in toward Dane. "Ask yourself this: Is there even the slightest chance Zachary would have let off that bomb in the vicinity of Chloe? I know that wasn't Chloe's plan, but can you be sure it wasn't his? Right now, I feel like we're living in an enormous spiderweb. Tangled as hell and sticky as fuck. We're going to look out for our woman. We have no doubt you plan to do the same thing. But remember something. Parker and I messed with her birth control. Zachary messed with a *bomb*. Who do you think is the greater threat?" He sat back.

"If you're not suggesting we work together then what?" Dane asked carefully.

"Just be on alert," Hunter said with a shrug. "No one will mind if you take out Zachary for overstepping. And he will. I'm willing to bet a big chunk of my trust fund he doesn't want to share with you. He might have a plan in place to get rid of you. Would you be all that surprised if he did?"

"I teach at Brutham Academy," Dane pointed out. "Nothing would surprise me less than a plot against me or anyone else. Hell, you two probably have a plan to get rid of me."

Hunter grinned. "Actually, we don't, but now you mention it, maybe we should. What do you think, Park?"

"He *did* hold us down so Zachary could inject that shit into our veins," I said slowly. "But I'd turn my back on Dane faster than I'd turn it on Zachary. Or Chloe, to be honest. Given the way Dane's cousin Ric has managed to get in with Caleb, I'd think there was an opening if Dane wanted to take it."

"Exactly," Hunter agreed. "We don't have to be enemies. We don't have to work together either, but we could be... Is 'allies' too strong a word?"

"I think so," I said. "How about non-enemies? As in we basically leave each other alone. Although, Dane did threaten us a moment ago."

"I'm sure he was just surprised to see us alive and well. To be honest, I'm slightly surprised myself." Hunter placed his hand, palm down, on the desktop and leaned on it. "Killing us is a lot harder than it sounds."

"They say the same about cockroaches," Dane drawled. "The world will end, but there will still be cockroaches crawling the earth."

I grinned. "Yes, we are very resilient. Thank you for pointing that out. We're also smart. Smart enough to know who the real enemy is, and who should be neutralised, even if it means sleeping with the enemy. Not literally," I added quickly.

"We all knew you didn't mean it literally," Hunter said. He hopped down off Dane's desk. "I think we've taken up enough of your time. All we ask is that you think about what we said. If you don't, you're probably going to end up dead...pretty soon. That would be a shame." He started towards the door.

I slipped off the desk to follow.

Hunter stopped, his hand on the doorknob. He turned back to Dane, a sly look in his eyes.

"It would be a shame if you died before you saw Mina again."

Dane stiffened. "What are you talking about?" He placed his hands on the desk in front of him and pushed himself to his feet. "What do you know about my sister?"

"Oops," Hunter said as though he wasn't deliberately provocative. "You didn't know?"

"Know what?" Dane demanded. "Mina got married young and

decided to stay away from this life." He didn't look entirely certain of that.

"Some of that is accurate," Hunter agreed. "But if you don't know, it's probably not my place to tell you." He started to twist the knob.

Dane lurched around the desk, and towards us. "What. Do. You. Know?"

"You should ask Asher." I had no guilt at all for throwing Dane's younger brother under the proverbial bus. Better him than us.

"I'm asking you," Dane snapped. He looked like he was ready to grab both of us by the throat and strangle us simultaneously. It might be entertaining to see him try, however unlikely it was that he'd overpower both of us at the same time. Or individually.

"Where the *fuck* is she?"

I glanced at Hunter. He shrugged.

My gaze returned to Dane. "She's with Reuben," I said. "And when I say *with*—"

"Bullshit," Dane snapped. "She would never..."

"It's a long story and you didn't hear it from us," Hunter said. "I promise you, she's fine. Happy." He paused for a moment. "As happy as she can be. Reuben, Damien and Gianni take good care of her. Better than her fucking asshole husband did."

I grunted. If there was anyone who deserved a slow, painful death, it was Kurt Lasalle.

Dane shook his head. "You're full of shit."

"Like we said, ask Asher. He's seen her. We saw him see her." He was as impressed as Dane, but Hunter wasn't lying when he said our brother and his right-hand men were taking care of her. Helping her heal. I never would have guessed I'd be thinking that about Reuben, of all people. Even fuckers like him can surprise you once in a while.

Dane looked conflicted. He clearly didn't want to believe us, but chances were he'd be on the phone to Asher the moment we stepped out of his office. When he discovered we were telling the truth, he'd wonder what else we were telling the truth about.

My second favourite kind of fuck was a mind fuck.

"Get out," Dane said, his voice dangerously soft. "Stay the fuck away from me and Chloe. And anyone else in my family."

Hunter smirked. "That could be difficult, we're practically brothers-in-law."

"Get. The. Fuck. Out," Dane ground out. His face turned pink with fury. If he had a gun in his hand right now, he'd likely shoot our balls off. Lucky for all of us he didn't. I was, personally, very attached to my balls.

"All right, all right, we're going. Don't get your panties in a twist." Hunter opened the door and waved for me to step out first. He followed me out and closed the door behind us.

"That was a lot more fun than it should have been." He grinned.

"Messing around with Dane is always fun." I leaned over and pressed my ear to the door. Just as I suspected, it sounded like Dane was speaking to someone, his tone demanding. I couldn't make out the words, but the gist was clear enough. I almost felt sorry for Asher on the other end of the call. Almost, because if he got the chance, the drummer would probably kill us. And besides, he could have told Dane the truth ages ago. That was definitely not my problem or fault.

"She's what?" Dane roared.

"Come on, Park, our work here is done. This bit of it anyway. Now it's time to have even more fun."

I grinned. As much fun as it was to screw with Dane, there were other people it was more fun to screw around with. Figuratively speaking, of course.

fourteen

LILA

"DO I want to know what's going on?" I eyed my drink carefully, even though I'd watched Hunter open the can and check my glass carefully before pouring the contents in. He did the same with his beer. So did Parker and Slade.

"You'll know soon enough." Hunter toasted me with his glass and took a sip.

"I'm sure you'll be interested to know Gavin, who worked behind the bar, quit yesterday," Slade said. "He was also a barista."

"He had his fingers in a lot of drinks," Parker remarked. "Literally."

"I presume his income was supplemented by Chloe," I said.

"That's our suspicion," Hunter agreed. "We have some people looking for him. When we find him, we'll get some answers out of him." He sipped again and smiled.

"He's going to regret his life choices." I took a sip of my vodka, lemon and lime.

"He really is," Parker agreed.

Slade jerked his head towards the entrance. "Here we go."

Chloe and Zachary.

They both hesitated when they saw us. Flashes of surprise and confusion laced their exchanged glance.

Chloe set her lips in a firm, pale line and tossed her hair before stalking to the bar to get drinks.

Zachary hurried after her, speaking low in her ear.

"Interesting," Hunter drawled. "Either they weren't working with Hades, or he wasn't forthcoming about us all getting away alive."

"Not gonna lie, if I was him, I wouldn't have told them anything," Parker said. "That would lead to a one way trip to, you know, Hades."

He and Hunter high-fived.

Slade shook his head at them but smiled. "I agree, I wouldn't have told them either. Let Brutus take the blame. There's no reason for Hades to step forward and take it. He's an asshole, but he's not stupid."

"It would be a lot easier if he was," Parker pointed out. His gaze was on Chloe and Zachary, clearly expecting something to go down.

"You're making me nervous," I told him.

He turned his face and gave me an apologetic grin. "You have no reason to be nervous. We have the situation well in hand. Right, Hunt, Slade?"

"Definitely," Hunter agreed.

Slade sat back and nodded. "Let's just say I'm glad I'm not on the opposite side to these two." He jerked his head towards the twins. "They don't get called evil for nothing."

Both of the twins grinned.

"Exactly, but this will top off all of that," Hunter said.

I glanced over as Chloe and Zachary settled on the couch on the other side of the room. She crossed her knees and leaned against the arm like she owned the place.

I wanted to scratch her eyes out.

"We should ask them to join our next Kink or Drink," Parker remarked. "Them and Dane. It would be fun to see the expression on their faces when one of them paddles Chloe while the other has to watch."

Hunter chuckled. "That would be fun, but this is going to be more fun." He rubbed his hands together and smiled like a cartoon villain.

"And we have front row seats," Parker added.

I turned back to my sister and former stepbrother as his phone rang. He pulled it out of his pocket and scowled the screen before pressing the device to his ear.

Whatever the person on the other end said, it quickly had him agitated. He gestured with his other hand while he spoke and listened.

Chloe put a hand on his arm and looked concerned. He shook his head and hung up the call. He said something to her as he tucked his phone back into the pocket of his jeans. She didn't look happy about it, but she lowered her hand and sat back.

Zachary leaned over to kiss her cheek, then rose and hurried out of the bar.

I frowned. "Is that what we're waiting for?"

"Nope, it gets better," Hunter said. "Keep watching, but don't look too much like you're watching. We don't want her to think we're up to something."

"We *are* up to something," Parker said.

"Of course we are, but we don't want her to know that." Hunter downed a gulp of beer.

"Right, play it cool." Slade sipped his own beer and draped an arm over the back of the couch behind me. "We're here to enjoy the fact we're all still alive. Nothing more."

"That is something to celebrate." My mind kept returning to Mary. She filled my dreams. Her and Brutus. Him trying to force himself on a dying woman... I woke with the urge to throw up. And to punch my sister and Zachary for having any part in that. They'd clearly taken women who looked like me in the hope of making it harder to find me. Hunting down one brown eyed brunette amongst several would have been difficult. Mary was dead because she looked like me. Not for any other reason.

"Here we go," Hunter muttered.

Chloe blinked hard and shook her head. Her head flopped to one side, then the other. Her eyes rolled back and she slumped onto the couch.

"She's—" I started to stand, but Slade pressed a hand to my shoulder, keeping me down.

"Not dead," he said. "She's not fully unconscious either. Just...incapacitated."

My eyes widened as a couple of fellow students, second years like the twins, approached Chloe, smiles on their faces.

Her eyes were still open. They widened. Fear. Understanding. Terror.

A chill passed right through me.

"They're not going to..."

"It's what she arranged for you to go through," Hunter said, his tone dark with simmering rage. Every drop directed at Chloe.

"She organised for you to be sold to someone who would force themselves on you. She wanted you broken. We're returning the favour." He smiled and gulped the last of his beer.

The two guys hooked their shoulders under Chloe's arms and pulled her to her feet. One held her upright before the other scooped her into his arms.

I must have imagined hearing her whimper, because the music in the bar was too loud for that. She was virtually paralysed. Completely unable to fight back against what they'd do to her. It wouldn't just be the two of them either. They would use her and use her until—

I shot up out of my seat so fast I spilled vodka all over my hand. I barely noticed.

"We can't let them do that to her. I know what she would have done to me, but... I just can't. Please. Make it stop."

"Of course—" Before Hunter could finish his sentence, Dane stalked into the room.

He saw the two guys with Chloe and his face turned red.

"What the fuck are you doing?" he demanded.

The one carrying her smiled as though they weren't up to anything. "Hi, sir. She fell asleep. We were going to take her to her room and tuck her in."

Dane gave them both a disbelieving look and all but hauled Chloe into his own arms. "I'll take her from here."

"I'm sure you will, sir," the other student said. He grinned and ducked away before Dane could respond.

Dane glanced over at me and my guys. His eyes narrowed, but he must have caught sight of the worry in my eyes. The sides of his mouth drew back, but he nodded and carried Chloe out of the bar.

"Mission accomplished." Hunter looked smug.

I sat back down, feeling numb. "You weren't planning to let them rape her?"

He shrugged. "If that happened, it happened. But this way, Chloe and Dane no longer trust Zachary. He bought her a drink and then left. Does that say suspicious as fuck to you?"

"Who was really on the phone?" I asked.

"His grandmother," Slade said. "Nice lady. Very receptive to a healthy deposit into her bank account." He looked as smug as Hunter.

I closed my eyes for a moment. "You bribed Zachary's grandmother to call him up and pretend there's some emergency?" After a moment I added, "Or was there a real emergency?"

"Oh, it's real." Parker grinned. "But I'm sure he'll be able to help get her kitten out of that tree."

If anyone would consider that to be an emergency, it would be my former step grandmother. She was very attached to her cats.

"She'll let us know when he leaves her place to come back here," Slade added.

"Trust you to sweet talk an old lady," I told him.

He grinned. "Like I said, she's a nice woman. I'm definitely going to try the cake recipe she emailed me."

"You sweet talk old ladies and you cook." I shook my head in amazement. "Who even are you?"

He laughed. "One of the guys who would do anything for you." He leaned in and kissed my mouth.

"You know if Zachary manages to get back in with Chloe, they're going to retaliate for this," I said. "If Dane hadn't arrived when he did..."

"You would have stopped it." Slade took my hand and squeezed lightly. "Chloe would have been grateful."

"Was that part of the plan too?" I asked.

The guys all exchanged a glance.

"That was a variable we couldn't one hundred percent factor in," Parker said. "There was every chance Tyson and Felix could have had her right here in front of everyone and you would have sat back and watched. Personally, I couldn't see you doing that. Not even after what she did to you."

"Don't mistake me for a good person," I warned. "I just... I couldn't see any woman go through what Danica did. What Mary almost did. Chloe might have been happy to have it happened to me, but that doesn't mean I have to do the same to her."

I exhaled softly. "Maybe my dad is right, I'm not cut out to lead the family. I'm not ruthless enough."

"You definitely are," Slade said. "There's a fine line between being ruthless and being an asshole. Hunter, Parker and I walk that line, so you don't have to."

"You all would have let it happen to her?" I looked from one to the other, to the other.

"I would have brought the popcorn." Parker grinned.

"I would have brought the beer," Hunter said.

"I would have helped them eat and drink it," Slade said. "It might have been the thing that forced her to step aside and stop competing with you. It might have prevented whatever she might do after this. There may come a day when you wish it happened."

I chewed over that thought for a moment. Long enough to realise he was right. If I was going to win this thing, I was going to have to toughen the fuck up. Whatever that took.

I should have been horrified that the guys would let my twin sister be raped, but it cemented the fact there was nothing they wouldn't do for me. No length they wouldn't go to.

"It makes you feel any better, I wouldn't have touched her," Hunter said.

"Me either," Parker agreed.

"Me three." Slade nodded firmly. "Not unless that was something you needed me to do." I couldn't tell what he thought of that idea.

There was no way that should have been hot, but it fucking was. For half a second I enjoyed the thought of Slade holding Chloe down and ramming himself into her. Her cries of pain and anguish...

Yeah, I was as fucked up as they were.

fifteen

LILA

I DIDN'T SEE Zachary before he grabbed me from behind, whirled me around and pressed me against the corridor wall, his body against mine. His hand closed around my throat.

"Fucking psycho bitch," he growled. "Don't think I don't know what you did to Chloe." His breath was hot on my cheek.

"I didn't do anything to Chloe," I said as evenly as I could with my heart racing. I hated the fact he took me by surprise, but I composed myself. My father would be proud of me for recovering so quickly.

"Never show them fear, or they know they have you by the balls," he would have said.

I tipped my chin up and stared Zachary down, unflinching. "You're the one who seems to enjoy spiking people's drinks."

His hand tightened. "I didn't do anything to her. I sure as fuck didn't *drug* her."

"Says you," I retorted. "What's wrong? Chloe and Dane don't believe you're not involved?" Judging by the flicker of anger on his face, that was exactly the case. Exactly what the twins and Slade wanted.

"Don't tell me, Chloe won't suck your dick anymore?" I gave him a smile laced with sarcasm.

He glared at me. "Maybe I should make you suck my dick instead."

"Only if you want me to bite it off." There was no way my mouth was going anywhere near his cock.

He pressed me harder into the wall, then stepped back and crossed his arms.

"It's a shame Chloe's plan didn't work. I would have paid money to watch whoever bought you break you. Hell, I would have settled for photos of the mascara running down your face."

"And you call me a fucking psycho," I retorted. "What sort of sick fuck arranges for women to be abducted and sold?"

"Your father," he suggested. "Have you ever done anything to stop him? Have you ever said a single fucking word? Or have you let it go on for years and years? How many women have been raped while you did nothing?"

I managed to contain a flinch. "I didn't know any better. Now I do. It won't be happening when I take over the family. I sure as hell wouldn't organise for someone to be taken just to get them out of the way."

"No, you'd organise for your sister to be drugged and raped by her classmates for your own amusement. Let me guess, Hunter, Parker and Slade were going to take their turns with her too. You're all as fucked up in the head as each other."

"Hypocrisy isn't a good look for you," I told him. "I did nothing to Chloe. If Dane hadn't stepped in when he did, I would have."

Zachary gave a bitter laugh. "Bullshit. You wouldn't have done a single thing."

"What would you have done?" I asked. "Like I said, you're the one who likes to spike drinks. Did you drug hers just to see if you could have some fun with her? Maybe you like fucking women when they're unconscious."

He dropped his hands, lunged towards me and pinned me to the wall again. "Maybe I should find out." He pressed his growing erection into the side of my hip.

"Maybe I should cut off your balls and have them made into dumplings for Chloe to eat." I managed to keep my voice even. "Oh, right. They'd only be a tiny mouthful. Barely more than a few crumbs."

"You think so?" He ground his now hard cock against me. "It seems like you need a reminder."

I looked him straight in the eyes. "We both know you're not going to cheat on Chloe, even if it means not getting to work your anger out on me." If he tried, he'd find himself in a thousand tiny pieces, courtesy of me and my guys.

He ground against me a moment longer before grunting and stepping back. "I wouldn't soil my cock on your tainted pussy."

I managed a short breath of relief.

"That might be the most romantic thing a guy has ever said to me," I said sarcastically. "My pussy is way too good for your cock."

He stalked over to a window that overlooked a courtyard. "This is all bullshit." He ran a hand over his hair. "You have no idea what you've done. Chloe and Dane both think I did that to her. Nothing I say... I wouldn't do that. I love her."

Cry me a motherfucking river.

"Is this where you expect me to go to her and tell her you weren't involved?" I asked. "That you didn't really try to blow her up?"

He turned around, looking stricken. "I did not try to blow her up. That was—"

"Meant for me," I finished for him. "Placed there by her to convince me to trust her. For what? To give her more time to put her plan together? Didn't have enough brunettes who looked like me?"

He averted his eyes.

"I thought so. I'm not saying I was involved in what happened to her, but the only way I'd tell her you weren't is if you convinced her to pull out of this competition with me."

If she did that, I wouldn't give a shit what she did and who she did it with. Let her, Dane and Zachary run off into the sunset together. If I never saw them again, that would be all right with me.

"She would never listen to me. Not while she thinks I drugged her." He looked delightfully miserable.

I shrugged. "Well, then, it seems we have nothing more to say to each other." I started to turn away.

"What if I told you what she had planned?" He looked desperate. "You can stop it from happening and then speak to her for me."

Now he had me thinking. If I knew what to look for, I could avoid it. I could stop my guys from getting hurt, or worse. Maybe I could turn whatever it was, back on her. She could be the one abducted and sold next time.

"What makes you think I'd believe a word you say?" I asked carefully. "This could all be an act to set me up."

"It could be, but it isn't." His eyes pleaded with me to believe him. "I don't give a shit about this competition between you and Chloe anymore. All I want is her." His thick brows lowered.

"Do you think she'll want you if you do anything that makes her lose?" I asked.

"I'll convince her she doesn't need to win this. There are more important things in life than power."

"If the idea of touching you wasn't repulsive, I'd check to see if you have a high temperature," I said. "Since when did Zachary Sinclair not care about power?"

It was what all of us were raised to want. To please my father and to gain as much power as possible. Personal fulfilment didn't factor into it.

"When I saw Chloe looking at me with mistrust." His brow crinkled as he frowned. "She asked me to organise for your drink and the twin's drinks to be spiked. She didn't know who it was behind the bar that did it. She didn't want to know. I swore to her the guy I hired left. Whoever you hired—"

"I didn't hire anyone," I said coldly.

He shook his head. "Whoever the fuck the twins hired then. Or Slade. Whatever. It wasn't me."

"Studying at Brutham Academy will teach you a lot of things." I folded my arms over my breasts. "Including the fact you should never trust anyone to pour a drink. Not unless you know they won't drug you. Your asshole quit and ran and you didn't think he might be replaced?"

He shrugged. "I should have anticipated. I didn't. I'm paying the price for that."

Boo fucking hoo, I thought.

"I'm going to be honest with you, Zachary," I said. "I don't think you've even begun to pay the price for what you, my sister and Dane did to me. Starting with the toxic gas and ending with the whole trafficking bullshit. Now I think about it, you've all gotten off lightly. I don't want to know what Chloe has planned for me, because we'll be ready for her. We will go after her again and there's nothing she can do to get ready for what we'll do. When we're done, she'll beg to step down."

He glared at me. "You're going to regret that. When Chloe is done with you, you'll be the one begging to step down." He stepped closer. "You'll be begging to be auctioned off to someone who will only use you. Because what's coming is going to be so much worse than that."

I wanted to slap the smug expression off his face. Instead, I rolled my eyes at his melodramatic statement. He should be studying theatre instead of chemistry.

"You have no idea what she's planning, do you? It absolutely kills you that you haven't got a clue and that whatever she does, you won't be involved. You might as well leave Brutham and go back to ANU. Make a life for yourself away from us and all this." I spread my hands to either side.

"You never know, you might even be happy." I would be. The farther away from me he was, the better.

He rubbed the back of his neck and exhaled in frustration. "I'm not going anywhere, Lila. If you won't help me voluntarily, then I might have to find a way to force you to."

"Have you ever considered asking nicely?" I asked. "Instead, you accosted me, threatened to assault me, then threatened me in three or four other ways too. I know for a fact your mother raised you better than that." Not much better, granted. She wouldn't have married my father otherwise.

"Yes, but your father didn't." He smiled viciously. "Your father taught us to be ruthless and merciless, and fight for what we want. Not to roll over and play dead."

"Then go out there and fight for Chloe." I waved down the corridor. "Don't let her tell you no. She might like it if you pinned her to the wall and made her listen."

He looked at me for a few drawn out movements.

"You're wrong about one thing. I do know what she's planning. She had a backup in case things went pear-shaped with the last plan. She probably has a backup for the backup. I believe you when you say you didn't drug her. It's something the twins would do. Something half-assed and ultimately doomed to fail. I mean, what have they really done? Changed her birth-control and put her to sleep for a while? Small potatoes compared to what we've done. What will they think of next? Putting hair dye in her shampoo so she accidentally dyes her hair green? They make all of this look like amateur hour in preschool. They call themselves evil twins, but pathetic twins would be more accurate. It's almost like they want you to lose."

He looked down his nose at me, then stepped away.

I pressed my head back against the wall behind me. He was right. We hadn't done anything that came close to what Chloe had done to us. I knew the guys fully intended drugging Chloe to go a lot further than it did. Were they disappointed I stopped it? Was I wrong to think about stepping in? This whole competition could be over if I'd kept my mouth shut and if Dane hadn't stepped in when he did.

I was going to have to do something drastic. Something that would have an impact on Chloe and on this stupid competition. Something that would put an end to it once and for all.

sixteen

"WE HAVE SOMETHING FOR YOU." Hunter waved Parker and Slade into my room and closed and locked the door behind them. He held up a tub of my favourite choc-mint ice cream. In his other hand, he held a bottle of chocolate sauce.

They sat down around me on my bed. Parker handed out bowls and spoons and Hunter started scooping ice cream into each.

"Are we celebrating something?" I put my laptop aside and nodded as Slade raised the bottle of chocolate sauce and looked at me in question. He squeezed a big dollop onto the top of my ice cream.

"We're celebrating being alive," Hunter said. "In my opinion, that's a good enough excuse for ice cream." He raised his bowl to me in toast before starting to eat.

"Works for me." I dug my spoon into mine. "You're sure there's nothing in this other than ice cream and chocolate sauce, right?"

"Slade and I drove into town to get it," Hunter said. "If there's anything in there, then someone was trying to drug the whole town."

"You realise that's not impossible, right?" I still scooped ice cream into my mouth and savoured the minty taste before I swallowed. "Mmm, so good."

Parker grinned around his spoon. "You have the exact same expression on your face right now as you do when you swallow my cum."

"What can I say? I have good taste in ice cream and men." And ice cream and cum both tasted delicious.

"I wonder how much of this I'd have to eat before my cum tasted like mint," Parker mused.

"There's only one way to find out," Hunter said.

"Are you offering to take part in that experiment?" Slade teased.

Hunter laughed. "Only on the coming side, not the swallowing. In order for this to be a true scientific experiment, we need a control group. Or a control guy."

"As interested as I am in scientific research and Lila swallowing my cum, I don't want to miss out on this ice cream." Slade shovelled a huge spoonful into his mouth.

"That experiment will have to wait for another day then," Hunter said. "I wonder if the Academy will give us a grant for the research."

"I don't think so, because it would be difficult to prove or replicate the results," I said. "But that doesn't mean we can't conduct the experiment anyway." I finished my ice cream and set the bowl aside on the table beside the bed.

"I propose a different experiment." Parker placed his bowl on top of mine and grabbed up the chocolate sauce. "It's called, let's see how delicious chocolate sauce is when licked off Lila's skin."

He pressed me down to the mattress and pushed my singlet up, over my bare breasts. He turned the bottle upside down and trickled sauce over my breasts and stomach.

"She certainly *looks* delicious." Hunter spooned himself some more ice cream and sat with his legs crossed, watching.

Slade put his own bowl aside, grabbed a handful of my singlet and pulled it up over my arms and head. "Wouldn't want to get sauce on that. Or this." He scooted down and pulled my shorts and panties down my legs and off my feet.

"She looks even more delicious like that," Hunter remarked.

"My theory is that the taste of her skin will make the chocolate sauce even better. My method will be to use my tongue to lick it off. I'll measure the results using a very scientific method; my taste buds." Parker grinned at me, then lay with his head over me before starting to oh-so-slowly tease me with the tip of his tongue.

He swirled his tongue around my nipple, stopping every few moments to swallow the sauce.

Slade parted my legs with his hands and lowered his face to my pussy.

"What, no scientific hypothesis?" Hunter asked with mock outrage.

Slade looked back up and grinned. "My theory is that if I lick Lila's clit, not only will she taste like perfection, I'll give her the best orgasm of her entire life. Best to date. There's always room for improvement."

Hunter nodded, evidently satisfied. "The first part of your theory is sound. The second part is presumptuous and, in my not-particularly-humble opinion, bullshit. While I can't scientifically prove the fact, I'm almost certain I have given her the best orgasms of her life. To date. However, I completely support this scientific research, if it means our queen gets an orgasm. Or two. Continue. The results of the second part of your theory will have to be measured by Lila herself. Parker and I will take note of how loud she screams. That will be factored into the results."

"Thank you Doctor Brantley," Slade said with a grin.

"You're welcome, Mr Lincoln." Hunter wiggled his eyebrows, then went on eating.

I shook my head at them all. They were too fucking adorable for their own good. I lay back and let my gaze drift to the ceiling while Slade lowered his mouth to me and resumed the experiment. I much preferred science to business, and this was definitely the kind of experiment I could get behind.

The combination of both of their tongues on my most sensitive places, had me trembling in moments. My whole body ignited slowly. My blood burned its way through my system, pulsing through my pussy and making me ache. The things these guys did to me was nothing short of absolute bliss.

"Chocolate sauce never tasted so good," Parker moaned. He had a mouthful of that and one of my nipples. "I'm spoiled now."

"To be fair, you were spoiled a long time ago," Hunter teased.

I glanced down as Parker flipped Hunter off. I watched Slade's head bobbing up and down as he licked me from top to bottom. He slid a finger inside me, working it in and around in circles.

I quivered and groaned from the sensation.

He locked his eyes on mine as he added another finger to the first.

"I don't remember fingers being part of the experiment," Hunter remarked. "However, since our subject matter is clearly enjoying herself, I'm happy to endorse this modification."

Parker raised his head from my nipple long enough to say, "You're such a nerd."

Hunter chuckled. "Only when it comes to pleasing our girl. There are no lengths I won't go to in the pursuit of that goal."

I snort-laughed and watched Parker sucking my tit while I drew closer and closer to the precipice. Even with everything crazy going on, I was still the luckiest woman in the country, if not the world.

Right from the start, the twins made it their mission to treat me like a queen. Slade had apparently accepted that mission too. I loved every minute of it. Every woman deserves to be treated like she's special. Like she's the centre of her partners' universe. The sun their existence revolves around. They made me feel like all of that and more.

"I'm so close," I whispered.

"Don't let her come yet," Hunter said. "I want this to be amazing for her. When she does come, I want her to scream the place down."

Slade slid his fingers out of me and traced circles around the insides of my thigh. He kissed his way down and back up the other one.

At the same time, Parker sucked and nipped my nipples and breasts, not letting up for a moment.

I made a small sound of annoyance in the back of my throat, frustrated at being denied an orgasm so close to the edge. Hunter was right, I would scream the place down, but it still drove me crazy, and he knew it.

After what felt like a year, Slade finally returned his mouth to the centre of my pussy. He drew my clit between his lips, then bit down lightly.

I moaned. "Mmm, that feels amazing."

"You taste amazing," Parker told me. He moved up enough to kiss me, his mouth tasting of chocolate with a hint of salt and mint. If we could bottle that, we'd make a fortune.

I licked his lips and plunged my tongue into his mouth. I couldn't get enough of him. Of any of them. They were as much a part of me and my world as breathing, or my heart beating.

Slade slid his fingers back inside, three of them now. He fucked me with his hand and tongue, driving me hard to bliss and over the edge.

I came, groaning into Parker's mouth. He swallowed my scream and gave it back with a moan of his own.

I rocked my hips against Slade's fingers and mouth, drawing out the pleasure, letting the light dance across my vision. Blood roared through me like a cascade of water rushing over a waterfall. It went on and on until I finally, slowly drifted back to earth. I flopped back against the mattress and panted through my nose, my lips never leaving Parker's.

"I think we can call that experiment more or less successful," Hunter said.

"It was very successful," Slade said. "I can confirm Lila tastes delicious." He grinned.

"I can confirm that finding to be accurate," Parker agreed, his mouth pressed against mine. "With or without chocolate sauce."

"You know what else tastes good with chocolate sauce?" Hunter asked. He arched an eyebrow at me.

"Beer?" I asked teasingly, knowing exactly what he was referring to. I laughed at the horrified expressions on all of their faces. "Right, you meant pizza."

"Getting warmer." Hunter undid his jeans and curled his fingers under his cock to pull it free.

"Sausage pizza?" I watched with interest as he worked his cock, making it hard.

"How about just sausage?" He moved over to me and handed me the bottle of chocolate sauce.

I took it and trickled a line of sauce from his head, halfway down his cock. I handed the bottle to Parker and leaned down to run my tongue across the trail.

"Sausage and chocolate, perfect combination." He tasted sweet and salty, hot from his blood and cool from the sauce. I licked pre-cum from his tip before sliding my mouth all the way onto his cock. I sucked him and the divine chocolate flavour. I always liked sucking cock, but this was next level.

He moved his hips, driving himself in and out of my mouth. He tangled his fingers in my hair and held me there as he fucked my mouth.

"So fucking perfect," he breathed. "Such a good, amazing queen. You have the best, fucking mouth." He thrust a few more times. "I'm going to come in your mouth. Right down your pretty little throat. But don't swallow. You're going to hold my cum."

He twitched, grinding into me before he came, squirting salty, hot cum out his slit.

"So fucking perfect," he breathed. "But we're going to try another experiment. Parker." He waved for his twin to take his place.

"We're going to see how much cum Lila can hold in her mouth before she has to swallow."

I raised my eyebrows at him, but this was a challenge I was happy to accept. I held his cum in the side of my mouth as Parker slid his cock inside.

Every few thrusts, he'd pull all the way out to let me breathe through my nose.

"You feel so good," Parker groaned. With every stroke, the tip of his cock dipped into his twin's cum, until he was soaked with that and my saliva, along with his own juices.

He grunted and pounded harder a couple of times before he squirted his own cum into my mouth.

"Can you hold it for a while longer?" Hunter asked.

I nodded. I focused on breathing through my nose and combining both releases into one. When I was ready, I opened my mouth again for Slade's cock.

"Holy shit," Slade said breathlessly. "I feel like it should be weird to stick my cock into two other guys' cum, but this is..."

I glanced up to see him shake his head. I had no words for it either. This was one of the hottest things I'd ever done.

I closed my eyes and concentrated on breathing, sucking and keeping myself from swallowing too hard. Fighting the reflex wasn't easy, but I wanted to wait until I had all three of them inside me. I wanted to combine all of them in one big, delicious mouthful.

Fortunately, Slade only took a few more thrusts before he came, adding his cum to the wet, salty ball of heat.

I drew my mouth back off him, took a couple of breaths through my nose, then slowly and deliberately swallowed down every single drop.

"Woman, you are a fucking goddess," Hunter said.

"And a goddess of fucking," Parker agreed.

"Hell yeah I am." I smiled. "I think that just qualified me for some sort of degree in science."

"I don't know," Hunter said slowly. "I think we need more experiments before we get to that level."

"A lot more," Slade said. "By the time you all graduate, you'll do it with honours."

"Yeah, we will."

We had to survive that long first.

seventeen

PARKER

"THIS IS SO UNFAIR," I stated.

"What is?" Lila sat on the step below me, between my legs. I played with her ponytail, twisting the soft strands around my fingers before letting them fall free.

"That we don't get to sit in on the board meeting," I said. "I'd like to be a fly on the wall in there."

"This will have to do." Hunter tapped the laptop that rested on his knees. "We'll see most of it through the feed."

"Unless they figured out we hacked it last time to watch," I pointed out.

"How would they know?" Hunter shrugged. "Most people here wouldn't bother."

"Most people here don't have the last name Bell or Brantley," Slade said. "We have a vested interest in knowing what the school board is discussing."

"Couldn't you wrangle an invitation?" I asked. "You do work here."

"Only the board and the department heads are invited," Slade said. "Not humble guys like me."

"I don't know if humble is a word I'd use to describe you," I told him.

He smiled briefly. "Probably not. I also have to pretend I don't know you're doing this. If the board found out, I'd be fired."

"Fired if you're lucky," Hunter said. "Shallow grave if you're not. The school board takes their meetings seriously."

"That's my father's car." Lila nodded towards the window beside the stairs. The window was covered with vines, giving us a limited view out, but making it difficult for anyone to see in.

"Looks like Reuben is right behind him," I said. "You'd think they'd share a car."

Hunter snickered. "I don't know who would kill whom first if they got in a car together."

"It wouldn't be pretty," Lila said. She craned her neck. "Yeah, that's Reuben. Mac D'Antonio is with him. And Hilton Blake."

"If they're not careful, the school will sink under the weight of all those billionaires," I joked.

I watched my brother and his—friends wasn't quite the word—until they disappeared into the building. Somehow, the air in the place got heavier, like a shadow passed over the Academy. That wasn't far wrong. The combined evil deeds of the school board would make the average person shudder. If their power didn't make them horny as hell.

"Here we go." Hunter tapped the keyboard and brought up the feed. The camera off to the side of the board room showed a table surrounded by thick, leather chairs. Several men and a couple of women already reclined in them. All of the men were members of the Brotherhood of Kings. The women were, no doubt, aware of its existence. Neither looked deterred. Of course not. If they had enough power to sit on the school board of Brutham Academy, they wouldn't be intimidated by anyone here.

Hunter already decided Lila would sit on the board someday. Him too if he could swing it. I'd be happy to watch from home. Or hear about it all later.

The sound of shuffling and low conversation came through the laptop speakers. No one seemed in a hurry to take their chair.

"Please be seated." The Academy's principal stepped around to the end of the table and stood with his palms pressed against the mahogany timber.

The shuffling persisted for another few minutes before silence fell.

"Thank you all for coming." The principal droned on with his stan-

259

dard welcome, along with a reminder of the minutes of the last meeting and notes about things which needed to be discussed at this one.

Most of it was boring as shit. School funding, the discussion to expand or contract certain departments, or combine others. The board could argue for hours over all of that and not come to any conclusions. No one ever wanted their department to be cut back. No one wanted their children or sibling's degrees to be compromised.

Reuben sat on the opposite side of the table from Samuel Bell. Every so often, one would look at the other like they expected trouble. That was nothing out of the ordinary either. This was the only time they tolerated being in the same room as each other.

Sometimes, I wondered if our hope for the two families to come together was in vain. Old hate and animosity seemed hard to put aside.

"Are these meetings always so boring?" Lila asked.

"Usually, unless someone gets shot," Hunter said. "That's when things get really interesting. Mostly we watch because sometimes they change things up with the trials. We don't want to be taken by surprise."

"Yeah, there was the time—" I started to say.

Hunter hissed at me to be quiet.

"I assume you received the request to consider the founding of a Brutham Academy campus in Dusk Bay?" Reuben asked.

"We did," the principal replied carefully. "That's on the agenda to discuss today."

"Let's discuss it now," Reuben said. "The funding is there. Adequate land was donated. I see no reason to delay."

"That's Reuben," I muttered. "Straight to the point." He'd be more interested in his own personal agenda than the rest of the board's priorities.

"Why does he want a campus there so badly?" Slade frowned.

"If I had to guess, I'd say Caleb is pissed about us disrupting his operation. He's probably the one pushing for this. If he could arrange it, he'd sidestep Reuben and Reuben wouldn't want that. In proposing it himself, he puts himself in charge. Caleb gets what he wants, but on Reuben's terms." Hunter waved at us again to be quiet.

"We don't want to be hasty," the principal said. "There is much to be discussed—"

"I suggest we put it to a vote," Reuben said. "We can work on the logistics later. Let's come to an agreement first."

"Your father looks like you when he's suspicious as fuck," I told Lila, speaking softly in her ear. "I can almost see him thinking. Wondering what Reuben is planning."

"I'm wondering that myself," she whispered. "Why would anyone want another Brutham campus?"

"More people to play Kink or Drink?" I grinned.

She choked back a snort. "I can't imagine Caleb taking part in anything like that."

I chuckled. "Probably not. Chances are, he and those he works with would like somewhere closer to home for their children and prospective children. I'm surprised it's taken them this long."

The principal looked uncomfortable, but nodded. "Very well. All in favour of a Dusk Bay campus, raise your hand."

Not surprisingly, Reuben, Mac and Hilton raised their hands. So did a few others. Samuel kept his hand firmly down at the table.

"One, two, three, four, five, six... Seven," Hunter counted. "That's more than half of the thirteen board members. Looks like the Academy is expanding."

"Reuben looks smug as fuck," I remarked.

"When does Reuben *not* looked smug as fuck?" Hunter asked.

I pointed a finger gun at him. "Good point. But he looks particularly smug right now."

"Well isn't this cosy?" Chloe drawled from behind us. "You know you're not supposed to be spying on the school board meetings, right?

"There's a lot of stuff we're technically not supposed to do, but do you see that stopping any of us?" I asked without looking back.

"It certainly doesn't stop you," she agreed. She walked down until she was standing beside Lila. "I'm sure you're pleased to see me alive and well."

"I don't think pleased is the word that comes to mind," Lila told her dryly. "Anyway, shouldn't you be having this conversation with Zachary? He was the one who drugged all of us at one time or another. That sounds like the behaviour of a psychopath to me. Thank fuck you found out now and not when you were in deeper."

"Zachary was in pretty deep from what Hunter and I heard," I remarked. "Balls deep."

Chloe gave me a dirty look. "We'll deal with Zachary when the time is right. He...misjudged."

I wanted to laugh in her face for really believing Zachary went after her. It's true what they say. It's hard to gain trust, but as easy as fuck to lose it. I had no doubt Zachary was working on some way to worm himself back in with her. If not, that was his problem. Personally, I didn't give a shit.

Lila did laugh. "Misjudged? He set you up. I'd call that a whole lot more than a misjudgement. What sort of person does that to a woman? Ah, right. Someone like you. You're lucky you didn't wake up in the back of a truck."

Chloe shrugged. "You don't seem the worse for the experience. You know what they say, what doesn't kill you makes you stronger."

"It makes you a whole lot more than stronger," Lila said. "It also makes you pissed off and vengeful. What you did was...disgusting. Cruel."

"You wish you'd thought of it?" Chloe asked with mock sweetness.

"I do," I said before Lila could respond. "But if we had, we would have been more successful. No one would have seen you ever again. Except whoever bought you." I looked her up and down deliberately, as though appraising her value.

"You're sick," she told me.

I grinned. "It takes one to know one. You were the one who came up with it. And the one who wanted to use Hunter and I as... What was it? Leverage. Did you really think Reuben was going to give you anything in return for us?"

"Who said anything about Reuben?" she replied easily. "He has plenty of enemies who would love to get their hands on you. *You* have plenty of enemies who'd like to get their hands on you, too. It's a very long list."

"You know what they say about needing to break eggs to make omelettes," I replied. "We do what we have to do, the same way anyone else in this world does. No one can blame us for that. And if they can, too fucking bad. At the end of the day, we're the ones still standing. Us and Lila. We'll be the ones standing at the end too."

I was tempted to push her down the stairs and be done with it, but I suspected the fall wouldn't be enough to end her. She'd break a bone or two at worst. Then go crying to daddy, no doubt. Pity.

"Keep telling yourself that," she replied. "That doesn't make it true. Honestly, I'm surprised you haven't given up yet. You can still do that. Make it easier on yourselves and walk away now. It will be a lot easier for you if you do." She gave Lila a filthy look before heading away, down the stairs.

"I can't believe we just accused Reuben of being smug," I remarked. "If anyone is smug, it's her."

Not for much longer.

eighteen

PARKER

"SHE'S GOT BALLS, showing up here," Hunter muttered.

He drank a gulp of beer and toasted Chloe and Dane as they made their way through the bar and sat on one of the couches. "How nice of you to join us. Kink or Drink wouldn't be the same without you."

"Of course it wouldn't," Chloe said. She wore a pale pink T-shirt that matched her nail polish, and a short black skirt that fell to mid thigh. The side of her short hair was held back by a bright pink hair clip.

I didn't know who she was trying to fool with the innocent exterior, but it wasn't fooling any of us. We knew how acidic her heart really was.

"Someone has to keep an eye on you." Dane draped an arm over the back of the couch behind Chloe. He gave us all a dark look.

"That's very noble of you," Hunter said sarcastically, but without his smile faltering.

"We have some new faces. And some old faces." Annoyance flickered in his eyes when Zachary entered the bar and strode over towards us. He sat down between a couple of women and crossed his legs.

My gaze slid over to Chloe. Neither she nor Dane seemed surprised to see Zachary, but they didn't seem happy about it either. Apparently they hadn't kissed and made up yet.

I exchanged a glance with Hunter. His smirk suggested he was thinking the same thing. I laced my fingers in Lila's and squeezed.

I leaned to whisper in her ear. "Any time you want to leave, just say the word."

She responded with a subtle nod of her head. "I won't let them ruin all of my fun. I came here tonight to show them I'm not broken, not even close. I want to do something normal."

I wasn't sure if our little card game was normal but I knew what she meant. She was a university student. That meant lots of study, but also lots of... Drinking and fucking. She didn't want to let the rivalry between her and her sister stop her from enjoying herself.

"Ah, here's Slade." Hunter rubbed his hands together and grinned.

Slade balanced a tray of empty shot glasses on the palm of one hand and held two bottles of tequila in the other.

"We figured with the unfortunate spate of druggings, we'd forgo pre-poured drinks." Hunter nodded his thanks to Slade as he placed the tray and the bottles on the table. "Anyone is welcome to inspect the bottles to make sure they haven't been tampered with." He looked around the gathered students, but no one moved.

"Very well then." Hunter picked up his pack of Kink or Drink cards from the table and started to shuffle them. "There have been suggestions in the past that I may have put the cards in a particular order. I might have been slightly remiss in not shuffling them. From now on, they will be carefully shuffled. If anyone wants a turn, you're welcome to do that too."

He split the deck before flicking the corners of the cards to combine the deck in a different order.

"I think we can see they are shuffled." Slade sat on the other side of Lila.

"Thank you," Hunter said graciously. "I wouldn't want to be accused of cheating."

Dane barked a laugh. "If the hat fits."

"I don't have as much life experience as you do," Hunter said slowly, "but I've noticed that people who tend to fling accusations are trying to deflect from their own shortcomings or guilt."

Dane looked ready to pick up one of the tequila bottles and smash Hunter over the head with it. Chloe placed a hand on his knee, keeping him from doing anything rash.

In the corner of my eye, I saw Zachary watching both of them like a stalker. He wasn't even trying to contain his envy. He wanted to be the one with Chloe's hand on his knee. No doubt he'd also be having the same thoughts about smashing a bottle over Hunter's head.

If I'm honest, I've had thoughts like that myself from time to time. Being a twin wasn't always torture and fucking around with people. Sometimes it was difficult, especially when we spent so much time together.

"Are we going to play?" one of the newer students asked. What was her name? Tina? She sat with a couple of women I'd seen her with before. All second years like me, most of them were studying business and marketing. Even businesses like ours needed good PR from time to time.

"Of course we are." Hunter placed the pack of cards face down on the table. "Would you care to go first?" He gestured towards Tina.

She looked uncertain now, but her friends giggled and waved for her to go ahead.

"You've got this." Angie was a perky blonde with perky breasts. Breasts I would happily have touched, if not for Lila. And by touched, I mean come all over.

Tina leaned forward, giving us all an eyeful of cleavage, and picked up a card. Her eyes grew round, but she looked excited.

"Get choked," she read. "I've always wanted to, but all the guys seem to think they'll hurt me." She pouted.

All the guys were silly if that's what they thought. It was just a matter of learning the right pressure by paying attention to your partner.

She looked around hopefully.

"I'll do it," Zachary said before any of the other guys could speak. Tina's friends moved aside to make room for him to sit beside her. He stroked his palm down the side of her face, over her chin and down to her throat. She tilted her head back as he gripped her with his large hand.

"Does that feel good?" He braced himself with his other hand on the back of the couch beside her.

"So good," she said breathlessly. "I'm so wet now." Her eyes were half closed. She looked like she'd come with a breath on her clit.

"Of course you are," he said, his voice deep. A moment before I thought he might take it too hard and strangle her, he slipped his hand away and moved to the other side of the couch. His eyes were dark. He'd come close to giving in to the temptation to kill her.

Lucky for him because he wouldn't be allowed to play this game again.

Lucky for her too, because being choked was supposed to be fun.

I glanced over at Chloe. She was visibly fuming. Of course, that was the exact reaction Zachary wanted from her. To piss her off, make her jealous.

She glared at him, then looked away. Apparently forgiving and forgetting didn't come easily to her.

Fair enough. It didn't come easily to me either. I was good at a lot of things, including holding a grudge.

Zachary grunted something, then stood and stalked out of the bar.

"He looks like someone who needs to get laid more often," Hunter remarked. "Parker, do you want the next turn?"

I shrugged. "Sure." Anything to break the tension.

I leaned over and snagged the card at the top of the pile. I held it in front of me for a few moments for dramatic effect before turning it around to read it.

I blinked a couple of times. My face heated.

"Bro, are you blushing?" Hunter asked. "What does the card say?"

I cleared my throat and swallowed. "Get pegged."

"May I remind you that taking a drink is an option?" Hunter asked.

"Yeah, I..." I rubbed a hand over the back of my neck. "I'll try anything once."

I looked sideways at Lila. She was watching me with dark, curious eyes. With no judgement at all.

"You want to?" I asked. "There's a strap on over there." I jerked my head towards the shelves of toys. Everything was cleaned and sterilised between uses, which meant they were constantly being cleaned and sterilised. Brutham Academy students tended to be adventurous. Probably because none of us expected to live long, so we might as well make the best of it.

"Only if you want to," she said.

I placed the card face up on the table and offered her my hand. She curled her fingers around mine and we made our way over to the side of the room.

"Any time you're uncomfortable..." She gave me a gentle smile.

"I know." I nodded. "The safe word here is banana." I wasn't used to the nervous excitement that passed through me. Excitement yes, but not nerves. This was something I had no experience with. The second later, I realised it was likely she didn't either. That helped to settle my nerves somewhat.

"Okay, let's see if we can figure out how this goes on." I grabbed the strap on and held it in front of Lila. She slipped out of her skirt and panties, totally unfazed at being half naked in front of everyone else. She never had been shy about stripping and fucking in public. Fortunately, neither had I.

She gripped the sides and held it in place while I walked around her to fasten and tighten it. Satisfied it wasn't going to fall down, I stepped back around to face her.

I grinned. "That's a good look for you." The straps were black, but the dildo that stuck out from the front was bright pink. It wasn't massive either, thank fuck. I didn't want to be split in two.

I stripped off my own jeans and boxers and tried not to look back at the group watching us as I went down on all fours.

Lila grabbed a tube of lube from the shelf and knelt down behind me. She squirted a ton of it on her fingers, then smeared it around my rear hole.

I shivered slightly. "That's cold."

She laughed softly. "Now you know how I feel."

I looked back at her and grinned. "Touché." I dropped my head down as she slid a finger inside me.

"Is that okay?" she asked tentatively.

I was almost certain I could feel her fingers trembling. At the same time, they felt so fucking good. Gentle, but hot at the same time.

"That feels amazing," I replied. I swallowed hard as she slid in another finger, stretching me, readying me. Then a third.

The sensation of her filling me made my cock rock hard. I gripped myself and started to stroke slowly.

"Are you ready?" she asked.

"Yeah," I said, my voice hoarse. "Do it."

She gripped the sides of my ass and pressed the tip of the dildo into my slick, needy hole.

"Fuck," I groaned.

She stopped immediately. "Are you—"

"No, don't stop. It felt better than I thought it would." No wonder she was up for anal. It felt incredible.

"Okay." She pressed in deeper. Slowly. Determined not to hurt me. As if my queen could ever hurt me. Except in ways I liked to be hurt.

She slid in almost all the way before pulling back out again. "I almost wish I had an actual cock."

I laughed softly. "I almost wish you did too, but then you wouldn't be you."

"That's true." She thrust the dildo into me a few more times, then slid all the way out.

She unclicked the strap on and set it aside before lying down beside me and pulling her over me. She hooked her legs around my hips and pushed my cock down until I slid into her wet heat.

I groaned. "Fuck, this feels good too." I fucked her hard against the hardwood floor, driving my cock into her over and over. In no way was I as gentle with her as she was with me. She didn't want me to be.

"Fuck, Parker, just like that," she panted. "Ah, I'm going to...to come."

"Good girl, come around my cock," I told her. Her muscles clenched around me as she came, forcing an orgasm out of me too. I came hard into her, spilling my cum deep inside her luscious body.

I was barely down from my high when the lights went out, plunging us into total darkness.

nineteen

LILA

"SHIT." I lay still, waiting for my body to come back down and the lights to turn back on.

The orgasm faded. The lights stayed off.

"We should figure out what the fuck is going on." Parker slid his cock out of me and patted around the floor before pressing my clothes into my hand. "Don't turn the light on your watch, in case something screwy is going on."

"Yeah," I agreed. The Academy's generator should have kicked in by now. Screwy was more likely than not. I dressed in about half a second. From the sounds beside me, he was doing the same.

He patted my back, then my arm before he found my hand and gripped it tight. "Stay with me. We'll be fine."

My heart raced like crazy. The bar wasn't a small space and it wasn't silent, with everyone shuffling around. Trying to stay quiet, but audibly anxious at the same time.

I still felt enclosed. The only light was starlight that came through the window. It wasn't nearly enough to steady my nerves.

Before I stood, I felt around for something to use as a weapon. The only thing I could find was the strap on dildo, still slick with lube. It was better than nothing. I gripped it in my fist and let Parker pull me to my feet.

"Where are we going?" I whispered in his ear.

"We need to find—" he started to say.

A hand grabbed hold of my arm.. Without thinking, I let go of Parker and swung the dildo. I connected with something hard. The dildo striking with a thud.

"Fuck!" Hunter cried out. "Ouch."

"Shit, I'm sorry." I dropped the dildo to my side and searched around in the dark for Hunter.

He grunted. "What the hell did you hit me with? Wait, never mind. I don't think I want to know."

Parker chuckled. "What the hell is going on, bro?"

"No idea. Slade, where are you?" Hunter asked.

"Right behind you," Slade said softly. "I suggest you keep your voice down. Otherwise you might as well turn your phone on and announce your presence to everyone."

"Good idea," Hunter whispered. "Any idea which way Chloe and Dane went?

"I wasn't really keeping track," Slade admitted. "As soon as the lights went out, I headed in the direction I saw Lila last."

"Same dude, same," Hunter replied. "Lila doesn't like dark spaces. We need to get her out of here."

"That was what I was trying to do," Parker said. "I could use a weapon right now."

"I might have grabbed both of the tequila bottles," Slade said. "I can share."

"Perfect," Parker whispered. "If we get stuck in here, at least we can get shitfaced."

"Let's not get stuck in here." I was almost at the point where I'd prefer to give away our location than be in the dark any longer.

I shoved the thoughts away. I couldn't give into fear and paranoia. Whatever was going on, the darkness might ultimately prove to be our friend.

"The door is roughly that way," Hunter said. "We'll make our way over and see what happens from there."

"Bro, if you're pointing, we can't see you," Parker said.

"Oh, right. Everyone hold hands or some shit."

One of them gripped my left hand and another my right wrist.

"I hope that's Lila and not someone else," Parker said jokingly. His tone was light but his nerves were showing, even in the dark.

"It's me," I told him.

"Perfect." His hand slid down my wrist and felt around for what I was carrying. "Is that—"

"Yes," I said. "Yes it is. I would have grabbed a paddle or a flogger, but this was closer."

"At least it's not still warm," he said with a chuckle. He moved his hand back to my wrist and hung on carefully.

"It's fucking hard is what it is," Hunter said.

"I think that's the point," Slade said.

"Yeah, but you're not supposed to hit people over the head with it. Anyway, let's go. We'll go slowly. The last thing we want is to fall over furniture."

"Especially when Lila is carrying a hard dildo," Parker said. "That thing could put out someone's eye."

"You could console yourself with a bottle of tequila if that happens," Hunter told him.

"I think I'd need more than that." Parker walked behind me as Hunter led the way.

We stepped as silently and carefully as we could. Here and there, the shuffling continued. No one turned on a light. No one shouted or became hysterical. Every single person in that room knew there was a potential for them to become a target even though they didn't know who might be aiming.

At any normal university in Australia, everyone would have their phones out. They wouldn't even stop drinking or having a good time. But Brutham was a different place.

A dangerous fucking place.

Ahead of me came the thud of bodies connecting. That was followed by a short grunt of surprise from Hunter.

"Who the fuck is that?" he whispered.

"Dane DiMarco and Chloe," Dane said. "Is this some bullshit you assholes are pulling?"

Speaking of fucking dangerous.

"Funny, I was going to ask you the same thing," Hunter said. "We were right here with you. How could we have pulled anything?"

"Because you're you," Chloe said.

Hunter chuckled. "Thank you for the vote of confidence, but this isn't us. And if it isn't us, and it wasn't you, then—"

"It's someone else," I whispered. I remembered what Chloe said a couple of days ago about the twins having lots of enemies. His family, my family, none of us were short of enemies. Straight off the top of my head, I could think of several who might come after any one of us.

"Have you had any death threats recently, Mr D?" Parker asked.

"From anyone other than you guys? No," Dane replied. "You?"

"Same," Parker replied. "But that doesn't mean someone isn't after one of us in particular."

"That sounds like a good reason why we should stay away from them," Chloe said. "If whoever is behind this is after them, then we should make ourselves scarce."

"I was thinking the same about you," I said coldly. "Who else have you pissed off recently?"

She didn't answer.

"This might not be about any of us," Slade pointed out. "But whatever this is, we'll deal with it. We'll need weapons for that."

"I know where we can get some," Hunter said. "We need to get to them first."

"Yep, let's do that," Dane said. "But there are several hundred students and teachers here. Chances are, this has nothing to do with any of us."

He didn't sound like he believed his words either. Anyone with the last name Bell or Brantley, or with affiliations to either family, were going to be the prime targets. Most of the other students were from less influential families. Except those with ties to the Yakuza, Bratva or the Italian mafia.

Standing around contemplating the possibilities wasn't going to get us somewhere safe.

"We'll keep going," Hunter concluded. "We can't be far from the door."

We resumed walking, moving even more carefully now.

"There's the doorway," Hunter said. The corridor beyond that was bathed in moonlight.

That would make it easier to see but it would also make it easier to be seen.

"Where are we going?" I whispered.

"We need to get out of the building," Hunter said.

"They might be anticipating we'll do just that," Dane said. "We could be walking into an ambush."

"If they're outside waiting for us, they won't wait forever," Slade said. "Sooner or later, they'll come in after us. I don't know about you, but I prefer not to be a sitting duck. If we get out of the building, we can get what we need to fight back."

Dane grunted. "Fine, but if you get me or Chloe killed, I'm going to be pissed off with you, Lincoln."

"Right back at you, DiMarco," Slade said. "I don't suppose you have a gun on you?"

"If I did, I wouldn't tell you," Dane said.

Slade paused for a moment. "Yeah, I guess you wouldn't."

We stopped on the threshold.

"I don't like how bright that moonlight is," Hunter said. "If I was waiting to shoot someone, I'd be aiming a gun at that window there." He gestured. "The minute we step out, we'll be visible."

"So we don't step out," Slade said. "We keep down low, stay out of the moonlight and out of sight of anyone outside the window."

"Are you suggesting we crawl?" Parker asked.

"That's exactly what I'm suggesting," Slade said.

"Cool, I thought so," Parker said lightly. "I can get down on my hands and knees."

"We noticed, Park," Hunter said. "You seemed to enjoy it very much"

"I did, Hunt," Parker agreed. He knelt down, pulling me with him. "This would be easier without carrying a tequila bottle."

We kept our heads down and crawled toward the exit.

A glance back showed Hunter and Slade right behind me, Dane and Chloe behind them. She was sticking close to Dane; clearly scared, but I wasn't sure if she was scared of us or whatever the fuck else was going on. Both, perhaps? They were somewhat outnumbered.

I looked away. Right now, I needed to worry about getting myself and my guys out of here in one piece. Chloe and Dane could look after themselves.

We reached the doorway without getting shot or seeing anyone else. Either the other students had left the building, or they were hiding in their rooms, or somewhere else in the building. Wherever they were, we seemed to be the only ones moving around the corridor. What did that mean, if anything? Maybe nothing. Maybe everything.

I couldn't rule out the possibility everyone knew this was coming but us. Until I knew otherwise, I had to assume everyone but me and my guys were the enemy.

A million possibilities tumbled through my brain, none of them good. No one had ever, to my knowledge, attacked Brutham Academy. It never occurred to me before to wonder why that was. Considering who we all were, something like this was inevitable.

Of course it had to fucking happen when I was here.

"The minute we step out, we may become a target," Hunter whispered.

"Can you see anyone out there?" Dane asked. He crawled up beside Hunter and Parker.

"No one, but that doesn't mean they aren't there," Hunter said.

"What if someone goes out first?" Parker suggested.

"Are you volunteering?" Chloe asked him.

"Hell no," Parker replied. "Ladies first. And before you suggest Lila, remember you're the big sister."

"What if the first thing out isn't a person?" I held up the strap on with the bright pink dildo sticking out from the front.

"It's worth a try to see if we get a reaction," Hunter said.

I crawled over closer to the door, drew back my arm and threw the dildo as hard as I could.

twenty

LILA

THE DILDO and strap landed on the ground with a plop. I waited with my breath held, but nothing happened.

"That was anticlimactic." Parker sounded disappointed. "I guess it's safe to go that way."

"Everyone wait here," Slade said. "I'll check it out first." He slipped past us and disappeared into the shadows.

"Assassin mode, activated," Parker said. "I need to learn me some skills like that."

"Just what the world needs," Hunter said. "Parker in stealth mode." His grin was a flash of white teeth in the dim light.

"Exactly," Parker agreed. "I'd be even more epic than I already am."

Chloe snorted.

Everyone's watches lit up simultaneously. Bathing us in light from a text message.

"Fuck." I cupped my hand around my watch to block the light while I quickly read.

> Brutham Academy alert, level five. All students shelter in place. Suspected incursion. More orders to follow

"Well, shit," Hunter said.

276

I pressed the crown on my watch to darken the screen. It would suck if a message meant to warn us, drew attention to us.

"It took them long enough," Dane said with a grunt. "We could have all been dead by now."

"Lucky for them, we're not," Parker said. After a moment he added, "Lucky for us too."

"That's a matter of opinion," Chloe muttered.

"My heart wouldn't break if you were dead," Parker told her. "But it seems like we might need each other to stay alive, so maybe we can stop being shit to each other for five minutes."

She gave him a scathing look but fell silent.

I peered out into the darkness. Every so often, I caught sight of a flash of light. Each time it was gone before I could pinpoint its location, but they seemed to be getting closer.

"There's at least a dozen out there," Slade said.

I jumped as he appeared in front of me suddenly. My heart thundered for a few moments, once it got going again.

"Fucking hell," Hunter whispered. "I need you to teach me that."

Slade gave him a quick glance, then said, "Follow me."

"How do we know we can trust you?" Chloe asked.

"You don't, but I don't want to end up dead," Slade told her. "You can follow me or you can stay here. That's your call."

"Personally, I'm not going to fuck around and find out," Hunter said. He put a hand on my lower back and moved forward slowly.

"Me either." Parker crawled along beside us until Slade gestured for us to stand.

"We're headed over to the sheds," Slade whispered. "If that text message was right, we will need those weapons."

I assumed by supplies, he meant guns. I'd feel better if we were armed with more than a couple of tequila bottles.

We kept to the side of the steps, where the shadows were deepest, and moved down in single file. I winced as our footsteps crunched on the gravel at the front of the building. Each step sounded like a clap of thunder.

I stepped past the dildo and considered scooping it up. If only so I had something in my hand to defend myself with. I dismissed the idea.

Even if I moved quickly, I'd be stepping out of the shadows into the moonlight. The risk of being seen was too great.

Slade led us off the gravel and onto grass, where our footsteps were muffled. We made it to a line of trees before the lights converged on the Academy building. Slade was right, there were about a dozen of them. Dark silhouettes with a phone or torch in one hand and a gun in the other.

"They don't look like they're here for a party," Parker whispered. "Chloe, are you sure they're not with you?"

"If they were, I would have told them where to find you by now," she pointed out.

"And if they were with us, we would have done the same," I said. "Chances are, they want both of us dead."

"Zachary looked pissed off the last time we saw him," Parker said. "They could be friends of his."

"I'm starting to think Zachary is unhinged," Hunter said. "That's saying something, given the company I keep."

"You can't see me right now, but I'm flipping you off," Parker told him.

"Let's keep going," Dane said.

"The more distance we put between us and them, the better." Slade led the way through the trees, somehow moving silently over the dry leaves.

"Make a note of the date," Parker said. "Mr D and Slade agreeing on something."

"We can all agree we don't want to die," Hunter said.

"Can we all agree that you should shut up?" Chloe snapped.

"I actually think that's a good idea," I said. "In the interests of not ending up dead."

Parker muttered something under his breath but the twins fell silent until we reached the sheds.

We stopped in the shadows about twenty metres away and watched.

"This isn't an inside job," Dane said softly.

"No," Slade said. "Unless they don't know what's kept in the sheds."

"That's possible," Dane conceded. "But if that's the case, they didn't do their homework."

"Either way, they're not—" Slade was interrupted by the sound of gunshots. Someone screamed. Another shouted, but that was cut short by another gunshot.

"We need to hurry." Slade trotted over to one of the sheds and pulled out a set of keys from his pocket. He slid one into the lock and opened the door.

The walls of the shed were lined with guns, ammunition, flame throwers, bats and what looked like a rocket launcher.

Hunter rubbed his hands together. "I love this place." He went straight for the rocket launcher.

"Trying to overcompensate?" Chloe asked.

"Sweetheart, I'm the only one with big enough muscles to pick this thing up." He grinned.

She rolled her eyes at him and grabbed up a handgun. I took the one beside it.

I thought Parker might opt for a flamethrower, because why not? Instead, he picked up a handgun of his own. But only after opening the tequila bottle and taking a swig.

"Now it's a party." He grinned.

Dane picked up a handgun for himself, hesitated for a moment then grabbed another. "Can never be too careful."

"Hey," a whisper came from the doorway.

I aimed my gun, but lowered it when I saw Tina and Angie.

"Looks like we weren't the only ones who thought to come here." Tina stepped past us and picked up a weapon of her own.

"Definitely not." Zachary entered next, followed by another handful of students.

"This went from a party to a battle," Parker remarked. "The battle for Brutham Academy." He put a fist to his chest. "They can take our school over our cold, dead bodies."

Chloe made a derisive sound in the back of her throat. "They can have the fucking school. I just want to get out of here alive."

"Me too," I agreed. Loyalty was one thing, getting killed to save our school was another. "Zachary, those aren't friends of yours?"

"I was going to ask the same question," he replied. "I thought you might be getting desperate, so you called in reinforcements."

"Nope, nothing to do with us," I said. "I guess this means we're on the same side, for now." If that was what it took to get out of this alive, then I'd do it. But I wouldn't turn my back on him or Chloe. Vice versa, no doubt.

"What's the plan?" Dane asked Slade. "Do we take them on or get the fuck out of here?" He winced at the sound of another few gunshots.

"You can get the fuck out of here if you want," Slade said. "I'm not going to stand by and let them kill everyone in the school."

"That's noble, but you might get yourself killed," Dane said.

Slade shrugged one muscular shoulder. "I'm not that easy to kill. Are you? Imagine the gratitude you'll get from the students' families."

Dane considered for a moment, then aimed his gun at Zachary's head. "Did you drug Chloe?"

Zachary didn't flinch. "No, I promise I did not. The twin assholes engineered that."

"Guilty," Parker said. "Now, are we going to stand here talking or are we going to go and kill some motherfuckers?"

"We could kill some motherfuckers right now," Dane said. He swivelled his upper body and aimed at Parker's head.

"Pull the trigger and we'll find out how well a rocket launcher works at close range," Hunter warned.

I sighed. "You all have big cocks, okay? Let's go before there's no one left alive."

I turned and stepped toward the doorway. I half expected to hear shots behind me, but I didn't. A few grunts of dissatisfaction, but then everyone filed out behind me.

"Men."

I glanced over to see Chloe walking beside me. I actually managed a half-smile.

"We can't really blame them for not trusting each other," I said. "We haven't been very good role models in that department."

"If you're trying to—" she started.

"I'm not trying to do anything," I whispered. "Just stay alive. After that, we can go back to being at each other's throats."

She didn't answer for a minute or two. "I'm not going to let myself get killed to convenience you, just so you know."

I laughed softly. "Me either. I wouldn't want to disappoint you by taking that away from you. I'm sure you'd prefer the satisfaction of killing me yourself."

"Exactly," she replied. "I'm sure you're thinking the same thing about me."

What I was actually thinking was, how did we get to this point? When everything was said and done, she was still my twin sister. We must have been close once. Maybe before we were born. I was almost certain neither of us tried to loop an umbilical cord around the other's throat.

I grimaced. If Dad was here, he'd probably tell me that was exactly what I should have done. If I had, it would have changed every aspect of my life. What would it have been like growing up without my twin? Boring, at worst.

"Just don't go getting yourself killed tonight, okay?" I said.

"Yeah, you too," she whispered.

If I didn't know better, I'd think she was being sentimental. I couldn't think about that right now. Even if she was, it didn't change anything. Once we dealt with this, the competition would continue and things would get brutal. Right now, I had to focus on tonight and getting through this with me and my guys intact.

We kept to the shadows, moving as silently as a group of about fifteen people could. Granted, all of us were trained for things like this. To fight, to kill.

Chloe and I had handled guns since before we could walk. I had no doubt Hunter knew exactly how to use a fucking rocket launcher. If anyone could, it would be him. And he'd laugh while doing it. That was all kinds of fucked up, but I loved it.

Gunshots rang out again from inside the Academy building. A couple of people shouted. The sound of running footsteps was cut short by another shot.

"It sounds like they're hunting them down," Slade said. His voice was ice cold fury. That was sexy as hell. Hearing him sound so protective made the pulse in my clit pound harder.

"At the risk of sounding cliché, the hunter just became the prey." Hunter brandished the rocket launcher. "And this Hunter loves nothing more than a good hunt."

"It's not fair that you got a cooler name than I did," Parker told him.

"When this is over, you can change your name to Tracker, if you want," Hunter said.

"Hmmm, I'll think about it." Parker didn't sound convinced.

Slade shook his head at him, gripped his gun in both hands and started up the steps.

twenty-one

PARKER

I KEPT CLOSE to Lila as we moved through the corridors. Every now and again, a shot would ring out, or a scream or shout would come from somewhere else in the building. They'd only last for a second or two before fading into silence again. That made it difficult to pin down the exact location of the attackers. They seemed to be moving through the building, some on the bottom floor, some on the second.

"Someone get the—" a voice shouted from up ahead. Whatever else he said, I couldn't make it out. He was definitely only ten or fifteen metres ahead of us. This part of the school contained the classrooms. At a guess, they were in one of the chemistry labs.

"This way," Slade whispered. "There has to be at least two of them in there."

"This wasn't what we were sent here for," a second voice said.

"Who cares?" said a third. "We can just... Did you hear something?"

Slade lunged toward the doorway, Hunter and I on his heels. Zachary and Dane weren't far behind.

Slade was illuminated by the light from the attackers. He raised his gun and fired.

A grunt and a thud said he hit his mark. He ducked sideways, narrowly missing return fire.

I got off a couple of shots. The first missed, but the second took an attacker right in the stomach. He cried out in pain and doubled over before falling to the floor.

The next thing I knew, Zachary was standing shoulder to shoulder with me, taking out the third asshole with a neat shot right through the centre of his forehead.

"Dude, nice shot." I didn't like the guy, but I had to give him credit. It was a better shot than mine.

"I have skills." Zachary shrugged.

Dane stepped into the room and ended the moaning of the guy shot in the stomach. A shot to the left side of his chest left the room in a few moments of silence.

"Three down, nine to go," Hunter said.

"What exactly are you going to do with that thing?" I ask him. "You can't use it without destroying half the school."

"It's a last resort," he told me. "If I have to decimate the place to get rid of the infestation of invaders, that's what I'll do."

"You've been watching too many science-fiction movies," Dane told him.

Hunter grinned. "There's no such thing as too many." He grabbed one of the attacker's guns and held it in his hand while he slung the rocket launcher over his shoulder. "For the record, it's shows like *Firefly* and *Stargate*. Not to mention *Buffy the Vampire Slayer*."

"Yeah, well don't get us killed by doing stuff that works on TV," Dane said.

"I'll try my best, but I make no promises," Hunter said. "Where to next?"

"We wait a couple of minutes," Slade said. "The noise we just made won't go unnoticed. They may come to us."

"Better than coming on us," I quipped.

"I'd prefer cum to bullets," Lila said.

I smiled at her and draped an arm over her shoulders.

"Me too, babe, me too." I loved the idea that this was going down while she was still sticky with mine. I definitely wanted to try that strap on dildo thing with her again. That felt incredible. And probably the closest I'd ever come to having a cock in my ass.

"Down this way," someone in the corridor called out.

We pressed ourselves back against the walls, keeping flat in the shadows. Without knowing if the approaching footsteps belonged to friend or foe, we held a collective breath and waited.

"Clark?" A male voice asked. "Calzone?"

Absolutely not friends. I frowned, trying to gauge who sent them. They were common enough names that they didn't stand out in my memory.

After what happened in Vancouver with Abbie and Wolf Venom, the Fiorelli family were still more or less in disarray. I couldn't rule out the possibility of their involvement. If that was the case, it was probably Hunter and me they were after. Hunter killed the family's eldest daughter. I've never known a Fiorelli to be particularly forgiving.

Lights flickered in the corridor. A phone or a torch being shone this way and that. Finally, it shone through the doorway into the lab.

"In—" He never got that word out before a bullet slammed into the side of his head, courtesy of Slade.

He barely hit the ground when four more took his place.

They first shot wildly. A couple of bullets hitting a shelf of bottles right behind me, igniting the contents.

"Fuck." I pulled Lila down to the floor with me. "That almost singed my hair."

"No one singes my brother's hair but me," Hunter declared before shooting the asshole in the hand. Then in the chest for good measure.

"Thanks for defending my hair, bro," I called out.

"Any time, bro," he replied.

The other two attackers ducked to either side of the door.

"We have the Academy surrounded." One spoke in an accent I couldn't quite identify. "There's no way out."

"I hate to break it to you, but that's very much untrue," Hunter said. "Also, if I was you, I'd leave while I was still alive. Just some friendly words of advice. I don't expect you to listen."

"The fucking Brantley twins," the attacker growled. "I'm particularly looking forward to killing you two."

"Will you do us the courtesy of telling us who sent you before you kill us?" Hunter asked. "It seems like the least you can do."

"Fuck off," the attacker called back. "I'm not telling you shit."

"Mercenaries," Slade said. "They're not telling because they don't know. They just got paid to come here and kill."

"It's a nice job if you can get it," I remarked. "But a cop out. Whoever sent them is trying to send a message. If we don't know who that is, how are we going to know what the message is meant to be?"

"No message." He sounded Italian. "Just your death."

"Hey, Dane." I squinted into the shadows, roughly in the direction I thought he was.

"What?" Dane asked.

"You said Hunter watches too many movies. What about these guys?" They were about as melodramatic as you could get.

Dane grunt-laughed. "Yeah, sounds like they watch too many of them too."

"Get the others down here," an Italian-voice snapped to someone, presumably speaking into his phone. "Last chance to give yourselves up."

"Oh?" Hunter said. "We didn't realise that was an option. Are you saying if we step out of here, you won't kill us?"

"No, but we might consider killing you quicker," Italian-voice said.

"No deal," Lila said. In my ear she whispered, "We need a distraction."

"We could use an exploding teddy bear right about now," I whispered back.

"We have something better," Zachary whispered.

He slipped over to a cupboard at the side of the room and started doing something I couldn't see. It sounded like he was pouring the contents of one bottle into another. That was followed by the sound of fabric ripping.

He held a bottle with a scrap of his T-shirt sleeve hanging out the top, up to the shelf which still burnt slightly. When the fabric ignited, he hurled the bottle out into the corridor.

The glass shattered, sending liquid and glass everywhere. The liquid ignited and exploded in a flash of flame and a bang loud enough to make my ears ring.

One of the attackers screamed in pure agony. He ran past the doorway, his clothes engulfed in flames.

"Ouch," I remarked. "That wouldn't tickle." I didn't want to be impressed with Zachary, but once again, I was. An impromptu explosive was impressive.

The corridor flooded with smoke thick enough to make my eyes sting. A second or two later, the smoke alarms sounded, deafeningly loud. That was followed by the sprinkler system kicking in and spraying us all with a torrent of water.

"This isn't how I like to get wet," Lila said.

"Me either. We need to get out of here," Slade said. "Everyone will know where we are by now."

"Time for the rocket launcher?" Hunter looked hopeful.

"There's a door at the other end of the corridor," Dane said. "We can head down there and wait for the rest of them."

Slade nodded. "Let's do it." He stepped toward the doorway carefully. Peered out. "I can't see anyone." He gestured for us all to move out.

Tina and Angie stepped out into the corridor first, guns raised. A shot rang out, then another. The first took Tina right between the eyes. The second slammed into Angie's chest.

"Fuck." Slade looked stricken as they fell to the floor. He stepped out, aimed and shot off several bullets.

Turns out a grunt of pain sounds the same in an Italian accent. Especially when it comes to an abrupt end.

"Motherfucker." Slade lowered his gun before gesturing again. "Come on."

I helped Lila to her feet and steered her out of the room. Her expression when she looked down at the bodies of the two other women was grim. Slade was going to beat himself up about that, no doubt.

The Italian asshole must have been hiding in another classroom, waiting to see what we'd do. He could just as easily have been killed in Zachary's explosion. The misjudgement was unfortunate, but not Slade's fault. I made a mental note to tell him that later. Whether or not it would make a difference was another thing.

We reached the door at the end of the corridor and ducked down low to wait. All of us had weapons raised, ready. Dane had a gun in each hand, looking like a character from a computer game. Ironic given how quick he was to judge us for watching TV shows and movies.

I never would have picked him for a gamer, but then again I barely knew the guy. He could be a furry for all I know. Probably a dog, or maybe a bilby. That mental image almost made me laugh out loud.

Nothing against the lifestyle, I just couldn't really picture Dane doing that.

I tilted my head back and let the sprinkler wash the smoke out of my eyes.

I took a moment to glance at Lila, who looked hot as fuck in dripping wet clothes. She looked hot as fuck in and out of everything, but the way her clothes clung to her body made my balls heavy.

Yeah, when were they not heavy? Especially around her. Especially when the fabric was all but transparent, her nipples visible as peaks in the cotton. I wanted to close my lips around one of them and suck.

I shook droplets of my face and focused my attention back up the corridor. If I let myself be too distracted, I could get her killed. No one would ever forgive me if that happened, including me.

The sprinklers shut off, leaving us in damp silence, except the sound of dripping, which gradually slowed. Clearly the electricity was still running to the building, or the sprinklers wouldn't have worked. The assholes must have messed with the fuse box to shut off the lights.

For mercenaries, they seemed to know what they were doing. They'd planned this in advance. They must have if they knew where the fuse box was. Although, they'd missed the weapons shed. Or had they? The more I thought about it, the less sense this made.

Who the hell had the time and money to send dickheads like this after us? It must have cost a small fortune. Who was so desperate they'd bother? We were hard to kill, but there were easier, cheaper methods than this.

I caught Lila in the corner of my eye as she turned her head.

"Fuck," she whispered.

"What is it?" A second later, I realised our mistake. Half a second before the door behind us opened and gunshots rang out again.

HUNTER RAISED THE ROCKET LAUNCHER. He pointed it at the four attackers.

"Die motherfuckers!" He pressed the trigger. It clicked but nothing happened.

"Fuck." He gripped it in two hands and smashed it into the head of the nearest attacker. The man went down with a cry of pain.

Hunter threw the rocket launcher aside and pulled out his gun to finish the job.

I put myself between the assholes and Lila, while at the same time shoving her back up the corridor.

The last three attackers surged inside the building. One of them took aim at Zachary. He ducked aside at the last moment and the bullet hit one of his friends in the chest.

I took the opportunity to shoot that guy in the head. The attacker, not Zachary, tempting though that was.

A second later, pain and heat passed through my shoulder. It took another few seconds to register I'd been shot. It wasn't much more than a graze, but it hurt like a bitch.

"Parker, are you okay?" Lila stepped out from behind me, barely glanced at me before putting a bullet in the chest of the guy who shot me.

"I am now," I said approvingly. She killed a guy for me, what could be hotter than that?

The last attacker turned and ran, but Dane put a bullet between his shoulder blades. He flew forward and slammed into the floor.

Silence fell, heavy and oppressive.

"Are we sure that's the last of them?" Chloe asked finally.

"I wouldn't assume anything," Lila said. "Not yet." She was wet and tired, but her chin was raised. If this was only the beginning, she'd keep fighting.

"Everyone hunker down," Slade said. "I'm going to take a look around outside."

"I'll go with you," Dane said.

Slade regarded him for a moment, then nodded. "Fine. Everyone else, stay here." They moved slowly towards the door and slipped out into the night.

I pulled off my shirt and pressed it to my shoulder.

Lila put a hand over mine to help hold the fabric in place. "That looks painful."

I started to shrug but stopped and winced. "I've had worse." I nodded towards the dead bodies lying on the floor. "I'm better off than them."

"That's true," she said. "We still need to get you to—"

The lights flickered and came back on.

I blinked against the sudden glare.

The floor of the corridor was covered with a combination of blood and water. It looked like a literal bloodbath. Here and there, bullet holes dotted the walls. I didn't *think* they'd been there before. No doubt they'd be patched up by the end of the week like they were never there.

The attackers all lay dead, each dressed entirely in black. Unless I was mistaken, none would carry ID, or anything to indicate who they were and who hired them. They were nothing more now than nameless, faceless mercenaries. Which was just how guys like them liked it.

"What a mess." Hunter clicked his tongue. "I hope they don't expect us to clean that up." He glanced over at me and realised I was injured. "Didn't duck fast enough?" He grinned.

"Fuck off," I said cheerfully. "I love you too, bro."

He laughed. "It's just another scar. You'll live. This time."

"Just trying to make it easier to tell us apart," I said lightly. As if my crooked nose didn't do that already. Although, statistically speaking, chances were Hunter would get punched in the nose at some point. It might even be someone other than me that did it.

Hunter patted my other shoulder. "Keep telling yourself that." He peered towards the window. "We should go and hide. There's a couple of cars approaching."

I looked in the same direction. Two black cars were headed up the driveway, both illuminated in the blazing lights at the front of the Academy building.

"What the hell?" Lila's face paled.

"What is it?" I asked.

It was Chloe who answered. "That's Dad's car. What the hell is he doing here?" She glanced over at Zachary, who shook his head.

"I have no idea," he admitted.

I squinted as the cars came to a stop outside the building. "This gets weirder and weirder. That looks like Reuben's car."

"It really fucking does," Hunter said. "I'm going to go out there and see."

"I'm coming with you," I told him.

I turned to say something to Lila, but she was already halfway out the door, Chloe right behind her.

"I guess we're all going," I said to myself. "What could possibly go wrong?"

My hand pressed hard against my shoulder, I headed out the door and down the steps.

Both of the cars were parked side-by-side. Reuben stood leaning against one, his arms crossed over his chest.

Samuel Bell stood beside the other in a similar pose. His brown eyes took in his daughters and Zachary as they stepped out of the building together.

For someone who would happily see Samuel Bell dead, Reuben had a remarkably similar expression on his face when he looked at Hunter and me. Although, where Samuel looked slightly disappointed, Reuben looked disapproving.

"You're alive, I see," Samuel drawled.

"You were expecting to come here and find us dead?" Hunter asked.

291

"I was hopeful you might be," Samuel told him. His gaze swung back to Lila and Chloe. "You survived this little test."

Lila sucked in a breath.

Time stopped while we all stared at him, trying to absorb what he just said.

"Little test?" Lila finally choked out. "You sent those mercenaries to attack the Academy?"

Samuel looked remarkably unapologetic. "The school board agreed that if I bankrolled another trial, it could take place." He tilted his head slightly towards Reuben.

I looked back at my older brother. His expression was unchanged. I should have guessed he and Samuel were behind this. Who else would be twisted enough?

"I guess we passed," I said lightly. "We didn't die. That sounds like a pass to me, right Hunt?"

"Right, Park," Hunter agreed. He looked like he wanted to pick up the rocket launcher, figure out why it didn't work the first time and use it on Samuel and Reuben. Failing that, he might pick up the dildo where it still lay on the ground and hit them over the head with it.

Pissed didn't even begin to describe it.

Lila looked even more furious. "You sent people to kill us? Who does that?"

Samuel ignored the question. "You four worked together?"

"Just this once," Chloe snapped. "Don't worry, it won't happen again."

"Definitely not," Lila agreed. "I can't believe you'd do something like this. What sort of monster—"

Samuel exhaled out his nose. "I was hoping this test would toughen you up. Make you reassess your priorities. Instead, it seems to have done the opposite. I'm starting to think none of you should take my place."

Lila must have remembered she was holding a gun, because she raised it slowly and pointed it at her father.

"You sent people to kill us," she said again.

"Did you die?" he said evenly. He actually seemed pleased she had a gun aimed at his head.

"She could have," I said, barely containing my rage.

"We all could have," Hunter added. "Those assholes could have killed everyone in the school. Even if they had orders not to kill Chloe and Lila, it was dark in there. It's only skill and us working together that prevented that from happening."

Reuben rolled his eyes.

Samuel settled his gaze on Hunter. "There was no such order. Just like there is no such order during the trials. If my daughters don't have the skills to get through this, then they won't survive in the long run."

"You're a special kind of asshole," I told him. He didn't seem to give a shit Lila could be dead right now because of him. I turned to Reuben. "You too. The trials are one thing. Armed mercenaries are another."

The sides of Reuben's mouth twitched. "Nothing you couldn't handle. Don't tell me you didn't enjoy yourselves."

I opened my mouth. Closed it again. The fucker was right, we had enjoyed it. It was exactly the kind of shit we got off on. And he fucking knew that too.

"I thought so." He nodded faintly. "They haven't nicknamed this place Brutal Academy for nothing. You should all be able to handle situations like this with one hand tied behind your back. As far as I'm concerned, this test was a success."

Samuel frowned at him. "We'll have to agree to disagree."

"Were you hoping one of us would die so you don't have to think too hard anymore?" Lila asked. "Or two of us." She jerked her head in Zachary's direction.

"Not at all," Samuel replied. "I was hoping this would make you fight harder for what you want. I was hoping to see one of you handle the situation better than the others."

"Lila used a dildo as an improvised weapon," I said helpfully. "And Hunter is handy with a rocket launcher. It was kinda epic." I couldn't stop a smile from creeping onto my lips.

"Zachary is an amazing shot," Hunter said. "Slade and Dane too." He glanced around for them. "And Zachary made a bomb. That was cool." He was almost smiling now too.

"Chloe held her own," Zachary argued. "She was amazing."

Samuel looked unimpressed. "Next time, I expect to see you all perform better."

"Next time?" Lila echoed. Her hand was steady. She didn't seem to have made up her mind about whether to use the gun on her father or not.

I could understand her conflict. This might be part of the test too. Part of me wanted her to go ahead and kill him, but she'd hate herself for it later. She wanted him to approve of her and choose her, not take his place by killing him. Personally, I think killing him would be a lot easier, but it wasn't my call to make.

"There will always be a next time," Samuel said. "It might be at the trials and it might be before that. Or after. You need to be on your guard against anything and everything. Always. That is the point of tonight's test. To remind you of that. You can never become complacent. Not for a minute, not for an hour, not for a day. The moment you do, someone will work their way under your armour and get to you."

"Like sneaking into your house and putting a virus on your computer?" I asked.

He barely glanced at me. "Like that, yes. That could have been much worse than it was. We have to be ready for every contingency. It could come from anyone." Now he looked at me. Accusingly.

"Nothing would ever make me go after Lila," I said firmly. "She can totally trust me, Hunter and Slade." After a moment I added, "Has anyone told you you have trust issues?"

He actually twitched. Apparently I hit on a raw nerve. Interesting. Who would have the guts to tell him something like that, apart from me? Instinct told me there was a woman involved. I didn't know why they did, but they did. I filed that away for later. You never know when information like that could come in useful.

"I should be on my way," Samuel said. "I'm sure you're wanting to get some rest after the excitement." He made it sound like we'd had a party or something. As if there weren't fuck only knew how many dead bodies lying inside the Academy.

"Just remember," he added as he opened the door to his car, "Don't let your guard down." He nodded to his daughters, then slipped inside and closed the door behind him.

It was Hunter who took the gun from Lila's hand and put his arms around her.

"That was some fucked up shit," he remarked.

None of us disagreed.

twenty-three

LILA

I STEWED on my father's words while we trudged back into the building. Staff and teachers appeared from wherever they'd been hiding, and started to clean up the corridors. None of them looked horrified or even surprised.

"This is all kinds of screwy," Hunter said.

"Yeah," was all I managed to say. My brain was overloaded with the attempt to understand everything.

I knew this year was going to be a challenge, but I didn't expect anything like this. I certainly didn't expect my father to send people into the school to kill. The problem was, I *should* have expected it. This was my father we were talking about. Whenever anyone describes the Bell family, they use the words 'the worst of the worst.' I didn't really stop to contemplate what that meant before now.

Apparently what it meant was killing your children if they don't meet your expectations.

What was his expectation anyway? I was supposed to tell Chloe and Zachary to stay put somewhere safe while I dealt with twelve armed assailants? Was I supposed to tell the twins to stay out of it?

Slade trotted up to us as we headed out of the Academy hospital. The doctor had patched up Parker. He hadn't even needed stitches, just a bandage and a warning to take it easy for a while. As if Parker knew how to take it easy.

"It's all clear out there. Was that your father I saw driving away?" Slade slowed to a walk beside us.

Hunter explained everything to him. He sounded as overwhelmed as I felt. Not to mention conflicted. I knew he and Parker had enjoyed themselves. Hunter was in his element carrying a rocket launcher around the school. The twins motto seemed to be 'enjoy life to the fullest.' If they died tonight, at least they'd look and feel good doing it.

That wouldn't be much consolation for me, if they were dead.

Slade's eyes widened with disgust. "Twelve mercenaries and at least ten students are dead. For what? So your father could play his stupid fucking games?"

I tried not to bristle. Instinctively, I felt like I should defend him, even though what he did was indefensible. He was my father and what he did was only to make me stronger.

I just wished he'd... find a better way to go about it.

"He—" I couldn't think of a single thing to say, so I shook my head. "You're right, it was fucked up. He did it because he doesn't think I'm strong enough. If I was, none of this would have happened."

"Hey." Hunter stepped around in front of me and put his hands on my shoulders to stop me. "This is not your fault. If he can't see how strong you are, then he's not looking close enough."

"Isn't he?" I said bitterly. "Maybe you're biased. Maybe the whole point of tonight was that I was supposed to take charge of the Academy. Hell, maybe I was supposed to take charge of *mercenaries* and hunt down Chloe."

I shook my head. "Either of those would have been better than protecting her and Zachary. Or letting Zachary protect us."

"I'm not saying hunting down Chloe with a bunch of mercenaries wouldn't have been fun," Hunter said slowly. "But that's not who you are. You had to protect yourself. Those assholes could have been after you. If you'd tried to take charge of them, they could have killed you. Or worse."

That reminded me of Danica and Mary. I didn't want to think what twelve men might do to me.

I shuddered.

"You couldn't have known your father was involved," Slade said. "If you had, you would have behaved differently."

"Would I?" I asked.

"Yeah," Parker agreed. "You would have called him up and told him to call off his dogs. Then we could have gone back and finished our game of Kink or Drink."

I groaned, remembering we'd only just started when the lights went out. Zachary trying to make Chloe jealous by choking Tina seemed so ridiculously childish now. Okay, it was childish then, but it was even more so now with twenty-two people dead.

"I suppose I would have," I agreed. "But he wouldn't have listened. They would still have come after us. If we knew he was behind it, we would have assumed they had orders not to kill Chloe or me. We might have hesitated."

"If we had, we'd be dead right now," Slade said. "None of us hesitated. We did what had to be done. If your father doesn't like it, too fucking bad. What matters is that we survived."

"Except Tina, Angie and fuck knows who else," I said. "This had nothing to do with any of them. Dad would call them collateral damage." Just like Mary.

"That's exactly what Reuben would say," Hunter said. "He probably got a good laugh out of all of this."

"Reuben laughs?" I asked dryly.

Hunter grinned. "Not out loud. He smiles once in a while though. Very rarely and usually when things have gone horribly wrong for someone else."

"That sounds like Reuben." I grabbed Hunter's wrists and pushed him a few steps back to my door.

"Right now, I want a nice, hot shower and to get out of these damp clothes." I let his wrists go and pulled out my key.

Tentatively I slipped it into the lock and turned it. The door opened easily. My room looked untouched. The sprinklers hadn't come on in this part of the Academy, thank fuck. Otherwise everything I owned would be saturated.

So would everything the guys owned. We'd have to leave and find a hotel for a few days. We could do that anyway.

I won't lie, that was a tempting thought, but I wasn't going to run. Whatever Chloe, Zachary or my father threw at me, I would deal with it.

Slade placed his hands on my shoulders and steered me into the room and towards the bathroom. We stopped at the threshold for him to pull my T-shirt over my head. He unhooked my bra and slid the wet lace down my arms.

Hunter started on my shorts while Parker turned on the shower.

A girl could get used to this. I couldn't say they didn't take good care of me. They called me their queen and treated me like one.

I stepped under the hot spray, surrounded by three even hotter, naked guys.

Parker stood with his shoulder raised, out of the water. It looked sore, but the bullet only grazed his skin. A few centimetres to the right, and he'd be dead.

I may not have hesitated to shoot my father if Parker died because of his fucking games. Screwing with me was one thing. Killing one of my guys was unforgivable.

Besides that, the whole attack could have led to me, Chloe and Zachary all dying. What would Dad have done then? Hunt down someone like Hades Turner to take his place? Or maybe he had something else in mind. He wasn't too old to have more children. I knew he wasn't sentimental, but this...

"Put it out of your head for a while," Hunter said. "We got through it. Everything they've thrown at us, we've survived. That's the important thing." He massaged my shoulders with his fingers and scented body wash.

"What he said." Slade squirted body wash onto his hands and started washing my breasts and stomach. "Also, we wouldn't let anything happen to you."

"No way." Parker washed himself quickly, then pushed Hunter aside to wash my hair.

"You know I can do this for myself, right?" I asked.

"We like doing it for you," Parker said.

Slade knelt down in front of me and washed my thighs carefully before he parted them to press his face between my legs. "You can't do this yourself." He traced a circle around my clit with his tongue.

I shivered. "That's true, I can't." I wouldn't want to. Having them lick me was much more fun.

Hunter rinsed himself off and stood to the side to run hot, wet hands over my breasts. He pinched my nipples gently, then more firmly.

Parker placed his hands to either side of my chin and tilted my head back to help him rinse my hair.

I closed my eyes and let the hot water rush down the back of my head and over my face.

"You're spoiling me."

"Yes, and we're going to keep on spoiling you," Parker told me.

"Yes we are," Hunter agreed. He leaned down to kiss my nipple with his tongue, before drawing it into his mouth and sucking. "You always taste so good."

"It's the body wash," I said.

He laughed. "No, it's definitely you. Nothing ever tasted as good as this."

"Or this." Slade licked my clit firmly, kissing and nibbling while running his thumbs up and down the insides of my thighs. "This tastes like heaven."

"It feels like heaven." I grabbed one of Parker's hands and squeezed tightly as I rocked my hips back and forth on Slade's mouth.

My other hand slid down to grip Hunter's erect cock. He was slick with water and hot and hard with need. I slid my hand from his head to his balls slowly, carefully. I didn't want him to finish too quickly.

He thrust into my hand, just as slowly. "I will never get enough of you touching me," he said. "You always feel so incredible. So fucking perfect."

"No, you three are so fucking perfect," I told them. I leaned back against Parker as I came hard. I wanted to scream all of their names at once, but all I could manage was a shout toward the ceiling.

I was just coming down when Slade stood. He gripped my ass and picked me up until my legs wrapped around his waist. With one thrust, he slid me onto his cock. Between him and Parker, they held my slippery, wet body. Slade started to pound into me with even, almost frantic thrusts.

If anything gave away his state of mind after the attack, it was this. He was more scared than he let on. For him, for me, for the twins. For all of us. He needed to let off steam and remind me, and himself, that we were still alive.

In spite of that, he didn't come quickly. He was so in control of himself he managed to keep himself from coming even when he was clearly right on the edge. His breathing was ragged with desire and exertion, his need great.

Finally, he gave in and let his orgasm claim him. Hunter came a moment later, squirting hot cum all over my hand.

I could have washed it off under the water, but instead I let his cock go and brought his hand to my mouth. My eyes on his, I licked his pearly release from my palm and fingers.

"Now this is delicious," I told him. Thick, salty and warm. With the slightest hint of his own personal flavour.

"Woman, you are next level hot," Hunter told me. "I'm starting to think we should run away and hide out somewhere."

I laughed softly. "Don't tempt me." A secluded island far away from the Academy, my sister, my father, Zachary and next week's exam, sounded like bliss. The exam in particular was something I'd love to avoid as long as I could. Yeah, that's how much I hate exams. Priorities.

"Let's get out." Parker turned off the water. He helped me slide off Slade's cock and back onto the floor. He stepped out and handed me a towel. "Get nice and dry on the outside. I intend to keep you nice and wet on the inside." He grinned and grabbed a towel for himself.

"Did I mention you're spoiling me?" I teased.

"Babe, we've only just started spoiling you," Hunter said.

"They're right," Slade said. "There's a lot more where that came from and we're going to give you every bit of it."

twenty-four

LILA

"HE'S RIGHT, YOU KNOW." Chloe flopped down on the chair beside me.

"Who is?" I barely glanced away from my laptop screen. I should have chosen somewhere more private to study than the library, but after the attack I didn't want to be alone.

Sleeping at night without having nightmares was hard enough.

"Dad." She leaned forward and rested her elbows on the top of the table. "What he said about not doing enough."

"Are you suggesting I'm not doing enough?" I closed my laptop and swivelled around in my seat to look at her. "Should I strangle you now and get it over with?"

She rolled her eyes. "No. I mean our first instincts should have been to turn the attack to our advantage. Not team up and run."

"We fought back," I pointed out. "We could have hidden in the bush until it was all over. We didn't."

"No, but if we were thinking right, one of us would insisted the other go and hide. If I dealt with it while you were trembling under a tree, I would have won."

I smirked. "If my guys and I went and trembled under a tree, you'd be dead and Zachary with you."

"Then neither of us would have won. Dad isn't going to let a coward take his place." She chewed on the tip of a bright pink nail.

"You got that vibe too?" When she gave me a questioning look, I added, "I got the impression he has a plan for none of us to take over. Like somehow all of this is a test he wants us to fail."

"Why would he want that?" She narrowed her eyes at me, but didn't deny the suggestion.

I considered for a moment, but slowly shook my head. "I don't know. I'm starting to get the impression nothing we can do will be enough for him."

"He is Dad," she pointed out. "When have we ever been enough for him? Maybe if we were born with cocks, he'd be more satisfied. Or if Zachary's mother gave him a little boy."

"That would have pissed Zachary off." I smiled. "Passed over for his own half brother."

Chloe frowned. "We would have been passed over for the same little half brother."

"Yeah, but then we wouldn't be trying to destroy each other." I toyed with a ring on my right hand. A gift from Hunter on my last birthday. Parker gave me a matching necklace. I'd protested that I didn't need any shiny things, but in typical twin fashion, they insisted I deserved it. I didn't usually wear them, but after the last few months, I felt the need to have something from both of them close to me.

"Was teaming up to stay alive such a bad thing?" I asked. "Would you rather die than lose?"

Something flickered in her gaze. "You don't get it do you? I've done nothing but lose. I was born first, but I might as well not have been born at all. Dad always preferred you. Then our stepmother did. Our mother probably did too. Even Zachary..."

She scrunched up her mouth and shook her head. "Just once, I want to be first."

"Dad does not prefer me," I protested.

Although... I always got the impression he saw more of me in him than in Chloe. My stepmother used to help me with my maths home-work, but Chloe never needed it. She was always better with numbers than I was. As for our mother, the memories of her were vague. If she had a preference, I couldn't remember, but I doubted she did. She was our mother, surely she wouldn't play favourites?

"Zachary cares about you," I told her. "You're all he wants. You're all Dane wants too."

"Both of them want power," she said bitterly. "They backed me because they knew they couldn't compete with the fucking Brantley twins. If you win, they'll hold so much power. Dane and Zachary would have had none."

She really was bitter.

"Dane and Zachary adore you," I said. "Yes, both of them want power, but they want you with it. Besides, I never would have had any interest in either of them. And vice versa. Dane has put everything on the line for you. He'd do it regardless of who you are."

She snorted in disbelief.

"Why don't you step aside from this competition and see?" I suggested. "Chances are, neither of them will walk away."

I wasn't completely certain of that. Dane, in particular, was desperate to claw back power for himself and his family. I doubted he'd go running to his cousin to do it. If that was an option, he would have already taken it.

Chloe laughed. "Good try. I'm not stepping aside from this. I want Dad to look us both in the eyes and say I deserve to win. I want him to be proud of me." She pointed her perfectly manicured nail at my face. "Don't say he already is. We both know it will take more than what I've already done."

"This is about more than you winning," I accused. "This is about you seeing the expression on my face when I lose. You want me to— what? Cry?"

She leaned in closer. "I want you to do more than cry. I want you to know— I want everyone to know— I'm the better sister. When you lie awake at night, I want you to regret all the things you did that made people think you're better, smarter, more competent than me. All the things that got me overshadowed and pushed aside."

I frowned. "I never—"

"Yes," she hissed. "You did. Don't pretend you have no idea what I'm talking about. If I got an A, you had to get an A+. If I fell over and skinned my knee, you had to fall and break a bone. If Zachary fucked me, you had to fuck him too. If any guy looked at me, you had to get his attention. If it took me two tries to get my driver's license, it only took you one. If..."

I rolled my eyes. "You act as though sibling rivalry is something new. As if I'd break a bone on purpose." I narrowed my eyes. "If I remember right, I broke my wrist because you tripped me."

She sat back. "I wished I'd broken your neck."

Breathing the same air as her was becoming difficult. "There's still time."

She smiled slightly. "No way. Like I said, I want to see your face when I win. After that..."

"I hear the psychology faculty here at Brutham is very good," I said with forced evenness. "You might consider going to see them and getting some therapy." She was starting to make Zachary seem sane. Hell, she might give Ice Miller a run for his money in the unhinged department.

"You know what they say about revenge being the best therapy," she said.

"Revenge for what?" I asked. "For living my life? For trying to live up to Dad's expectations? For breaking a bone after you made me fall? Fuck that. I have nothing to be sorry for. Whatever picture you have painted in your mind, it's fucked up."

"It doesn't matter, I'm still going to win," she insisted. "You say you have no regrets now, but that will change. You will eventually. I promise you that."

Her cold fury knocked the air out of my lungs.

"I don't think you care about winning," I told her. "I don't think you really care one way or another if you lead the family. You have this idea in your head—" I waved a hand in the direction of mine. "That somehow my existence is the reason why your life isn't perfect. If there was no competition between us, you'd make one. You would have done the things you did."

"Yes I would," she agreed. "Every bit of it."

I regarded her for a full minute or two. "I get it," I said softly. "You have nightmares about the rooms in the basement too, don't you?"

She shook her head faintly. "I don't know what you're—"

"Yes, you do," I kept my voice gentle but insistent. "Let me guess, he told you you needed to spend time in there because you weren't good enough at something." Her flinch told me everything I needed to know. "What was it?"

She averted her eyes. "You're wrong."

"No, I'm not. What did he tell you weren't good enough at?" I didn't expect her to tell me, but she needed to understand there was more to all of this. It wasn't about what I did. It was what Dad made her think about me and herself. Our whole lives were a mind fuck.

She scrunched her eyes closed like she was holding back tears. "He told me I needed to be better at everything than you, because I was the oldest. He told me I needed to think about what I'd done and how I could do things better. He said time down there would give me the chance to think."

"But all it did was scare the shit out of you?" I guessed.

"I was weak," she whispered. "I let it get to me because I'm not as strong as you."

I stared at her in disbelief. "Is that what you think? You think I handled being down there better than you did?"

"Didn't you?" she asked. "Did you scream and cry and beg to be let out?"

I hesitated. "No. I curled up in a ball in the corner and hoped like hell he wouldn't forget I was down there." My eyes glazed as I thought back. The memories, the fear, were as fresh now as they were back then. I doubted they would ever disappear into a cloud of the past. They lingered too long and too close to the surface.

"After a while, I had myself convinced he had forgotten. I was sure I was going to die down there. Eventually, I thought dying might be easier than being in there any longer. I was ready to give up when finally the door opened."

"But you didn't give up," she said. "I did. I disappointed him and I disappointed myself. But I won't do that anymore." She wiped the tears from under her eyes with a vengeance. "I will never give up again. Even if one of us is dead at the end of this."

I sighed. "You realise we're messed up because of what Dad did to us? Right?"

"He only did what he did because he wanted us to be tough," she said. "I'll prove to all of you that I can be tough."

"By making my life miserable," I said.

"If that's what it takes," she agreed.

I frowned at her. A disturbing flash of understanding popped into my brain. One I didn't want to contemplate too much, but I had to. Even if my stomach turned and my hands trembled.

"You're terrified that if you lose, he'll put you back down there?" The thought had occurred to me before. Judging by the way she shivered, it occurred to her too.

"If you win, he'll make you lock me in there," her voice wavered.

My blood went cold. "And if you win..."

She looked back at me for a solid minute before she stood and walked away.

The problem was, I wasn't sure if he had to make her lock me in one of those dark, unrelentingly miserable rooms. I would die before I let her do that to me.

I would kill.

twenty-five

LILA

"SOMETHING MAKES me think we're not out here enjoying the sunshine," Parker said. He held my hand in one of his, while the other toyed at something in his pocket. I suspected it was the panties he stole from me the night before. While Slade was marking and Hunter was studying, he and I had a rare night alone. He'd made the most of it.

"Of course we are," I said lightly. "It's a beautiful day out here. The sun is shining. The kookaburras are laughing. I survived yesterday's exam. Why not step out and enjoy ourselves?"

Hunter raised his eyebrows at me. "It's not as though we don't appreciate your good mood, because we do. It's just that—"

"We've been worried about you," Slade finished for him. "You've been quiet for the last while. Since the attack."

I shrugged. "I've been busy with essays and exams." I cocked my head at him. "Whose fault is that?" I smiled teasingly.

He grinned. "Brutham Academy. They tell us how many major assignments and exams we have to assign you. Ultimately that goes back to the school board."

"So it's all Reuben's fault," Parker concluded.

"Blaming him seems like as good a strategy as any," Hunter said. "And Lila's dad."

"If they don't kill us with mercenaries, they'll kill us with coursework," Parker groaned, a hand to his chest as though he was about to die under the pressure of study.

I frowned at the mention of my father but turned my attention to Slade. "Did you ever find any evidence that the school board endorsed that attack?"

"Not really." He draped an arm over my shoulders. "Either no one is talking or Reuben and Samuel did that all on their own. Of course, they contribute so much money to the Academy, the board can't kick them off."

"I don't get why Reuben and Samuel would work together," Hunter admitted. "What does Reuben have to gain?"

"Me dying?" I suggested. "Chloe and Zachary too. Getting rid of us would be guaranteed to make him smile. Even if you two were killed too."

"Chances were, Samuel wouldn't have been able to conduct his test without Reuben's backing," Slade said. "Reuben really had nothing to lose."

"Hey," Parker protested. "Hunter and I are not nothing."

Slade leaned over and patted his shoulder. "I know you're not. People like us are expendable to people like Reuben and Samuel, even if we're related by blood."

"You're not secretly a Brantley, are you?" I tilted my head back to look at him.

He chuckled. "Not that I know of. We're just brothers from different mothers."

"Sibling zoned," Parker looked slightly disappointed.

"Sorry dude," Slade told him. "I'm a one person guy and that person is Lila. For what it's worth, if I was going to screw another guy, it would be you."

That perked Parker up. "Thanks, dude. That means a lot. I always suspected I was hotter than Hunter, but this proves it once and for all."

Hunter barked a laugh. "Dream on, bro. You could wish to be as hot as me."

"All three of you are just as hot as each other," I said firmly. I looked down the driveway at the sound of a truck rumbling towards us.

"What is this about?" Chloe demanded. She trotted down the steps out of the Academy, her phone in her hand. She must have made up with Zachary, because he was right behind her. Dane was nowhere to be seen.

"You know as much as I do," I told her. "Assuming you got the same text I did. Mine was from Dad, saying he had a gift for us for surviving his test."

"That's what mine said," she said carefully.

I shielded my eyes from the sun as a truck rolled into view. It came to a stop outside the building, maybe twenty metres away.

The driver opened the door and slipped out. "Chloe and Lila Bell?"

"That's us," I called back.

He grinned. "These are for you." He waved to the back of the truck where two brand-new Mercedes glimmered in the sun. One black, the other silver.

"Apparently they don't come in pink for Chloe." He shrugged.

"Good thing they had black," I said.

We stood back to watch as he drove the silver car off the back of the truck. He climbed out and handed the keys to Chloe before going back for the black one.

"This is very generous of Samuel," Zachary said carefully.

"Maybe he feels bad for almost killing us," Parker replied. "It seems like a couple of cars is the least he can do."

"Definitely," I agreed. It wasn't unusual for him to send extravagant gifts, but I doubted he'd ever done it out of guilt.

I accepted the key from the driver and toyed with it while he drove the truck away.

"Want to go for a ride?" Chloe asked Zachary. She dangled her key in front of his face.

Did she wonder what he thought about not getting a car himself? Honestly, he didn't seem too concerned. If anything, he seemed happy for her.

"Of course." He grinned. "I always want to ride you, and ride with you."

She batted his arm lightly, before unlocking her car and sliding inside.

"Drive carefully," I told her.

She rolled her eyes at me and slammed the door shut. The engine started with a purr. She gunned the engine, all but flying down the gravel, towards the road.

"Three... Two... One..." Parker said.

In the distance, tyres squealed, followed by a loud bang and the tearing of metal.

I leaned against Slade and exhaled softly.

"Oops."

vengeful

one

LILA

"ARE THEY..." I stepped out of the back of Slade's SUV. With tentative steps, I walked towards the twisted wreckage of my sister's brand-new car.

The front of the silver Mercedes was a crumpled mess of smoking metal resting against the base of a thick gum tree. Dust drifted down, kicked up by high-speed and the impact of the crash.

"Dead?" Slade took my hand, his fingers warm and firm around mine. Reassurance I probably didn't deserve.

"Yeah." We followed Hunter and Parker, stepping over long skid marks to the wreckage.

A groan from inside the twisted Mercedes suggested Chloe or Zachary was still alive.

For now.

I couldn't tell who from the brief, muffled sound. Didn't dare to guess.

"We'll have to go in from the back, Park," Hunter said. "The front doors are kinda fucked."

"I noticed that, Hunt," Parker said. "I'd suggest it was a waste of a car, but..."

He grabbed hold of the handle of one of the rear doors and yanked it open. Knees first, he crawled into the back of the car.

"I hope this thing isn't going to explode," Hunter remarked before he did the same on the other side.

"Yeah, it better not." Slade peered at the front side window, into the driver's seat.

I bit my lip hard enough to draw blood. How did I feel? I wasn't sure. We did this to Chloe and Zachary. Parker hacked her phone to make it look like our father sent a message. I bought both cars, pretending they were a gift from him. Slade organised for the brakes on Chloe's car to fail when she drove at speed.

I did this.

I did this because I couldn't let her win. Not if it meant being confined to the dark, soundless rooms under my father's house. If that's what losing meant, I'd rather die. Or kill my twin sister.

It was fucked up.

I was fucked up.

We both were. This whole competition came down to nothing more than us reliving our childhood terror of being locked in there.

Did either of us really give a shit about heading the family?

Until this moment, I hadn't grasped the extent of the trauma inflicted on both of us. So much trauma it became everything.

If Chloe was dead, I never had to worry about being locked away down there again. Unless Zachary survived and Dad decided—

A shiver of panic-edged fear passed through me.

I wrapped my arms around myself. Whatever happened, I *had* to win. I couldn't let anyone...

"Chloe is alive," Slade said. "So is Zachary by the look of him. We're going to need that..." He glanced around at the sound of an approaching ambulance.

One I'd called after hearing the impact. After all, the world thought my father sent the car. I had absolutely no shred of hesitation in pinning this on him. The money had come from his account, courtesy of Hunter. Slade knew how to cover his tracks. People could and would assume, but no one could trace this back to me.

"I don't think we should move them," Hunter called out. "We wouldn't want to cause any permanent injury, or death." No one missed the irony in his tone.

"Or we could move them," Parker said cheerfully.

"Fuck off," Chloe growled. "We don't need your help." She tried to push her door open, but it was stuck, too twisted to move.

She shoved past Parker and climbed into the back of the car. Blood trickled down her face from a gash in her forehead. Her face was pale, she looked dazed, but otherwise she seemed unhurt.

"Lucky your father sent you such a sturdy car." Parker stepped out behind her. He glanced at me and shrugged. Both he and Hunter seemed disappointed to see her alive.

My own feelings were conflicted. Part relief, part reemergence of fear.

I could almost *hear* my father telling me I failed.

"You tried to kill her but she's still alive. You can't even do that right, can you? Maybe you deserve to be locked away in the dark forever."

I pressed the heel of my hand to my temple, as if I could physically push the thoughts away.

"I don't know what happened." Chloe shook her head. "I tried to stop, but the brakes... I guess I was going too fast and the car skidded on the gravel."

"You were going fast," Slade said. "Some may say you were driving recklessly."

She squinted at him. "Yeah." She seemed confused.

"I'm no doctor, but hitting your head might have given you a concussion," I said. "Maybe you should sit down." I gestured towards the back of Slade's SUV.

I should find a weapon and finish her off here and now. People would believe a blow to the head was from the accident. If they didn't, I could pay them off to say that.

I couldn't bring myself to move. Some small part of me wanted to put my arms around her and comfort her. To tell her I was glad she was alive. I wanted her to hug me back the way Hunter and Parker would have done to each other. Right before they killed whoever did this to them.

Instead, I watched her slump down in the back seat and turned away as the ambulance skidded to a stop beside the wreck.

Time stood still.

I watched as though I was watching a movie. The paramedics climbed out of the ambulance and tended to Chloe. One of them slipped into the Mercedes and placed one of those collars around Zachary's neck to keep him from moving too much.

Words were spoken, but only a handful filtered through into my brain. Concussion. Potential broken neck. Very lucky.

They forced Zachary's door open and carefully lifted him onto a wheeled gurney.

I stared down at him as they pushed him past me. His face was covered with blood. He looked paler than Chloe. If the paramedics hadn't said he was breathing, I might have assumed he was dead.

Somewhere in the middle of this, Dane DiMarco pulled up. His face was a mask of worry until he saw Chloe. He gently pulled her into his arms and cradled her, comforting her in a way I never could. I knew he loved her, but I'd never seen him demonstrate it until now. If he lost her, he'd be devastated. Just as I'd be devastated if I lost the twins or Slade.

Someone said something to me, but I didn't hear until the second or third time.

"Lila? Lila? Hey, babe." Hunter wound his arms around me and drew me to him. "They're taking Zachary and Chloe to the hospital. They think they'll both make a full recovery."

I looked up at him through teary eyes. "This wasn't supposed to—" I couldn't finish the sentence. I was cold and numb all over.

"No, but with any luck, they'll blame your father for this. If Chloe thinks he's trying to kill her, she may choose to walk away."

"He'll deny it." I blinked until the tears trickled onto my cheeks.

Hunter wiped them away with the pad of his thumb. "So will we. This isn't the first time your father tried to kill all three of you. We'll say it was another of his tests. He can deny it all he likes; Chloe won't know what to think."

"Right." The last time was armed mercenaries attacking Brutham Academy. Cars with tampered brakes was something very different, but not implausible. The more I thought about it, the more it sounded like something he'd do.

He'd want to see which of us would just jump into a car, apparently gifted by him, and drive away in it. Honestly, if he'd sent them, I would have had the vehicle checked out thoroughly before I went anywhere near it. If there was anything I learnt this year, it was not to trust anyone except Hunter, Parker and Slade. *Maybe* myself.

Chloe evidently hadn't learned that lesson. That thought shouldn't have given me a surge of satisfaction, but it did.

"I see you understand," Hunter said proudly. "We can totally use this to our advantage. Your father will approve."

His words gave me a sliver of hope. "You think so?"

"I know so. You said it yourself, he wants you to beat her, not kill her. This couldn't have worked out more perfectly." He kissed my forehead.

"I hate to say this, but Hunter is right," Parker said. "I'd go as far as to say it went exactly to plan. I mean, if you really wanted to kill her, you would have bought a cheap, plastic car, not one designed to protect the driver and passenger in a crash."

I chose the cars because my father wouldn't have sent anything cheap, but maybe deep down he was right. I didn't want her dead, just beaten.

"First of all, I'm always right," Hunter said. He paused for effect before adding, "There's no need for a second point."

Parker chuckled. "Keep telling yourself that. It might be true some-day. Although, that's kinda unlikely."

Hunter lifted his hand from my shoulder long enough to flip him off.

"Are you all right?" Slade had been talking to the paramedics and helping them move Zachary, but he stepped over to us now.

I managed a faint smile. "Yeah. I'm okay. Thank fuck Chloe and Zachary are okay too."

He gave me a slightly surprised look, but quickly rolled with my response and nodded.

"This could have been much worse. They're going to need some time off from the Academy for a while. Zachary in particular. It won't be for more than a few days."

"It's wonderful," Hunter said a little louder than necessary. "I hope no one minds if I organise to have someone give Lila's new car a thor-ough going over. I'd hate to have this happen to her too."

Chloe stopped to frown at him before letting herself be led over to the back of the ambulance. She glanced over at me, then at the car. Whatever she was thinking, she clearly hadn't come to a firm conclu-sion yet. She would, soon enough. No doubt she'd blame it on me. I was going to have to work hard to play it cool.

In the meantime, I'd need to speak to my father.

"I don't mind," Parker said. "We don't want this happening again. Although, a whole new car would be better."

"Yes, don't drive that one," Slade said softly.

I glanced at him sharply. Did he really say that? Like so often, his blue-green eyes were hard to read.

"I couldn't be sure she'd take the silver one," he explained. "And if only one was faulty, people might ask questions. Don't worry, I wasn't going to let you get behind the wheel."

"You better not," Hunter growled. "If anything happened to Lila, I'd rip your fucking head off. I mean that in the most caring, brotherly way."

Slade snorted softly. "Of course you do, bro. If anything happened to her, I'd rip my own head off."

Parker cocked his head at him. "I'd like to see you try that. I mean, not literally, but how would that even work?"

They talked in low voices which I mostly ignored while watching the paramedics help Chloe into the back of the ambulance. One of them sat her down and wiped the blood off her face.

For the first time in I didn't know how many years, she reminded me of the little girl she used to be. The one who'd cry if she skinned her knee, or if her balloon flew away.

I pushed away the sliver of guilt that tried to worm itself inside me. If the tables were turned, she'd be laughing over me being hurt. Or she'd be regretting that I wasn't dead. Or that the twins weren't dead too. Remorse didn't seem to be in her vocabulary.

On the other hand, I understood why. All the things she did came from a dark place. One where she was still a scared little girl. Everything we did to each other was because of that.

Could we ever get past this without adding to our own trauma?

two

LILA

"ARE YOU SURE ABOUT THIS?" Parker gripped my hand and squeezed.

"We didn't come all this way to walk away," I said. If only I felt as confident as I sounded. On the inside, it was my turn to be the scared little girl.

I hated that feeling. I pushed it away as violently as I could.

Fuck being vulnerable.

Fuck being scared.

"We're right here with you." Slade killed the engine. He got out of the SUV and came around to open my door.

"I could have done that myself," I told him.

He responded with a smile that made my heart skip several beats. That look never failed to melt me, inside and out. Maybe instead of knocking on my father's door, we could go somewhere private instead. Just the four of us. It was fucking tempting.

"I know you could, but I wanted to do it," Slade said easily. "I can't let the twins have the monopoly on doing things for you. Or to you." One side of his mouth twitched upward slightly.

"Yes, you can," Hunter told him. He grinned and hopped out of the car.

"No, I can't and I won't." Slade didn't take his eyes off me. He ran his knuckles down my cheek. "After everything that's happened, I thought

323

you should know something. If anything happens to either of us, I'd hate it if you didn't know."

"Not know what?" I asked softly. "Is this where you tell me you're breaking up with me because my lifestyle is too crazy?"

He chuckled and leaned in closer. His breath brushed my cheek and the side of my nose, warm and smelling like coffee and spice.

Him being so close like this threatened to make me wet as hell. A breath on my clit might make me come.

"Exactly the opposite," he said finally. "I love your crazy life. I love being part of it." He paused for a moment, then added, "I love *you*."

I exhaled, letting my breath mingle with his. "I love you too."

I couldn't blame him if he had wanted to walk away. I was relieved he didn't. He was no less important to me than the twins were. Losing one of them would be like losing a part of myself.

"Awww," Parker said. "You two are so cute. Almost as cute as Lila and I are together."

Slade's eyes stayed on me, but his smile widened. "We're much cuter."

"Says you, dude," Hunter said. "Everyone knows she and I are the cutest pairing. Right Lila?"

"I'm not playing favourites," I told him. "I couldn't choose one of you over the other, even if I wanted to. Which I don't."

"That's one of the things we love about you," Slade said. "Your heart is big enough for the three of us."

"But only the three of us, right?" Parker asked. "I mean, if you wanted someone else —"

"I only want the three of you," I said immediately, firmly. "Three is the perfect number for me."

"Good, because we like it too." Slade brushed his lips over mine, lightly at first then more demanding. He pressed me back against the side of his SUV and slid his hands up and down my sides.

I shivered under his touch. I was definitely wet now. The pulse in my clit was pounding like crazy.

He ground his quickly hardening cock against the side of my leg. "I want you."

"I want you too," I said breathlessly. I didn't care that we were parked by the side of the road and that it was daytime. We'd stopped a street over from my father's house. He wouldn't see us coming, in both meanings of the word.

Slade pushed up the hem of my skirt and slipped his fingers under the front of my panties. He ran them over my clit and up into my pussy. "You're so fucking wet for me."

He slipped his fingers out of me and pressed them to my lips. "Suck. I want you to know how good you taste."

I opened my mouth and sucked. "Delicious."

He opened the front of his jeans and let his erection spring free. Pre-cum already glistened on his tip.

He gripped my thighs and picked me up. He pressed my back against the side of the SUV while I wrapped my legs around his waist and pushed my pussy onto his cock.

"Fuck, that's hot," Parker said softly.

Literally, anyone could walk past right now. Several cars already rolled on by. For all I knew, people were watching out their windows.

Let them watch. I wasn't shy. I didn't even flinch when Slade pushed up the hem of my red singlet top and tugged down the cups of my bra. I didn't care if the world saw my bare breasts.

Or my nipples tighten as Hunter leaned in to lick all around one of them.

Or when Parker did the same to the other.

Slade started to thrust inside me with slow, even strokes, filling me all the way to the brim with his cock. He slid all the way out, then slammed back in with a grunt.

"Fuck," he breathed. "So fucking incredible."

"You're incredible yourself," I replied. All three of them were. One deep inside me, the other two sucking and licking, lavishing attention on my breasts. Hunter was leaving bite marks here and there, while Parker reached down to keep me steady against the car.

Always so thoughtful.

"Come for me," Slade insisted. "I want you to come around my cock."

"What if I don't?" I asked teasingly.

He paused in his pounding for a moment. "If you don't, I'll have to punish you when we get back to Brutham."

I laughed, low and husky in the back of my throat. "Sounds like I win either way. If I come for you, will you spank me later anyway?"

"I'll spank you, choke you and come down your throat," he promised. "Then I'll tell the twins to do the same. By the time we're done with you, you'll be completely boneless. You'll be begging us to stop and let you rest."

I moaned. "Yes please, sir." I couldn't have stopped myself from coming if I wanted to. The mere idea of all of that was perfect enticement. If they weren't touching me and spoiling my body, I probably would have come anyway.

Slade made an incoherent sound of pleasure and a shout tore out from between his lips. He ground against me, enjoying his own orgasm while my world splintered into a thousand pinpoints of light and pleasure.

I finally came back down and slumped back against the car, struggling to catch my breath.

"Now I'm horny as hell," Parker said. "Yeah, yeah, I know. When am I not horny as hell?" He grinned, but reluctantly pulled up the cup of my bra. "I'm even more so right now."

"So am I, but I'm willing to wait for the punishment session Slade mentioned." Hunter pulled up my other cup, then tugged my singlet back down into place. "I'll conserve my energy."

Slade slowly slid out of me and put my panties back in place. He lowered me to the ground and let my skirt fall back over my thighs. "I'll enjoy speaking to Samuel Bell while his daughter has my cum dripping down her legs." He looked smug.

Parker groaned. "Dude, you're going to make me lose my load in my jeans."

Slade chuckled. "It's not my fault you can't contain yourself."

"You only have to take one look at Lila to realise why I struggle so hard with that," Parker retorted. "I know she makes your balls as heavy as she makes mine."

"So it's my fault?" I teased. I lightly ran my fingers over the bulge in Parker's pants.

He groaned. "You're a cruel woman."

Maybe I wanted to relieve his tension and maybe I wanted to put off seeing my father, but I locked my gaze on his and lowered myself to my knees.

"Oh, hell yes," he breathed as I undid the button of his jeans and worked the zipper down slowly.

I pushed them and his boxers down far enough for his cock to pop free. Not surprisingly, he was already rock hard.

My eyes still on his face, I wrapped my lips around the head of his cock and swirled my tongue around the tip.

"If you really wanted to be cruel, you'd stop right there," Hunter remarked.

"Fuck off," Parker told him. He tangled his fingers in my hair and held me there as if he thought I might actually pull away.

Instead, I worked my mouth down further, taking him in deeper. I let him set the pace, moving my head back and forth along his cock. He pushed himself in deep enough that I gagged.

"You're such a fucking good girl," Parker groaned. "Such a goddess. You take my dick so fucking well."

His praise was exactly what I needed to hear. It was so easy to get lost in the things my father did and the way he made me feel. Knowing someone thought I was good was beyond gratifying. It reminded me that maybe there was hope for me.

Combined with the taste of him and the delicious slide of his cock in and out between my lips, I felt stronger, powerful. Whatever the world threw at me, I'd deal with it.

"I changed my mind about conserving my energy," Hunter said. He took my hand and wrapped it around his thick, red cock.

I gripped him firmly and slid my hand up and down his length while sucking Parker. If anyone was watching out the window, they were getting one hell of a show.

"I'm going to come," Parker said. "I'm going to come in that sweet little mouth of yours."

"She's going to swallow every drop, then suck Hunter's cock," Slade said. "If she does, I'm going to add to her punishment."

I glanced up at him, but he didn't elaborate. Whatever he might come up with, I'd enjoy. All three of them had a way of knowing exactly what I liked and gave that, and more, to me. As far as I was concerned, I was the luckiest girlfriend in Australia.

I sucked Parker harder, one hand massaging his balls while the other slowed in my working of his twin's cock. I didn't want Hunter to come too soon. Not to mention, while it was a turn on to think of talking to my father with Slade's cum running down my thighs, having Hunter's all over my face might not be a good look.

Parker grunted a couple of times. His balls tensed and then he was squirting a load of salty cum into my mouth.

I swallowed down every drop.

"Fuck yeah." He sagged forward for a few moments before pulling me off his cock and turning my head so Hunter could slip his in between my lips.

"Yes, just like that," Slade said. "You're perfect."

"She is, isn't she?" Parker agreed. "She's so perfect."

"The most perfect," Hunter said breathlessly. "The most beautiful, smartest, most amazing."

If they weren't careful, all of this praise was going to go right to my head. Instead, I focused on swirling my tongue around Hunter's cock and grazing my teeth lightly across his tip.

"Holy fuck," Hunter groaned. "Woman, your mouth is beyond perfection. I can't even..." His balls tightened and he exploded in my mouth, shooting himself down my throat.

I looked up at him and swallowed.

"That deserves spanking, choking and choc-mint ice cream," Slade said.

I smiled as I slid my mouth off Hunter's cock. "I can't wait."

The sooner we got this conversation over with and got back to Brutham, the better. I was looking forward to getting thoroughly spoiled after dealing with my father.

three

LILA

"WAIT." Slade grabbed my wrist as we stepped up to the gate leading into my father's opulent, harbourside mansion. A wrought iron and brick fence obscured the view of the lower level, but the upper two were visible.

Stark white contrasted with black roof and windows, the whole effect an architectural study in slants and angles. My father always preferred modern architecture to classic. Modern furniture to antique. Unless it was ridiculously expensive, if it was more than a year or two old, he'd have it replaced.

Instinctively, I froze, my alert level shooting up even higher.

"What is it?" Nothing appeared to be out of place, or ticking.

The gates clanged and slid open, revealing the short driveway and garage big enough to fit six cars.

"Looks like he knew we were coming after all," Hunter said.

"I've never felt so welcome here before," Parker added.

"That's not it." Slade's grip on my wrist tightened.

I glanced over at him, then back at the house as the front door opened. A woman stepped outside. Her hair was a tangle of red falling down her back. She wore loose, linen pants and a white T-shirt with a colourful flower in the centre. She stepped away from the door in bright red flat shoes.

I frowned.

Who the hell was she?

My eyes widened as my father stepped out behind her and drew her towards him. He said something in her ear which made her giggle, then kissed her.

"What the—" I rubbed my fingertips over my forehead. I knew my father wasn't celibate, but in no universe I was aware of was she his type. Except the red hair. That was definitely his thing. Usually he went for women who wore pencil skirts and heels. Not black linen pants with — was that paint? —on the front.

She broke off the kiss, placed her hands on his chest and pushed him away playfully. "I really have to go."

"You don't have to." He pulled her back and nuzzled his face into her hair. "You could—"

He somehow became aware he was being watched. He raised his head and looked right back at me.

"I'll see you later." His relaxed posture became all business. He lowered his hands and stepped away from her.

"If you're lucky," she teased. She smiled at him over her shoulder as she walked away. Only when she turned back did she see me and my guys standing outside the gate. She gave me a warm smile and a brief finger wave before she slipped into the driver's seat of an old van. That was covered in more paint than her pants. Some artistic and intentional, others looking as though someone threw balloons full of paint, letting them burst however they wanted.

"Did you want something?" My father stood with his arms crossed over his button down shirt.

"Dude, nice socks," Parker remarked.

Dad and I both looked down at his feet.

I'd never seen him with cartoon character socks on before. Only a small sliver was visible between his patent leather shoes and the hem of his suit pants. Even that little bit was out of character for him.

He looked back up, but offered no explanation about the woman or the socks.

"I asked you a question, Lila. I presume you didn't come all the way to Sydney to stand there and stare." He gave the twins a look like they were bugs that crawled out from the sewer. The glance at Slade was only slightly more welcoming.

"You're right, we didn't," Hunter said. He waved us all in through the gate and up to the door. "We're not vampires, so we don't need an invitation to enter, but the polite thing to do would be to extend one anyway." He smiled pleasantly.

Dad didn't smile back. Without another word, he turned and stepped back inside.

"Well, he didn't slam the door in our faces." Parker trotted up the steps and followed him into the house.

"No, but he might shoot you in the face instead," Hunter said.

"I won't say I'm not tempted." We found Dad in the kitchen, standing by the coffee machine. "But I'm not in the mood to have blood cleaned out of the carpet today. Unless you push me too far."

"Who was the woman?" I reached for four cups and set them on the island.

"None of your business," Dad snapped.

"Daddy's got a girlfriend," Parker said in a singsong voice, half under his breath.

I grimaced at him. "If you say anything like that again, *I* might shoot you in the face."

Parker raised his hands to either side and grinned. "There's nothing wrong with having relationships. Is there, Hunt?"

"Nothing at all," Hunter agreed.

"But we really should get down to why we're here," Slade said. He glanced over at me, letting me take the floor. The slightest sparkle in his blue-green eyes told me he was thinking about his cum on my thighs.

I rolled my eyes at him slightly. Men.

I decided to be blunt. "Chloe was in a car crash. Zachary too."

Dad flinched slightly. "Are they..."

"Dead? No." I flicked my ponytail back off my shoulder. "We made it look like you sent the car, but we fixed the brakes. She didn't hesitate to get into the driver's side and drive away. The car is totalled, but she's fine. Zachary may take a bit longer to recover fully."

Dad listened, visibly absorbing what I was telling him.

"You tried to kill her?" he asked evenly. He gave away nothing of his thoughts.

"Not exactly," I replied. "The cars I bought were made to withstand the impact. If that wasn't what happened, then... That would have been too bad."

My stomach twisted and I resisted the urge to turn and run. I hadn't ruled out the possibility he might throw all of us in the basement rooms.

Fuck.

Should I have called him instead? I didn't because I wanted to look him right in the eyes and tell him what we did. Okay, I wanted to see a hint of *something* in his face. Pride, or...something like it.

"She didn't question that the cars came from me?" He didn't seem particularly concerned by how much of his money was spent on those cars.

"Not for a second. She took the key from the guy who delivered them and drove away. I'm sure you'd agree she let her guard down." My heart raced. I wanted to beg him to agree with me. To say that he approved of what I did and that Chloe failed this test.

Yeah, it was all kinds of fucked up, but I needed to hear that from him. Some reassurance I wouldn't end up back in the darkness.

"It certainly sounded like she did," he said slowly. He turned away and finished making a cup of coffee.

"That's it?" I asked. Was that all he had to say about it?

"What more is there to say?" He added sugar to his coffee and gave it a quick stir.

"You could offer us a cup," Parker said helpfully. "Although, it might be laced with something, and I've been drugged enough for one lifetime."

Dad raised an unsympathetic eyebrow in his direction and sipped his coffee.

"You know Lila deserves to lead the family," Hunter said.

"Do I?" Dad sipped again before lowering his cup. "Or is this just more proof none of you deserve it?"

I glanced down at the hardwood floor. "I don't know what more I'm supposed to do."

"That's exactly the problem." He turned his lack of sympathy back toward me. "None of you seem to have a clue. Am I supposed to believe you didn't try to kill your sister? Yes, she let her guard down, but you tried to kill her and you failed."

I took a step back and bumped into Slade.

He placed his hands on my shoulders. "We all know killing is easy," he said. "It's far harder to outsmart people."

"That depends on the people." Dad's eyes flicked towards the twins and back again.

"Rude," Parker muttered. "At least we're on Lila's side."

"Yes, we are," Hunter agreed. "Maybe you should try it sometime. You might find out how amazing she really is. She's—"

"I'm perfectly well aware of what my daughter is like," Dad said coldly. "She conducted a little test and her sister failed. I'm impressed with her ingenuity, but it ultimately proves nothing." He returned his gaze to me.

I lifted my chin. "It proves Chloe trusts you more than she should. That may change after this. For all she knows, you sent those cars."

Dad chuckled.

It took me a second to realise why. Of course, how could I be so stupid?

Hunter chuckled. "Cute that you didn't think we'd tamper with any recording equipment you have in the house before we stepped through the door."

For half a second, Dad actually looked surprised, possibly even slightly impressed. That faded quickly.

"Was that Lila's idea?"

"I'm starting to think you're missing the point," Hunter told him. "Lila and the three of us are a team. Whether you like us or not doesn't matter. Parker, Slade and me intend to stand by Lila's side forever. Before you say that takes her out of the running, remember Chloe is very attached to Dane DiMarco."

Dad's lips twitched with displeasure. "Poor taste in relationships notwithstanding, Lila needs to stand on her own two feet. So does Chloe."

"Is that what this is about?" I demanded. "You'll only be happy when I'm alone?"

"Possibly," he said vaguely. "Possibly not. Whoever ends up leading the family needs to learn how to answer to themselves. Not to anyone with the surname Brantley, or DiMarco. Or Lincoln," he added after a moment.

Hunter tipped his head back and laughed. "You actually think she answers to us? You really don't know her at all if that's what you believe."

Dad stared at him, his face expressionless. "If I were you, all of you, I'd focus on the upcoming trials. That will be the real test."

His expression gave me chills. What could he, or the school board, throw at me that was worse than anything he'd already done? What could Chloe try to do to me?

Mercenaries, dark rooms, being kidnapped, drugged and almost blown up by a teddy bear. How the fuck could anything be worse than any of that?

"We're very much focusing on those," Hunter said. "I have complete faith in Lila to kick ass and get through the trials without breaking a sweat."

"So do I," Parker said.

"Me as well," Slade said, his voice low and deep. "I presume we can't leave with an assurance you won't test Lila again before the trials."

"Of course not," Dad said. "Everyone here knows that complacency in this life gets you dead. It seems as though that lesson hasn't fully sunk in. You might be better off assuming something is coming. Hopefully this time Lila won't disappoint me."

He fixed his gaze on me, his eyes colder than chips of ice. "She knows what happens when she disappoints me."

Hunter grabbed Parker before he lunged at Dad.

"You won't be doing anything to Lila," Hunter's tone matched Dad's. "Like Slade said, killing is easy."

"Don't threaten me, you little prick," Dad growled. "I could have you killed before you step foot out the door. That would immediately reduce two of my problems."

Rather than being intimidated, Hunter took a step forward. "I happen to have a big prick, but thanks for bringing my cock into the conversation. I think you might be threatened in that department."

I grimaced. The last thing I wanted to think about was my father's body parts. Especially that one.

"I suggest you get out." Dad's eyes flashed an angry warning. "The next time I see Lila, I expect her to have done better."

I gave him a long look before I followed the guys out the door.

four
SLADE

"I DON'T KNOW what the fuck he wants." Lila kicked a foot full of sand away from her. "He doesn't want us to kill each other, but nothing else is good enough. Am I missing something?" She glanced over at me.

I draped an arm over her shoulders. "If you are, then so am I. I've heard he was... Difficult. I get the distinct impression whatever you do, he'll poke holes in it. Even where there are no holes."

"Maybe that's the point." She looked so defeated. "There are always holes. Whatever I do, there's always something not quite right." She sighed and leaned against me. "It's more than that though. *Everything* I do is wrong."

A refreshingly cool wave washed onto the shore and over our bare feet. A slow walk on the beach always helped to put things into perspective. Even on a sunny day.

During a storm, I loved to come down here. It was a reminder that mother nature didn't give a fuck about us. She'd happily sweep us into the sea and swallow us. If we were lucky, we'd get spat out afterwards. If not, then the sharks and whatever else was hungry were the lucky ones.

"Not as far as I'm concerned," I assured her. "I know the twins agree."

I glanced over my shoulder. They were trailing along behind us.

Hunter was staring out at the waves, a thoughtful expression on his face. Parker seemed to be gathering shells.

"I wish I knew what he wanted me to do." She kicked the sand again, narrowly missing touching a bluebottle. The sting of the small jellyfish would be worse than anything her father could inflict. Although, the effects wouldn't be as long lasting.

"Am I supposed to drag Chloe off to one of the family's brothels and lock her in there? Or hack into the school's records and give her failing grades?"

"I wouldn't recommend trying to hack into anything at Brutham," Hunter said. Apparently he was listening after all. "Listening in on school board meetings is one thing. Tampering with your grades could end up with you in a shallow grave, if you're lucky."

"That doesn't sound lucky," I remarked. "On the other hand, there are worse things than being dead."

"Like being sold and raped?" Lila asked wryly. "That would definitely be worse."

"Anyone who touched you would end up worse than dead," I told her. "Before they died."

"Hell yeah they would," Parker said. "Do you think we're going about all of this the wrong way?"

"Going about what, Park?" Hunter asked.

"This whole competition with Chloe," Parker said slowly. "Maybe we're supposed to go after Samuel instead. I mean, it's unlikely, but it's fucking tempting. Right?"

I glanced over at Lila. She didn't look so tempted.

"I'm starting to think this is like a cryptic puzzle," she said slowly. "The only way we get to find the answer is if we know what the question actually is. All the clues are so confusing, I have no idea how to figure it out. But I don't think my father wants us to kill him."

"He probably wouldn't mind if you killed Parker and me," Hunter said. "Maybe that's the question."

Lila glanced back at him. "If that's the question, I refuse to answer. I don't care what he does to me, I wouldn't kill either of you." The look in her eyes was haunted. It was the same one she often got whenever she talked about her father.

"It's because of him you don't like dark places, isn't it?" I asked gently.

She pressed her lips together so hard they turned white. "It was a long time ago."

"What did he do? You don't have to tell me if you don't want to, but I see it bothers you." I squeezed her shoulders gently.

She closed her eyes for a few moments. "He has rooms under his house. They're designed for various different kinds of torture. Some have chains and torture equipment. Some have nothing, including light and sound."

"Sensory deprivation?" I asked.

She responded with a faint nod.

It took a full minute for the meaning of her words to sink in. I rubbed the stubble on my chin.

"Fuck. I've heard of some screwed up things in my life, but that..." I wanted to jump back in the SUV, go back to Samuel's house and rip his head straight off his shoulders. Or better yet, wrap my belt around his throat and watch him die, nice and slow.

"He could have had us skinned alive, or made us skin his victims," she said in a small voice.

"Just because he didn't, doesn't mean what he did to you was okay," I said firmly. "He doesn't deserve you defending him." He deserved a lot of things, but not that.

"Do you think I'm strong enough to be head of the family?" She looked up at me. "I'm not sure I am. I could have gone against his wishes and killed Chloe and Zachary. That might be what he wants. For us to stand up to him and do whatever we need to do to be rid of each other. Could that be the thing I'm missing?"

I couldn't tell how she wanted me to respond to that.

"Is that what you want?" Maybe answering her question with a question was a cop out, but I wasn't going to tell her to go and end her sister's life. Not unless that was what she needed to hear.

"No. I don't know." She glanced down at the sand. "I just...don't want to end up back in those rooms. I don't want to end up sold. I don't want to do anything that would hurt you guys."

"But you wish your father would explain what it is he wants so you can decide if that's something you're prepared to do. What if he did that and you weren't? What if he told you to put a gun to Chloe's head and pull the trigger?"

She didn't answer straight away. When she did, it was in a small voice.

"I have no idea. There were times, especially when I was on the back of that truck, I would happily have blown her brains out. What she did to me was...unforgivable."

"But now?" I prompted.

"Now I realised she's scared of the same thing I am. She's scared of not winning because in Dad's eyes, that's losing. And if we lose, we risk getting punished. Not in the good way either." She offered me a faint smile.

I flashed her one in return. "Would you get punished if you wanted to step aside in favour of your sister?"

"Probably," she said after another moment of hesitation. "Chloe would never believe I'd ever fully get out of her way. She'd assume it's some kind of trick. That the moment her back was turned, I'd try something."

"She'd assume that, or you'd assume it from her if she stepped aside?" I asked.

"Both," she replied. "You must think our family is a special kind of fucked up."

I smiled. "My family is pretty fucked up itself. My cousin plays American football for the Dusk Bay Sharks, of all things. It's a growing sport here in Australia, but still..."

She snorted softly. "That's terrible. Much worse than anything my family gets up to." A smile tugged at the corners of her mouth.

"Exactly," I said with a laugh. "His parents have never recovered from the shame." Truthfully, they were just as proud of Walker as my parents were of me. Sometimes, I thought he was the lucky one, being as far from this crazy life as he was.

Lila sighed out her nose. "I'm sure being a professional athlete isn't easy, but at least you know what the expectations of you are. He probably has a coach yelling at him constantly, telling them to correct this or that."

I grinned. "Basically, yes. He seems to enjoy himself."

VENGEFUL

"Why did you become a teacher?" She asked. "Why business law?" She wrinkled her nose.

"Why not business law?" I shot back. "Who would suspect the business law professor is also an assassin? It's a near perfect cover."

"Near-perfect?" She glanced at me questioningly.

"The perfect cover would be one that involves making and eating more cake." I nodded decisively. "What?" I added when she gave me a funny look. "I like baking. There's something satisfying about turning a bunch of ingredients into something tasty."

"You don't do that fancy cake decorating shit, do you?" She poked me in the chest with a manicured, black fingernail.

"What if I do?" I asked teasingly. "Are you saying you don't want a birthday cake shaped as a teddy bear?"

She barked a laugh. "I definitely do not. But feel free to send one to my sister. Maybe throw in a bomb or some GHB for shits and giggles. I know, throw in both."

Suspecting she didn't really want her sister dead, no matter what her father might think, I said, "How about a cake that when it explodes, it sprays pink icing all around the room? Wait, pink icing and glitter. No one would ever wash all of that shit out as long as they lived."

She laughed. "And they call me wicked."

"Who calls you that?" I asked. That didn't seem especially accurate to me. Nicknames often weren't. Like the weird habit of calling a redhead Blue.

She shrugged. "Hunter and Parker are the evil twins, Chloe and I are the wicked sisters. I can't remember the first time anyone said that about us, but I can't say they're wrong."

"They're definitely wrong," I assured her. "You're not wicked. You're the victim of what your father did to you. The person he tried to make you become. But he didn't, because in spite of everything, you're not a bad person."

"I'm not a good person either," she said. "I'm not convinced I didn't deserve what he did."

Her expression was so troubled my heart ached for her. I shoved away the mental image of my hand sliding a knife between Samuel's ribs. That was a temptation I couldn't give into unless it was necessary. Right now, we needed him alive.

339

I stopped and turned her to face me. "There's nothing you could ever do that would justify what he did. Nothing that would make you deserve it. Punishment like that is for people who would buy women, or people who would lock children in a dungeon. You would never do either of those things."

I fixed her with a firm gaze, determined that she should believe me. I meant every word. She was beautiful, smart and extraordinary. I fell for her the moment I lay eyes on her, in the Academy bar. The second my cock sank into her pussy I was gone, head over heels. If the twins hadn't agreed to share, I would have been forced to get them out of my way.

She said she wasn't a good person. She was wrong. It was me who wasn't. Not even close.

"I wouldn't do those things, but I'd do other things," she said. She looked like a sad, lost little girl for a moment. Sometimes it was easy to forget she wasn't a mature, worldly woman. She was only nineteen. Right at the beginning of her life. She was a badass, and not as innocent as many women her age, but she was still so young.

Could I protect her from the big bad world before it destroyed her?

five

SLADE

"SO, ABOUT THAT PUNISHMENT." Lila slid a hand up my arm.

We arrived back at the Academy a few hours ago. As far as I could tell, Chloe and Zachary were still in hospital, with Dane watching over them. Okay, watching over her. My sneaking suspicion was, if Zachary died, Dane wouldn't shed a tear. He might even have a hand in it.

I thought about driving over there and quietly ending all three of them. Doing that would take little effort on my part, as long as Lila was somewhere public so no one could immediately pin it on her. Unfortunately, my absence wouldn't go unnoticed, and if all three of them turned up dead, it wouldn't take a PhD graduate to figure out what happened.

I didn't give a fuck what anyone else thought, but if Lila didn't want them dead, then they could live for a while longer.

If I had any regrets in life, it was that I hadn't disposed of them months ago. Long before anyone knew about the connection between me and Lila. I should have stayed away from her long enough to get the job done, but I let my emotions get in the way. And my cock. That was the first and last time that would happen.

"You're eager to have your ass spanked, aren't you?" I teased. "You like the sting of my hand that much?"

The smile she gave me in response triggered a competition in my

341

body. One between my heart and my cock, to see which would react the most vigourously. I think it was a tie.

"That looks like a yes to me," Parker said. "Wouldn't you say so Hunt?"

"Without doubt," Hunter agreed.

"It is." Lila dropped her hands to her sides. "But I keep thinking about the trials."

That made my cock soften slightly. "What about them?" I could be all business if she needed me to be. Considering the importance of the trials, I could put anything aside, even thoughts of burying myself balls deep inside her.

"Not so much the trials themselves." She stepped towards the door that led out of her room and slid the tips of her fingers around the knob like it was one of us. "I keep thinking about the practice run we did."

"What about it, babe?" Hunter frowned and took a half step toward her. "Whenever you want to do another trial practice, we can—"

His concern was palpable, almost equal to my own. If I could do the trials for her, I would, in a heartbeat. All three of us would.

If we thought she'd forgive us for taking her place. Which she wouldn't. She want to confront this head on and get through it. Otherwise, she'd always wonder at her own abilities. She shouldn't. Her self-doubt was misplaced as far as I was concerned. No one was more incredible than she was.

"I definitely do," she replied. "The sooner the better." She glanced down at the floor, then back up at us, a secretive smile on her luscious lips.

"I was thinking since we all enjoyed the chasing part so much, we could do that again." She twisted the knob and yanked the door open. "Catch me if you can." She darted out the door and swung it shut behind her.

I was a step behind Hunter as he pulled the door open and raced out behind her. My heart and cock were in definite agreement now. We needed to catch her before either of the twins did.

Hunter headed down the stairs, but I caught a glimpse of white dashing around the end of the corridor.

I glanced over my shoulder. Parker was hesitating. Clearly torn between following his brother and following me.

I didn't bother to wait and see what choice he made. I bolted down the corridor, hoping that *was* Lila I saw rounding the corner. If not, I just gave the twins a huge advantage.

I slowed before I reached the corner. Now was a good time to put my skills to use. If I found her first, she wouldn't see me coming until I was virtually on top of her. Figuratively and then literally.

I ducked into the shadows and peered around the corner.

Moonlight illuminated another long corridor, slanting in from a couple of windows that overlooked the front of the building. At the end of that corridor was another bend leading to another set of stairs.

Judging from the slowed, gradually fading footsteps behind me, Parker decided to follow his brother. I contemplated whether or not I'd made the right decision when I caught another glimpse of movement up ahead. It was the slightest flash. If I wasn't looking in that direction, I would have missed it.

I smiled to myself and slipped around the corner.

A shadow flowed further down the corridor towards that second bend. They moved slowly at first, but then darted across a beam of moonlight.

I grinned. There was no mistaking that luscious shape. Those perfect hips and generous breasts. The body that begged to be fucked. Her silhouette alone made my cock stand up at attention. She was so fucking gorgeous. She genuinely had no idea how beautiful she was. To me, she was absolutely breathtaking. So much more than a queen or a goddess. She was the woman who held a pincer grip on my heart and my balls.

She darted across the second beam and flew off to the end of the corridor and out of sight.

I broke into a quiet trot, but I wasn't trying to stay unseen. Let my prey know I was behind her, stalking her every step. Her heart would race, knowing I was there, just out of reach.

Her footsteps headed towards the stairs.

I visualised the layout of that part of the school. Smiled again.

I caught another glimpse of her as she started down the stairs, her hand on the banister. By the time I reached the top, she'd reached the bottom and disappeared.

I trotted down and headed straight into the darkened library.

Whether or not she'd come here was a guess, but an educated one. No pun intended.

She could have slipped into a dozen different places, but instinct told me she was here. Instinct that was proven correct a moment later with a whiff of her perfume in the air. The scent was subtle, but lingering, enticing.

"I know you're in here," I called out softly. "The hound is on the scent of the beautiful fox."

"Maybe," she called back. "But the library is a big place."

I followed the sound of her voice to the section containing legal books. Only her scent remained.

"I like a challenge," I told her. I stood still and listened.

A faint shuffle sounded from only a handful of metres away. Silently, I followed the sound, stalking my prey more like a lion than a hound. When I caught her, I was going to fuck her on her hands and knees. After I spanked her ass red.

I circled around to where I thought she'd be, hoping to cut her off. When I reached the stack of history books, she wasn't there.

"Come out, come out wherever you are," I teased.

She giggled. "No way. I'm not making it easy on you."

"But we like it easy." That was Parker's voice. The twins must have finally found out where we'd gone.

"Not *too* easy," Hunter said. "Too easy isn't fun."

Fuck. I was hoping to catch her long before they showed up. I didn't mind sharing, but I had a competitive streak almost as long as my dick. That was one thing I shared with the twins. We hated losing.

Lila streaked out of one stack and into another.

Stealth wasn't going to help me now. I raced after her. If I was going to win, I was going to do it with speed, not with assassin skills.

I almost caught up with her in the study area, but she bolted around a wide table and stopped, putting it between us. She was panting, the rise and fall of her chest making her breasts move tantalisingly.

"Now what?" she teased.

I grinned and chased her around the table, gaining ground but not enough to catch her.

Not yet.

She ducked away and into another stack.

"I've come to the conclusion, if we're going to catch this sneaky fox, we need to work together," Hunter said.

"Only if I get to take part this time and not sit back and watch," Parker said sulkily.

Apparently he still hadn't gotten over that practice trial. I couldn't say I blamed him. Watching Hunter and I fuck Lila must have been a special kind of torture.

"Deal," Hunter told him. "You good with that, Slade?"

"Works for me," I said. I needed to be inside her, and soon. Whatever that took.

"You have to catch me first," she taunted.

Once again, I followed the sound of her voice, and circled around where I thought she'd be. The twins made no effort to be quiet, which made it easier to pinpoint their locations and try to keep Lila between me and them.

I stepped forward slowly, keeping all of my senses open. Her scent lingered here, but it mingled with twins and books. A hint of something else tickled the back of my memory, but I couldn't place what it was. Something from my past long forgotten, and better left there.

I lunged towards the shuffle of movement ahead of me and grabbed what felt like an arm.

"Shit," Parker hissed. "You scared the hell out of me."

"Sorry." I dropped my hand. "Lila should have been here."

"That's what I thought." Hunter was right behind Parker. "She's a slippery little minx."

In the deeper shadows, a couple of stacks over, she giggled.

I raised my voice slightly. "She's a brat who is going to have a very red ass when we've finished with her. I think she needs more lessons in doing as she's told. Wouldn't you say, guys?"

"Definitely," Hunter said. "She's very naughty sometimes. I might even spank her a time or two myself."

"Promises, promises," Lila taunted. "Maybe I should spank you."

"You can spank me anytime," Parker said. "Before or after you peg me. I'm good with either."

He was so fucking adorable I almost regretted not being into other guys. I meant it when I told him if I was, I'd be into him. Either way, Lila was the only one for me. No one else I ever met came close to being as incredible as her. She was a hundred times hotter, sweeter and sexier than anyone else.

"I might have to catch you some time," she told him. "Although, at this rate you'll be old and grey before you catch me."

She darted out of the stacks and into a pool of moonlight that shone through the transom window high up in the wall. She placed her fists on her hips and grinned. "I thought you guys were better at this?"

"That's what we want you to think," Hunter said. "The second you let your guard down, we'll be all over you. Wouldn't want this to be over too quickly."

Lila snorted. "That's such bullshit, Hunter Theodore Brantley."

I barked a laugh. "Your middle name is Theodore?"

Hunter huffed. "Yeah, but it's still better than Parker's middle name."

"Dude," Parker groaned, "leave my middle name out of this. I'm sure Slade's is just as bad."

"I'll tell you mine if you tell me yours," I said. If he was that touchy about it, it must be pretty terrible.

"It's after our great-grandfather, Albert," Parker said.

"I think it's cute," Lila said. "Parker Albert Brantley."

He groaned again. "Okay, Slade. Time to share. What's yours?"

I grinned. "I don't have one."

"Motherfucker," Parker growled.

I laughed, but that stopped abruptly when Lila turned and bolted toward the library door.

I raced after her, the twins right behind me.

We couldn't have been more than a second or two behind her, but when I reached the doorway and stopped, there was no sign of her. She'd completely disappeared.

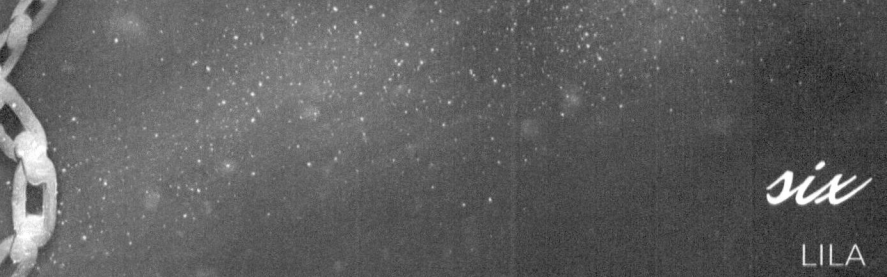

six

LILA

MY PULSE WAS RACING and my pussy throbbing, but I didn't want this to end too soon. I'd shivered slightly when I entered the shadows, an edge of fear creeping up my spine. Knowing the guys were close behind me, and occasionally stepping into the moonlight, I felt safe. As safe as I could in a place nicknamed Brutal Academy.

Okay, the absence of my sister and her guys contributed. For an hour or two, I could put aside everything and enjoy the chase.

I ran out of the library and dove into one of the nearby lecture theatres. I hesitated for a moment before trotting down the steps between the seats, all the way down to the floor.

Fuck only knew how many people had paced back and forth here, lecturing students who were half listening at best. Most of them would have been daydreaming about their futures, or whoever they fucked the night before.

Whatever, I didn't want to get a job here. Although I wouldn't take over from my father for years, I still expected to work in the family business before then. A shit ton of things always needed to be done. Starting with dismantling any trafficking operations and working instead to expand into other countries and make alliances all over the world.

I'd often wondered if I could somehow convince the Brotherhood of Kings to allow women. One of my goals was to be powerful enough to force them to, if they wouldn't voluntarily comply. Then, of course, I'd take over. Absorb the brotherhood into the rest of the family interests.

Whatever my father might think, I never lacked ambition.

The guys walked past the doorway, three shadows barely illuminated, moving slowly.

A thrill of excitement passed through me.

Should I slip in between the rows of seats and hide there? No, where would the fun be in that? I could be there for hours, crouched down in a confined space. That wouldn't get me spanked or fucked.

"Looking for something?" I called out instead.

The three shadows stopped.

"We might be," Hunter replied. "Have you seen a cute brunette around anywhere?"

"I'm right behind you," Parker joked.

Hunter laughed. "I should have been more specific. I meant a cute, female brunette. One with perfect tits and the best pussy on the face of the planet."

"That's definitely not me," Parker said.

"Let's spread out," Slade suggested. "We have her pinned down this time." He sounded amused and excited.

Me too, gorgeous man, me too.

"Are you sure about that?" I teased. "You seemed very certain in the library and yet I'm still unpinned." I clicked my tongue in mock disappointment.

"We noticed that." Slade started down the steps slowly, moving like he was stalking me. Like I was the fox he called me.

"Yes, we did." Hunter headed to the other end of the room and started down the steps there.

"We're observant that way." Parker moved down the centre. "Especially me. I've noticed because of the absence of your hot, wet pussy around my cock. How wet do you think she is, guys?"

"Very wet," Slade replied.

"Very, very wet," Hunter agreed. "Dripping wet. Trickling down her own thighs."

Accurate. I was so turned on it wouldn't take much effort for me to come. I was so aroused, I was almost tempted to touch myself, instead of waiting for them to catch me.

The anticipation as they closed in on me sent an inferno through my body. Fire, boiling, lava, all at once.

I stepped to the very front of the room, closest to the wall, and waited. The moment they all reached the floor, I ran, ducking and weaving around the lectern and heading for the space between Slade and Parker.

I bounded up two steps before one of them grabbed me around the waist, pulling me down on my hands and knees.

"Caught you!" Parker's voice was triumphant. His arms slid around me, yanking me back down to the floor and pinning me face down on the cold hardwood.

"Nice work," Slade told him.

"Thanks." Parker pushed up the hem of my skirt and bit my ass so hard I squealed. "Shit, too hard?"

I managed a breathless laugh. "No. Not at all." It was perfect.

"Good." He slid his lips across my skin and bit me again. He wound his fingers on the waistband of my G string and pulled them down before tucking them into his pocket. "Consider those a trophy."

He shifted his weight off me long enough to pry my legs apart and trace his thumb around my rear hole. He pressed a couple of fingers inside me until I moaned.

"She makes the best sounds, doesn't she?" he asked.

"She definitely does." Slade crouched beside my head and grabbed my wrists. He pulled my arms up over my head and held them hard. "But she still deserves that spanking. Especially after running away from us." He brought his hand down hard on my ass.

I jumped at the sting, but between that and Parker's fingers, I was on the verge of coming.

"Don't let her come too soon," Hunter warned. "What sort of punishment would this be if we let that happen?"

"Exactly." Slade spanked me again a couple of times on the same cheek then gave the other cheek the same treatment. Each time pushed me closer and closer to the edge. Right before I plunged over, Parker took his hands from me.

I groaned in frustration.

"Something to say?" Hunter sat down in front of me and rested his chin on his fist.

"I need to come," I panted. "Please."

"Please, what?" Hunter asked. "I think if you call Slade sir, it's only fair you call Parker and me that too. Don't you, Park?"

"Definitely." Parker was running his hands up and down the insides of my thighs, driving me even more wild.

"Please, sir," I moaned. Fuck it felt good to surrender control like this. It made me feel powerful. Like out in the forest, I knew if I said banana, or even mango, they'd stop immediately. "I need to come."

"I don't know if she's learned her lesson," Hunter said. "Roll her over."

Slade and Parker rolled me onto my back, Slade holding my arms and Parker holding my legs. The moment they set me down, Parker opened my legs again and resumed running his hands up and down the insides of them.

Hunter scooted over beside me and lightly wrapped his hand around my throat. "Little fox." He clicked his tongue. "Are you going to run away from us again?"

I smiled. "Yes."

He squeezed a little tighter while at the same time pushing up my top and landing a light slap on the side of my breast. It felt so fucking good.

"Are you going to run away from us again tonight?" he asked.

Parker slid his hands up to my core and ran the heel of his hand up and down my pussy, barely touching my clit. That slight touch was almost enough to shatter me.

"No, daddy," I replied teasingly.

Even in the semi-dark I saw Hunter's eyes widen. "Fuck, that was hot. I think I like it better than sir."

"Good," Slade growled. "Sir is mine, get your own."

Hunter chuckled. "Okay, Park, let her come."

He didn't hesitate to increase the pressure on my pussy. The heel of his hand rubbed up and down my clit while he slid his fingers inside me.

My back arched. I came so hard it almost hurt. So hard there wasn't a cell in my body that didn't scream out in pleasure. Moisture squirted out of me, splashing Parker's hand and onto the floor. It was like nothing I ever felt before. A perfect moment of absolute, pure bliss, surrounded by and surrendered to the three guys that loved me.

"Now *that* was hot," Parker said. I didn't even see him undo his pants or slide down his boxers before he slammed his throbbing cock inside me.

I groaned at the sudden sensation of being filled while Slade held my wrists and Hunter gripped my throat. I was theirs to do whatever they wanted with and I loved every minute of it. In their hands like this, I felt truly alive. Nothing else in the world mattered but here and now and us. The pounding of Parker's cock, sliding in and out of my wet heat. The friction we created.

"Do I need permission to come, daddy?" Parker joked.

"I hadn't thought about that, but yes," Hunter replied, half laughing. "From now on, no coming without permission from your big brother."

"I'll think about it," Parker said distractedly. "In the meantime, I think I'll just enjoy the way she feels around me. Right now, in this exact moment, I am the luckiest guy in the entire fucking world." He pulled all the way out before sliding back in to the hilt.

"Yeah, you are," Hunter said so softly I almost missed it. "All three of us are, but right now you're the luckiest." He squeezed my throat, then leaned down to kiss my mouth. Nothing more than a brush at first, it quickly became heated, his tongue sliding in and out between my lips.

"You always taste so fucking good," he said against my mouth.

"You too, daddy," I replied. I loved the way his breath hitched when I called him that. I knew his cock would be hard as a rock. Just picturing his head red with blood, pulsing veins running through him made me want to see him and feel him.

He unbuttoned his jeans, slid down the zip and pulled out his always impressive length. He slid his hand up and down, from his balls to his head, making himself harder and dripping pre-cum onto my belly.

"I'm going to... Ahhh." Parker grunted and emptied himself in my body. He panted. "Come," he finally finished. He half closed his eyes until he caught his breath. "I'll never get enough of doing that."

He slid out of me and shuffled over awkwardly with his pants around his knees, to make room for Slade.

Slade grabbed my legs and draped them over his shoulders. He gripped my hips and drove himself into me deep and fast.

I let out a gasp of surprise. "Fuck, sir." He filled me even more than

Parker, particularly at this angle. His cock filled every centimetre of me, the fit so tight I'd almost swear I felt the pulse in the base of his head throb.

"Tell me how you want me to fuck you," he insisted.

"As hard as you can, sir," I replied. "Don't hold anything back."

He didn't. He pulled all the way out and slammed back into me harder than the first time. Over and over. Harder and harder until I was almost screaming with pleasure and pain. He was that wild animal who'd hunted down his prey and now he was taking his spoils. It was like we forgot we were human and became something else. Something completely wild and untamed.

I screamed out, "I need to come."

"Then come," Slade insisted. "I want my wild little fox to come around my cock before I come inside your beautiful body. Come for me. Right. Now."

I screamed my release to the ceiling of the lecture theatre, not caring if the whole Academy heard me. I screamed out Slade's name until my throat was raw from shouting.

Slade's orgasm followed mine by half a heartbeat. His cry wasn't quite as loud as mine, but hearing him call out my name as he spilled his cum inside me made me come a third time.

Hunter came almost simultaneously, the tip of his cock sending his release all over my breasts. The rush warmed one of my nipples with the pearly wetness. He released the pressure around my throat and sat back, cock still in his hand.

"That was something else."

I had no coherent words to respond with but every part of my body completely agreed with him.

seven

LILA

IN THE CORNER of my eye, I saw Chloe enter the library. She glanced around before her gaze seemed to settle on me. She wound her way through the tables before sitting opposite me. I let her sit silently for a few minutes before I glanced up. I didn't say anything, I just raised my eyebrows.

Her tongue swiped over her lips. "He tried to kill us."

I closed my laptop and rested my arms on the table in front of me, one folded over the other.

"I know, I was there. Armed mercenaries. Death and destruction." I knew that wasn't what she was referring to, but the reminder of what dad did would add weight to what she actually meant.

She leaned forward and placed her elbows on the table. "The cars he sent. The brakes were tampered with. The accident wasn't an accident. I know your car was messed with too."

The surprise on my face was genuine. She was right, but I didn't know how *she* knew that.

I shrugged and picked up a pen to toy with. "Dad said he'd send us another test."

She glanced down at her hands, miserably. "And I failed. I jumped straight into one of the cars and almost killed Zachary and me."

"I didn't see Zachary trying to stop you," I pointed out. "How is he?"

She looked back up. "He'll be okay. The doctors were worried about his neck, but they did all of the x-rays and shit and he's fine. They let him out of the hospital this morning, but told him to rest for a couple more days."

She chewed on her lip. "You're right though, he didn't try to stop me. I might not have listened. I believed the car was a genuine gift. I *wanted* to believe it. It never crossed my mind that..."

"Dad had an ulterior motive?" I suggested. "I think at this point we have to assume pretty much everyone has an ulterior motive." I was surprised she didn't try to blame me.

"You did," she said. "You didn't get into your car and drive it into a tree. You must have suspected something was up." She tilted her head and regarded me warily.

"I suppose I did," I said as blandly as I could. Of course I did, something *was* up. "I spoke to Dad about it."

Her skin paled. "You told dad I didn't hesitate?"

"Yes, I did," I said as evenly as I could. Should I feel bad about pinning this on our father? My sense of self preservation left me feeling somewhat numb. I was doing nothing less than what I *had* to do.

"Don't worry about it too much," I added. "He didn't seem to give a shit. All he said was that I wasn't doing enough."

I didn't bother trying to keep the bitterness out of my tone. "Don't get too cocky, he doesn't think you're doing enough, either."

"He never will," she whispered. "I don't think either of us will ever do enough or be enough to please him. What does he want from us?"

I sighed softly. "I have no idea. I'm not even sure this is about us and Zachary anymore." When she gave me a puzzled look, I added, "He was with someone. A woman. They seemed...intimate."

Chloe grimaced. "I'm sure it's not the first time."

"No, but something about this was different," I said slowly. "She's not his usual type. He might be thinking about replacing all of us."

Chloe blinked a couple of times. "You think she's pregnant? Or influencing him in some way?"

"I don't know, and possibly." I tapped the side of the pen on my fingertip. "She didn't look like the sort of person who would suggest he send us cars with tampered breaks."

She looked more like the kind of person who would suggest he send us kittens, but I knew better than to judge a person by their outward appearance.

"If she's pregnant and he's planning to replace all of us..." Chloe frowned.

"We should find out," I said.

"That too." She nodded slowly. "I was thinking more along the lines of...all of this is for nothing."

My blood froze. I hadn't considered that before.

"If it's for nothing, then—" Fuck. I couldn't get my head around the implications.

"Then he really meant to kill us?" She swallowed visibly. "To get us out of the way of a new baby."

I considered telling her the truth about the cars, but put the thought aside for now.

"Why would he bother?" I asked. "All he has to do is name his heir and be done with it."

"Would you accept that and move on with your life?" She cocked her head. Some of the colour had returned to her face. "He might think we'd go after the baby."

"Would you?" I asked. "We've gone through all of this. If it's for nothing, would you be pissed off?" Would I? He'd put us through hell. Why shouldn't we return the favour if he tried to put us aside?

"Of course I would," she replied quickly. "Be pissed off, I mean. If he was never going to hand it over to us, then why do any of this?"

I tapped my pen a little faster. "Hedging his bets? He might have thought he wasn't capable of fathering another child. He still might not, we're only speculating here."

She put her hand on mine to stop me from tapping. "That's so annoying."

I dropped the pen onto the tabletop beside my laptop. "Not sorry."

She rolled her eyes. "I assume you guys are hunting down who this mystery woman is? The sooner we find that out, the sooner we get some answers."

"We could try asking Dad," I said.

We both snorted, identical sounds of wry amusement.

"Giving us straight answers hasn't been his strong point recently," Chloe said.

"Was it ever?" I sighed. "You're right though, he has gotten worse. The only thing we *can* assume is that there might be more tests and that even if there aren't, we need to concentrate on surviving the trials." In the unlikely event we formed some sort of truce, fuck only knew how many others may want to come after us.

"He might combine the two," she said slowly. "Throw an extra test into the trials, just for shits and giggles. More mercenaries, some man eating tigers, a landmine or two."

"I'll take my chances with the man eating tigers," I said. "We're not allowed to be armed during the trials, so mercenaries are unlikely, but they'd suck. I don't want to think about how difficult it would be to avoid landmines."

"Allowed." Chloe used air quotes.

I smiled. "The rules at Brutham Academy do seem to be made to be broken."

"But we weren't," she said firmly.

She surprised me by including me in that. For a moment, I almost felt close to her. Maybe there was hope for us after all of this was over and done.

"No, we weren't. Also, yes, the guys are trying to find out who she is. Whoever Dad's girlfriend is, she's low key. No one affiliated with the Bell or Brantley families. Or the Fiorellis, as far as they can tell. She's not a politician or a judge, or anyone with that kind of influence or position."

Chloe wrinkled her nose. "Can you not use the word 'position' when it in any way has something to do with our father?"

I laughed softly. "My brain hadn't gone there, but now it has, yuck. Parent sex."

Watching Dad and the woman kissing was bad enough. No doubt he didn't want to hear about my sex life either. Especially since he couldn't stand the twins. Some day, he may get to know them. He might even start to like them.

Would that be before or after hell froze over?

"Ewww." She stuck out her tongue. "Who do you think she is?"

I ran a hand down my ponytail and gripped the end. "She looked like someone perfectly ordinary. She actually looked...nice."

"What is a nice person doing with our father?" Chloe asked. "He must have her fooled. Or else it's love. It is blind after all. So they say."

They did say that, but I didn't believe it. I went into my relationships with my guys with my eyes wide open. I looked for all the warning signs and listened to my instincts. If the guys were working against me, they were all excellent actors. None of them gave me reason to doubt their loyalty or their love.

"When I find out who she is, I'll let you know," I said. "Until then, I'm sure we can agree it changes nothing."

I wasn't going to let my guard down around her, or anyone else apart from my guys. I'd tell her if I found out about Dad's girlfriend because I'd want to know, but that was as far as it went. For now.

"Of course it doesn't." Her smile faded and she sat back. "I appreciate you telling me about her. You could have kept it to yourself."

I picked my pen back up and rolled it in my hands. "I could have, but I didn't see any point. If it involves the family, it involves you. I assume you'll tell Zachary?"

"I suppose so," she said uncertainly.

"You two still haven't quite made up?" I guessed. "The twins admitted they were the ones who drugged you."

That was all their idea, but I didn't bother to point that out. If she didn't realise that already, she wouldn't believe me now anyway.

"Not that you care, but no," she replied. "I mean, we have but...it's difficult to know who to trust. He does have a vested interest in the outcome of all of this."

"So does Dane," I pointed out. "For that matter, so do Hunter, Parker and to a lesser extent, Slade. I'm sure the Brantley family would be ecstatic if we imploded."

"And yet, you seem to trust them," she said. "Are you sure they're on your side?"

"I've thought about that a ton of times," I said slowly, honestly. "Maybe I shouldn't be certain of them, but I am. I trust all three of them with my life. For what it's worth, I think you can trust Dane."

"But not Zachary?" Her brow creased slightly.

I took a moment to respond. If she was going to ask me questions like that, I was going to do my best to answer in a way that was to my advantage.

"I think he genuinely cares about you, but like you said, he has a vested interest. If Dad looked at him the right way, he may decide his allegiance is only with himself."

I didn't *necessarily* believe that, but it didn't hurt to nurture the seeds of doubt that were clearly in her mind already. A little bit of paranoia could go a long way.

"Exactly," she said softly. "He's ambitious, but I'm not sure if it's for me or for himself."

"Do I need to suggest you don't turn your back on him?" I asked.

"I can't turn my back on anyone," she replied. "Including myself, apparently. I want to smack myself for getting into that car without having it checked first."

"I can smack you if you like," I offered. I placed the pen down and raised my hand as if I was about to do just that. "How hard do you want it?"

She raised her hands in front of her face and laughed slightly. "That's okay. If I want to be smacked, I have Dane for that."

"TMI." I lowered my hand. "Let me know if you change your mind."

She shook her head at me then stood to leave. Before she did she said, "Sometimes I wish it didn't have to be like this."

I didn't respond until she walked away. Under my breath I said, "Sometimes I wish that too."

eight

LILA

MY SOMBRE MOOD continued until after Slade stopped the SUV beside the forest road.

The trees and bush were dense on either side. Thick enough to block out a lot of the sun. A flock of birds startled and took off out of the canopy. Fuck only knew what else we'd scare off before we were done. Snakes, spiders, kangaroos, wombats...

I reminded myself I had to focus on the next few hours. I had to push Chloe, Zachary and any other interruptions out of my mind.

My father was the only one I couldn't put aside. Him and the trials. Specifically, what he might pull before, during, or after the trials.

"Remember to look out for anything different from the last time we were here." Slade killed the engine.

"That could be difficult, considering how dense the bush is." I opened the door and slipped out. "If he's done anything out here already, they would have erased the tracks."

"Erasing them completely is difficult," Hunter said. "It hasn't been that long since we were out here, and it's only rained a handful of times. A bent branch here, or footprint there might still be visible. Keep your eyes peeled."

"That's a strange expression," Parker remarked. "Who wants to peel their own eyes?"

He mimed popping out one of his eyeballs and pulling off the skin like it was a grape. He pretended to pop it into his own mouth and grinned.

"Yuck, bro," Hunter said. "Only you would think about eating your own eyeball."

"Actually, I prefer other people's eyeballs." Parker closed the SUV's door behind him and draped an arm over my shoulders.

"You're not having my eyeballs," I told him. "I need them."

He leaned over and kissed my temple. "Yes you do. You need them for admiring my cock."

"Amongst other things," I agreed.

"Yes, *my* cock." Hunter pressed a hand to his groin.

"As fascinating as all our cocks are, we need to get this practice trial started," Slade said.

"So you admit my cock is fascinating." Parker wiggled his eyebrows at Slade.

"They are fascinating, but Slade is right. I'd like to get this practice over with before it gets dark."

I cast my gaze toward the sky that wouldn't be dark for hours. I'd much rather think about fucking them, but for now I had to focus on surviving another practice and memorising the terrain.

"Slade is usually right," Slade said.

Parker groaned. "Great, now Slade is turning into Hunter."

"What is Hunter turning into?" Hunter asked. He seemed genuinely curious.

Parker shrugged. "If you're really lucky, you'll turn into me. Don't hold your breath though, I don't think even you could be that lucky."

"I'm way luckier then," Hunter protested. "I'm me. The only thing I'm turning into is an even better version of myself."

"Keep telling yourself that." Parker patted him on the shoulder with the hand that wasn't lightly touching mine.

Hunter flipped him off. He pulled out his phone and tapped on the screen. "We have three hours and twenty-seven and a half minutes until the sun sets. Plenty of time."

He shoved his phone back into his pocket. "Just like last time, head north. You know what you're looking for this time, the road."

He turned to Slade and pointed his finger right under his nose. "No driving around there to get in front of us this time. No helicopters or any shit like that either. If we're chasing Lila, we do this on foot."

"Yes, daddy," Slade teased.

Hunter's eyebrows shot up. "Hey, that works, coming from you too."

"Only if you want to call me sir until the end of time," Slade retorted.

"Hard pass," Hunter told him. "At the risk of spoiling anyone's fun, we won't be chasing Lila down today."

"We won't?" Parker looked unimpressed.

"No, Park, we won't. We will be moving in roughly the same direction, keeping our eyes peeled for any changes. Or any sign of intended changes, tampering, human activity, skulduggery or any kind of fuckery."

"Okay, but what's the difference between skulduggery and fuckery?" Parker asked.

"One is worse than the other," Hunter said. "Hence the reason I put them in that order. The difference is subtle but significant."

"You might have to explain that one to us later," Slade said. "Maybe when we've had a beer or two. It might make sense then."

"It makes perfect sense," Hunter protested. "Just keep your eye out for shit, okay?"

Parker pointed a finger gun at him. "Shit. Got it." He nodded. His eyes shone with humour and mischief.

Hunter rolled his eyes. He stepped over to me and pulled me out from under Parker's arm. He kissed the tip of my nose. "Be safe, okay?"

"Of course I will; I have you three to keep me from getting into trouble." I kissed his mouth, hoping to reassure him.

So much had happened since last time we were here, it wasn't surprising he was nervous. So was I. If my father did anything to mess with the trial area, chances are it would suck. Right now though we had no proof he'd done anything. I'd have to be careful, but this may only be a nice stroll in the bush.

Yeah, right, that'd be the day.

"You three stay safe," I told them. My gaze may have lingered slightly longer on Hunter and Parker. They put on identical brave faces, but I knew being taken and chained up had an impact on both of them. It made them angry and more cautious. Vengeful.

They wanted to make people suffer for what was done to them. I wanted that for them. After we got through all of this alive.

"We always do," Parker said. "Dane said we were like cockroaches, almost impossible to kill." He looked smug, as though Dane hadn't meant that to be an insult. Of course he did. Parker never took much to heart.

"It's the *almost* I'm worried about," I told him. I sighed and glanced down at my watch. "I should get going."

"We won't be far behind." Hunter kissed me, then turned me around and gave me a swipe on the ass. "You've got this, babe."

"Remember you're the sneaky fox," Slade said. "Stealthy and smart."

"And foxy," Parker added. "I think that means hot." He frowned, then shrugged.

I flashed him a grin before I headed away towards the trees.

Like last time, I stepped into the bush, keeping my hands in front of me to clear the way and protect my face where necessary.

Unlike last time, I walked slowly and carefully, not needing to hurry to make it to the end before the guys caught me.

Okay, I wasn't in that much of a hurry last time, and being caught was one hundred percent worth it. Still, this time was much slower.

As far as I could tell nothing was out of place. What would I look for if it was? Freshly turned dirt where landmines were buried? Huge tiger footprints? A group of mercenaries boiling water over a fire to make coffee while they waited for me?

All right, they'd be hiding in the bushes. Unless they didn't expect us to come here today. That was unlikely. People saw us drive away from the Academy building a couple of hours earlier. Plenty of time to alert any potential attackers to hunker down.

When did extreme caution become paranoia? It seemed to me it was a fine line and I had the tip of my toenail right on it.

Was that the idea? Dad wanted us to be paranoid? I knew very well paranoia came with the territory, but it seemed excessive to take it to an extreme. That might be one of his lessons. To teach us how far we could go before we snapped completely.

If that was what this was, then it was a thousand different kinds of fucked up. At least a thousand, if not more.

I moved through the bushes as quietly as I could, but the ground was drier than last time, leaving sticks and leaves to snap and crackle. Trying to find places where there were none was virtually impossible. Although, as an added bonus, I could hear the guys behind me, albeit at a distance. From the sound of them, they'd spread out and were scouring the area. If there was anything to be found, one of us would find it.

Once we did, we could figure out how to get around or through it. We'd be ready.

I hoped.

The trials were stressful enough without adding in an extra...anything.

Had Reuben gone through this bullshit before he took over as head of the Brantley family? Had any of the Brantley guys? Hunter and Parker never mentioned anything about that to me. As far as I knew, they'd only dealt with the standard bullshit of the trials.

Fuck only knew that was bad enough.

I stepped over a fallen log I was almost certain I didn't see the first time. That didn't mean a whole lot, I probably wasn't walking the exact same way.

Whatever, as long as I headed in the right direction.

Still, I crouched down to have a look around, searching for any signs of anything suspicious. I was no expert, but it didn't look as though anyone had taken a saw to it. It was too big to have been pushed down with brute strength. Especially with the roots as big as they were. Nothing looked exploded, imploded or otherwise weird.

I decided it was nothing more than a tree that fell because it was time. For all I knew it had been dead for ages and waiting to fall. Like I said, I'm no expert.

I stood and clambered over the trunk before dropping clear on the other side.

Something scurried away as my boots hit the ground. Whatever it was, it sounded small, and probably harmless. Unless it was a snake and I mistook slithering for scurrying. Either way, it headed away from me, which as far as I was concerned, was the right direction.

Remembering a fallen tree was a great place for snakes to make a home, I hurried on.

To go through everything I'd been through, only to die from a snake bite, would suck, to say the least. Definitely not my favourite kind of sucking. Or biting for that matter.

I peered through the trees, trying to locate the area with the massive rocks I saw the last time. I couldn't be that far from them. I knew when I reached that point, I was close to the end of the practice. I also knew I could take the easy way around this time, without one of the guys right on my tail.

I stopped to glance back. They couldn't be too far behind, but I saw no sign of any of them.

The only sounds—crickets and the occasional bird. No crunch of leaves. No snap of twigs. If I didn't know better, I'd think I was out here alone.

Don't panic, I told myself. *They have to be close. If you called out, they'd call back. And then they'd worry you were calling for some terrible reason.*

I didn't want them to think I was scared or anything like that. I wasn't. Much.

I continued on, my eyes ahead, searching for the rocks and the precipice beside them.

On the ever growing list of things that would suck, was falling down that precipice.

Hunter had said something about disposing of one of their rivals down there during their trials. I didn't like the idea of a one-way trip down a cliff, or the landing at the bottom of it.

I stepped forward slowly, bit by bit, eyes scanning. Where the fuck were the rocks? I checked my watch to make sure I was headed in the right direction. No, I was slightly off. I readjusted and moved through a set of young gum trees.

There. Up ahead, there were the rocks.

I smiled to myself. I was almost there.

I took another step and the earth disappeared under my feet.

nine

SLADE

I WAITED until the twins moved away before I headed into the bush. Neither of them were in a hurry, but they weren't making much effort to be quiet either. Admittedly, they'd be almost silent to most people. To me, they sounded like a pair of Brontosauruses walking through the undergrowth.

What? I was dinosaur obsessed as a kid and I never fully got over it. For a long time, I wanted to be a palaeontologist. That never happened, of course, but my fascination for the creatures remained.

Once the twins were more or less out of earshot, I was able to focus on listening as well as looking. Sometimes it wasn't what you saw that mattered but the things you heard or didn't hear. The absence of birds or cicadas in certain parts of the forest, for example.

On this occasion, the sounds were peculiar by not being unusual. If anyone came here recently, they knew how to keep a low profile. Nothing I saw suggested anyone passed in a long time. Not even anything as big as a kangaroo.

I was a good twenty or so metres away from Lila or either of the twins, drawn here by pure instinct. The same instinct that told me not to go too far from her. For once, it wasn't about her magnetic personality, just...

I was twitchy after the mercenary attack, but today I was on edge. My skin tingled with the need to be vigilant, like every nerve stood on end. Something was up. What the fuck was it? What the hell had Samuel Bell done?

I'd like to suggest I was shocked at his response to his daughter, but I wasn't. Men like my father, and him were unbending when their children were concerned. They were absolutely determined what they were doing was for their own good. That someday, Lila would look back and appreciate the tough love.

For that reason, I wouldn't put it past him to anticipate her coming here today and pulling something.

If not him, then Chloe or fuck knows who else.

I just finished that thought when a faint crunch sounded from up ahead. I paused mid-step, the heel of my hand pressed against the trunk of the gum beside me. Slowly, I lowered my boot down beside the other one, careful not to make a crunch myself.

I lowered myself to a crouch and waited, watching, my eyes on the undergrowth ahead.

Another crunch. A hint of movement. Something was definitely up ahead. It might be nothing more terrifying than a kangaroo. My instincts told me otherwise.

Up until now, those instincts had kept me alive. I wasn't going to ignore them now.

Someone was there and it wasn't the twins or Lila.

I moved forward slowly, centimetre by centimetre, looking for patches of bare dirt or rock that would mask my footsteps. At the same time, I searched for signs of whoever it was, having passed here. Bent grass, snapped twigs. They didn't tell me much until...

The imprint of a shoe in a patch of dirt. The side of a shoe and part of the heel, to be precise. I almost missed it. If I wasn't looking carefully, I would have.

Definitely a person then. Male, judging by the size and depth of the imprint. Someone at least as big as me.

I crouched again. Where there was one, there may be several. Chances were, they weren't out here alone. If they were after Lila, they definitely weren't. If they'd split up, they'd die alone. Excuse me if I didn't spare any pity for them.

A voice came from up ahead. I froze. Listened.

I caught a word or two before the wind blew any further conversation away. Either they weren't alone or they were speaking to someone on the phone. Since we were out in the bush, it seemed unlikely they got a decent signal unless they were using a satellite phone.

I decided to proceed on the assumption I was dealing with at least two people. Possibly more.

I caught a couple more words, this time from a different voice. Definitely at least two then. Sloppy enough to let themselves be overheard.

They may not die alone, but if they were after Lila, their deaths were imminent.

I took a couple of breaths, suppressing the surge of adrenaline at the thought of killing. I didn't need that right now. I needed a clear head.

I pulled back any emotion and tied it tight before tucking it away in the back of my mind. This was one of the first things my assassin training taught me. Something I'd always been good at. I had to be cold-blooded and ruthless right now.

When I was operating, I was one of the most feared assassins in Australia. Second only to the Sparrow, when they were operational. They'd disappeared some five years ago. No one was ever able to explain why or where they'd gone. I always presumed they'd made enough money to retire to some nice island in the Whitsundays, where they lived their days drinking cocktails on the beach.

Why not? Even now, their codename sent a shiver of fear through most sensible people.

"Won't be long now." That was definitely a male voice, only a handful of metres in front of me. Seemingly totally unaware of my presence. Exactly how I liked it.

"Hope so, this place gives me the fucking creeps." A second voice, also male. The click of a lighter was followed by the smell of cigarette smoke.

Fucking idiots. The bush was so dry, they'd be lucky if they didn't start a fire with the butt.

"Me too," the first voice agreed. "Give me a dark alley any day."

I frowned. Did I recognise either of those voices? They sounded familiar, but I couldn't quite place them. They weren't the twins. They weren't Zachary or Dane either. Chances were, they were just some random assholes hired to fuck around with us.

"Are we in the right place?" That was a third voice. Male as well. "They said the trial area was pretty big."

"Yeah, but the other teams are—"

I couldn't make out the rest of the comment. He must have turned away from me, or lowered his voice. Whatever, I had confirmation they weren't working alone. That meant I had to hurry. If I didn't deal with them, then another team might deal with Lila.

My emotions threatened to escape from the corner of my mind. I shoved them back and started forward.

I slid a knife out the side of my boot and held it while I approached the approximate location of those voices. I stayed down low, keeping the underbrush between me and them. They knew we were here somewhere. That limited the amount of surprise I had on my side. I'd have to make it count.

I ducked behind a thick trunk at the first sight of one of the men. He was dressed in black jeans and a T-shirt, dark hair tied back at the nape of his neck. He turned towards a tree and unzipped his jeans. He was about to pull out his cock and take a piss when I gripped the back of his shirt from behind and sliced his throat without a sound.

I grabbed him before he could fall too loud and lowered him to the forest floor.

I took a moment to get a good look at his face. He was vaguely familiar, but I couldn't place him. He looked like one of many street thugs I'd met in my day. Nothing about him was extraordinary. If I saw him in the street, I wouldn't look twice. Which was why he was hired for this in the first place. Forgettable faces were highly desirable in our world. They got away with a shit load of things the rest of us couldn't.

I listened for the other two men. It wouldn't take them long to realise their companion hadn't come back from relieving himself. When they did, they'd come looking for him.

I'd be ready.

"Jayden, where the fuck are you?"

Shit. That voice was closer than I realised.

I ducked down low and waited. A minute or two later, he walked past, making as much effort to move quietly as the twins had. Sloppy for trained mercenaries.

His back to me, I shot up and wrapped an arm around his neck. I drove my knife into his throat before he could make a sound. His eyes widened with surprise. Blood sprayed over the sleeves of his black T-shirt. He raised his arms to try to fight me off. A futile gesture at best. He was dead a moment later.

His body joined the first on the forest floor.

Now, where was the third asshole?

I quickly moved away from the second body and crouched back down, senses open. I couldn't rule out the possibility I'd made noise without meaning to. If he'd heard them, he'd be waiting for me. Fortunately, I was a patient man. I could wait a while for him to make a mistake. Unfortunately, my worry for Lila was starting to unravel again, out of my bundle of suppressed thoughts.

I pushed it away for a while longer. I needed to concentrate on dealing with the third asshole first.

I ran through both faces again in my mind while I waited. Nothing popped out. No sudden recognition. Nothing but a feeling of familiarity I couldn't put my finger on. Hell, they could have been former students for all I knew. I hadn't been teaching for long enough to forget them though, had I?

No, they were from somewhere else. None of that mattered right now.

Crunch.

I froze still, listening for more.

"Fuck." The word was muffled, the meaning clear. Which body had he found? Not that it mattered all that much. Clearly neither men were killed by a kangaroo or even an angry magpie. More like an angry lion. One who would protect his pretty little sneaky fox, no matter what it took.

I circled around slowly, again wanting to get behind the asshole. If I could take him out quickly and cleanly, I could go after Lila and the twins.

Yeah, they'd all say they could take care of themselves, but I wouldn't live with myself if anything happened to any of them. Having Lila was taken and trafficked on my watch was bad enough. I'd let my guard down just long enough for them to slip in and grab her. When I'd realised what they'd done, I was ready to slice open throats and tear people apart.

When I saw her standing in front of me, dressed in her transparent underwear... I'd never known relief like it. It felt like a shattered world had come back together and been reborn. My world. She was the sun we all orbited, basking in her fire and light.

She was the perfect combination of sweet, sexy and badass. I wasn't even slightly surprised she led the revolt against those who dared to keep her and those other women captive. And fuck me, she looked smoking hot doing it.

Ignoring the sudden ache in my balls, I moved through the bush, following the occasional crunch and snap, and a second, "Fuck," as he found the second body.

I caught sight of movement up ahead. He crouched and knelt beside the body, then stood. He turned around slowly, scanning the bush, looking for me.

I smiled to myself. Gotcha, asshole. He wasn't going to live long enough to regret taking this job. Instead, his bones would be bleaching out in the bush along with his friends. The bugs and other creatures were going to have a feast tonight.

Hand around the hilt of my knife, I almost strode forward. He knew I was coming, I could feel it in the air. That moment when death steps up, making itself known before it takes you.

This was exactly the reason my codename was Death Adder. I was stealthy, deadly and slippery as fuck. I was the last thing a lot of people saw.

"Freeze, asshole." A voice came from behind me. That was followed by the cocking of a gun. "Unless you want your brains spread out all over the Australian bush."

ten

SLADE

I KEPT MY BODY LOOSE, ready. It wasn't often I was taken by surprise. I was irritated as fuck with myself. How had he crept up on me without me knowing? I was so focused on the man in front of me and all the noise he was making, I missed the silence behind me.

Fucking idiot, I told myself.

"I'd prefer to keep my brains intact," I said lightly. "Do you always sneak up on people out for a bushwalk?"

His response was half huff, half laugh. "Drop the knife."

"I'd rather not." I chanced a glance back over my shoulder. "I should have figured you'd be lurking around here somewhere."

"And yet, you seemed oblivious. Drop the knife. I won't ask again."

"You're not going to blow my brains out," I told him.

"Don't count on that. The last time I saw you, you pissed me off. I've been looking forward to an opportunity like this. I'm not sure why I shouldn't take it."

"Is that any way to talk to an old friend?" I asked.

"That depends what you're doing out here," Kent replied. "Don't try to tell me you're here for a bushwalk."

"Why not? I like it out here." My hands raised, I slowly turned around. The same age as me, Kent and I had always had an interesting relationship. We were always in competition with each other, but at the same time we were relatively close. We both played every sport we could get our hands on and loved beating each other at it. Neither of us excelled the way my brother Walker did, but we weren't bad either.

If I was honest with myself, I'd admit that Kent's greatest strengths were my greatest weaknesses and vice versa. Whenever a coach would put us in roles we had to support each other in, we were almost unbeatable.

"Slade Lincoln, out for a bushwalk. Now I've heard everything." He lowered the gun, but only slightly. "With a knife covered in blood in one hand and two of my men dead. I was never that good at maths, but two and two make suss as fuck to me."

"The fact you're out here with them is pretty suspicious too," I said. "Who hired you?"

He responded with a sardonic smile. "Who said anyone hired me? I might also be out for a bushwalk."

His companion made no effort to hide the fact he approached. Any louder and he'd be heard in Sydney. He stopped beside me, gun in his hand.

"Isn't this cozy?" I jerked my head towards him. "Who is this guy?"

Kent's gaze didn't waver from me. "He works for me. I'd appreciate it if you didn't kill him."

"Funny, I was hoping you'd say the same thing to him about me," I said. I raised an eyebrow expectantly.

"You know this motherfucker?" the asshole growled.

"Yeah, Dave, relax," Kent told him.

"He killed two of—" Dave started.

"I know," Kent snapped. "He didn't know it was us, right Slade?"

"Not a clue," I said honestly. "You still haven't told me why you're here and who hired you. Actually, it doesn't matter. Whatever they paid you, I'll double it."

Guys like Kent only had loyalty to their bank accounts. We might need his help to deal with the other teams. Chances were, they were led by men not as easily influenced as someone I've known since I started school. Men who might actually be loyal to their employer.

"Why?" Kent looked even more suspicious. "Why would you do that? Are you a billionaire now?" He looked at me sideways.

I smirked. "No, but my girlfriend is. You were sent here to deal with Lila Bell?"

"In a manner of speaking," Kent said. "I guess we're working with her now."

"No way, we have a job to do," Dave argued.

"Plans change," Kent said evenly.

"I'm not going to—" Dave's words were rudely interrupted by Kent turning his gun and shooting him in the centre of his forehead.

"I fucking hate when these hired assholes argue with me," Kent growled. "Dave was really getting on my nerves." He put his gun away and spread his hands in front of him. He raised an eyebrow until I lowered the knife and slipped it back into my boot.

"You should keep some better company," I told him.

"Like yours?" He laughed. "That's fucking hilarious, dude."

I grinned. "There's nothing wrong with my company. I'm fucking awesome and you know it."

"Yeah, yeah." He rolled his eyes. "What's the plan, champ? You better be serious about paying me double. A guy has expenses. This job was going to take care of them. Double and I'll be on an island in Tahiti, drinking beer and fucking pretty women."

"How many other teams are there? What are our chances of being able to convince them to walk away?" I asked.

"Three, and slim to none. Most of those guys have a major grudge against the Bell family." He stepped over to Dave and grabbed up his gun.

"Which Brantley hired them?" I asked. They had a bigger grudge than most. Who else would it be? "Do they know two of their brothers are out here?"

"I'm not sure, and one with a grudge against his brothers." Kent tucked his spare gun away. "Probably not Zeke." Kent and Zeke were also friends back in school.

"Hunter and Parker have a tendency to piss Zeke off, but I doubt he'd do anything of this scope," I agreed. "If I was a betting man, I'd assume it was Caleb. Lila and the twins disrupted his human trafficking operation. That's the kind of thing Caleb doesn't take very well."

"What *does* he take well?" Kent asked. He was as big a fan of Caleb as I was. Not to mention he despised the abuse of innocent people to at least an equal extent. Guys like us, we went after people who deserved it. There was satisfaction in killing assholes and preventing them from hurting anyone else ever again. To me, justice was a bigger motivator than a power trip. People like Caleb and Reuben, and Samuel Bell were all about power trips. Maybe it was just their way of compensating for other shortcomings.

Me, I didn't need to do that.

"As far as I know, nothing." I pulled out my phone, sent off a text to the twins and searched for Lila's location. I hoped the text would get through with the limited coverage here. Trying to pin down the location of the tracking chip in her earring should be easier.

It *should* be, but it wasn't. I frowned at the screen. Closed the app and opened it again.

"That can't be right." I shook my head.

"What is it?" Kent glanced over my shoulder.

"I'm trying to track Lila, but this is giving me nothing. Her tracking chip isn't responding." I closed and opened the app again. Nothing changed. According to the app, no tracking chips were within range. I should have received a signal from several hundred kilometres away.

"I hate to say it, but that's not a good sign," Kent said. "It's not too late for me to kill you and get my original pay." His hand hovered loosely over one of the guns.

"Just try it," I growled. "It's the reception out here. It's fucking with the signal. Or one of the teams has it jammed." I narrowed my eyes and pressed my face closer to his. "Do you have it jammed?"

He raised his hands to either side again. "Not me. My job was to wait for whichever one of you came this way and take you out. Another one of the teams was supposed to deal with her."

His words sent white hot fury through me. Not aimed at him necessarily, but the other teams and Caleb or whoever the hell was behind this... Anyone would think she was some kind of monster, to go to this extent to get to her. Did they not understand she was a nineteen year old woman, trying to figure things out? That, on some level, she was a scared little girl. She'd hate that analogy, but it was accurate.

"You better hope we find her before they do," I said. "Otherwise no Tahiti for you at best. At worst, I'll kill you myself."

"There's nine other men out there," Kent said as if I hadn't just threatened his life. "Between us, we make approximately six." That might have been slightly ambitious.

"Hunter and Parker can take care of themselves. Lila evens out the nine. Those sound like good odds to me." He grinned as if it was all as simple as that. We had skills, but nine versus six out here was still going to be tricky. Nothing we couldn't handle, but not as easily as he made out.

"Not if we stand here talking about it." The twins hadn't responded to my text. As far as I could tell, they hadn't received it. They better still be alive. I might need them to help Lila. Not to mention the fact I'd miss the hell out of them both if they were dead. They were closer to me than my siblings. Not to mention much more entertaining.

I turned away, then turned back. "You must have something to tell you the location of the other teams?"

He cleared his throat. "I might have a satellite phone." He pulled it out of his pocket.

I snatched it out of his hand and tapped on the screen. It opened to an app with three blinking dots.

"Three other satellite phones?" I asked.

"Something like that," he agreed. "They're still spread out."

"And moving north," I added. "Following, but not converging. Chances are they haven't found the others yet, but they have a fair idea where they are."

I tucked his phone in my opposite back pocket and ignored his grunt of protest. I needed it more than he did at this point. I didn't bother checking again to see if the twins saw my text. Chances were, they were well aware they were being followed and had their phones turned off. They were likely leading them away from Lila, or toward a place they could deal with them. That left the middle team. That's where we'd head first. We'd deal with them and then make a decision after that.

"Come on." I started off as quickly as I could. I didn't bother trying to be quiet right now, we were too far from them to be heard. Once we drew closer, we'd slow down.

"Tell me about these assholes," I said. "Anyone I know?"

"No one you want to know," he said. "But probably several you're acquainted with. Casper is leading that middle team."

"Fuck," I said under my breath. That was not what I wanted to hear.

Casper wasn't his real name, as far as I knew, and he was far from friendly. He was one of the meanest sons of bitches I ever met. If he lay a hand on Lila, he'd be one of the deadest ones.

Yeah, I know that's not a word. I don't give a shit.

"I'm guessing his days are numbered." Kent followed along behind me. "To be honest, I've been looking for an excuse to kill him for a while now. No, that's not true, I have plenty of excuses and even opportunities, but not when it won't come back to bite me in the ass. I'm averse to being bitten in the ass, unless it's by one of those hot women we were talking about."

"You have my blessing to take the shot if you get one," I said. "Don't miss and get me instead."

He laughed. "I'll try not to, but I make no promises."

I stopped. "Don't make me kill you now before it becomes a problem." I stomped on before he could respond.

eleven

LILA

I WOKE WITH A GROAN. My head hurt like a bitch. What the hell happened?

Right. One minute I was walking through the forest, then the ground gave way under me. I tumbled, windmilling my arms. A searing pain went through my shoulder and the side of my head and...everything went black.

Hoping like fuck I wasn't in the back of a truck, I forced my eyes open.

Fuck.

Not a truck. It was worse than that.

The sky was a long way above me. Little more than a glimpse of darkening blue in gaps in the canopy. All around me were steep dirt walls. I lay on a flat patch of dirt and leaves. A section of rock dug into my hip.

I pushed myself up into a sitting position. My breathing was already ragged with the beginning of a panic attack. The dark, hand dug walls started to press in on me. Dirt slithered down from the mouth of the hole and scattered around me. Loosened by my footsteps and fall, it added to the growing fear.

Trembling, I glanced up. The dirt was going to fall in on me at any moment. I was sure of it.

I was going to die here, buried alive.

Alone.

I bent my knees and pressed my head down between them. Each breath came with a whimper or a sob. I struggled to calm myself.

Giving into panic wasn't going to help me.

What the fuck is? I asked myself.

I was alone in the dark and it was only going to get darker. Once night fell, I wouldn't even have starlight to see by. Maybe that was a good thing. I wouldn't be able to see the walls crumble until they collapsed on me.

I'd be able to hear them though. The rumble, the slither, the slide of dirt on dirt as it piled onto me bit by bit. Or maybe it would fall quickly, burying me in a second or two. That would be the merciful way to die.

Tears dripped off my cheeks and onto the ground.

Calm the fuck down, I told myself. *The guys are out there...*

The guys.

My head shot up. I winced at the jolt of pain. A light touch to the side of my head with my fingertips felt wet with blood. A gash down the side of my face, and across my ear. The earring holding the tracker was smashed. I must have landed on it somehow.

The irony that I may be suffering concussion wasn't lost on me. Chloe's was my fault and so was this. I was distracted by the sight of the rocks in front of me and excitement at the prospect of almost being at the finish.

Once again, I let my guard down and screwed myself.

I leaned my head back against the wall of the pit. I had to think rationally about this. My first instinct was to stand up and scream for help. The guys would find me and get me out of here somehow. Knowing Slade, he kept a rope in the back of his SUV for occasions like this.

I sucked in a few breaths and blew them out through pursed lips. First instincts weren't always right. Someone put this pit here. That same someone might come back. I had no way of knowing how long this lay here, waiting.

Rationally, it must have been here long before the last time the guys brought me out here. No one could have come in here, dug anything this deep and left without leaving signs. For all I knew, it was done years ago.

None of that ruled out the possibility of someone coming and finding me here.

"At least your paranoia is intact," I muttered to myself. I pulled my phone out of my back pocket and tapped on the screen. How it wasn't shattered into a thousand pieces, I didn't know. It even turned on. That was nothing short of a fucking miracle.

Unsurprisingly, there wasn't even a single bar of reception. Even in the middle of Sydney, I might get nothing at the bottom of a pit. Out here, I had no chance.

I resisted the urge to throw my phone. Instead, I shoved it back in my pocket. Only after dismissing the idea of using it as a source of light. If someone was looking for me, other than the twins and Slade, then the light would draw them here.

I sat back again and considered my options. I couldn't climb back out. The walls of the pit were too steep. If I had a knife or stick, I could dig handholds, but those would take forever, and the dirt may not be strong enough to hold my weight. With my luck, I'd bring it all down on me sooner.

I could sit here and wait for someone to find me, and hope that someone was the twins. Or I could give in to that first instinct and shout for help.

Rationally, if I sat and waited, I may never be found, even with the guy's skills.

I glanced back up at the sky. It was darker now. How long had I lain unconscious?

According to my watch, two hours had passed since I entered the trees. I walked for a bit over an hour and a half. Or at least, I thought I had. If I had a concussion, I could be way off. Either way, I was knocked out for twenty minutes or so. That was about average as far as I knew. Any longer than that and I might have had permanent damage. Hell, I still might.

I took another few breaths and tried to ignore the way the walls pressed in tighter.

"They're not moving," I told myself out loud. They'd stood for this long, they could stay up until I got the fuck out of here. As long as I didn't move around too much, they may stay stable.

They also might tumble in at any second.

Panic started to rise again. Along with memories of those slow, terrifying hours locked away in the dark. If someone wanted to find a way to new, unique way to torture me, this was perfect. This was as close to my worst nightmare as it could get. Even when my father locked me away, I knew the ceiling wouldn't fall and crush me. Dirt was considerably more fragile.

"I need to get out of here." I blinked away more tears and rolled over onto my knees. I pushed myself slowly and gingerly, until I was standing.

The rush of dirt and rocks that fell around me made me wince.

I stood completely still until it stopped. The rush became a slow slither which gradually faded to one or two rocks falling before the pit became silent.

Silent except for my racing heart that pounded through my chest and my ears. It exacerbated the pain in my head.

"Hello?" I called out experimentally.

A chunk of dirt broke off from the lip of the pit and narrowly missed me before it landed near my feet.

Okay, don't shout too loud, I told myself.

How the hell was I going to get out of here then? If I didn't shout loud enough to be heard, they wouldn't find me, but if I did, I risked bringing the whole fucking pit down around my ears.

"This is payback for what I did to Chloe, isn't it?" I muttered. If that was the case, then when did she get payback for the things she did to me? Granted, she hadn't tried to kill me, not exactly. I was the one who went too far.

My shoulders sagged. This might be exactly what I deserved. Destined to die down here, alone in the dark. Justice for trying to kill my twin. The universe was certainly a vengeful bitch.

"If you do nothing you may die, if you do something, you may die," I told myself. "You're Lila Bell. You don't wait around and do nothing. You take risks."

I took a chance on all of the guys and they hadn't let me down. I always grabbed life by the balls and lived it. That was what I had to do now. I had to take the chance that I could shout loud enough to be heard.

Hell, for all I knew, the walls would stand for years after I got out of here. The opening of the pit would be covered over again and it would lie in wait for someone else. This year's trials, or one years from now. Sooner or later, someone else would find themselves down here. That was a problem for a future someone. I couldn't dwell on that right now.

I tilted my head back, raised my chin and shouted.

"Hello! Can anyone hear me?"

The walls of the pit trembled. Chunks of dirt broke off from the lip and poured down around me. A couple of fist sized rocks hit my arm and bounced off painfully.

I threw my hands up in front of my face to protect myself from debris.

The trembling and crumbling seemed to go on for ages. Truthfully, it was no more than a handful of seconds. It finally stopped, followed by an intense silence. Even the birds and insects made no sound. They'd probably fled when I shouted.

I listened for any sign I'd been heard. A return shout. Running footsteps. Something. Anything.

I heard nothing.

I shook my head and raised my chin again.

"Hello! Hunter! Parker! Slade! I'm down here!"

Please hear me this time, I pleaded silently.

The sky was getting darker and darker and I was struggling to hold on. The only saving grace here was that no one could see me come apart. No one was here to witness me panicking, on the verge of losing my mind.

"Down there," a voice said.

I froze. That wasn't one of my guys.

Was I right after all? Someone set this trap for me and that someone had come back?

Fuck. If that was the case, I might be better off dead. After she tried to sell me, I wouldn't put anything past Chloe. I might end up in a different truck, or worse.

I pressed my back against the wall as though I could possibly hide down here. It was a ridiculous instinct, I knew. I could no more hide than I could run.

"This looks precarious," the same voice said. "You really want to risk yourself to get her out of there?"

Another couple of chunks of dirt fell away, as if punctuating his words.

"See what I mean? The whole fucking thing is ready to crash in on itself. People these days can't even dig a decent hole."

I chewed my lip. Who was he? I got the impression he knew exactly who I was. He certainly knew exactly *where* I was. Who was he talking to? I hadn't heard anyone answer him yet. Friend or enemy, he was not alone.

I swallowed hard. My palms were sweating.

A light shone down on me, so bright I had to raise my hand to shield my eyes.

"Well, what do we have here?"

twelve

LILA

"DON'T MAKE me poke your eyes out, Kent."

That was Slade's growl. Thank fuck.

Kent chuckled. "Do you want my help or do you not?"

"Let's just get her out of here. Are you all right, little fox?" Slade's tone softened.

"I will be when I'm not stuck in a pit anymore," I replied. I had no words for how relieved I was to hear Slade's voice. I had no idea who this Kent was, but if he was a friend of Slade's, I'd happily accept his help. Hell, at this point I'd happily accept help from just about anyone.

"We have a rope. We're going to tie one end around a tree and one of us will anchor it. The other will climb down to you," Slade said.

I shook my head and blinked against the glare. "It's not safe for either of you to come down here. If you can throw me a rope, I'll climb out to you."

I didn't want to risk Slade being stuck down here with me. I definitely didn't want his body weight to bring the pit down on us both. Dying down here would suck. Having him die down here with me would suck even harder.

Slade huffed. For a moment I thought he might disagree. Finally he said, "Fine. But if it looks like you're getting into trouble, I'm jumping down there with you."

"Noted." I nodded. "I'll be okay." I would be now. It was still an uncomfortably small space, but the glaring light almost balanced that out.

Almost.

"Give us a couple of minutes, all right?" The light moved as one of them placed it on the ground beside the mouth of the hole.

"That tree there," Slade said. "That should be sturdy enough. We'll both anchor for her."

"For double, I can tie some pretty good fucking knots," Kent said.

"You better," Slade growled. "If anything happens to her, you don't get jack shit."

"If anything happens to her, I'm pushing you in too and I'll take my original payday from Caleb," Kent retorted.

I frowned. What the hell did *Caleb* have to do with any of this? A lot by the sound of it. I'd have to wait and hear the story later. No doubt it would be interesting and aggravating all at the same time.

"Are the twins with you?" I called out.

"No, they aren't," Slade said. "They have things to deal with, but they won't be too far away."

Things to deal with? I mouthed to myself. Did I *want* to know what that meant?

Probably not, but I'd have to anyway, sooner or later. The lack of worry in Slade's tone went a long way to soothing any worry I had before it formed. If he wasn't concerned about the twins, then I wouldn't be. Unless Slade was a good liar...

But no, I suspected he was telling me the truth.

"Okay, try that," Kent said.

"It feels solid," Slade replied.

I pictured him tugging on the rope, testing that it was properly tied and would hold my weight.

"Of course it's solid," Kent said. "I tied it, didn't I?"

Slade didn't respond to him. He appeared beside the light, a tall, burly silhouette against the evening sky.

"I'm going to toss this end to you." He raised his hands and I saw part of the rope before it disappeared out of sight. "Are you ready?"

I raised my hands. "Very ready."

He nodded and threw. I snatched at the air and managed to grab one end.

"Nice catch," Kent said.

I smiled and tugged experimentally on my end of the rope.

"No one believes I can tie a rope," Kent complained.

"I tied a knot at the other end," Slade said to me. "If you stand on that, we can pull you up."

"No one believes I can climb," I teased.

"I'm sure you can, but I can see the blood from here," Slade told me. "Not to mention climbing up the side of that could bring it down on you. Lifting you out would be safer, as long as you can hang on tight."

"I can hold on," I insisted. I had to, otherwise he wouldn't hesitate to jump down to me. I appreciated the thought, but not the risk.

I grabbed the rope above my head with two hands and stepped onto the thick knot at the bottom. I had to press my boots in hard against each other to hold me in place. Hopefully it would be enough.

"Okay, I'm ready." I scrunched my eyes closed tight and clung to the rope as Slade reached down and grabbed up a handful.

"Got it?" Slade called back behind him.

"Yep," Kent replied. "Let's do this."

"On three." Slade started to count. "One. Two. Three." He grunted and started to tug on the rope.

I swallowed hard as my feet were pulled off the ground. Half a metre in the air, I bumped into the side of the pit, bringing still more dirt down around me. I managed to contain a yelp of pain, but my eyes stung.

"Fuck," Slade said softly. "Sorry."

"I'm fine," I said quickly. "Don't stop now."

He exhaled hard and resumed pulling, tugging the rope hand over hand.

Twice more, I bumped into the side. Both times painful, but always telling him to keep going. A few bumps and bruises were worth it, if that was the worst I got for this.

"Almost there." His voice strained, but he didn't pause.

I glanced up.

Only about a metre was left between me and the mouth of the hole. My heart raced harder than ever. I didn't want to come this far and have something go wrong. What if my curves were too much for the strength of the rope? What if the tree wasn't strong enough? One snap and I'd be sent back down into the darkness.

In the back of my mind, I heard a shitty voice telling me if I didn't get out now, I never would.

It wasn't rational, I knew that, but that was what went through my head. That and another rising wave of panic.

Without knowing I was going to speak, the words slipped out from between my lips. "Please, get me out of here."

"Open your eyes, Fox," Slade said gently.

I wasn't even aware of closing them.

I opened them and looked up into his face. He was crouched beside the pit, rope wound around his hand. Close enough to touch.

He reached out his other hand. "Grab on to me. I'll pull you the rest of the way. I've got you. I promise." The expression on his face was almost enough to make me sob.

Fingers shaking, I took one hand off the rope and reached for him.

Instead of taking my hand, he gripped my wrist and tugged me toward him.

For a couple of heart stopping moments, I was sure I was going to lose my hold on the rope, or him. I pictured myself falling harder than the first time. The impact might crumble the hole, taking Slade and Kent down with it.

And then he was hauling me over onto solid earth beside him.

I lay there for a long while, catching my breath and trying to get my head around the fact I was actually safe. I was out of that long, dark, fucking piece of literal hell.

"Are you all right?" he said in my ear. "You can let go of the rope now if you like."

I realised I held it in a death grip, which I slowly, gradually released.

"I'm all right." I managed to sit up and throw myself into his arms. "Thank fuck you heard me. I thought—"

"We would have found you, one way or another." He squeezed me so tight it was difficult to breathe, but I didn't protest. It felt good to be held by someone who loved me.

"We had a fair idea of where you were. Sooner or later, we would have stumbled on that hole."

"As it is, we were lucky not to fall in too," Kent said.

I glanced over to see a guy dressed head to toe in black, with dirty blonde hair that was longer on the top than it was on the sides.

"Do I know you?" I asked him.

"No, but you owe me a shit load of money." He grinned.

I raised my eyebrows at him.

"I'll explain everything later," Slade said. "We need to find the twins and get you out of here."

"Did you say something about Caleb?" I asked.

Slade hesitated. "I did." He briefly told me about meeting up with Kent and convincing him to work with him instead of against me.

"Like I said, shit load of money," Kent said.

"Worth every cent," I said. After a moment I added, "I would have paid you triple."

"I'll take triple." Kent said brightly. "Triple could buy me an island and a bunch of hot women. Um, I mean, I'd buy an island, the women would come voluntarily. And by come I mean, a lot."

"Friend of yours?" I asked Slade.

"I'd like to say I've never seen him before in my life, but the truth is I've known him for a long time," Slade admitted. "Kent is all right. When he's not working for Caleb Brantley."

Kent raised his hands in surrender. "It was one time." He headed over to the tree and started to untie the rope.

"One time too many," Slade told him. He nestled his face into my hair. "I was worried they'd get to you first." When he exhaled, it was slightly ragged with emotion.

He might have actually been more worried about me than I was about myself, which was saying something. If I knew there were people out there hunting, I would have been terrified for him and the twins. Knowing they already took care of three men was reassuring. Five against six were pretty good odds for us.

"They didn't. You got to them first," I said. "Now we have to make sure we get to the twins before they get into too much trouble."

"Given this is the Brantley twins we're talking about, trouble seems to be inevitable." Slade sighed. He reluctantly unwound his arms from me and stood before offering me his hand to help me to my feet. "I should send you back to the SUV with Kent."

"You can try, but we both know I won't go," I said. "I meant it when I said I was fine. I'm not going to sit by and wait until I know we're all safe."

"So stubborn," Slade grumbled. "Fine, but only because I know you'd follow me if I didn't let you come with me."

"I like coming with you," I teased.

He groaned. "Don't distract me, woman. If I start thinking with my cock, we'll never leave here." He looked down at me like he might tear my clothes off and fuck me then and there, in the dirt.

I grinned. "Under other circumstances, I'd be okay with that. But not while Hunter and Parker are out there." I would definitely take a rain check. The idea of him fucking me on the ground was hot as hell.

He reached into his back pockets and pulled out a phone from each. He turned the screen on one.

"Hunter read his message, but hasn't responded. Parker still hasn't read his."

He checked the other phone. "The two other teams are still moving."

Kent glanced over his shoulder. "If I didn't know better, I'd assume they've gone around in a circle."

"That sounds like the twins," Slade said approvingly. "Leading them on a wild goose chase." He went back to the first phone and tapped out messages to both of them.

We all watched the screen for a minute or two until first Hunter, then Parker read their messages. Three dots bounced across the screen as Parker typed quickly:

Little help here?

Slade responded with—

On our way

Of course he didn't finish the message with a full stop. He wouldn't want to be seen as aggressive or uncool.

Three dots bounced as Hunter typed.

Meet at SUV

Be there in thirty

Slade followed that with a thumbs up emoji.

Hunter responded with a running person emoji, then three laughing emojis. I took that to mean hurry the fuck up, but with his sense of humour intact for now. Typical Hunter.

Slade tucked both phones away and nodded at us. "Let's go. No doubt the twins have something in mind."

"I'm sure they do." I brushed dirt off myself and hoped Slade had something in the SUV for this headache.

I clung on to his hand as we made our way back through the bush.

thirteen

SLADE

I KEPT a close eye on Lila while we moved through the forest. She could claim she was okay as much as she liked, I didn't buy it for a minute.

The blood on her face and clothes, the dazed look in her eyes— They said otherwise.

If I let her, she'd push herself until she dropped. I wasn't going to let her. I was tempted to tie her up with Kent's rope and stash her away in the bushes for a while.

She'd kick me in the balls if I did something like that, even if it was for her own good.

Not to mention the fact I wanted to keep my eyes on her anyway. She shouldn't be alone right now. If I had my way, she wouldn't be alone ever again.

"Stop giving me that look," she said.

"What look?" I asked, feigning innocence.

"The one that says you think I'm going to break in half at any moment." She raised an eyebrow at me without breaking her stride.

"You did fall in a pit," I reminded her. "I think some concern is justified. If anything happened to you..." I would personally hunt down whoever dug the hole and fill them full of holes. Then throw *them* in a shallow one where no one would ever find them.

While they were still alive.

She shuddered. "Nothing happened to me. Just a few cuts and bruises. Did you pull me out of there so you could play mother hen?"

"More like Daddy cock." I managed a smile. "It's my job, as one of your boyfriends, to take care of you. That includes worrying about you when you've been through something."

"That sounds like a yes to me," Kent said.

I looked back at him and glared.

He raised his hands to either side in surrender. "I'm just saying, is all. I've known you long enough to know you fuss over people you care about. Although, you've never fussed over me."

"Like you said, I fuss over people I care about." I smirked.

"Ouch," he said playfully. "Stab me in the heart, why don't you?" He pressed a fist to his chest.

"Don't tempt me." I turned back to Lila. "He's harmless."

"He's also right," she said.

"Does that mean I get triple?" Kent asked.

"No," she said over her shoulder. "No one needs to make a fuss about me. What we need right now is to help the twins and get out of here."

"I can deal with six armed assholes and worry about you at the same time," I said. "But if I tell you to stay back out of sight, you'll do it. No argument."

I tightened my grip on her hand when she looked like she was going to argue. "If you're the distraction that gets them killed, you'll never forgive yourself. Do what I tell you to do and we'll get out of here in one piece. Understood?"

She pressed her lips together for a few moments. "Yes, I understand."

"You understand, what?" I tapped my thumb against the back of her knuckles.

"I understand, sir." She glanced sideways at me.

"That's better," I told her. I didn't want her meek, but she had to realise how much was at stake here. Not just the twins, her as well. If the other two teams knew where she was and that she was alive, she'd immediately become a target.

Once again, I considered tying her up and leaving her, but if they found her before I got back...

"That goes for you too," I told Kent. "If I tell you to do something, I expect you to do it."

"As long as I get paid, I'll do whatever you want," Kent said. "Within reason. I'm not going to suck your cock unless I get paid quadruple."

"Everyone has their price," I said. "Now we know what yours is."

"What can I say, I'm a sucker for a beach and a good cocktail. There's not much I wouldn't do to make that dream come true. But a guy has standards."

"Since when?" I quipped.

"Since—"

My head snapped back around. I yanked Lila down to the ground and shielded her with my body.

"What—" she started.

"Shhh," I hissed.

Kent lay on the forest floor, a neat bullet hole through the centre of his forehead. A hint of blood glistened in the last rays of the sun.

Fuck. We had our moments, but he was like a brother to me. I could tell some wild stories about the stuff we used to get up to. Now...

"Shit," Lila whispered.

"Yep. Stay down." I pulled out my gun and peered between the thick branches of a Grevillea.

Two men stood near a stand of gums. Neither was Casper. They must have lain in wait for us. Now, they were doing nothing to hide their presence.

Of course not; killing Kent was like waving a flag above their heads. It was also the last thing they'd ever do.

"Keep an eye out for Casper," I told Lila. We might be dealing with both teams here, I was well aware of that. Let her assume it was only one for now. We could deal with three men. Hell, we'd deal with six if we had to.

In a crouch, I moved over to Kent's body and pulled out both of the guns he had on him.

Sorry, buddy, I told him silently. He didn't need them anymore and we might. *I'm sorry you'll never get to drink cocktails on a beach and fuck beautiful women.*

He would have known, going into this, he may not get out of it alive. His death still sucked.

I crawled back over to Lila and pressed one of the guns into her hand. I knew she wouldn't hesitate to use it if she needed to.

"How far are we from the SUV?" she whispered in my ear.

"About ten minutes," I whispered back. Where the fuck were the twins? I had a couple of theories. Some of them weren't good.

Judging by the expression on Lila's face, she was thinking some of the same things. A flash of fear crossed her features, but she shoved it away. Her tough-as-stone mask was back in place.

I wanted to grind my teeth. She was too young to be so hardened. Kent had the right idea. A beach in Tahiti, far away from all of this, would be perfect. If she'd leave, which she wouldn't.

"I'm going to deal with these assholes. Stay down. Keep out of sight." I quickly kissed her mouth.

"I'm coming with you," she said.

"They know we're here," I said before she could argue any further. "Chances are, the third asshole is coming around behind us. I need you to get him before he gets me. Understood?" I needed her to do as I said or we might both be fucked.

She paused with her mouth open, then closed it and nodded. "Consider him dead."

"That's my girl." I nodded my approval and kissed her again before moving away through the bushes.

I stopped to scoop up a rock and threw it as hard as I could in the opposite direction to where Lila lay. It was the oldest trick in the book, but rarely failed to achieve the desired result.

"Over there," one of them said. He started to move towards me.

I did say *rarely*, not never. Either way, he stepped in sight, giving me the chance to raise my gun and shoot him squarely in the left side of his chest.

The shot sounded like thunder on acid. It rang loud enough to make me wince.

The other asshole stepped in sight as his companion's body hit the forest floor. I decorated his face with a shot to his temple. He looked much better that way, with blood and brains, and bits of skull going everywhere.

"Don't move, motherfucker." A voice came from the left of me. This time it definitely didn't belong to a friend. "I'll blow your knees off and leave you to die."

I started to turn my head slowly.

"I said don't move," Casper snapped. "On your feet."

Those weren't confusing instructions at all. Pointing that out would result in me being dead, so I held my hands out and slowly rose.

"Drop the gun." He moved closer.

I opened my hand and let the firearm drop clear. "Now what?"

Lila rose from the bushes, took aim and shot Casper three times in the face. "Now he dies."

What was left of Casper hit the ground with a thud.

"Huh, he had more brains than I realised." I exhaled a slow breath and scooped the gun back up. "Nice work."

No one was going to recognise the body. His face was almost completely destroyed.

She was definitely not holding anything back. What is it they say about hell not having as much fury as an angry woman? Lila Bell was not someone to cross.

"No one pulls a gun on my boyfriend." She lowered the one in her hand. "Unless it's me, if you and the twins deserve it." She smiled faintly.

"Remind me not to piss you off." I stepped over to the other bodies and took their guns before searching for any identification, or something that would indicate who exactly they were.

As I expected, I found nothing on them. On Casper, I found two phones. One satellite phone and one with a Bugs Bunny phone case.

"That's Parker's phone." Lila took it from my hand and tapped on the screen. "It's unlocked. He never leaves his phone unlocked."

Her brow creased with worry for a moment before she screwed her eyes shut and grimaced. A sure sign her head was giving her discomfort. The sooner I got her out of here and to a hospital, the better. Or at least into a nice, hot bubble bath with a couple of pills for the pain. Maybe an orgasm or two if she was up to it.

"He might not have had a choice." I glanced at the satellite phone screen. It gave the location of the one in my back pocket and another one, maybe a hundred metres from my SUV.

"If they're still alive, that's the last team," I said. "We need to take care of them. They may have Hunter and Parker with them."

The twins might also be dead, but I didn't need to say that. She knew as well as I did that was a possibility. This team may have killed Parker after unlocking his phone and sending us messages to tell us where to go.

The idea gave me a pain in my chest. I pushed it away. The twins were like cockroaches, I reminded myself. They wouldn't be killed that easily.

"They're fine," I found myself saying. "We'll find them. Their brother hired these assholes, they may be under orders not to kill the twins."

I'd never known Caleb to be particularly sentimental. He was a ruthless asshole, like his older brother Reuben and their father before them. Like Samuel Bell. The animosity between them was ironic given how alike they all were.

"They have to be fine," Lila said. "I'm going to be really angry with them if they're not."

"Of course you are." I managed a brief smile. "Let's find them then. We have three more assholes to take care of."

"Caleb is going to be really annoyed we killed all the people he hired," Lila remarked without a shred of sympathy.

"Caleb is going to be annoyed we're not dead," I said slowly. "He'll probably be ecstatic he didn't have to pay any of them. We've saved him a couple million dollars. He might even reward us for doing it."

She snort-laughed and followed me through the forest.

fourteen

SLADE

I DROPPED TO A CROUCH. This whole practice trial was a better leg workout than going to the gym. I hadn't crouched so often in months.

"They should be right ahead of us," I told Lila as she crouched beside me. "Keep your eyes and ears open everywhere around us."

"You think they left the phone for us to find it and moved away?" she guessed.

"That's exactly what I'd do," I agreed. "Then I'd set up an ambush for us. Probably using the twins to draw us out."

"Knowing we'd guess that, they may do the opposite," she pointed out.

"That is a distinct possibility." I nodded briefly. I ran through a variety of scenarios in my head, but came to no conclusions. There were too many variables here. Too many ways they may act that I couldn't anticipate. The uncertainty put me on edge. I liked to be in control of the situation and I wasn't. Not yet. What I needed was an opportunity to force them to show their hand.

"Give me Parker's phone." I held out my hand.

She didn't hesitate to pull it from her pocket and place it on my palm. She trusted that whatever I needed it for, was necessary. I appreciated her confidence.

I tapped on the screen and opened the contacts app. I found

Hunter's number and pressed on it. A second or two later, the sound of a song from Blazing Violet rang out through the forest.

"Hunter," Lila whispered excitedly. She sighed. "Or Hunter's phone."

I put Parker's phone to my ear and waited. The ringtone stopped and a voice crackled down the line.

"Hey." That was Hunter's voice. He sounded strained, like he was forced to answer the call.

"Hey, this is Felicity. We met at a party the other night," I said.

"Cute brunette?" Hunter replied. "I remember you. You have huge tits."

I rolled my eyes and suppressed a laugh. "That's me. I was wondering what you're up to?"

"Just...lying around," he replied. "To be honest, I'm a little tied up right now. I'm having car trouble. You know how it is."

"I do know," I agreed. "If you're too busy to hang out with me, what about your brother? He's pretty cute."

"He's a little tied up too," Hunter replied. "You really think he's cute? I mean, he's okay, but I'm still better looking."

"Of course you are." I rolled my eyes. "How long do you think you'll be held up? I'd really like to get together again."

"So would I," he agreed. "I'm not sure how long, maybe...three hours? No longer than that. You could come on over then if you like. You'll be expected."

"I thought I might," I said. "I think I will head on over. I'll bring a friend. She's also a cute brunette." I quirked an eyebrow in Lila's direction.

"Don't tell my girlfriend, she's the jealous type," Hunter said. "She'd take one look at you and put a bullet in your brain."

"Not if I stick one in her first," I said, not meaning bullets.

"If you stick anything in my girlfriend, I might get jealous," Hunter said with a faint, high-pitched laugh.

"I thought you were into sharing?"

"Only with the right people," he replied. "If the wrong people try to touch her I tend to kill them."

"I can get behind that," I said. "I should let you go. I'll see you soon."

"I'm looking forward to it." The line went dead.

"Hunter and Parker are alive." I handed Parker's phone back to Lila. "There's three people with them and both of them are bound. The assholes are waiting for us near my SUV."

She nodded. "You were right, they left the satellite phone for us to find. It's probably attached to a landmine or something."

"That wouldn't surprise me one bit. It also wouldn't surprise me if they listened to that call. Assuming they did, they know what we know." I thought quickly. "We have to anticipate what they think we'll do."

"What would you usually do?" she asked.

"Usually I'd wait until it was fully dark and sneak around behind them," I said. "They'd be dead before they knew I was there."

"They won't expect us to attack them front on then," she reasoned.

"No, but if we do that, chances are they'll kill the twins the moment they see us."

I rubbed my pointer finger back and forth across my lower lip slowly. "We need a distraction. Something convincing."

"You don't know who any of them are?" she asked.

"Only Casper, and we took care of him," I replied. "Why?" She was getting at something, but I wasn't sure what it was.

"If you don't know them, then what are the chances they recognise you on sight?" she asked. "It seems to be me and the twins they were after."

"I can't be certain, but I'd say there's a reasonable chance they don't know my face," I said slowly.

"But they know mine," she said.

"No," I told her simply.

She looked back at me evenly. "Why not? You said we need a distraction."

"I'm not letting you walk straight up to them," I said just as firmly.

"I wouldn't be alone," she said.

I sighed. "This better not end badly."

* * *

"You don't have to do this," I told her.

"As far as I can tell, you haven't come up with a better idea," she

398

said. She cocked her head at me challengingly. Did she have to be so hot, even with blood on her face and her clothes torn here and there? If it wasn't for the twins, I'd would have bent her over the nearest stump and fuck her silly.

"I haven't, which is the only reason I'm agreeing to this," I said.

We'd backtracked far enough for me to swap clothes with one of the dead mercenaries. My black jeans were too faded to pass as one of them. My button down shirt said 'teacher,' not mercenary. Fortunately, my black boots would pass.

I rubbed my fingertips over my forehead. "I still don't like it."

She stood on her toes to kiss my mouth. "I know you don't, but we don't have a choice. Let's do this before night falls completely."

That couldn't have been more than twenty or so minutes away.

"All right. Turn around and put your hands behind your back. Keep them there and do exactly what I tell you to do."

"You're so hot when you're bossy," she said teasingly.

"I'm hot all the time," I joked. I raised the gun and pointed it at her back. "Now, walk, woman. And remember, you're scared of me. You don't know if I might kill you or not."

She blew out a breath through pursed lips. "I'll think back to Brutus. If I pretend you're him, I might pull this off for long enough."

"Enough talking," I snapped. I had to get into the role myself.

Her mouth shut so quickly her teeth clicked. She was brave as fuck to think this up, much less want to go ahead with it. Only Lila Bell would walk straight into the wolves' den.

Back straight, she marched forward, stepping carefully through the trees. I followed right behind, glancing at my watch every so often to make sure we were headed in the right direction. I didn't want to contemplate how ridiculous it would be if after all this, we got lost. We could laugh about it later. Nothing was funny right now.

"Over there," I barked. I waved past her, in the direction of my SUV. "Move." I put a hand on her back and gave her a shove.

She shot me a resentful look over her shoulder, which might have been genuine. She clearly wasn't impressed with being pushed around like that. I'd apologise later.

We kept walking until we reached the road. Hunter and Parker were tied up, sitting on the ground beside my SUV.

Three mercenaries, all dressed in black melted out of the trees nearby. All three trained their guns on Lila and me.

"What the fuck are you doing?" I snapped at them. "I have her. Put your fucking guns down." I shoved her forward again.

I half expected a growl from the direction of the twins, but neither of them said anything. Clearly they'd cottoned on to the plan.

Uncertain, two of the mercenaries looked to their leader. He looked back at me for a moment before nodding and putting his gun away.

Lila and I both raised ours and shot the mercenaries to either side. One was hit in the head, the other in the stomach. The latter got off a shot, but it missed us by about a week.

Before the leader could react, the twins lunged forward, barrelling their bodies into his legs and knocking him off his feet.

Lila put a bullet in his head. Then, for good measure, one in the chest of the man who lay on the ground, clutching his stomach. He groaned and fell still.

Hunter flopped back against the road and looked up at us. "Felicity, your tits have shrunk."

I laughed. "It's good to see you too." I knelt down beside him and started to untie his wrists and ankles.

Lila did the same with Parker before giving him back his phone.

"I'm always happy to see you." Parker rubbed his wrists. "But I'm even more happy to see you right now than usual. I'm also really tired of being tied up and held at gunpoint. It's not fun anymore."

"When was it fun?" I asked.

"Exactly never," Hunter growled. "Caleb is definitely my least favourite brother right now. He's a massive prick."

"How did they catch you?" Lila asked.

Parker looked embarrassed. "They followed us and pinned us both down separately. Also at gunpoint. They had the audacity to make me unlock my phone before they took it."

"Poor baby." Lila patted his cheek, then kissed his mouth.

"I can't decide if I want to kill Caleb quickly or slowly." Hunter pulled himself to his feet and shook out his wrists. "Maybe one, then the other."

"If I didn't know better, I'd think he and Reuben are working with Samuel Bell," Parker said slowly. "But I do know better and this is just an asshole thing Caleb did. He wanted to fuck with us after what we did to his human trafficking shit. I thought we were supposed to owe him a big favour. What's with coming after us?"

Hunter shrugged. "Who knows with Caleb? He'll probably ask us for a favour after doing this to us. This was all probably to remind us that he's a big, bad asshole and we shouldn't fuck with him."

"I don't want to fuck with him," I said. "If anything, I'd like to thank him and maybe shake his hand."

"Shake his hand?" Parker stared at me in disbelief. "I want to high-five him. In the face. With a brick. Maybe a baseball bat." He mimed swinging a bat at his brother's head as hard as he could.

I smiled. "Think of this as another test. A part of the trials. One, I might add, that we passed with flying colours. All of us are still alive."

"I hate tests," Lila spat. "I'm getting really sick of them. I'd like to get on with the real trials and not ever think about them ever again. I'm starting to think I should have gone to a regular university and made a life for myself doing something else."

"If that's what you want to do, we'll support you," I said. "But after everything, is that what you really want?"

She looked uncertain. Shook her head. "I have no idea. I know one thing though. I'd like a nice, hot bath and a stiff drink. And then three nice, hot guys and some stiff cocks."

fifteen

LILA

"I TOLD YOU I WAS OKAY." I batted away Slade's hand when he went to touch my forehead. "I didn't even need stitches or anything."

A couple of pills for the pain and a sleep in the SUV on the way back to the Academy, and I was almost myself again.

"You'd say that even if you were missing a couple of limbs," he pointed out.

"I think you might be exaggerating a little bit." I held up my hand with my fingers spread as far apart as they'd go.

He grabbed my wrist and brushed his lips over my knuckles. "Only slightly. We all know you're a badass, strong, independent woman. You don't need to keep proving it to me."

"I might need to prove it to myself," I suggested, more curt than I intended.

After everything that happened, I wasn't sure if the expression 'whatever doesn't kill you makes you stronger,' was accurate. I suspected it made me more brittle. More inclined to shatter or wither, rather than growing tougher.

I *hated* that. Fragility was a weakness I couldn't afford.

He kept hold of my hand and led me out of the Academy's hospital.

"If you do, I'm here for it. Whatever you need." He glanced over at me, worry clearly etched on his features. Concern both for me, and that maybe he'd say the wrong thing. "Have you given more thought to what might be?"

I managed to contain a wince at the pain in my head from sighing deeply. "No. All I can think about right now is why Caleb sent people after me."

I was pissed off, but it went deeper than that. "Is there's even a *chance* of making peace between his family and mine? Trying to kill me kinda suggests he doesn't think there is. Or— He doesn't want that."

According to Slade and the twins, Caleb didn't want me dead. If that was the case, what *did* he want? Why not kill us all and get it over with? I asked myself the same question several times in the last few hours. Would it be easier to wipe out most of the Brantley family and move on?

"Hunter and Parker will get to the bottom of it," Slade assured me.

"I don't like the idea of them going to see him," I admitted. "I'd prefer they were here with us." Where I could see them and know they were safe and alive.

They'd left soon after we returned to the Academy. Not until they made sure I was all right. Both of them smiled and insisted they were fine and wouldn't kill Caleb unless they had to.

Behind their expressions was the acceptance that he may not return the favour. If their brother *did* kill them, that would destroy any chance of ever having peace between us. I'd have no choice but to go after Caleb. That would force Reuben's hand. The retaliation would go on until most of us were dead. I had to trust the fact Caleb knew that too. So far, we avoided full-blown war. How much longer could that last?

"I'd prefer that too." Slade started up the stairs, gently drawing me behind him. "They'll be okay. If Caleb wanted them dead, they'd be dead."

We walked in silence for a few steps, each contemplating the situation and the long day behind us. Finally, I turned to Slade and managed a smile.

"I'm surprised you're letting me walk on my own two feet," I teased. "I'd have thought you'd throw me over your shoulder and carry me up the stairs."

"I would, but you'd fight me. I'd probably get a knee to the groin. We'd both end up in a pile at the bottom of the stairs," he said. "Trudging up slowly seems safer to me."

"I am not trudging," I protested. I didn't argue with his assumption he'd get kicked in the cock. It was a distinct possibility. "I'm walking carefully in case a hole opens up in front of me. Can you guarantee it won't?"

"Actually, no, I can't." He eyed the staircase doubtfully. "It doesn't *look* like anyone's tampered with it, but we have some of the smartest minds in the country studying here. If anyone was going to come up with an invisible booby-trap, it would be a Brutham Academy student."

"Or graduate." I nodded towards him.

"Or that," he agreed. "I can one hundred percent guarantee you I didn't tamper with the stairs." After a moment he added, "Yet."

I laughed and bumped my shoulder against his arm. "What does a business law professor know about booby-traps anyway?"

"Not much." He bumped me back. "Assassins on the other hand know quite a bit about them. They can be a useful distraction at times."

I grabbed onto the banister and pulled myself up the last couple of steps. "Why assassin?"

He shrugged and followed me to my door. "Why *not* assassin? It pays well. Better than teaching here. When my victim is an asshole, I get the satisfaction of dispensing with them."

I pulled my key out of my pocket and inserted it into the lock. "And when they're not assholes?" I turned the key and opened the door.

"I don't know, it's never happened." He grabbed my shoulders to stop me, before stepping past and into my room first. He turned on the light and looked around carefully. "No new teddy bears. Nothing seems out of place to me."

I peered past him. "It looks just how we left it." I walked inside, taking in every surface, even glancing under the bed.

"Stay here." He left me near the door and went to inspect the bathroom. "It looks all right in here too."

I exhaled and relaxed my shoulders before closing and locking the door behind us.

"Thank you." I walked up behind him and took a moment to scan the bathroom. I trusted him implicitly, but wouldn't relax until I'd seen for myself.

"What for?" He turned around and cupped my cheeks with his hands.

I looked up into his blue-green eyes. They mirrored my emotions. Relief, tiredness and love.

"For being you. For pulling me out of that hole. For killing people for me. For not walking away from me when most guys would have." Most guys would run at the first sniff of my crazy life. Hell, I probably should too.

"Any guy who walked away from you is an idiot," he told me. "And someone who doesn't know how amazing you are." He leaned in to kiss my mouth.

"How amazing am I?" I teased.

He slid his hands down my shoulders, over my shoulder blades and gripped my ass.

"Very amazing. Beautiful, smart and capable. If I hadn't pulled you out of that hole, you would have found a way. Then you would have killed all of those guys, single-handedly."

I choked out a laugh. "There you go, exaggerating again. I might have managed five or six of them. But not getting out of that hole by myself." He was right though, I would have found a way eventually. Or died trying.

I glanced down at his muscular chest, then back up to his face. "I might have unravelled slightly. When I was down there, I mean. It was...scary."

He smiled tenderly. "Of course it was. I would have been shitting myself. Whoever dug that didn't make it to hold parties down there."

I cocked my head at him. "Big, bad Slade Lincoln? Scared of a pit?" I wasn't teasing, it was a perfectly rational fear.

He exhaled slowly, his breath brushing my temple. "I know, right? It's like I'm human or something. Do me a favour and don't tell anyone."

I smiled. "They wouldn't believe me anyway. I expect you to return the favour and don't tell anyone I'm only human." Although, tonight, I felt it acutely.

"If I did, I'd then be forced to take a hit out on myself," he said. "That could be awkward."

I laughed softly. "This conversation is very silly."

He grinned. "I think we need a bit of silliness, don't you?" He gripped my ass more firmly, picked me up and tucked my legs around his waist. "I can think of something else I need a bit of. You mentioned stiff cocks?" His certainly was. His erection pressed against the gusset of my panties, hard through his jeans.

I wound my arms around his neck and wriggled against him, making him harder still. "I did, as it happens. What are you proposing, sir?"

He carried me over to my bed and laid me down before starting to peel off my clothes. "I'm proposing orgasms. For both of us."

"I like this proposal." I lifted my ass off the mattress to let him slide my jeans off my legs and over my feet. My panties went next. My shirt and bra were close behind.

"Me too." He shed his shirt, tossing it carelessly onto the floor. "I like this view." His eyes raked up and down my naked body.

"I like my view." I could stare at his chiselled chest, abs and ridiculously muscular biceps all day. He was one of the hottest guys I ever saw. Hands down the hottest teacher at the Academy.

Everywhere he went, women watched him, trying to catch his attention. As far as I could tell, he was oblivious. He certainly wasn't interested. He better not be. If any other woman touched him, I'd be forced to kill them. Same with the twins.

Touch one of my guys and die.

"Even if I don't have big tits?" he joked.

I laughed. "I'm glad you don't. You're big in all the *right* places."

"My head?" he suggested, grinning.

I rolled my eyes and made a face at him. "Only the one on the end of your cock." I climbed to my knees and opened his jeans to let his erection pop free.

"See?" I ran the tip of my finger all the way around his engorged head and down the vein at the underside.

He looked down. "I do see. That is impressive, if I say so myself."

I laughed and slapped his ass. "You're such a brat, sir."

"Funny, I was going to say the same thing about you, missy," he teased.

He pulled off his boots and jeans and pushed me back against the mattress. With one hand, he grabbed my wrists and held them above my head while straddling my body. He supported most of his weight on his knees, careful not to put too much on me.

"What do you say now?" He ran his tongue from my collarbone to my chin.

"I still say you're the brat, sir," I said. A brat who was making the blood pump harder through my body, from my neck right down to my clit.

"Do I have to punish you, remind you who is in charge here?" He licked his way back down to my collarbone.

"I definitely need reminding," I agreed.

"I was hoping you'd say that." He leaned over the side of the bed and, with his free hand, tugged the belt out of the top of his jeans.

My eyes widened. A flutter of excitement passed through me. "What are you planning to do with that, sir?"

"Wait and see." He flipped me over onto my stomach and knelt beside me.

I wasn't disappointed. He curled the buckle end of the belt around his hand and flicked my ass with the other. The sting of pain sent the pulse in my pussy racing like crazy.

"Did you like that, brat?" he asked.

"I think I need another reminder, sir," I said over my shoulder.

He flicked me again, harder this time. He did the same to one cheek several more times, then the other. Every sting made my pulse race faster, until blood pounded through me like a runaway train.

He leaned down to whisper in my ear. "Do you trust me?"

I didn't hesitate. "I trust you." If he wanted to hurt me, he would have done it by now. He knew exactly how far to push without going too far.

He lifted my head with one hand and looped the belt around my neck. He slid one end through the buckle and drew it tighter, until the leather pressed into my throat, choking slightly. Just enough to make me wet as hell.

"That's a good look for you," he told me. He slid his hands down my body, over my ass, and drew my legs apart.

He pressed his face between my thighs, his tongue skating over my skin and down to my pussy. "You taste delicious."

He rolled me over and bent my knees to open me out to him further before diving back in. Firm, even strokes of his tongue around and over my clit had me balanced right on the edge so quickly I surprised myself.

If there was anything my guys were good at, it was making me come faster than I could by myself. Not that I needed to touch myself with my three guys around.

He drew my clit between his lips and sucked like a baby trying to get milk. Like I was the tastiest meal he ever had.

I grabbed fistfuls of the bed covers and rolled my hips, grinding myself against his face.

"I'm going to come, sir," I said breathlessly. My blood was racing around my body so fast, it was a virtual miracle I could speak coherently. Every part of me was on fire, ignited by his every touch.

"Not yet," he said between licks. "Not until I tell you you can."

I groaned in frustration, but didn't stop moving against his mouth. My body was begging to come, but his order held me on the brink, balanced like a tightrope walker over a chasm. There was no net underneath me. If I fell, I'd never stop falling. I wanted to throw myself over and lose myself forever.

"I can't hold on," I said between pants.

"Yes, you can." He didn't even pause to reply. His mouth was relentless, licking and sucking. His tongue diving into my pussy and snaking out again.

I gripped the covers tighter, my hands white from the pressure. "Sir," I begged. "Please..."

"Okay, you can come now," he said finally.

I saw stars. Fireworks. A volcano erupted, releasing hot lava and smoke into the air. On and on it went, a rush of heat and light and glittering air. The pressure on my throat and his mouth both drove me harder than I've ever gone before. The entire world disappeared, leaving nothing but a universe where only orgasms existed. A place I'd happily have stayed in forever.

Finally, reluctantly, I started to float back down to earth. Back down to the mattress, where I lay trying to catch my breath.

His mouth slick with my release, Slade crawled up the bed and curled his hand around the buckle-end of his belt. Holding it tight near my throat, he knelt between my legs and drove his cock into me hard and fast.

I gasped with the sudden shock of having his thick length inside me.

Unapologetically, he drew all the way out and slammed back in. All the time, keeping the pressure on my throat.

"You feel so fucking good." He pulled out and drove back in again. Over and over, grunting each time. He was completely in control and I let him have it. Feeling him pounding into me made me feel alive. It reminded me I didn't die in a hole today. Slade wasn't shot, and neither was I. The twins didn't die. Whatever Caleb's game was, we all survived.

I pushed him out of my thoughts and raised my knees to let Slade in deeper. I wanted to feel him all the way through me. As far as he could possibly go. I didn't want to let one centimetre of his cock go to waste.

He grunted in appreciation. His balls slapped against me every time he thrust. He had his eyes closed, his lips pressed tight together as he concentrated on working us both.

"I want you to come again," he panted. "Be a good girl and come around my cock."

"I don't know if I've ever been a good girl, sir," I said with a throaty laugh.

"Be a good girl now," he insisted. His grip on the belt tightened. Not enough to cut off my air, but enough to fill my whole body with renewed need. "I want to feel you come around me."

My body couldn't resist his order. Muscles tightened, clenched around him as I came harder and faster than before. My whole body stilled, at the same time as him. The only sound was our breathless groaning and the twin pounding of our hearts. My blood sang with pleasure, doubled at hearing him come at the same time. Feeling his balls clenched as he came inside me left me breathless with pure bliss.

He ground hard against me, milking us both for every drop.

Finally, we both came down and flopped together on the mattress. He panted for a few breaths before loosening the belt and slipping it off over my head.

"That was so fucking hot." He dropped the belt down on the floor beside the bed.

It really was, but I could only respond in a breathless murmur before I snuggled up to his side, completely spent and boneless. He wound his arms around me and stroked my hair as I fell into an exhausted sleep.

sixteen

LILA

"I'M MIXING things up a bit tonight," Hunter said. He shuffled the cards in his hands. He only held a handful, maybe ten at the most.

"We figured you might be, because we've never played Kink or Drink in one of our rooms," Parker remarked. He gestured around mine.

"I thought that, under the circumstances, it might be better to keep this evening's proceedings amongst ourselves," Hunter said. "This way we're less likely to be interrupted by armed assholes, drugged alcohol and whatever the fuck else." He sat cross-legged on my bed with a covered tray beside him.

"Perhaps you could tell us what Caleb said first," Slade suggested. He leaned against the wall, legs crossed at his ankles, arms crossed over his chest. His blue-green eyes were intent on Hunter. Determined to get a straight answer. So far, the twins had been evasive.

I was relieved to see them alive, but my patience was wearing as thin as Slade's.

Hunter sighed dramatically and continued to shuffle. "In typical Caleb style, he said he had nothing to do with those teams out in the forest. Of course, he's full of shit. He knows it. I know it. Parker knows it."

"Yes I do," Parker agreed.

"Caleb knows we know it," Hunter continued. "Unfortunately, we can't prove it. Caleb knows that too. In the end, we had to pretend we believed him. I'm not sure if he bought it though." He shrugged. "Probably not. For some reason, he's a mistrustful prick. It might have something to do with Parker threatening to kill him if he went anywhere near Lila."

Parker shrugged. "I don't trust him around her." He frowned. "I don't trust him even when he's not around her. Fun fact though, he seems to have a girlfriend."

I wrinkled my nose. "Anyone I know?"

"No. And by that, I mean I don't know who she is either. He was being cagey as fuck, more so than usual, but the signs were there." Parker ran his finger around the rim of an empty shot glass.

"Women's underwear was drying on the washing line," Hunter remarked. "I wouldn't judge him if it was his, but none of it looked like Caleb's size."

I stuck out my tongue in disgust. "Excuse me if I don't want to imagine any of your brothers in women's underwear. Or men's underwear, for that matter." Okay, maybe Zeke. He was almost as hot as the twins, and since he kept his nose out of family business, much more harmless.

"Caleb might have a houseguest that isn't his girlfriend," Slade pointed out. He dropped his arms and sat on the edge of the bed. "Although, a girlfriend might distract him from coming after us again."

"We can hope," Hunter agreed. He cleared his throat. "All right, welcome to our final round of Kink or Drink before the actual trials take place. I should remind you that anything that happens in Lila's room stays in Lila's room."

"Obviously," I drawled.

He grinned. "Because of the nature of this evening's proceedings, being that we are an adventurous lot, I've modified this round's game. Instead of Kink or Drink, this is Kink *and* Drink. Drinking is optional, but you may wish to avoid being sober by the end of this."

"So, just Kink," Parker concluded.

"Yes, but that word by itself sounded...boring," Hunter said.

"Only Hunter would find kink boring," I teased.

He grinned. "Not tonight. We also have a theme for this evening. That will reveal itself in due time. Mr Lincoln, would you care to take the first card?" He set the pack down on the bed between us.

"I'm game." Slade shrugged. He leaned over and picked up the first card. He looked at me speculatively.

I tilted my head and raised my eyebrows. "What?"

He read from the card. "Feed Lila a chocolate covered strawberry."

Hunter grabbed the edge of the cover with one hand and ceremoniously flicked it off the tray. Underneath was a plate of chocolate, chocolate covered strawberries, ice cubes, a feather and a bowl of honey with a spoon sticking out the side.

"Challenge accepted." Slade threw the card down on the bed and reached for a strawberry. Instead of offering it to me straight away, he placed one end between his lips. His eyes smiling, he leaned over to me and pressed the strawberry against my mouth.

"Extra points for being creative," Hunter said approvingly. "No one ever said *how* you should feed her."

Slade laughed and pressed the strawberry harder until I opened my mouth and closed my lips around it.

"Mmm." Chocolate, strawberry and his lips were a tasty combination. I swirled my tongue around the chocolate before biting down. When I had a firm hold of the strawberry with my teeth, Slade let go and sat back.

I chewed quickly and swallowed. "Delicious."

"Parker, your turn," Hunter said.

"Okay." Parker snatched up a card. "Feed Lila a piece of chocolate. I think I'm starting to see a pattern here."

So did I, and I didn't mind a bit. If they wanted to spoil me, I wasn't going to complain.

"Here's the problem." Parker rubbed a hand over the back of his neck. "Slade here set the bar high. How am I supposed to compete with that?"

Slade shrugged unashamedly. "Don't try. It's okay to admit I'm fucking epic." He grinned.

"Yes, you are, but I'm not ready to give up that quickly." Parker picked up the chocolate and thought about it for a few moments. Finally he smiled slowly and placed the chocolate back on the tray.

"Giving up?" Slade asked.

"Not at all." Parker grabbed my thighs in his hands, rucking up my skirt, and bent my knees to open me out to him. He hooked his fingers into my panties and tore them in two.

"If you guys keep doing that, I'm going to run out of panties," I said.

Parker grinned and shoved the fabric into his pocket. He picked the chocolate back up and slid it up my thigh.

"Sorry, not sorry." He traced circles around my clit with the chocolate before sliding a corner of it inside my pussy.

I shivered at the strange sensation. It was cold and hard but he was gentle. He slid it in and out of me a couple of times, before pulling it out and pressing the chocolate against my lips.

"I'm not beaten, but that was awesome," Slade said.

I opened my mouth and accepted the chocolate, glazed with my juices. "Tasty."

Parker grinned and hopped up to grab a washer from the bathroom. He lightly ran the damp towel over my pussy and inside, over the tip of his finger. "You never know where that chocolate has been. Wouldn't want you getting a nasty infection."

"You're so thoughtful," I told him.

He grinned and tossed the washer onto the floor.

"My turn," Hunter declared. He picked up a card and read it. "Feed Lila some honey. Excellent. I was hoping to get this one."

"There is definitely a pattern here," Parker said.

Hunter chuckled and undid the front of his jeans. He pushed them and his boxers down to expose his cock. He was already hard, his head red, veins pulsing under the skin.

He picked up the spoon and trickled honey onto his cock, careful not to get any in his slit. Satisfied, he tossed the spoon back in the bowl and knelt beside me. He pressed his sweet, sticky cock against my lips.

"Open up so I can feed you," he told me.

I licked along his length, swirling my tongue around his skin, tasting his saltiness mixed with the sweet honey.

"Honey never tasted so good." I lapped it all up before closing my mouth over his length and sucking.

"Your mouth never felt so good," he told me. He rolled his hips, pressing his length deeper into my mouth. All the way to the back of my throat. "You have the best fucking mouth."

I smiled at him around my mouthful and went on sucking and licking. I ran the tips of my fingers and my fingernails over his balls lightly at first, then more firmly as they started to tense. He was already so close.

He thrust harder and harder, with even strokes and groans. "Yes, yes..." He ground into me hard and exploded in my mouth. His hot cum tasted of honey, or maybe it was the lingering flavour in my mouth. Either way, it was delicious. I slid my lips off his cock and swallowed.

"I think you can all agree, I get the most bonus points for creativity." He looked smug.

"Bullshit," Slade told him. "All of us would have done the same thing."

Hunter flipped him off. "Keep telling yourself that, if you like. We know the truth."

"The truth is, Slade is right, that's what I would have done too," Parker said.

"Whose side are you on?" Hunter asked.

"The side of truth apparently." Parker shrugged and grinned.

"It's my turn," I said. "Am I supposed to think up some inventive way to feed myself?" Without waiting for an answer, I reached for a card. I turned it to face me and read what was written on there in Hunter's handwriting.

"I can't help feeling somehow you managed to rig this." I raised an eyebrow at Hunter.

He grinned. "You saw me shuffle them. Read it out."

I rolled my eyes but read. "Have honey licked off your breasts."

"That would have been awkward if one of us got that," Parker remarked. He glanced down at his chest. "I seem to be missing mine."

"So is Felicity," Hunter teased. He grinned at Slade. "You know, that's how people get nicknames."

Slade looked unworried. "Why do you think I didn't say I was Boob McBigtits? Or Pussy O'Shea?"

"Touché." Parker chuckled. He raised his hands when we all glanced at him. "What? It rhymes. O'Shea. Touché."

"Yeah, we got it," Hunter told him. He turned back to Slade and grinned. "For the record, those would have been awesome nicknames. Don't tell me you don't want to be called Pussy O'Shea?"

Slade laughed. "No, but I'm happy to call you that, if you like. That might be a cooler name than Hunter."

"There is no cooler name than Hunter," Hunter said. "Hunter is the coolest name. Except maybe Lila."

"Thank you, but I think Pussy O'Shea is kinda cute." I picked up the bowl of honey and the spoon and held it out in front of me. "Who's going to do the honours?"

"I will," Parker said quickly. He took the bowl from my hand and waved for me to lie down.

Smiling in anticipation, I lay back and placed my hand on a pillow.

"You are so fucking beautiful," he told me before dipping the spoon into the bowl and scooping out some honey. He held the spoon over my breasts and let it trickle down slowly all around and over my nipples.

"Honey never looked so good." He trickled out another spoonful, then set the bowl and spoon aside. He knelt beside me and lightly ran his tongue over my skin, tasting me and the honey. "Fuck, it never tasted so good either. Everything tastes better when I eat it off you. I think, from now on, I'm going to put all of my food here and eat it like this."

"Not if it's hot or cold," I told him.

"I'll make sure it's just right," he assured me. He closed his lips around one of my nipples and sucked. "Mmm, so fucking good."

"I could take your word for it or I could..." Slade knelt on the other side of me and licked my other nipple. "Yeah, you're not wrong. This is perfection."

I closed my eyes. "It feels amazing from here too."

Hunter parted my legs and started some licking of his own. Teasing my pussy and nibbling on my clit.

The attention from all three guys had me panting and wanting to scream out all of their names at once.

Hunter slid a couple of fingers inside me and hooked them around to massage my G spot, while his tongue lavished attention on my clit.

"How long should we make her wait until she comes?" Parker asked. He sucked a mouthful of nipple between his lips and looked at me, his eyes smiling.

"Not too long, but just long enough," Slade said. "It's more fun when she's going wild and begs."

"You suck, sir," I told him.

He raised an eyebrow at me while he sucked my nipple.

"I meant the other kind of suck." I let my head flop back and my gaze went to the ceiling. Every touch ignited my body more and more. I loved having one on one time with each of the guys, but all three of them together was incredible. They knew exactly what I wanted and were generous in giving it to me. Even though sometimes that meant making me wait.

I bent my knees to open myself out further to Hunter's mouth.

"That feels so good. I'm going to come." I slowly rocked myself against his lips and tongue, wanting to last as long as they wanted me to. I could have done this forever.

"Not yet." Parker moved away from my breast and kissed my mouth. He tasted of honey and tequila, mixed with his usual, delicious flavour. His tongue slid between my lips, stroking across my teeth and tongue.

I kissed him back, hungry for every drop of him. I grabbed onto his bicep and squeezed tight as I got closer and closer to the edge. My nails dug into his skin, but that seemed to spur him on further. He kissed me harder, pressing his tongue to the back of my throat.

"Let her come," Slade told Hunter. Just as well he did, because I couldn't have held back another second anyway.

I came hard against Hunter's mouth, my lips clamped around Parker's tongue. I held him there like that while I shattered into a million pieces, gasping and groaning with heat and pleasure.

I only let him go when I finally came down. I kept my grip on his arm as Slade swapped places with Hunter, knelt between my knees and drove his cock into me. He thrust a few times before rolling us over so I straddled his hips.

Hunter grabbed a bottle of lube out of the drawer and tossed it to Parker.

Parker worked the lid loose and squirted some onto his fingers. "Lean forward," he told me in a voice choked with need.

Eagerly, I did what he said, lowering my upper body until my breasts brushed Slade's chest. I shivered slightly with the sensation of cold on my ass as Parker spread lube around my rear hole.

He slid his fingers inside me, lubricating and stretching my muscles, readying me for his cock. Finally, he gripped my hips and straddled

Slade's legs. He positioned his cock outside my ass and slid the tip inside. He stopped still, letting me get used to having him there.

I took a couple of breaths and forced myself to relax. After a few moments, he slipped in deeper, then stopped again to let me stretch. After a few more moments, he slipped all the way in, his cock filling me as deep as Slade's was filling my pussy.

They both felt so fucking good inside me.

Hunter crawled over to massage my breasts with his hands and mouth while both guys thrust slowly in and out of my body.

"You're so fucking gorgeous," Hunter whispered. "Watching both of them fuck you is hotter than hell."

"Being fucked by all of you is hotter than hell," I told him. I never wanted to stop.

Parker set the pace, thrusting into me and driving me onto Slade's cock. "You feel incredible."

"She definitely does," Slade agreed. His eyes were half closed, his expression one of bliss.

"No, all of you," I half laughed, half whispered. "I'm so fucking lucky."

"I'm so fucking close," Slade said.

Parker grunted. "Me too."

"Think you can come at the same time?" Hunter rolled my nipples between his thumbs and forefingers.

"Challenge accepted," Parker said. "We can do this, right Slade?"

Slade's only response was to groan and thrust up into me, harder than ever. Only a thin wall of skin separated his cock from Parker's. Every time they drove into me, they must have felt each other. The thought of that drove me wild. Wild enough to come again.

My orgasm stole one from Parker and Slade, making us all come at the same time.

The only sound I heard past the rushing of blood through my ears was the slapping of skin on skin, and the groaning of both guys as they shattered with me.

The universe ended, splintered into a million pinpoints of light and heat. Nothing was left but full, sweating pleasure and the feeling of two incredible guys releasing themselves into my body.

"Now that was fucking hot," Hunter said appreciatively. He didn't let up messaging my breasts until the three of us flopped down together and the guys slid out of me. "I think I like this version of the game much better."

I sagged onto Slade's sweaty chest and lay there catching my breath. When I was finally able to speak, I said, "I like both versions."

As long as my guys were there, I didn't care if I played Kink or Kink and Drink.

In the back of my mind I remembered: we had to survive the trials first.

seventeen

SLADE

I CLOSED and locked the door to my office. The expression that locks only kept honest thieves out was as true here at Brutham Academy as it was anywhere else. I did it anyway, out of habit. Fuck only knew why anyone would bother to break in anyway.

The students who attended were usually rich enough to buy whatever they needed. They didn't need to steal from anyone's office. If they did, they'd be disappointed at what they'd find in mine.

I headed down the stairs, toward the corridor that led to the Academy assembly hall. I had no idea why they called this meeting. That made me nervous as hell. The Academy rarely gathered all the students together in one place, and then only for the first day of a new semester, or a graduation ceremony. Today was neither.

I hurried down the corridor and was about to step inside when I caught sight of a couple a few metres past the door. Their voices were low, but the conversation sounded heated. The man, his suit perfectly tailored, stood with a hand pressed against the wall beside the woman's head. His whole posture screamed dominant alpha. The tension in his body suggested he was pissed off.

I couldn't make out who he was, but I knew her. Francine Young, the head of the IT faculty, was only a couple of years older than me. Her chocolate brown hair was kept in a neat bun back from her face. Her heels were so high, she was almost as tall as the man she was speaking to. She looked pissed off too, but not intimidated. She clearly knew him.

"I'm not getting into this now," she hissed.

"This is fucking—" he lowered his voice again.

"No," she said firmly. She placed a hand on his chest and pushed herself away from him. She started off down the corridor, heading in my direction.

It wasn't until he turned that I recognised Joshua Brantley, the third oldest of the Brantley brothers. He usually kept his nose out of their shit in public, but occasionally represented Reuben or Caleb. In private, he was in it as deep as they were. Apparently he had other things going on in private too.

"Francine." He growled at her back. Literally growled. He sounded like a feral dog, a stark contrast to his navy Armani and a white shirt that looked like it wouldn't dare to crease.

She raised her hand but didn't look back. "I said later, Joshua." She gave me a slightly embarrassed smile. "I assume you're going into the meeting, Mr. Lincoln?"

"Uh, yes." I gestured for her to go first and ignored Joshua's glare. Whatever was going on between them was none of my business.

Joshua muttered something under his breath and followed us, but headed to the far side of the hall.

"Trouble in paradise?" I asked. We both moved to the back of the room where several other teachers stood and waited.

"I wouldn't call it paradise," she replied. "How are things with you, Slade?"

I shrugged. "Same shit, different day." If she didn't want to talk about it, I wouldn't push. I turned towards the seats set in lines in the centre of the room. Students were starting to file in and sit down. Lila already sat in the second row, looking anxious.

"This is going to be carnage," Francine remarked. When I turned towards her, she elaborated. "This year's trials. The whole switching it up thing. We'll be lucky if any first years remain when it's done."

"Why do I think you know something I don't?" I asked.

She offered a faint smile. "Because I do. I sit in on school board meetings, remember? I'm privy to all sorts of things you probably don't want to know about."

I regarded her thoughtfully for a few moments. "I'm sure you get approached all the time to make changes to suit certain factions." Was that what Joshua was doing here? I got the impression there was more going on than that. Were they intimate?

I couldn't blame Joshua. She was intelligent and beautiful. If it wasn't for Lila, I'd pursue her myself. She was also one of Hunter and Parker's professors. I couldn't help wondering if Joshua was the only Brantley she was ever intimate with. Before Lila, they had a reputation for getting their dicks wet anywhere and everywhere they could.

"It comes with the territory," she agreed. "Nothing I can't handle."

She was keeping her cards close to her chest as far as Joshua was concerned.

"I can't imagine anything being beyond your ability to handle, Frankie," I told her.

"I've always thought you were wise, Slade," she replied. Her gaze scanned the room. She seemed more on edge than usual.

"I'm not sure I'd go that far." I kept my tone as light as I could. "Anything I can do?"

She turned back to me, hazel eyes serious. "Don't lose your shit, whatever happens. If at least one of those girls doesn't survive the trials, we're in for a world of pain."

I didn't need her to tell me which girls she was referring to. "Samuel Bell will use it as an excuse to blame the Brantleys," I said.

"Exactly," she agreed. "If they go to war, we'll all get caught in the crossfire."

Her words chilled my blood. "Joshua wants you to pick a side."

"Everyone wants everyone to pick a side," she said. "No one will remain neutral for long. Not even me."

"Are you really that neutral?" I cocked my head at her. If she was fucking Joshua Brantley, then people would assume where her loyalties lay. It's me, I'm people.

"I try to be, just like you do," she said. "You've always been affiliated with the Brantley family, but now...what will you do if this escalates? Who are your loyalties with?"

"Lila," I said immediately. She was right though. It would be natural, easy, for me to return to the Brantley fold. Why would I owe

Samuel Bell any loyalty? He'd put Lila through hell. The only thing I owed him was a punch in the face. With a bullet.

"Nothing is so simple." Her tone was laced with meaning. "My mother was a Bell."

"And now you're sleeping with Joshua," I said without thinking.

The sides of her mouth twitched. "It looks as though the meeting is about to start."

The chancellor entered the assembly hall. The students gradually began to settle down.

I spied Chloe and Zachary sitting near the back. The twins weren't here. This meeting was only for students who'd take the trials this year, and relevant staff. No doubt Hunter and Parker found some way to watch. Knowing them, they were lurking just outside the doors.

"Thank you for coming," the chancellor said when those gathered were quiet enough to be heard. The hall wasn't big enough to need a microphone. The student body at Brutham was a lot smaller than the average university. Even if everyone was gathered here, there was no need for audio equipment.

"We love coming," one of the students shouted out.

Everyone laughed. I glanced over to see Francine smiling and shaking her head.

The chancellor cleared his throat. "Yes, well. I'm sure you're all wondering why you're gathered here."

"Because you told us to," someone else shouted.

"Yes. I'm sure you're wondering *why* I told you to," he said. He was visibly starting to get annoyed. He paced across the front of the room and back.

"It's come to the attention of the school board that various individuals have been taking it upon themselves to go to the trials' site and undertake various activities there."

"How about that?" I whispered.

"You wouldn't know anything about that, would you?" Francine asked teasingly.

"Me, Frankie? Not a clue." I offered an innocent smile.

She rolled her eyes toward the ceiling. "Of course not."

I turned my attention back to the chancellor.

"The school board has suggested those activities constitute cheating," the chancellor continued.

A rumble went through the gathered students. Lila turned around to look at me, worry etched on her face. I gave her as reassuring a smile as I could manage. Honestly, I had no idea what this meant either.

"In light of this, the school board has decided to change the location of the trials," the chancellor said.

I released a breath of relief. For a moment there, I thought he'd automatically fail anyone thought to have gone to the trial site. I wasn't sure how they'd prove that, but if there was a will, Brutham would find a way. Hell, Frankie could probably hack all of our phones with her eyes closed.

When the room settled again, the chancellor continued.

"No one will be told the location of the trials in advance." His gaze scanned the room and settled on Lila for a few moments before moving to Chloe and then Joshua of all people. Of course, that was why he was here. This was something to do with him or Reuben. Maybe Caleb too.

"In two days, transport will arrive to convey students and staff to the new trial site. The trials will take place as planned. Depending on the outcome, we may adopt this model for future years. Cheating will not be tolerated at Brutham."

"Hide the bodies next time," Francine told me. "For the record, I managed to get you added to the staff who are going to the new trial site."

I looked at her in surprise.

"Like I said, if at least one of those girls don't survive, there will be carnage," she said by way of explanation. "Don't get too excited, Dane DiMarco is coming too. That puts you both on equal footing."

"I'd rather be a few steps ahead," I said. "If Hunter and Parker—"

She shook her head just slightly. "The chancellor won't allow any students who aren't taking part in the trials. You know as well as I do, they'll find a way."

"They will, with or without the help of any of their professors," I said. "With would certainly be preferable."

"Do you realise how big a favour you'd owe me if I help them?" she asked lightly.

"Name your price," I said without hesitation. "Or better yet, think of it as preventing carnage."

"If I help Chloe and Dane, I achieve the same result," she pointed out.

"I'm sure Joshua would appreciate it if you help his brothers." I watched her expression carefully.

"Do I need Joshua's appreciation?" she replied.

I didn't know how to answer that. "Like I said, name your price. Lila is the right one to back, I promise you that. When she wins, you may not have to worry about picking a side. She wants to make peace between the families. Wouldn't that make life easier for all of us?"

"You make a compelling argument, Mr. Lincoln," she said. "I make no specific promises. It may be all I can do is what I've already done in getting you included."

I knew when I couldn't push any harder. She was at least as stubborn as Lila.

"Thank you, Frankie," I said graciously. "I know you must have had to pull some strings to do that. I appreciate you sticking your neck out."

"My neck is firmly in," she said. "I just did what needed to be done."

"Of course you did." We both knew there was more to it than that, but the gracious thing to do would be to leave it at that.

"Are there any more surprises I should know about?" I asked.

"Without doubt, but nothing I can disclose." She didn't bother to look apologetic. It was what it was. "I can wish you luck though. I have a feeling we're all going to need it."

"Funny, I have exactly the same feeling."

eighteen

SLADE

"WELL, THAT'S BULLSHIT," Hunter said evenly. "We get attacked and suddenly we're the bad guys?"

"To be realistic, plenty of people thought of us as the bad guys before that," Parker pointed out. "They call us the evil twins. They don't do that for no reason."

"Yeah, but in this case, we're the victims," Hunter argued. "Caleb sent those pricks after us. But we're the ones getting penalised for it." He stalked the four or five steps from one end of the room to the other.

"I agree with Hunter," Lila said softly. "I was relying on all of you to be there. Without you, I don't know if I can..." She shook her head.

"Hey, babe." Parker scooted over and wrapped his arms around her. "Like Slade said, we'll find a way. Even if Frankie doesn't help us, we'll figure it out. They said they're sending transport for you, we'll just follow that bitch. The transport, not Frankie. She's not—"

"We know what you meant," I said. "Whatever Lila and I are in, you'll be right behind us."

"Yeah," Hunter agreed. "I'd like to see them try to stop us."

"No you wouldn't," I told him. "If they wanted to stop you, you'd be stopped. They could tie you down again."

"Fuck that," Hunter snarled. "The next person who tries that is getting a one-way trip to a mangled face."

"That won't help Lila," I pointed out.

"It would help me and my rage," Hunter snapped. "We haven't done all this work to end up being left behind and letting Lila down."

"Then we get ahead of them," Parker said simply.

His twin swung around to stare at him. "What are you talking about, bro?"

"They said they're not telling anyone where the trials are, but someone knows and has made a digital record of it," Parker reasoned.

"Fuck," Hunter spat. "Since when are you the rational twin?"

Parker grinned. "Since you're pacing around the room like a caged lion, losing your shit. Someone has to be cool, calm and collected."

"That's usually my role," I pointed out. "But Parker is right. The Academy isn't just going to pick the students up and take them to fuck knows where. They have to know where to tell the driver to go. They would have had to make all sorts of plans."

"Unless..." Lila said softly.

"Unless what, babe?" Parker asked gently.

"Unless they were offered a place," she concluded.

"Fuck." Hunter punched the wall. He left a neat, fist-sized hole in the plaster. "Owww, fucking hell." He shook out his wrist. "I'm going to pretend that was Caleb's face. That was why he didn't want us dead."

"I thought it was because he loves us," Parker said.

Hunter laughed bitterly. "It's because he and Reuben are fucking with us. Joshua too by the sound of it."

I shook my head. "What are you guys talking about?" I got the fucking around with us part. None of that surprised me for a moment. Whatever else the three of them were referring to, I was missing something.

"Caleb owns a piece of land out in the middle of nowhere," Hunter explained. "Probably more than one, but this is a specifically crappy one. One perfect for nefarious activities and killing people who will never be found."

"It's where I was held with all those other women," Lila said softly. Her expression was haunted. She was clearly thinking back to those horrible days and nights. Her face paled. Her lips didn't tremble, but they were pressed in a tight line, making them white.

Like always, a pang of guilt went through me like a blade. A blunt, rusty one. I *should* have been able to prevent that. I'd never forgive myself for failing her the way I did. She forgave me, but I didn't forgive myself. I still beat myself up about it. Some day, I'd find a way to make it up to her.

"And where Hunter and I were chained up," Parker added. "If anyone is going to volunteer a location, that would be it."

"Okay," I said slowly. "If that's the case, we know where it is and what to expect when we get there."

"Nothing good," Hunter said. "If Caleb wanted to leave booby-traps, that's where he'd do it."

"Would Samuel Bell agree to use Caleb's land?" I directed the question to Lila.

She frowned in thought. "If the Brantley family is engineering this, maybe he doesn't know. This could be a way for them to get me, Chloe and Zachary all in the same place to get rid of us. Or maybe he knows and doesn't care."

She looked halfway defeated already. She was obviously convinced her father wasn't on her side, no matter what she did. Even if she figured out what it was he wanted, it wouldn't be enough.

I thought my father was difficult, but he was a lamb compared to Samuel Bell. Raising children to be tough was one thing. Breaking them down bit by bit was another. If Lila decided she wanted him dead, I'd be out of the door like a bullet. He wouldn't see the sunrise in the morning.

"If this is a move by the Brantleys, then Frankie did us a huge favour by making sure I was included," I said. "She could have made sure I was left behind or incapacitated, so I couldn't do anything."

"That might explain why Joshua was pissed off," Hunter said. "If she fucked with their plans, none of them would be pleased."

"No, they wouldn't," I agreed. "But Frankie doesn't take risks like that. Not unless she's very sure she can smooth it over after."

"I'm sure Joshua would forgive her after a blowjob," Hunter said. "He's not as complicated as Reuben or Caleb. He reminds me more of me than they do."

"They seemed pretty close." I rubbed a hand over my stubble.

For all I knew, she was on her knees with her mouth around his cock this very moment. That was a visual image I really didn't need, but I couldn't help wondering if she let her hair down before she fucked. The hot librarian look was cute and all, but she struck me as a wild woman in private. Someone who knew exactly what she wanted and how to ask for it. That being the case, Joshua was probably the one on his knees, his mouth between her legs. Yeah, I didn't need that visual image either. I shook my head to try to dislodge it from my brain.

"Can you find out if the trials are going to be at this location?" That was at least a billion times more important right now than the sex lives of other people.

"Are you suggesting I hack Brutham Academy?" Parker asked lightly. "You know that's usually grounds for a shallow grave, right?"

In spite of his words, he looked ready to tackle the challenge. More than ready, excited. Of course he was. If a shallow grave was guaranteed, he'd probably do it anyway. Firstly, to see if he could, and secondly, because of the basic enjoyment he got from fucking with people and the establishment in general. One day, his excitement and curiosity would get the better of him.

With any luck, it would wait until *after* the trials.

"Usually I wouldn't suggest doing anything like that," I said slowly. "But the only alternative is trying to follow and that's too unpredictable."

"That's not the only alternative," Hunter said. "Frankie seems to like you."

"If you're suggesting I try to seduce her just to find out—" I started.

Hunter shrugged. "I'm just saying, we all have to make sacrifices to get where we need to go. It's not as if she's not hot."

If he'd slept with her before, his expression gave away nothing. Good, I really didn't want to know. Whatever he did before Lila was in the past and his business. I was sure he didn't want to know about my past encounters either. Which I had no intention of telling him about anyway. Some things were better left unsaid, especially that. Everyone before Lila felt faceless and meaningless. Practice before I found the real thing. Practice I enjoyed, but nothing more than that.

I glanced at Lila. "No."

I silently insisted she not agree with Hunter. I'd do whatever was necessary, including fuck Frankie, but I'd feel like shit if I did it. I genuinely liked the woman and I didn't want to do anything that would feel like cheating on Lila. I liked to think I had more integrity than that. But if Lila's life was at stake—

"No," Lila said softly. "I don't want anyone using anyone like that, no matter what else happens. Also, if Frankie touched Slade, I'd have to kill her, and she seems like a relatively decent person, for Brutham."

I smiled. "Thank you." I had a feeling Chloe would have insisted on Dane or Zachary doing it, but Lila had more integrity and a stronger sense of 'touch him and die' than Chloe.

Parker scratched the back of his head. "Hacking it is then. If I end up dead from this, it was nice knowing you all." He kissed Lila's mouth. "I love you."

"I love you too." She pressed her cheek to his and stayed there for a few moments before Hunter handed Parker his laptop.

Parker took a deep breath and opened his computer. He tapped on his keyboard and focused his bright blue eyes on the screen.

"This may take a while. These systems are designed to be hack proof. Although, there is no such thing as hack proof, even if Frankie designed the system. Hell, even if Kennedy had." He glanced up for a moment. "If they worked together, they could probably invent something hack proof."

"Get on with it," Hunter snapped. He gestured at Parker to hurry up.

"I am, bro, calm your tits," Parker told him.

I sat down beside Lila and put my arm around her. "Are you all right?"

"I thought I had some idea what to expect during these trials," she said. Her brow was furrowed with a deep frown. "Now I don't. I can't help feeling there's no way I'm going to survive this. Maybe I should walk away right now and never look back."

"You would always look back," I told her. "You'd always wonder what might have happened. If you walk away now, you'll spend the rest of your life looking over your shoulder. If that's what you want, you know we'll support you, but I don't think it is."

"Would you really have fucked another woman if I asked you to?" she asked. She looked at me evenly, clearly seeking an honest answer.

"Sweetheart, I would do anything for you," I assured her. "I wouldn't have enjoyed a moment of it. And I would have felt like the biggest asshole in the world for doing that to you and her. But if it was necessary..."

She smiled faintly. "Lucky it's not necessary then. Because I really would have had to kill her."

I smiled back. "I believe you. If any man who wasn't already in this room touched you, I'd kill him. Unless you didn't want me to. In which case, I'd be fucking conflicted, but I'd still go with whatever you want."

"I love you," she told me.

"I love you too," I replied.

"Okay, I'm in," Parker sounded excited. "Anyone want their grades changed while I'm here?"

I raised an eyebrow at him.

"No? Okay. Let's see here. Student information. Past trials. Missing, presumed dead. Deceased students. Deceased staff. Dining hall menu for the next two months. Oh, we should definitely check that out. I hope pizza is on there."

"Parker," Hunter said warningly.

Parker glanced up. "What?" He looked back down. "Repairs to the building. Dusk Bay campus progress. Here we go, trials for this year." His hands moved over the keyboard quickly.

"Due to numerous deceased persons being found at the trial site, the trial site has been abandoned. Presumed compromised. Huh, you don't say? Alternative location is out in the middle of fucking nowhere." He glanced up again. "It doesn't actually say that. Just the address which happens to be out in the middle of fucking nowhere."

"We got that," I told him. "Is it the place you thought it was?"

Parker glanced back down, eyes shifting back and forth as he read across the screen. "Sort of, but it's a lot worse than that."

nineteen

LILA

"YOU'VE GOT THIS."

Everyone else on the bus gave me and Chloe a wide berth, leaving the seat beside me open for Slade. If I was honest with myself, I'd admit everyone was giving everyone space and wary looks. A few with obvious alliances stayed in small groups, but most kept to themselves.

There was no way I was the only one thinking how nasty as fuck all of this was.

I placed my hand over his, where it rested on my thigh.

"I don't feel like I've got this," I admitted. "The odds are, I'll be dead in a few hours."

"You will not," he said firmly. "I'll make sure of that. And if I don't, you will. Or the twins will. Between the four of us, we'll make sure nothing happens to you."

"Nothing better happen to you three either." I looked over at him and wondered for the millionth time why he was with me. He was so fucking gorgeous, smart and skilled. He could do better than me. If I tried to tell him that, he wouldn't listen. Stubbornness was something we all had in common. It would either keep us alive or get us all killed.

"We already know Hunter and Parker are invincible." He smiled. "What you might not realise yet is, so are we. We must be, to have made it this far. Right at the end of your first year at Brutham. Of all the students who started, these are the ones who got to this point." He gestured around the bus.

Thank fuck it wasn't a truck.

He lowered his hand. "Most of these students will make it to the end of the day. That greatly increases their odds of finishing their degrees."

I knew that. First year was always the most difficult. The students who didn't die, often dropped out. To actually *finish* the year, you had to be dedicated, smart and hard-core stubborn. The fact that Hunter, Parker and Slade all made it through spoke for itself.

I had to do it too. At the risk of sounding cliché, failure was not an option.

"Which ones won't?" I asked rhetorically. I glanced ahead to where Chloe sat with Dane. Zachary sat in the seat opposite her. She appeared outwardly calm, but inside she'd feel turmoil, the same as me.

"Has there ever been a year where everyone survived the trials?" I asked.

He looked thoughtful. "Once or twice. For the record, there's never been a trial where no one survived."

His words were punctuated by a distant flash of lightning.

"There's a first time for everything." I looked out the window. Heavy clouds were rolling in. The wind had picked up, judging by the way branches were tossed around the tress we passed. "I'm guessing they've never been cancelled due to bad weather."

"Never," he agreed. "I remember once they considered moving the trials to the middle of winter, to add snow to the level of difficulty. Luckily they kept it at the end of the year. and that we aren't in the northern hemisphere. Otherwise you'd be facing a blizzard."

"No thanks." Fat drops of rain scattered against the glass. Fuck, that was just what we needed.

"Use it to your advantage," Slade said. "Rain will reduce visibility. It will slow everyone down."

"Including me." I turned back to him.

"Then you concentrate on moving smart, not quickly." He made it sound easy. "I'll be right there with you as much as I can."

"I know you will, I just..."

"I know," he said when I couldn't find the words to finish the sentence. "Everything comes down to this. By the end of the day, you'll be the one to take over from your father. Your future will be set. It's a big deal."

"Unless he changes his mind," I said. "I could do the trials first and he might still decide to give it to Chloe. Or Zachary. Or insist Kennedy take it. Or..." I shrugged.

"Fuck knows who else. Frankie is a distant relative. He might give it to her. She's competent, smart—"

"Frankie would never take it," he said confidently. "That's way too high-profile for her. She doesn't want to take sides. Not openly anyway. She wouldn't want to make herself a target."

"Like I am," I said bitterly. "Sometimes I think I'm too young to have so many enemies."

He actually laughed. "Don't think of them as enemies. Think of them as allies you have to prove yourself to. This is the last hurdle to doing that. When you beat Chloe, you'll have Reuben and Caleb's respect. Getting that is three quarters of the battle. With me and the twins on your side, we'll convince them to come around."

"You make it sound so easy," I told him. We both knew it wouldn't be. Nothing ever fucking was.

He turned his hand around under mine and laced our fingers together. "Don't worry about any of that now. Focus on today. The trials should only take a couple of hours. It will be over before you know it."

"It could be over right now," I said softly. "All I have to do is ask the driver to stop the bus and let me off." I could walk away from all of this. Step out into the rain and never look back. I could take up a hobby, like knitting, and never think about being a Bell ever again.

"You won't," Slade said. "You haven't come this far to walk away now."

"Did you ever think about walking away?" I asked.

"A bunch of times," he admitted. "By the time I did my trials, I'd been working for a couple of years. Killing was nothing new. I'd done it several times already. But those were hits on people who deserved it. People like Brutus and Zachary. The other students in my year were nothing like that, for the most part. We were just living our lives. Trying to, anyway. One or two were assholes. One guy liked to hurt women. Another was a serial killer in the making. They should have been expelled long before they got to the trials. They weren't, so we dealt with them. It shouldn't have been up to us to do that."

His expression was reflective, troubled. A mirror of my reflection when I looked at myself in the morning. If this life didn't kill us on the outside, it killed us a little bit more each day on the inside.

"It's barbaric," I concluded. "What would happen if we all refused to take part?"

"That happened once." His eyebrows dipped slightly. "The whole year refused. They were failed and expelled. No other university would take them after that. Brutham Academy is definitely not for the faint of heart."

"And they want to open another campus in Dusk Bay," I said sarcastically.

"Dusk Bay is the perfect place for it," he said. "A lot of people there are already shady as fuck. It's a beautiful place to visit though. Some of those cliffside mansions are incredible." He sighed wistfully. "A guy can dream."

"My father owns one of them," I said. Of course he did. "I'm sure he'll let us use it if we make it through the day." I'd insist. After everything he'd put Chloe and me through, it was the least he could do.

"*When* we make it through the day," Slade corrected. "I'd like that. We could go and take in a game of hockey or football. Depending on when we go."

"Are the Dusk Bay Demons really that bad?" I asked. I'd heard rumours of their head coach working for Caleb, who owned the team.

"They're worse," he said with a smile. "But the Dusk Bay Sharks are on track to win the Down Under Bowl this year. That's the Australian version of the Super Bowl."

"I didn't realise you were into sports that much," I observed.

He shrugged. "I can get behind local teams. Especially when I know most of the guys on them. Most of them are friends or friends of friends. Or enemies of friends."

"You're full of surprises," I said. "I presume you know most of the Dusk Bay Smashers too."

"The twins are into rugby more than I am, but yeah, I know a lot of them. They're not a bad bunch of blokes."

"For people who are shady as fuck." It was my turn to smile.

"Exactly." He nodded. "A university in Dusk Bay might not be a bad thing. The area is big enough for one."

"I guess it is," I agreed. "I just wish... It was a normal university." I was quiet for a couple of minutes. I broke it by asking, "Has any school board tried to end the trials?"

"I'd be surprised if they don't have a conversation about them every year," Slade said. "Speaking as a law professor, they are a legal nightmare. The contract every student has to sign before they start at the Academy is worded to cover every conceivable scenario."

"What about the inconceivable ones?" I asked.

"One of those and the Academy will have problems." He ran his hand over his chin.

"Problems as in getting sued?" I asked. As far as I knew, that never happened. I remember signing pages and pages of the contract. Some of it I'd read, most of it I only skimmed. It wasn't as though I could send it back to have clauses removed. I'd had no choice but to sign it, regardless of what it contained.

Of course, my father told me I should have read it thoroughly before I put pen to paper. Chloe read it all and didn't say a word before she picked up a pen and signed hers.

"Problems as in people wanting to sue them," he agreed. "There's a clause in the contract stating that they can't be sued, but the right lawyer might find a way around it someday. Not that it would get that far. The Academy would deal with everyone involved long before that."

"They'd have them killed," I concluded. "Should one establishment have that much power?"

"Whether or not they should, they do," he said. "But the right people on the school board could end a lot of it."

"If they survive long enough to make change," I pointed out.

"That's true," he admitted. "It would take very powerful, influential people with balls or uteruses of steel."

"What you're saying is I need to get through today so future students don't have to," I said slowly.

"That's up to you," he said. "I would never tell you how to think. You're more than capable of doing that yourself."

I smiled. "Right, but what's the point of being rich and powerful if you can't make change when, where and how you want to?"

If the Bell family was going to be more powerful than any government, then I wanted to be more powerful than the board of Brutham Academy too. Yes, I was fucking ambitious and I wasn't going to apologise for it. For the first time in I didn't know how long, I had another, better reason to fight my way through the trials. Something even more important than leading my family. When I was done, Brutham Academy first year trials would be a thing of the past. If students wanted to kill each other, they'd have to find another way to do it.

"If I haven't told you lately, you're fucking gorgeous and I love you." He leaned over and kissed me, apparently not giving a shit about what anyone else thought.

I kissed him back. "*You're* fucking gorgeous and I love you too. We've so got this."

Now I wanted to get off this bus, but only to get the trials underway. I was ready to kick all the ass.

twenty

LILA

THE RAIN WAS FALLING HEAVIER by the time we reached our destination.

The black clouds matched the mood inside the bus.

No one spoke. I wouldn't have been surprised if no one breathed.

Everyone was on edge, even Slade, and little seemed to ruffle him. Believing in me was one thing, having nerves on my behalf was another. He was pretty good at hiding them, but the set of his mouth and the tension in his body gave him away.

Any other time, I would have knelt down in front of him and taken his tension away with my mouth on his cock. I'd do it in front of everyone. I didn't give a shit.

Today, that would have to wait.

The bus drew up in front of the gate I remembered all too well. One of the women tried to escape, only to be thrown off the electric fence. Hades and Brutus had laughed.

Assholes.

I curled my hands into fists so tight my nails dug into my palms.

The gate grated open wide enough to let the bus pass through. It slid closed behind us with a final clang. Shutting us in. There was no way out now, only through. My blood turned to ice.

We rattled to a stop beside the big shed.

The driver turned off the engine, leaving us in silence that drew out for an eternity.

Several of the school board stood outside the shed, umbrellas shielding them from the rain. I couldn't make out my father or Reuben, but Frankie Young stood near Joshua. He must be here representing his brothers again. Or he was trying to get Frankie's attention. If that was his goal, he didn't seem to be succeeding. Her face and body were angled away from him. His mouth was tight, suggesting he'd noticed.

Whatever, none of that was my problem.

"Let's go." Slade rose and drew me along behind him as we shuffled off the bus.

We stepped out into the rain. No one offered us an umbrella.

My gaze went over to the dam, where Hades almost drowned Danica, trying to make a point.

"Let's make our way inside," one of the teachers instructed. Jason Pang was an older man with almost entirely grey hair. He was the one who herded us onto the bus before climbing up behind us. He seemed to be in charge of today's trials.

Inside, the shed was completely devoid of any signs women were kept here. The foldout beds were gone, along with the towels and sheets.

The place still gave me the shivers.

"I'll ask the staff and board members to step back against the wall," Pang ordered. "Students stand in a circle. Place your hands behind your backs."

We all moved to do as we were told. Several of the students muttered and exchanged glances. So far, none of this was what we were told to expect. One or two didn't look surprised, suggesting they also hacked the Academy servers for information.

That included Chloe and Zachary. And, I realised a moment later, Dane. None of that came as a shock, but I wondered who did the hacking. Hopefully not Kennedy. She didn't necessarily need to take my side, but I didn't want her to take Chloe's.

Another of the teachers pulled out handcuffs and moved around, placing them on our wrists, one by one.

"How are we supposed to do anything like this?" one of the students mumbled.

I wondered the same myself. The Academy files mentioned hand-cuffs, but not in detail. I glanced over to Slade. He looked like a solid wall of calm, which helped to settle my nerves somewhat. I'd feel better if I knew exactly where the twins were though. We'd seen no sign of them for hours.

Thunder rumbled outside, accompanied by a couple of flashes of lightning. The rain was heavier now.

"To the north of our location," Pang started, "there is a beach. All you need to do is reach that beach." He made it sound like nothing could be simpler. "Along the way, you'll find keys." His gaze scanned us all.

"When I give the word, you will begin your trials."

I caught Chloe's eyes and held them for a moment. Something passed between us.

Something more than the reminder we were twin sisters. This was something deeper than that. A shared fear. Fear of failure. Fear of not being enough. Fear that whatever happened today, there would be no going back.

I gave her a slight nod, which she returned. Zachary gave her a funny look before giving me a dark one.

I smiled at him and mouthed, "Fuck off."

He glared, but didn't mouth anything in return. Or maybe he did and I turned away before I saw.

"The trials commence...now." Pang dropped his hand down in front of us and gestured towards the door.

Several of the students took off at a run.

I walked calmly to the door and out into the rain. If I was going to succeed, I'd do it by remaining calm, not by letting fear or panic get the better of me.

My hair and clothes were plastered to me within moments of step-ping outside. Naturally, all the teachers and board members stayed inside where it was dry. All of them except for Slade and Dane, who followed us out.

Officially, to supervise. Unofficially? I could only guess.

Honestly, I couldn't see the point of supervision anyway. It wasn't as though they were going to intervene. Maybe they were there to make sure no one chickened out and ran away at the last moment.

"This is bullshit," Shannon, a fellow business student, muttered as we trudged through the mud. "How are we supposed to know which way is north?"

"I guess we just follow them." I nodded toward the students who ran ahead of us.

"How do we know they're going in the right direction?" she asked.

"Have you got a better idea?" Ronnie, a cybersecurity student, cocked her head at Shannon.

Shannon hesitated. "Nope. What do you think the keys will look like? I mean, should we be crawling on the ground looking through the mud for them?"

Lightning lit up the sky, followed by a massive crash of thunder.

"That sounds like something they'd make us do," Ronnie said. "But I'm keeping an eye on the trees. They might be dangling from there." She glanced at me.

"It sounds like as good an idea as any." Shannon was right though, making us crawl around in the mud *did* seem like something they'd do. "They're not gonna make this easy."

"Fuck," Shannon swore. "This really is bullshit."

The ground was getting wetter and wetter, forcing us to step off the dirt and into the sodden high grass. Water trickled down under my clothes, making me shiver with cold and discomfort.

"Stumps," I said without thinking. They both stared over at me. "If I was going to hide keys, I'd hide them in stumps."

"So would I," Ronnie said. "But this is Brutham Academy we're talking about. What's a million times worse than sticking your hand into a stump or mud?"

"So many things," Shannon said. "Shit. Jason Pang's asshole. The middle of a fire, but nothing is burning out here on a day like this."

"We're heading in the wrong direction," I concluded. I wasn't sure if I should be helping them, but neither seemed to have a grudge against me for anything. I never had a run in with either of them. I may regret it, but this was better than doing it alone.

A part of me wished I was doing this with my sister.

"What do you mean?" Shannon asked.

"The dam." I turned around and headed back in the other direction. "Even if we were going north, we won't get far with these fucking hand-cuffs on."

I trudged back through mud and grass, past a bemused Slade, and stepped straight into the water.

For the first time, I didn't give a shit I was wet. I was going to get wetter. Not in a good way either.

I lowered myself down in the brown water and felt around behind me with my fingertips. It didn't take me long to touch something. It felt like a bone. Was it human or animal?

The twins said something about tossing a couple of bodies in the dam. I grimaced, dropped the bone and went on searching. A few moments later I touched something metal. A thick, metal ring. I hooked my fingers around it and drew it up out of the mud and water.

A key dangled from the end of the ring.

"Lila for the win," Shannon said. "Can you try that on your handcuffs?"

I rolled the ring around, trying to grab the key, but it kept falling back to the bottom.

After several tries, I finally managed to grab the key, but no matter which way I twisted my wrists, I couldn't get it into the lock.

"Fuck. I don't think so."

"If you unlock mine, I promise to stick around and unlock yours," Shannon said.

I looked over to her. I hesitated for at least a minute or two. In the end, I came to the only conclusion that made sense. What choice did I have but to trust that she'd keep her promise?

"Turn around." It was awkward as fuck, but I managed to find the lock of her handcuffs and wiggled the end of the key inside. "It won't go. Ronnie?"

"I'll make the same promise as Shannon did." She turned her back to me.

I tried again, but once more, the key wouldn't go into the lock.

"Try on mine." I managed to hand the key over to Ronnie.

I stood still and waited.

"Son of a fucking— Oh." Ronnie sounded surprised. The handcuffs fell off my wrists and landed in the dam with a pop. "That worked."

"I'm going to take a wild guess that every pair of handcuffs has a different key," I said. Of course they did, there was no way the Academy would make it that easy. On the other hand, if there was only one key,

441

we could have taken off with it, leaving the other students in their cuffs.

Both women looked at me speculatively. I hadn't made any promises, but I bobbed back down in the water, both hands out, searching for more rings.

"You're sticking around?" Shannon looked surprised, with a hint of scepticism but, at the same time, relief. Finding her key would do her no good if we left her here with it. She'd either have to walk around cuffed or wait for another student to come and hope like hell they'd help her.

Strange, I couldn't remember the twins saying anything about working together. Although, they wouldn't have, because working together came naturally to them. They wouldn't have given it a second thought. What about Slade though? That was a question for later.

"I might find your keys for you," I said. "But also, no one said what we could do with the other keys we find." I glanced up and smiled briefly.

"That is sneaky as shit." Shannon grinned. "I like it."

We all felt around for a while before I found several rings and keys in the same place, along with more bones and what felt like a skull. I did my best not to think about it too much. Killing people was one thing, finding their remains was another. Even if they deserved it.

I tried the keys in Shannon and Ronnie's locks before finally finding the two that unlocked their cuffs. The other five or six, I shoved into the back pocket of my jeans, leaving plenty more to be found.

Ours, we all threw back in, to confuse any of the other students if they figured out where the keys were hidden. Judging by the sound of returning voices, some already had.

"Let's get out of here," Shannon said, a smug grin on her face. Why shouldn't she be smug, we'd figured out something the others hadn't.

I glanced down at my watch and pressed on the compass app.

"The really good news is north isn't the way they're going." I nodded past the big shed. "It's that way." Sooner or later the rest would figure that out and be forced to turn around. Hopefully by then, we'd have found the beach.

I slogged out of the dam, waterlogged as hell, but satisfied we'd passed the first test.

Slade looked me up and down, drenched to the skin, my clothes leaving nothing to the imagination. He grinned.

I rolled my eyes and stomped past him, heading north.

twenty-one

LILA

"SNAKES OR CROCODILES?" Shannon asked.

I turned to frown at her. "What?"

"Snakes or crocodiles?" she said again. "Which one are they more likely to throw at us next?"

"I prefer neither," Ronnie said. "Especially if the throwing is literal."

I snorted. "I don't think even Brutham Academy would make crocodiles fall from the sky."

I glanced up, just in case. The conversation was ridiculous, but like with the twins, humour kept us somewhat sane. I came to a realisation, I should have made a bigger effort to get to know my fellow students. Especially other women. They could be future allies or maybe even friends.

Right now, though, we should concentrate on getting through the next few hours.

"That would make snakes more likely," Shannon said. "I would have said balls of fire, but in this rain—"

Lightning flashed, striking a tree a few metres from us. Both women squealed in fright.

I barely managed to contain a flinch.

The trunk of the tree was split in two. Blackened wood and bark smoked.

"That could have been us," Shannon said.

"Thank fuck it wasn't," I said. After a moment I added, "Brutham can't control the weather either."

"No, but they could have put a lightning conductor in the tree," Ronnie said.

I was about to scoff when I realised she might be right. If they knew a thunderstorm was coming during the trials, fuck only knew what they might do. I wouldn't put anything past either the Academy or the older Brantley brothers.

"Should we look?" Shannon eyed the tree cautiously.

"It might be good to know what we're up against," Ronnie said slowly.

"I guess it couldn't hurt," I said. "We'll know to stay away from the trees." We knew that anyway, but we'd take extra precautions if someone fucked with the foliage.

"I'll go." Shannon said. She wiped water off her face and stepped towards the tree. "It looks like there's a—"

The tree blew apart. Bark, branches and bits of Shannon were thrown in a several metre radius.

I threw my hand to shield my face. Heat and debris rained down all around me. I tried hard not to think about what struck my arm. It might have been tree and...it might not. My stomach turned.

"Fucking hell," Ronnie said when the air was finally still. The smoke already washed away by the rain. The ground surrounding the tree was scorched and bare. Only blood and shredded items of clothing remained of Shannon. "Since when does Brutham kill its own students? Aren't we supposed to do that?"

I glanced back at Slade. His mouth was set in a firm line of annoyance.

"I'm guessing all bets are off." I eyed the remains of one of Shannon's shoes. Not even the thick leather could withstand the force of the explosion. Only by sheer luck were Ronnie and I far enough away to avoid the worst of it.

Did the Academy even know the extent of these trials? Had they actually endorsed this?

"Is it safe to continue?" Ronnie asked.

I turned back to her. Her eyes were wide, face pale and wet. More than rain poured down her cheeks.

"Do we have a choice?" I asked. "We can't be that far from the beach. We just need to be careful and stay away from trees." Now it was my turn to speak like things were easier than they really were. Neither of us bought it.

"I guess so." She glanced down at a chunk of her friend and sniffed. "She wouldn't want me to stop because of her."

"Then do it for her," I said. "We can see this through to the end." I wasn't going to waste time feeling bad. Not yet. I'd leave that for after the trials were over. I could get angry or unravel then. Maybe both. Someone deserved a punch in the cock for this.

Ronnie nodded and gripped my arm as we continued north.

* * *

The tall, unkempt grass gradually gave way to thicker trees and a downward slope. The going here was slower. Partly due to the terrain and partly due to an overabundance of caution. If there was such a thing.

If I was going to set another trap, or challenge, I'd do it here. Which may well be a reason there wasn't one here. If all of the Brantley brothers had something in common, it was the enjoyment of a good mind fuck. Letting us assume we had something to look out for, would give them something to laugh about.

Assholes.

"Keep an eye out for concealed pits," I said. Staying away from the trees as much as we could meant having to step on potentially dangerous ground.

"How will we know they're there if they're concealed?" Ronnie asked.

I stopped for a moment to scoop up a long stick off the ground. "With this." I placed it on the ground in front of me and let it scratch a path for us to walk. If the thick leaf matter concealed anything, the stick would fall in first.

In theory.

"You know what I'm doing after this?" Ronnie said.

"Getting drunk?" I suggested. That was high on my list of things to do afterward.

"Before that. My boyfriend said he'd propose after the trials. He has something amazing planned for tonight. I know whatever it is, it will be amazing. He's really sweet. He's the most romantic guy I ever met."

"Congratulations," I said. "He sounds like a good guy."

"He is," she said. "He's the best. I—"

I sensed she wasn't following me anymore.

I turned back around slowly. She was lying on the wet leaves with her throat sliced open.

Fuck.

Fuck.

I dropped down to the base of a tree and scanned the area. How the hell had someone crept up behind us without either of us knowing? Unless...

Slade appeared from between some of the trees and glanced down at Ronnie's body in surprise.

That ruled him out then. I couldn't have thought up a single reason why he'd kill her anyway. That didn't mean he didn't have them. Slade was a mystery to me at times. I suspected he always would be.

He trotted forward until he saw me crouched down.

"Thank fuck. Did you see anything?" He took my hands and pulled me to my feet.

"Nothing," I said. "I'm guessing one of my fellow first years is an assassin. Any idea who?"

He frowned, but shook his head. "Not a clue. Whoever they are, they're good. Keep your eyes open."

"What do you think I'm doing?" I snapped. I regretted it immediately and sighed. "I'm sorry. I shouldn't take it out on you. I hate being taken by surprise."

"Me too, little fox. Me too. Since it seems the rules have gone out the window, I'm staying with you. This whole thing is a shit show."

"You're telling me." I was glad to have him with me. Apparently my instincts weren't good enough. I'd need his too. "I should have told Ronnie to quit. She could have turned back."

"If someone was determined to kill her, they would have done it either way," he said. "We can't worry about that now. Let's keep going." In spite of his words, he looked regretful. If Ronnie had any enemies, which apparently she did, I was unaware of them.

I took a moment to give Ronnie's body a long last look before I nodded and let Slade lead me through the trees.

* * *

"Shouldn't we be there by now?"

The land continued to slope downwards, but the trees thinned. We hadn't stumbled on any concealed holes, or other students. If it wasn't for the continuing, heavy rain, it might have been a nice walk in the bush.

"Maybe that's the next part of this. There's really no beach. We're going to keep walking until we're so lost, we'll die out here." If that was the case, I was going to be very pissed off.

"You underestimate my ability to keep us alive," Slade said. "If we have to catch rabbits and kangaroos to eat, that's what we'll do."

"You know how to skin an animal?" I gave him a sceptical glance.

He raised his eyebrows at me.

"I meant animals other than humans." I wiped the rain off my face with my sleeve. It was falling so heavily now, the gesture was almost futile.

"I haven't done it, but how hard can it be? I wouldn't let you go hungry. Since you have a new tracker in your earring, the twins would find us long before we had to resort to that. They'd bring pizza and burgers."

"Where are they anyway?" I ignored the way my stomach turned at the thought of food. "I thought the idea was to neutralise the additional shit Caleb put here."

The file on the Academy database wasn't extensive, but there were mentions of additional challenges. In retrospect, that sounded benign compared to what we'd faced already. We knew it would be difficult, but not as hard as this.

Honestly, I was worried about Hunter and Parker. They might have been killed by a tree-bomb or fuck knows what else. They could be lying out here somewhere, waiting for us to stumble over their bodies.

"It was," Slade said. "I'm guessing they missed the tree that killed Shannon. They might have disabled a bunch more though." He didn't look so certain.

"I'd feel better if all four of us were doing this together," I said.

"So would I." Slade glanced back over his shoulder.

"What is it?" I asked.

"We're being followed. For the last few minutes, at least." He glanced back again.

"Should you be seen with me?" I looked back too. "You're supposed to be supervising. If they think you're helping me, you'll get fired."

"I'd rather lose my job than lose you," he said, without looking at me. "They've changed the rules this year. As far as I'm concerned, they've broken them. And if they've broken them, then we get to do the same. If they don't like it, they can get fucked."

"In that case, should we do something to get whoever it is to reveal themselves?" Was it Chloe, Zachary or whoever cut Ronnie's throat?

My heart raced. The shivering wasn't just because I was cold and wet. The hint of panic in the back of my mind was getting more and more difficult to ignore. It made focusing more of a challenge. I forced a few breaths in and out until I regained some of my composure. What little composure I had today.

"Yep." Slade guided me into a patch of wattles. We ducked down to wait.

For the first time, I was grateful for the rain. Hunkering down this close to dried wattle flowers would make me sneeze. Nothing would give me away quicker.

I made out the sound of footsteps slogging through the mud. Whoever it was, they weren't trying to conceal their presence from us. They sounded determined to keep walking. To reach the beach.

Slade pulled a knife out from his boot and handed it to me before pulling out another one. He mouthed, "Be ready."

I nodded. I gripped the hilt of the knife in my wet hand and scanned the trees for movement.

There.

And there.

More than one person.

Slade gestured that he'd take the one on the left, while I dealt with the one on the right.

I nodded again that I understood.

"She has to be here somewhere," Parker said.

I sagged with relief and lowered the knife.

"She can't be— There you are." Hunter grinned as Slade and I stepped out of the bushes. "These are some wild trials. Much more fun than ours."

"Fun?" I echoed. I shook my head at him. "You're out of your mind."

He laughed. "I think we've established that already. We're only about a kilometre from the beach. If it wasn't for the rain, we'd smell the salt air." He sniffed as though he could anyway.

His words should have been a relief, but they filled me with dread instead. If I set up this shit show, I'd leave the worst until last. What could be worse than exploding trees and having to slog around in a cold, muddy dam?

Okay, plenty of things. At this point, I'd prefer it rain crocodiles to whatever was to come. The only thing I was sure of was that it was going to suck.

twenty-two

LILA

"THIS IS TOO QUIET," I said. "I keep expecting a hundred armed mercenaries to jump out of the trees and kill us."

"That would be overkill, even for Caleb or Reuben," Hunter said. "Seventy-five, maybe, but not a hundred."

I snorted softly. As if the number mattered. Seventy-five or a hundred, we'd be equally dead. "What about Joshua? He might supply the extra twenty-five, just to round it up."

"And risk pissing off Frankie Young?" Slade glanced back over his shoulder. "From what I saw, I'd be surprised if he hadn't tried to talk his older brothers out of the additional challenges."

Parker made a noise in the back of his throat like a game show when a contestant gave the wrong answer. "He failed. Hunter and I have spent the last two days dismantling... I don't know how many explosive devices and trip wires."

"Twenty-three explosive devices and thirteen tripwires," Hunter supplied. "We probably missed several. Obviously we missed one of them. I was surprised it didn't go off when the lightning hit that tree."

"No lightning conductors in the trees then?" I asked.

"I'm sure if they thought of it, there would have been," he said. "But no, none of those. Excuse me if I don't suggest it to them for next time. Poor innocent trees shouldn't be the victims of the Academy."

"People are okay then?" I asked curtly.

"That depends on the people," Hunter said unapologetically. "You know I'm at the point where if Caleb inspected a tree and blew himself up, I wouldn't be too sad. I mean, a little bit, but not too much."

"No offence, but right now, he can go to hell," Slade said.

"I take no offence whatsoever to that sentiment," Hunter said. "I both understand and agree with it. When this is over, I'm going to go back and have words with him again. I don't appreciate him fucking with us."

"Me either," Parker agreed. "Reuben doing it is bad enough. Caleb is starting to become Reuben two-point-oh. If Joshua is joining in on that, I'm going to be really pissed off."

"It's going to make forming peace between our families more difficult," I said.

I'd considered having Reuben assassinated, but now I pencilled Caleb in as well. Potentially Joshua too. So far, Lucas kept his nose out of everything, and Zeke was more or less harmless. The situation would be much easier if the twins were the head of their family.

Unfortunately, having three Brantley brothers assassinated would put a target on my back that I didn't need. The one I already had was big enough. I didn't need Daisy Lasalle, her boyfriends and connections coming after me. She was one of the more reasonable people I knew. Tough as fuck, but smart and savvy as well. Not to mention increasingly influential.

"How much further?" I asked after a few minutes of silence.

"Where are our fucking keys?" Zachary's voice growled from behind us.

We all stopped to turn around. Chloe and Zachary were trotting towards us, their hands still cuffed behind their backs.

The twins burst out laughing.

"Sucks to be you," Parker told them, a huge grin on his face.

Zachary glared at them, then turned to me. "Where are they? We went through every fucking key we could find. At least ten are missing."

"What makes you think I have anything to do with that?" I asked evenly.

"Did you?" Chloe asked.

I glanced at Hunter, who was still grinning and looking smug. "I might, but I don't think I'm the only one." I didn't have ten in my pocket.

"You might not be," Hunter agreed. He rubbed his hands together. "What's it worth to you?"

"I don't rip your nuts off and shove them down your throat," Zachary snarled.

Hunter clicked his tongue. "I don't think you're in a position to make threats, bro."

"*I'm not your fucking bro*. Where are the keys?" Zachary's face was pink with rage.

"If we have them, and give them to you, will you back off?" Slade asked. He stood with his arms crossed, eyes narrowed at Zachary and my sister.

Chloe and Zachary exchanged looks.

"I can't finish the trials like this," she said softly.

"Alive?" Slade asked.

She looked at him resentfully. "Handcuffed. Even if I'm alive, our father will call it a failure. I might as well die."

"Works for me." Parker shrugged and started to turn away.

"*Please*," Chloe added.

I hesitated for a moment longer, then reached into my pocket and pulled out the keys. "Turn around."

She looked at me like she was certain I'd stab her in the back, but turned around anyway. What choice did she have? I had keys and she didn't.

I tried one key after the other, handing each one to Slade when they didn't work.

Finally, the sixth key slid into the lock and Chloe's handcuffs fell open.

She turned back around, shaking her wrists, clearly relieved. She looked slightly like she'd prefer to suck a lemon, but she said, "Thank you."

"You really want Zachary's cuffs unlocked?" Hunter asked.

"Yes, she fucking does," Zachary snapped.

In the corner of my eye, I saw Dane approach. He must have been the dutiful teacher and kept his distance. In Zachary's present mood, I didn't blame him. I didn't want to be near him either. I gave Dane a slight nod and turned away.

"If you have his key, please use it," Chloe said finally.

"Turn around," Slade told him.

Zachary looked resentful, but turned his back on Slade. Slade tried them all, but none of the five keys I kept worked on his lock. One by one, Slade hung the rings on a branch where they could be seen by any students who came this way. If any of them were left alive.

"Hunter." I raised my eyebrows at him.

He sighed. "For the record, this is against my better judgement." He pulled out a handful of keys and gave them to Slade.

Slade took them and started trying to fit them into Zachary's lock. Three, four, five were added to the tree. A sixth. The seventh. Finally, the eighth key worked and Zachary's cuffs fell from his wrists.

He shook his wrists out, but when he turned around, he had a knife in his hand. He lunged at me.

Slade threw himself between us. He twisted his upper body and caught the knife in his shoulder instead of straight in his heart. He let out a grunt of pain and fury.

"Slade!" I shouted. Fucking hell. The expression on his face was one I'd remember until the day I died. Shock, agony and cold, hard anger. His emotions were there and then they were gone, tightly packed into the corner of his mind.

Faster than I've ever seen anyone move, he pulled out his own knife and drove it straight into Zachary's throat.

"Zachary!" Chloe shrieked.

Zachary's eyes widened with surprise. He let out a strangled gurgle before slowly falling to his knees.

Slade tugged the knife clear and let Zachary fall to the ground with a wet thump and spray of mud and water. He stood watching him for a while, the knife held loosely in his hand, his face the cool, calm assassin.

Dangerous, deadly and sexy as hell.

Chloe dropped to her knees beside him, her head bowed over his body. Her shoulders trembled, but she didn't cry. She didn't make a sound.

"Thank you," Dane said. "You saved me having to kill the little prick myself."

"You're welcome," Slade winced and tentatively touched the hilt that stuck out of his shoulder. It looked painful as fuck. A few centimetres to the right and he'd be dead. If not for his lightning fast reflexes, Zachary would have taken him from me. And me from him and my guys. Zachary would have ended up just as dead. I'd forever be grateful Slade wasn't.

Dane pulled his shirt off over his head and wrapped it around the blade to stem the flow of blood. Apparently killing an annoyance was a good way to create a bond.

I stepped over to Chloe and knelt beside her. "I feel like I should say sorry, but he did try to kill me." Sorry, not sorry, might be more appropriate. Zachary brought this on himself.

She sniffed. "It's okay, I understand. For the record, I promise I didn't know he was going to do that. We were supposed to finish the trials and go from there. You know?"

"I do know," I agreed. "This is crazy. It wasn't supposed to go like this." I sucked in a breath, difficult thoughts tumbling around my brain. "I've been thinking."

She turned to me. "I've been thinking too." She shook her head. "This isn't worth it. The killing, the dying. Dad's bullshit. I don't want to be head of the family any more. You can have it. I'm going to walk away and live my life. I won't contest it any time in the future. If you need me to sign anything to say that, I will. Whatever you need."

I stared at her for a moment. I hadn't expected her to say any of that. For a full minute, I considered taking her up on her offer. With Zachary dead and her stepping aside, there was every chance our father would choose me.

A flutter of excitement passed through me.

I shoved it away. I hadn't realised until that moment that I'd already made up my mind. My stubbornness wouldn't let me back down now.

"I was going to say the same thing. I don't want it either. Not if it means making ridiculous sacrifices and going through hell. I feel like I've lost my twin sister because of this and I'd do anything to get you back."

She gaped at me, then threw her arms around me and squeezed me hard. After a moment, I hugged her back.

We stayed like that for at least a few minutes before we pulled apart.

"What do we do now?" she asked.

"We finish this thing," I said firmly. "We finish it *together*. If Dad decides to disown both of us, then fuck it. He can go to hell as far as I'm concerned. He can make an heir or whatever. We're done with him. You and me against whatever the world throws at us."

She smiled. "Fuck yeah, I'm in. Let's do this."

Together, we stood and linked arms.

"Does that mean we have to be friends with Dane now?" Parker asked.

"Yes, it does," I told him. "Let's hurry up and finish this so we can get Slade to a hospital." I reached my spare hand out to him and laced my fingers in his. "Are you all right?"

"I won't be playing tennis for a while, but I'll live." He was clearly in pain, but determined to be as badass as ever.

"You play tennis?" Hunter asked him.

Slade smiled. "No, never. If I did, I'm right-handed anyway."

"Good, that leaves your stabbing hand for whoever fucked with these trials," Dane growled.

"My stabbing hand is at Lila and Chloe's disposal." Slade bowed his upper body, but then straightened up and winced. He gave Chloe a glance like he didn't quite trust her, but nodded for Hunter to lead the way toward the beach.

"Dane and I will bring up the rear," he said. He reluctantly let my hand go and stepped around behind Chloe and me.

"Good idea, any further booby-traps can get the Brantley twins," Dane said, smiling slightly.

Hunter and Parker simultaneously flipped him off. They both grinned and turned to march on down the slope and through the last stand of trees.

Finally, I heard the sound of waves licking the beach. The rain finally started to ease and the thunder and lightning only rolled in the distance.

"We're almost there," I said softly.

"Yeah we are," Chloe said. "Do you think—"

I shook my head "I don't know what to think. I guess we'll find out soon enough."

twenty-three

LILA

WE STEPPED out of the trees and onto the beach. A wet, muddy, eclectic group if there ever was one. Two teachers. Two sets of twins. Literal blood, sweat and tears.

But fuck me, we made it here alive.

The feeling of sand under my boots was sweet.

The pleasure was short-lived.

A hundred or so metres away, a track led down to the beach. Several cars were parked beside it. Each one dark, with tinted windows.

"Looks like we've got a welcoming committee," Parker said.

Arrayed around the cars were around twenty people, each with an umbrella in their hand. Most of those umbrellas were black, but one or two dark blue or green.

I squeezed Chloe's arm as we approached, both of us equally reluctant.

"Reuben," Parker said. "What a— Is pleasure the wrong word, Hunt?" He gave me a reassuring smile before turning to his twin.

"It definitely is, Park," Hunter agreed. "But I'm happier to see Reuben than I am to see Caleb."

The two older Brantley brothers stood side-by-side. Joshua stood a little away from them, hovering deliberately near Francine Young.

Caleb himself looked characteristically unapologetic. I doubted I was the only one who felt the urge to drag him towards the ocean and hold him under for...an hour should do it.

"Dad," Chloe said softly.

Speaking of people I'd happily hold under the waves.

"We can do this," I whispered. "We're not going to be victims of his bullshit anymore, remember?"

"I remember." Her voice was shaky. Shock was to be expected after watching one of her boyfriends die. Not to mention the fear of facing our father down.

I should probably have felt something, but when I thought of Zachary, I was nothing but numb. I couldn't reconcile the stepbrother I grew up with, with the person who tried to kill me today. They didn't seem like the same person. They weren't the same person. Zachary had grown bitter, to the point where he thought killing me would give the solution to Chloe's problems. I had a feeling she wouldn't have forgiven him if he was successful.

Walking beside Chloe didn't feel real either. We had a long way to go before we made up for the past. If that was even possible. I was willing to try if she was.

We stopped in front of our father. His expression was unreadable. For a second, I was that nine-year-old girl again, pleading with him to reconsider.

I shoved the thought away with force. I wasn't that little girl anymore. I hadn't been her for a long, long time.

"You both made it," he said blandly.

"Yes we did," Chloe said. "Zachary didn't."

A flicker of something passed across Dad's face, but it was gone quickly. If I didn't know better, I would have thought it was regret.

Regret for what? That we survived the trials and Zachary didn't? If that was what he thought—

I pushed away the flare of anger too. Letting that get the better of me wouldn't help me right now.

"Working together?" Dad asked.

I raised my chin. "A little bit, yes. And with others." I gestured to the twins and Slade. I silently added Shannon and Ronnie, who didn't deserve what happened to them. They should be standing here with us.

"We've also decided we're not in competition with each other anymore," I added. "We're done playing your games and dancing on your strings. If you want to hand the family over to someone like that, it won't be either of us."

His eyebrows twitched. "Do you feel the same way, Chloe?"

A moment or two of silence was broken by her saying, "Yes. Neither of us wants it enough to hurt each other anymore. We've done some horrible things to each other, just to please you. None of it's ever enough. We're done."

Dad made an indeterminate sound in the back of his throat.

My heart hammered. It was one thing to take a stand, and another to deal with his response. We may be the ones who ended up with our heads under the waves. If he could get past Hunter, Parker, Slade and Dane to do it.

Dad actually smiled. "It's about time."

I blinked. "What?" That was not what I expected to hear. Did he actually look...pleased?

"I've been waiting for you to stand up to me," he said. "I don't care if you work together. In fact I was hoping you could. I wanted you to figure out a way to lead together. After all, you have some big shoes to fill." One side of his mouth tugged up higher than the other.

"Smug prick," Parker said loudly.

Hunter grunted his agreement.

Slade didn't say a word, but I felt his anger and frustration from a metre or two away. Same with Dane. Not to mention a laugh that came from the direction of Reuben or Caleb. I didn't look to see which one it was.

"I don't understand." I shook my head. "All this time, all you wanted from us was to stand up to you? Everything else was completely unnecessary? The teddy bears, the trafficking, the mercenaries, the cars, all of it?"

He shifted his umbrella to his other hand. Shame it wasn't struck by lightning.

"The mercenaries weren't unnecessary," he stated. "But if you stood up to me and told me you had no regrets about working together, it would have ended right there."

"And the asshole of the year award goes to..." Hunter said darkly.

"Which is saying something, because Caleb was way ahead of everyone else up until now."

"I see you survived too." Dad's eyes took in the twins with his usual level of disapproval.

"Of course they did," I said, drawing his gaze back to me. "I'm in a relationship with them and Slade and I'm not giving them up. If you don't like it, that's too bad."

If he wanted me to stick up for myself, that's what he'd get. My guys and I were in this forever. Nothing he, or anyone else, could say would change that.

"And Dane and I are together," Chloe said. "We don't need your permission or approval either."

Dane stepped over to place a hand on her shoulder. "No, we don't."

"Of course you don't," Dad said. "I don't care who you're with, as long as they treat you right."

"I must have misinterpreted all those looks then," Parker said. "I was pretty sure you looked at Hunter and me like we were something you scraped off the bottom of your shoe."

"You didn't misinterpret them," Dad said. "I'm sure Lila could do better than you two, but if she's determined to be with you, I can't stop her. She had to want it enough to stand in front of me and insist. And she's finally done that."

That was a backhanded fucking complement if I ever heard one, but I'd take it. It was easier than dealing with the barrage of thoughts bouncing around my brain like a ball pit in zero gravity.

All the pain Chloe and I caused each other, we could have avoided. If we'd stood in front of him and refused to accept his ridiculous competition, we could have had a very different year. How many people died because we didn't have the guts to defend ourselves to him?

Fucking fuck.

"You want Chloe and I to lead the Bell family together?" I asked carefully.

"That's exactly what I want," Dad agreed. "Together, you two could take over the world."

I wanted to tell him to fuck right off.

"How do we know this isn't another game, or test?" I asked coldly.

"If we agree, you may just turn around and tell us we failed and that you wanted something else."

"No more games or tests," he said. "It took you a while to pass this one, but you got there in the end. Even though it took some help from the Brantley family." He was clearly displeased at that. A quick look in the direction of Reuben and Caleb showed they shared the sentiment.

"Why work with them then?" I asked. "You all hate each other."

"The rest of the school board refused to endorse these final trials—" Dad started.

"Final trials?" Chloe interrupted.

It was Francine who stepped up to answer. "The school board decided the trials were...barbaric. The only reason the students were permitted to participate was if this was the last time it ever took place. One time too many, in my opinion." She turned to briefly glare at my father and all three of the older Brantley men.

"Why hold this one last trial?" Slade asked. His fingers were white where he had them pressed around the knife in his shoulder. What I could see of Dane's shirt was soaked in blood.

"Because we didn't stand up to him," I said softly. "If we had, this whole thing never would have taken place." My father was definitely the one who deserved to be held under the water.

"It still would have." Reuben's gaze raked over Chloe and me. The message was crystal clear. He'd had a hand in this, in the hope it would rid him of us.

I lifted my chin and returned his animosity. If he thought he could intimidate me, he'd have to think again. The one good thing that came out of all of this was I knew what I wanted and I'd fight to get it. Nothing and no one was going to stand in my way.

I turned back to my father. "If Chloe and I agree to take over from you some day we have some conditions." I didn't give him a chance to respond before I continued. "First, you will support our choice of partner or partners. Second, no one goes into those basement rooms who isn't an actual enemy of the family."

I might have kept Reuben and Caleb in the corner of my eye when I said that.

"Third, no more trials under any circumstances," Chloe said. "No more games. No more competitions. No cars with tampered breaks. No mercenaries. No assassins sent for us by you."

"Or vice versa," Dad said dryly.

Clearly he understood we were pissed off. I won't say it didn't cross my mind. It very much did. For now, we needed him as a buffer between us and Reuben. When we didn't...

We'd discuss that when the time came.

"We want any human trafficking operations to stop immediately," I said. This was something I wasn't backing down on. Not one centimetre. If Dad didn't agree, I was walking away now and never looking back. This was my hill to, figuratively, die on.

"That goes for you too," Hunter said to Caleb.

"I don't answer to you," Caleb snarled.

"Then Parker and I will make it our life's work to disrupt any operations you try to run," Hunter said unflinchingly. "There's plenty of other ways to make money. Maybe you should put some more of it into that hockey team you bought. The Dusk Bay Demons don't have to suck."

Caleb grunted. "Maybe I should put you in charge of them, if you give a shit so much."

Parker grinned. "I could get behind that."

Caleb gave him a withering glance.

"That didn't sound like a no, did it Park?" Hunter asked.

"No it didn't, Hunt," Parker agreed. "Hey, Reuben, what do you think?"

Reuben raised an eyebrow, clearly not caring one way or the other. "I think you two have too much time on your hands. I can easily remedy that."

The twins grinned more broadly. "By making Caleb give us a hockey team?" They high-fived each other.

Here we stood, wet, muddy and covered in blood, and the twins were still having the time of their lives.

"If you'll excuse us, we need to get Slade to a hospital," I said. Evidently I was the only one who remembered he had a knife sticking out of his shoulder. Apart from him, of course. He was clearly in a great deal of pain.

"I'll drive you," Frankie said. She ushered us toward one of the cars as more students started to stagger out of the trees. It seemed more had survived than hadn't.

That was one small mercy at least.

twenty-four

LILA

"I CAN'T DECIDE if I should laugh or cry," I said. "Maybe a whole lot of both."

I stood beside the window, glass of vodka and lemon in hand. Below, the lights of Dusk Bay twinkled. Yachts worth a good chunk of my trust fund bobbed on the water. From here, it looked like the world didn't have a care. Like the trials never happened. No one died. No one's life was changed forever.

"Definitely laugh." Hunter stood behind me and wrapped his arms around me. "You survived the first year of Brutal Academy. You survived the trials. Only four students died, which is probably a record. You made up with your sister, and you don't have to worry about meeting your father's expectations anymore."

"I don't know about the last one." I leaned back against him and inhaled his clean, masculine scent. "I still have to pass the next two years of study. With good grades. And you and Park only have one more year. What am I supposed to do there by myself?" I downed the last of my drink and let Parker take the empty glass from my hand.

"You won't be by yourself, and I can think of a few things." Slade grinned. He moved to stand beside us and leaned his shoulder against the glass. His stitches were removed a few days ago. According to the doctors, he'd regain full use of his shoulder as long as he did the exercises they told him to. He was no longer in any pain and the scar the knife left behind was pretty fucking cool.

"Hunter and I have no intention of leaving you and Slade there alone," Parker said. "I'm thinking of doing postgrad. At least for a year."

"Me too," Hunter said. "A guy can never have too much education. Besides, I'm not ready to hand Kink Or Drink over to anyone else. I might even get a job teaching there, so I can continue to supervise my favourite game."

"Did you just suggest you'd corrupt your students?" Parker asked. His reflection in the glass beside us grinned.

"Firstly, yes," Hunter said. "Secondly, you make that sound like it's a bad thing. It's not, is it Slade?"

"I wouldn't know," Slade said innocently. "I think you three corrupted me."

I snorted a laugh. "Hardly. I don't think any of us have been innocent for a very long time."

"We wouldn't want it any other way." Hunter squeezed me tighter, then ran a hand down my side and up under my skirt.

"Of course you wouldn't." I placed my palms on the floor to ceiling window and leaned against it as he tugged my panties off my hips and let them fall to the floor. My skirt joined it a moment later.

He grabbed the hem of my shirt and pulled it up over my head, to my elbows. I removed one hand from the glass so he could slide it off, then swapped to the other hand. He unhooked my bra and let my breasts fall free.

I lowered my hands long enough to let it slide off my wrists to join the rest of my clothes.

Hunter ran his hands up my stomach and over my breasts. "Have I told you lately how fucking beautiful you are?"

"Yes, but I don't get tired of hearing it," I said with a slight laugh.

"You're the most gorgeous woman I've ever seen," he said. He palmed my nipples until they were stiff peaks.

"Me too," Slade agreed. He placed a couple of fingers on my cheek and turned my head so he could kiss me.

"Me three," Parker agreed. He stood on the other side of me and tangled his fingers in my hair. "So fucking gorgeous."

"You're all so fucking gorgeous." I traced around Slade's lips with the tip of my tongue. He tasted of bourbon and his natural, musky flavour. "Zachary could have killed you." My voice was a hoarse whisper.

"I'm not that easy to kill," he whispered back. "He could have killed you."

"He got what he deserved," Parker said. "If Slade hadn't killed him, Hunter or I would have. And if we didn't, Dane would have."

"Someone would have," Hunter agreed. He moved his hands slowly down to my pussy and around my hips. He squeezed my ass cheeks before gently prying my legs open and slipping his hand in between them. One arm went around my waist to bend me over, while he ran his fingers up and down my already throbbing seam.

"You're always so fucking wet for us," he marvelled. He slipped his fingers inside me, deftly massaging my G spot and making me wetter still.

"Because you're all so hot," I told him. I kissed Slade's mouth and let our tongues dance.

"No, you." Parker stepped around to roll one of my nipples between his thumb and forefinger.

"We might all be hot," Hunter said. He worked me harder until I was panting, my breath misting the window in front of me.

Could anyone out on the Bay see me up here, naked and surrounded by three gorgeous guys? If they could, they'd probably be envious of me. They should be, I was one lucky girl.

Slade swallowed my breath as I panted against his lips. I wanted to say I was coming, but I couldn't bring myself to break off our kiss. Instead, I just came, hard and fast, my vision making the lights on the Bay blur and shimmer.

"Good girl," Hunter purred. "Keep coming." He kept working me, harder and harder, making my orgasm last and last. By the time I finally came down, he already had his jeans undone, his cock ready to push inside me.

He gripped my hips with both hands and thrust firmly.

"So fucking good," he breathed. "Look at us."

I reluctantly drew my lips away from Slade's and turned my gaze to our reflection in the glass. I was leaning forward, breasts hanging, Hunter behind me, thrusting into me.

Watching him fuck me made my need grow again. It must have done the same for him, because he began to thrust faster and faster, the rhythm always even. His breath got more and more ragged the closer he came to coming.

"Tell me what you want," he insisted.

"I want you to come," I said breathlessy. "I want you to come inside me."

He grunted. "Hell yeah. That's exactly what I'm going to do. I'm going to fuck you hard and then come inside your beautiful body." He pounded into me, teeth gritted until he went still and spilled himself inside me. "Fuck. *Fuuuck...*"

He sagged against my back, clinging to me and trying to keep us both upright. "So fucking perfect."

He slid out of me and Parker gave him a shove before turning me around to face him. He'd already stripped and now stood in front of me in all his muscular, naked glory. He gripped my ass and picked me up until my legs wrapped around his waist. He pressed my back to the glass and slid me onto his erection.

"I'll never be tired of being inside you," he said breathlessly.

"I'll never be tired of having you inside me," I replied.

He smiled and fucked me up against the window, my skin sliding against the cool glass, the friction building until I came again. He followed a moment later. Grunting and grinding against me, his panting matching my own.

His eyes were half closed, lips turned up in a smile of pure bliss. "I could stay inside you forever."

If it wouldn't create complications, I'd happily have one of their cocks inside me all the time. No doubt they'd find a way to allocate a certain amount of time to each of them.

Parker leaned forward to kiss my eyelids before pulling out of me and setting me down on the floor. He stepped aside to let Slade take his place.

He put his hands on my shoulders and pushed me down to my knees. I knelt with my shoulder almost touching the glass, his cock thick and erect in front of my face.

He wrapped his fist around it and pumped himself a couple of times.

"Open up and suck my cock like a good girl." He pressed his tip against my lips.

"I don't know where any of you got the idea I was a good girl," I said, but I opened my mouth and let him slide his head inside. I swirled my tongue around his tip and sucked gently before he pressed more of himself inside my mouth.

"You're good at sucking," Slade said.

"And fucking," Hunter added.

"And being awesome," Parker said.

My only response was to suck harder, taking Slade all the way to the back of my throat. I loved the feeling of him in my mouth and the way he responded to what I did to him. He gripped my hair with one hand, but let me set the rhythm, surrendering all control to me. When and where and how he came was up to me.

I sucked slowly, then faster, then slowly again. I wasn't going to let him come until I was ready.

"Woman, your mouth..." His breath came shorter and shorter. He was close. So close.

I looked up at him and sucked harder and deeper. I wrapped my fingers around his balls and massaged them at the same time.

"I'm going to..."

I took him all the way down to the back of my throat, encouraging his balls to tighten and explode his pearly, sweet cum into my mouth. My eyes still on him, I pulled back off him and swallowed.

"You are amazing," he told me. "I love you."

"I love you too." I let him pull me to my feet and lead me over to curl up on the couch with him and the twins.

I lay back and nestled down, their arms around me, my legs draped over Hunter's. This was what life was about. Being surrounded by my guys. Not having to worry about trials or challenges, or random attacks. Just existing in the moment, tangled with the most amazing guys in the world.

"I love you guys too," I added.

The first year of my university life was over, but I wasn't naïve enough to think the rest of it would be easy. This was only the first part of the road, not the end of it. Chloe and I had a lot of work to do to make up for the past. If we wanted to mend our relationship with our father, that would take even more work. Could I ever forgive him for the things he did? Some day, maybe, but not today. Today was just for enjoying myself and living my best life.

"We love you too," Hunter said.

"Yes we do," Parker agreed. "Now and forever."

"Now and forever," Hunter echoed.

"Forever sounds perfect." I closed my eyes and exhaled softly. Forever sounded like exactly what we all needed.

It might almost be long enough.

epilogue

LILA

"CAN YOU BELIEVE WE MADE IT?" Chloe squeezed my hand.

The rivalry between us for the last two years was fierce. The competition for head of the family was over, but my sister and I couldn't help vying with each other for the best grades. That was made slightly more challenging with Chloe changing to an arts degree and studying history and writing instead of business. She gave me no chance to beat her in the same classes.

The upside was we could both top our classes without either of us being second. At some point in the middle of our third year, we even started to cheer each other on.

"Of course I can," I said, only half lying. "We made it through first year. Everything after that was a breeze." I adjusted my cap with my spare hand, then leaned over and adjusted hers. Queens fix each other's crowns, they don't tear them off.

"It was a lot easier when we weren't trying to kill each other," she agreed. "But I won't miss classes, essays or exams."

"We might miss all of those things when we have to live in the real world again." I sighed. "Maybe I should stay and do a Masters degree or PhD."

She gave me a disbelieving look. "We both know you better than that. There's too many changes you want to make. You wouldn't want to stay here at Brutham and put that off any longer."

"That's true."

We stood when the Chancellor stepped up onto the stage. Right behind him was Frankie Young. A few weeks ago, they announced she was going to be Chancellor of Dusk Bay Academy, the new campus affiliated with Brutham.

I would have bet anyone they'd never hold any trials there, but no one would take that bet. The board lived up to their declaration not to hold them anymore. The entire first year class for the last two years survived until the end of the year. No mercenaries attacked the Academy. No one tried to blow up the building.

The twins complained how boring it was, and took to practical joking every chance they got.

Everyone but Slade and me. They knew better than to target either of us.

I scanned the crowds in front of me and locked eyes on my three guys. They actually stood beside Dane DiMarco. The four of them were almost friends these days. They might actually have been friends, but Dane was often the recipient of Hunter and Parker's pranks. He'd threatened to get them expelled, but no one could prove it was them. In the end, no real harm was done to anything but Dane's ego.

He couldn't complain too much anyway, he got what he wanted: Chloe and power.

My gaze shifted over to where Dad stood with his new wife Siena. An artist, she always seemed to have paint on her somewhere, no matter what she was doing. It was hard not to like her. She was sunshine to his cynical doom and gloom. He smiled more when she was around. And didn't dare suggest locking Chloe and I away anywhere.

We'd already agreed if he tried, we'd make sure he ended up there instead of us.

According to my therapist, that wasn't the right approach, but it worked for us.

The Chancellor tapped the microphone to silence the audience. "I'd like to welcome you all to this year's graduation ceremony. I'm proud to stand in front of some of the brightest minds in Australia and congratulate them for surviving three long years at Brutham Academy."

I only half listened as he prattled on, tuning back in as he started to call us up by name to receive our degrees.

This was one time I couldn't argue that Chloe should go first. Even if she wasn't the eldest sister, her name was alphabetically before mine. For once, I didn't mind. I got to watch her step forward and accept her degree from Frankie before shaking the Chancellor's hand.

I might have even gotten a little teary with pride. I wiped my eyes quickly, before anyone saw.

The Chancellor called out my name.

I lowered my hand quickly and stepped forward.

"You're both going to do big things," Frankie said softly. "If you need anything, you know where to find me."

I smiled at her. "I might just take you up on that. The first thing I want to do is open the Brotherhood of Kings up to women."

Her eyebrows rose slightly. "That's ambitious, but I can totally get behind it. Count me in."

I smiled back, took my degree from her hand and shook the Chancellor's hand.

We stood back to wait for everyone else to get their degrees before we hurried off the stage and into the waiting arms of our guys.

University was over, but the biggest challenges were yet to come. Personally, I couldn't wait.

* * *

Hello, Slade here, your friendly neighbourhood assassin and business law professor. If you love this series as much as I loved being a part of it, you know what to do. Tell your friends, leave a review or rating, join the authors' Facebook group or sign up for their newsletters.

For a bonus scene of Hunter and Parker clearing up the trial area, grab it here.

If you want to find out if the Dusk Bay Demons suck as much as the twins keep saying they do, check out the first book of the series, Puck Drop. Yeah, that's puck with a P.

about the author

Maggie Alabaster writes reverse harem romance.

She lives in NSW, Australia with one spouse, two daughters, one dog, and countless birds.

Sign up for Maggie's newsletter! Sign Up!

Join Maggie's reader group! Join here!

Follow Maggie on Bookbub! Click here to follow me!

Check out Maggie's website- www.maggiealabaster.com

also by maggie alabaster

Ruthless Claws

Book 1 Ivory

Book 2 Crimson

Book 3 Elodie

Harmony's Magic

Book 1 Summoned by Fire

Book 2 Summoned by Fate

Book 3 Summoned by Desire

Shifter's Vault

Book 1 Discarded

Book 2 Deceived

Book 3 Disgraced

My Alien Mates

Book 1 Star Warriors

Book 2 Star Defenders

Book 3 Star Protectors

Academy of Modern Magic

Book 1 Digital Magic

Book 2 Virtual Magic

Book 3 Logical Magic

Complete Collection

Summer's Harem

Book 1: Shimmer

Book 2: Glimmer

Book 3: Flicker

Complete collection

Short reads

Taken by the Snowmen

Jingle All the Way